*Also by Arthur A. Cohen*

FICTION

An Admirable Woman    (1983)
Acts of Theft    (1980)
A Hero in His Time    (1976)
In the Days of Simon Stern    (1973)
The Carpenter Years    (1967)

NONFICTION

Herbert Bayer: The Complete Works
The Tremendum: A Theological Interpretation of the Holocaust
Osip Emilevich Mandelstam: An Essay in Antiphon
Sonia Delaunay
If Not Now, When?
(*with Mordecai M. Kaplan*)
A People Apart: Hasidic Life in America
(*with Philip Garvin*)
The Myth of the Judeo-Christian Tradition
The Natural and the Supernatural Jew
Martin Buber

EDITOR

Contemporary Jewish Religious Thought
(*with Paul Mendes-Flohr*)
The Jew: Essays from Buber's Journal *Der Jude*
The New Art of Color: The Writings of Robert & Sonia Delaunay
Arguments and Doctrines: A Reader of Jewish Thinking
in the Aftermath of the Holocaust
Humanistic Education and Western Civilization

# Artists &
# Enemies

# Artists & Enemies

## THREE NOVELLAS

Arthur A. Cohen

DAVID R. GODINE · Publisher

First edition published in 1987 by
DAVID R. GODINE, PUBLISHER, INC.
Horticultural Hall
300 Massachusetts Avenue
Boston, Massachusetts 02115

"Hans Cassebeer and the Virgin's Rose" and "The
Monumental Sculptor" were first published in *TriQuarterly*
in 1975 and 1978.

Library of Congress Cataloging-in-Publication Data
Cohen, Arthur Allen, 1928–1986
Artists and enemies.
1. Artists—Fiction.   I. Title.
PS3553.O418A89   1987   813'.54   86-45535
ISBN 0-87923-650-7

First edition
Printed in the United States of America

# Contents

# Hans Cassebeer and the Virgin's Rose

## One

Count Viktor von Preissendorf, who had profited from the advice of Adam Cassebeer respecting a splendid mare he had recommended for the count's purchase some years before, repaid the modest debt by suggesting his son, Hans, for the appointment. Adam Cassebeer —the shrewd connoisseur of horseflesh, by training and avocation an agronomist, a specialist, in fact, in the nurture of an alfalfa strain resistant to the cold winds of northern Prussia—had but a single son, who proved not nearly so resilient as his alfalfa.

Young Cassebeer, lately of the University of Berlin, more recently a docent at the Kaiser Friedrich Wilhelm Museum, a very junior colleague of the great von Bode, had just recovered from what was called at that time extreme exhaustion. We know, today, of course, that such exhaustions are exactions of the mind, but then they were still regarded as languors and humors, flaggings of the spirit, fissiparations of inclement environments, unsuitable companions, excessive or deficient self-abuse—and the result, *poof*, extreme exhaustion. But after four months at a seaside resort near Danzig and a winter of skiing and taking the waters at Bad Gastein, Hans Cassebeer was restored. Or so it was thought until the great scandal.

Hans's father never learned the cause of his son's illness; and being a widower, his wife having died and left him to care for his growing son and an older daughter, he had no one with whom to share his confidential anxieties. It is quite possible, moreover, that young Hans himself never inquired profoundly into the source of his own startling behavior. Nonetheless, early one morning—it was during August 1919—he quite simply took up the palette knife with which he was mixing an Umbrian earth color to execute a stroke on a copy he was making of a *cinquecento* masterpiece in the collection of the Kaiser Friedrich Wilhelm Museum (it being his custom, before his duties as docent began, to paint before a masterpiece) and was about to plunge it into the eye of a brooding Virgin when a large hand seized his wrist, twisted it, and, knife falling, young Hans collapsed. He foamed a bit, thrashed about, and fainted. It was two months before he spoke again, and by the time of his return to Berlin the following spring, he had determined to leave the museum and assume an entirely new vocation. He decided to become a restorer of paintings rather than an art lecturer and copyist.

It should not be thought that someone who had come close to mutilating the eye of a Virgin would be for that fact unsuitable to the vocation of restorer. Not at all. Quite the contrary, in fact! At that time in the history of the conservation of art, the mutilator in spirit was quite often the most promising restorer. Or, put another way, one who was so profoundly ambivalent about masterpieces of art—he who would sit day in and day out seeking to reproduce exactly the tones and textures of a painting (and often succeed in making not just a likely copy, but a splendid fake)—acquired in the course of his diligence an almost incantatory competence. He could prepare the panel like a medieval craftsman; he could make colors from the powders and mix the paints like an adept; he knew which colors were used where and what subjects were most likely to inhabit whose imagination. He could, in fact, so come to love another time, another culture, another sensibility that he could restore a masterpiece but could not create one. These Hans Cassebeers—and they are even today seated on little campstools in the Prado, the Rijksmuseum, the Accademia, the Metropolitan, the Albertina, everywhere in fact, diligently copying with a faithfulness and commitment—may seem to all of us who observe them no different from drones and craftsmen anywhere. But wrong! What you miss, if you conclude thus, is the secret fantasy, the fantasy nourished, for instance, by Hans Cassebeer himself. Would you believe it? Hans Cassebeer, that day in August, repainting that masterpiece, hoped not only to copy it so that it would be exact but, in his concentration, to prize the image from the wall and stick it to his brain so permanently that when it emerged once more onto his canvas, his would become the masterpiece and the original the faithful copy. What a reversal of divinities, and what a delusion! Delusion? Exactly. But that is what Cassebeer confessed. He wanted to be Sasseta, to be Cimabue, to be Mantegna, and his talent was insufficient to be Cassebeer. No wonder that when Cassebeer recovered his senses and returned to Berlin in the spring of 1920 he should decide to put his extraordinary fund of information and knowledge of technique to a more prudent and wholesome work. If he could not be those masters, he temporized, he could at least restore them.

## *Two*

Young Cassebeer was welcome in the homes of Berlin society, the homes of the wealthy, and the homes of the aristocracy—not always the same homes. His father had made for himself, and thereby for his son, something of a reputation. Adam Cassebeer was a Tolstoyan character, a true Levin, though not a Levin of great means. But he had Levin's theories and Levin's grave crankiness, and for Germans gravity and crankiness were what eccentricity had become for the English: marks of serious purpose embedded in unconventional behavior. He talked of grains the way other men discussed events of the day. Wheat, soy, alfalfa had personalities, and to signify his intimacy with them he habitually inserted in his hatband a tasseled stalk of wheat whose full grains not infrequently tumbled over the brim of his hat as he discoursed with his friends. His serious purpose and his somewhat unconventional behavior were endearing—he did not threaten power, not at all, and he was therefore welcomed as an original contributor to the race. They—the bankers, department-store magnates, war-department officers, estate managers, and landed aristocracy—called him Alfalfa Adam.

Count Viktor von Preissendorf ran into Adam Cassebeer as he was walking down the Unter den Linden one morning shortly after Hans's return to Berlin. "Alfalfa Adam," he called out cheerfully, slapping Adam's arm with his gray suede gloves, "how are you, old friend? Berenice is doing splendidly, although she is out to pasture now." (Berenice was the mare that Adam had brought to the count's attention. That mare had foaled a half-dozen times, producing four good saddle horses, a poor lame creature, and one celebrated racer.)

Adam beamed with pleasure at the chance encounter. "I haven't seen you since the war ended," the count continued. "How are you now? Enduring these times? Hardly, I should think. Foolish times, foolish country," he expostulated, turning his pink nostrils toward the sky. "Come round, Sunday afternoon. Many old friends. We have missed you, the countess and myself. And bring young Hans. He's recovered, I'm told. I have an idea for him. Perhaps? Perhaps?"

Adam Cassebeer nodded acceptance. The count used his "perhaps" more as an inducement than as a disguise of indecision. Most men said "perhaps" when they possessed no clear idea of their intention,

but Count Viktor was a count—a count, moreover, of many generations of authentic standing and service. His "perhaps" was thus more
in the manner of a *lèse majesté*, an expression of mystery and disdain
and therefore to be taken quite seriously.

The following Sunday, Adam Cassebeer and his son Hans drove
up the curved pathway to the mansion of the von Preissendorfs,
situated on the outskirts of Berlin amid a thinning forest of birch,
ash, and maple trees. The garden was unkempt, wild with a baroque
aspect of arrayed disorder, small fountains with urinating cupids and
satyrs fluting water into marble basins spilling upon goldfish in the
concrete pools below. The spirit of the mansion was adumbrated by
the grandeur and slight madness of its exterior flora, and Hans, having
heard his father's interpretation of the count's "perhaps," shuddered
as the liveried footman showed them into the conservatory where tea
was being served.

The conservatory. The glass, the crystal, the ormolu, the marble,
the china, the tapestries, the silks, the heavy chintz, the flocking:
each chair, each table, each secretary, each music stand, lamp, each
chandelier (there were eight—cascades of glass breathing like a rainbow in a clarified sky), all were of exquisite refinement, but of the
ensemble one could only gasp *enough, too much.* Each stood by itself
in magnificence, but at the *tout ensemble* one was appalled: heaviness,
not grace. The craftsmen were extraordinary, but the patron was
merely rich. In a word, the count (or perhaps it was his countess—
but one thinks not, for she was a small and, one thinks, a timorous
woman) had a taste for auction rooms and for collections; but he
lacked measure, and without measure even magnificence is slightly
vulgar. At all events, Adam and Hans, father and son, disappeared
into the large room and were soon swallowed up by the sounds of
clinking glass and cups, riffles of fans, clucks of guttural contentment,
and the swirling pleasure of a Mozart divertimento offered by a rigorous
troupe of hired musicians, complemented by the count's youngest
daughter, Adele, playing clavier in the corner.

Shortly before seven o'clock, when Sunday teas languish to their conclusion, the count approached young Hans and, pincering his elbow, guided him to the fireplace; and their conversation began. "My young friend, I have an idea which may be to your liking. You know Kastein?" Hans did not. He had never even heard of Kastein, though it is a commonplace of aristocrats to assume that everyone of their acquaintance should be known—and if not known personally at least be bruited abroad, discussed, and considered. Hans nodded as though the name were familiar, and the count rushed on. "In any event, Kastein—would you believe, Cassebeer, his amusing Christian name (if one may say that of a warty little Jew) is Lazare? Heaven only knows how he came by such an elegant name. He's from Riga, a cosmopolitan Balt, but then you know him, so I needn't rehearse his credentials. In any event, our Kastein is an art dealer. Terribly clever, some say wise, and most certainly shrewd. He's a specialist, among other things, in Old Master paintings and drawings, although he personally collects contemporary pictures. He sells only what he doesn't collect. He says it keeps his hands clean. What a clever little fellow he is. Well, then. Our friend Lazare has at this moment a little Giorgione. It's a ravishing picture, but I'm afraid the poor Virgin looks a bit dissolute; her face is blistered, and the paint is flaking from her forehead. She needs a bit of brightening. Do you think you could turn your hand to this? There's a first-rate fee, and I'll pay it, since I've bought that Giorgione for my collection. She is already mine, you see? If you think you're up to this sort of thing, ring up Kastein tomorrow and tell him I suggested you."

Hans became nervous. He drummed his fingers on the marble pediment of the fireplace as the count spoke. He saw the wriggling eye of the Virgin falling from the socket where Giorgione had emplaced it, and he became slightly nauseated. But the feeling passed. His lips opened into a smile, half disbelief, half irony. "I—I restore a Giorgione?" he replied modestly. Can I do it? Can I leave the Giorgione a Giorgione? he thought to himself, and his heart raced. "May I think about it for a day or two?" he asked.

"Of course, dear boy, of course," the count replied amiably, confident Hans would accept the assignment. "The Virgin's waited now at least a hundred years for such a treatment; she can wait another few days," he chuckled, and left Cassebeer's side to join a young cavalry officer in red-striped britches and high black boots who bowed and clicked his leave.

### Three

The following day Cassebeer visited the library of the Kaiser Friedrich Wilhelm Museum. He had not entered that vast neoclassical complex since his abrupt departure nine months earlier. The sleepy doorman greeted him lazily, as though he had never been gone. *"Guten Tag, Herr Cassebeer."*

He made straight for the library, not looking about, avoiding the hall in which the Virgin he had nearly mutilated hung, unenvied. The library had just opened its doors, and the chief librarian, pince-nez in place, was peering over a large portfolio of steel engravings. "Herr Gimpstedt, good morning. Cassebeer here, restored," he added nonchalantly.

Herr Gimpstedt looked up, smiled, but did not extend his hand. "And what can I do for you, young Cassebeer?" he asked.

"Giorgione. Giorgione of Venice. Books, reproductions, photographs. Anything. Everything," he replied enthusiastically. The reading room was empty, but Herr Gimpstedt put a finger to his lips and squinted his eyes to censure Cassebeer's excessive, and theoretically disturbing, exuberance.

"Yes, indeed. Giorgione. Do we have one here?"

"I'm afraid not, but there is one at the Stattliche Museen, a *Portrait of a Young Man.* No, my dear professor, I wish a Virgin, a most particular Virgin of Giorgione. Maybe it is, maybe it isn't, but I have some business with her," he replied, bursting to tell the news of the count's invitation.

"Very well," Gimpstedt replied, removing his pince-nez and squeezing his eyes. Cassebeer was familiar with Gimpstedt's deliberative mechanism. Beginning with eye pinching and brow wrinkling, thoughtful and distant gazes and slow speech, Gimpstedt was merely borrowing time while he consulted his vast mental card catalogue. His mind, unlike the minds of ordinary forgetful creatures, was composed of tens upon tens of thousands of little index cards on which author, title, and annotation were neatly printed, accompanied by judgments and valuations that he appended, having consulted in fact all the books to which he made reference. The prodigious Gimpstedt was warming to the subject. "Giorgione, is it? Well, then, you must have our own von Bode's study of the *Portrait of a Venetian Nobleman* in the Altman Collection—if only out of courtesy. I am sure the Venetian nobleman was no virgin, but still it is by our own von Bode. And then the volumes by Frizzoni. Several tendentious and opinionated essays by that interloper Berenson, but still suggestive and not to be ignored, even if he's good for little more than a general viewpoint of the period. Camavitto? No. But most certainly, indeed most certainly, the second edition of Vasari's *Lives*, the edition of 1568. It contains much that he learned after another visit to Venice in 1566. Most assuredly Vasari. And then, dry though it is, a mere inventory but useful in its way, Marcantonio Michiel's *Notizia*. These should start you." Gimpstedt smiled knowingly. Indeed he did know. He knew all the complexities. A good librarian, an even greater bibliographer, he knew the controversy surrounding the name and production of Giorgione da Castelfranco, born during the last quarter of the fifteenth century, dead in the Venice plague of 1511 or dead of a broken heart in 1510, but most assuredly dead in either the dramatic thirty-third year of his life or the more pedestrian and unmystical thirty-fourth.

Gimpstedt disappeared and left Cassebeer to make himself comfortable at one of the vast oak desks that filled the library. An hour later he returned with an assistant and put down before Cassebeer some twenty volumes, several illustrated with engravings of the pictures in question, others, many fewer, with early photographs of the works. The remainder of the day—that is, from ten-thirty in the morning, when Gimpstedt returned, until the late afternoon, when the west light began to wane—Cassebeer applied himself. During those hours he requested other volumes, principal sources about the Bellinis and Titian, the former having been colleagues and teachers of Giorgione's youth, the latter a young disciple—younger by some ten years—of the mature Giorgione. Hans had begun to draw certain conclusions.

Clearly, most assuredly, though he had not seen the Virgin in question, he already had doubts that she was painted by Giorgione —or, if she was, neither his judgment nor his knowledge would ever be sufficient to demonstrate her provenance. It was indisputable, he knew, that the Virgin and the events of her life were a favorite subject of the artist; that Giorgione, like the Bellinis, was charmed by the intense loyalty of her life and work; that her glow and passion came from the inside; and that Giorgione, master of what was regarded by Vasari as "the modern style," had managed to give her the radiance of pearls rather than the glitter of diamonds. Giorgione was the master of a soft and harmonic internality, whereas the Giovanni Bellini, in Vasari's cuttingly unsympathetic phrase, was "crude, dry, and forced." He knew, then, something about his artist, but he knew that Giorgione had been so beloved and honored in his abbreviated life that no one had taken the trouble to record with matter-of-factness that he had painted such and such a picture, that his workshop had so many artists by name, that these attended him, applied their hands to backgrounds because the artist preferred the subject or to anatomical appendages because the artist preferred to detail the grand motions. In a word, nothing was known about how Giorgione worked, and, as a result, now, four centuries and a bit after his death, the warring scholars took the extreme positions, crediting his hand with either too few or too many masterpieces. It would be impossible to know if the count's Virgin were by Giorgione, and most certainly the count, already behaving like the owner of uncertain goods, had fallen into the familiar habit of speaking of "my Giorgione." Of one thing alone the count could be certain—that he was authentically Count von Preissendorf; but his Virgin might not be by Giorgione da Castelfranco.

Cassebeer was not in the least alarmed by the state of Giorgione scholarship. Finally, it didn't matter to him. What mattered only was that the work was a genuine work of the period, that it was a work by a Venetian master of the late fifteenth and early sixteenth century, that it bore the marks of the incomparable Giorgione, that its subject was wasting from inattention and ingratitude, and that he, Hans Cassebeer, was being asked to put things right. A fake, a vulgar copy, would have bored him. Since he was without avarice, much less cupidity, he could not have been bribed to make a crooked path straight; but whether the work was a contemporary copy, the work of another hand, the work of many hands—the left hand of Giorgione and the right hand of Titian—a work by Titian ascribed to Giorgione, or simply a work fought over by scholars constantly changing their minds as they struggled to feel their way back into the Renaissance, did not matter to him. He was a restorative artist; he was a member of the atelier of Giorgione or, as he later hoped, of Rembrandt, whom he adored, or of Delacroix, whom he had just discovered. He was an itinerant, a vagabond of the painting arts, who had brushes and pigments for all works, and that flexibility of spirit genuine to craftsmen who lack the temperament to be creative in their own right. Who needs, he had taught himself to say, another second-rate painter when the world needs first-rate restorers to conserve and perpetuate?

The next morning Hans called Lazare Kastein, and his secretary arranged that he should present himself at the dealer's home the following afternoon at three. He was somewhat put off by the secretary's manner, for when he mentioned the purpose of his call, the young man—and Hans mistook his rudeness for youth rather than any more serious maladjustment—snorted and referred to him no longer as Herr Cassebeer, but rather as a workman would be addressed, simply as Cassebeer.

### *Four*

Punctually the following day at the agreed hour, Hans Cassebeer appeared, and a houseman answered the bell. Cassebeer entered a generous waiting room appointed with furniture that he recognized to have affinities with the still-popular Jugendstil movement and art nouveau: chairs whose backrests reminded him of drowning Ophelias, desk tables decorated with mortal and decadent conceits (entwined snakes and ivy), a settee covered in mottled green leather, ink sets curlicued with leaves and flowers, pots iridescent and opaline, lamps faceted with cut chips of colored glass. But the walls . . . the walls were indescribable: alternate panels of cut velvet and mahogany, and upon each velvet panel was hung a picture: a still life by Cézanne, a Moroccan landscape by the dead soldier Macke, a ballet dancer of Degas, and many more, some by artists he did not know (a vivid cavalier, for instance, in incredible color, by a Polish artist, he imagined, or Russian perhaps?), one by Egon Schiele. He sat waiting for half an hour. A young man—his youth was palpable—with a delicate mouth and his hair in either natural or enforced curls, put his head through the door and examined Hans from foot to head, beginning with his boots and ending with his straight black hair (indeed, Cassebeer thought, from foot to head; what a curious young man, he scoffed), and then withdrew, closing the door silently, without saying anything.

A few minutes later he heard laughter, marvelous laughter, the sound of tumbling gaiety, perfumed like the laughter of radiant women, and the double doors were thrown open and the most beautiful woman he had ever seen entered through the doors, which were held open obediently by a startlingly unattractive middle-aged man. The woman dominated the room, but her attendant spoke. "Good of you to come, Herr Cassebeer. I am Kastein." Cassebeer rose and shook the man's damp palm. "Thank you for inviting me," Hans replied politely. The woman had taken up a position behind Cassebeer, her hands resting on the back of the settee, one to either side of his head, and a single rose index finger scratched at the yellow damask with which the settee was covered. "And me, dear Kastein, what of me?" she rebuked with a renewal of laughter. "He's so very funny," she said to Cassebeer, as if to explain Kastein's neglect of her presence. "Forgive me. My dear Cassebeer, I have the pleasure of presenting you to the redoubtable and singular Lily Schwann, singer, dancer, friend of Reinhardt and Jannings, and my adored beauty, whom I love most tenderly and faithfully." Kastein bowed toward his mistress, and she acknowledged his introduction with a toss of her head, raising her chin to reveal that most fatal of beauties, a long and slender and magnificent neck, on which glittered a thin strand of diamonds.

Hans Cassebeer, flustered by the intimacies unfolded in his presence, bowed and kissed her hand, his lips closing over the scent that rose from her white knuckles. He lingered a moment, her hand grazed his hair, and he lifted his head, stepped back, and bowed once more as though having completed a reverence to royalty.

"Dear Herr Cassebeer, it has been agreeable meeting you, and I am certain we shall meet again." She smiled, and her even teeth parted once more in a smile. She was all energy and joy. As she passed Kastein, who held the door open for her, she brushed his forehead with her lips, and her hand rested a moment on his shoulder. She whispered something that Cassebeer did not hear, but her eyes moved back to him and narrowed for an instant. The door closed, and they were alone. Kastein returned to the settee and invited Cassebeer to make himself comfortable.

"The count tells me he believes you have the gifts of the witch," Kastein began peremptorily.

"Me? A witch?" Cassebeer replied quizzically, though not at all offended.

"Indeed, *the* witch. Or shall I say, more accurately, witch in the making. You've not joined the coven, but you will, he believes. Let me be precise. We all regard—we dealers in art, we collectors of art—we all regard restorers as witches. You've heard of Prezniewski, the Pole, the dean of restorers, the dean of witches? No? Excellent. That proves the point. Prezniewski is a true witch. No one has heard of him. No one has met him, but I can tell you something: he is the Raphael master. Raphael is his guardian demon. He has restored virtually all the Raphaels in the world, but no one has met him. The first Raphael that he touched, more than forty years ago now, was brought to his sister by an old Italian prince in whose family collection it had been for more than three hundred years—a fabulous portrait, and one the prince had adored since his childhood. Indeed, he confessed he could find no one in the world whose majesty and arrogance equaled that of the young cavalier, and, lacking brothers and sisters, he had made that young gentleman his consort and friend, often taking counsel with him. The prince was, of course, quite insane. Rather like the fairy tale of the princess and the magic mirror, he looked to his Raphael to requite his own diabolic self-infatuation.

"One day, late in the dry summer of 1877, when the fields were parched, the roads of the north dusty, his country estate infested with mice and locusts, the prince observed that his Raphael had begun to peel. The greens in the background of the canvas, and the rose pinks in the doublet of the cavalier, obviously responsive to the deadly sun of that summer, gave up their struggle to adhere and began to peel away. The darker colors, the shining blacks of night that surrounded the subject, held firm; only the lighter areas were afflicted. Prezniewski had settled in Florence with his sister several months earlier and had busied himself with small jobs of cleaning and freshening some mannerist pictures in the Pitti. He had heard of the prince's predicament and knew, since he was the only restorer in Florence at the time, that the prince would seek him out. In due course, the prince presented his card and requested that Prezniewski visit him at his estate. Prezniewski sent his sister with a brief but uncompromising message. He would come, but only on the condition that he met no one, that he was neither seen nor interviewed, that the picture be placed in an empty room from which all light but that from a single window had been excluded, and that, should he undertake to restore the work, he be allowed to determine the hours and the fee without negotiation. The prince, for obvious reasons, had no choice but to accept.

"Prezniewski worked never more than three hours a day, arriving by coach in the late afternoon and departing at nightfall. The restoration was completed in seven months, and the prince was charged a considerable sum, which was still modest for the achievement. The prince returned to his beloved, and Prezniewski was launched. What was it, all this shrouding and mystery? We moderns would call it style, perhaps salesmanship, but I think it was something else. The restorer's art is alchemical. Is it any different from the distillation of gold to be able to make a Rembrandt cloak, a Virgin's drapery, the green of a velvet not simply resemble but resume the actual life of the work? The restorer is a vitalizer, a spiritual elixir of culture, and hence a witch. So, my dear fellow, I ask you, are you on your road to witchcraft?"

Cassebeer had listened to Kastein's story with utter fascination, for he could not help regarding Prezniewski as a pretentious Pole and Kastein as a necromancer who undoubtedly loved the drama of pictures more than he loved the pictures themselves. But Kastein spoke with a spittled rapidity and enthusiasm that could not but impress the lean and somewhat austere young Cassebeer. When Kastein stopped, Cassebeer's eyes widened in amazement, for he realized at that instant, then, for the first time, that the restoration to which he had been called was really the beginning of a new life, that he had ascended to maturity. All the precocities of childish talents and pursuits, the idle fantasies of self-glorification, indeed his near self-immolation before the Virgin of the Kaiser Friedrich Wilhelm Museum, were simply diversions preceding adulthood. But here before him, this warted, sad face, speaking to the rhythm of moving hands, expressive and veined like a violinist's, was beckoning him into manhood.

"Are you ready to assume your secret vocation, young Cassebeer?" Kastein asked after a reasonable silence.

"I think I am," Cassebeer replied gravely.

"Splendid. Look over your shoulder." Cassebeer obeyed and saw, to the right of the draperied window, a music stand on which stood what he took to be a small picture, covered with a heavy silk shawl rosetted with pink and yellow flowers. He returned to Kastein's glowing smile. "Yes, that's it. Examine it. Be a professional and examine it. Let's have your opinion."

Cassebeer approached the stand and lifted the edge of the shawl, rolling the fabric tentatively over his index finger, not daring to make contact with the surface of the picture. At first he saw the brownish-black stones of an interior floor, then the drapery of her robe, rose-red, the window to her right, the glazed landscape beyond, miniaturized and detailed, but set off in the distance; and the Child, her finger touching his toe, not holding it, not caressing it, but merely in contact, the wrinkled body, the small head with curly, matted hair; her tightened bodice of rich green velvet, bordered with an intricately stitched yellow silk, the cream-white neck, the face of unearthly gravity and beauty, her hair invisible beneath a yellow head-covering that dropped down about her shoulders.

"Not a large picture. So much there, and so little." Cassebeer spoke, amazement dropping his voice to a whisper. "A cabinet picture. He was fond of them. He painted so few that scholars accredit, perhaps because he rarely sought large commissions. But I don't know. It seems so unlike Giorgione to redo a picture. It's a version of two pictures, I should think. The intimate ease of the portrait reminds me of the *Madonna with a Book* at the Oxford Ashmolean, yet the hieratic sadness of the face and the position of the Child are so much like the Bergamo *Virgin*. But my opinion is really worthless, Herr Kastein. I'm not a Giorgione expert. I'm not an expert at all. I trust one thing, however. My instinct. My instinct says it looks right. It looks the period, the mood, the grace of the time. It's nothing but north Italian. It's nothing but the grand Renaissance. And why not Giorgione? Why not? Proto-Giorgione? Mezzo-Giorgione? But not mock-Giorgione, not a fake. Absolutely not. There are none of the trivializing gestures of the fake—not the dullness of a dreary fake nor the creative effusion of an original fake. Whether it's real, real Giorgione, who could ever tell? Certainly not I. But one thing is certain. The picture's filthy, and unless something's done soon, the poor Madonna is going to look like a ragpicker in a few more decades. She needs a cleaning. So does the Child. He looks sickly already. So there. A cleaning first of all. Some caretaking in the corners, filling in the drapery, and most of all serious restoration on the Virgin's face. Well, you know already. The paint is lifting. It needs to be rebound and sealed."

Cassebeer paused. He stood back from the little picture, resting his weight on his right leg, his back curved, his head tilted to the left, finger to his lips, and smiled at his Giorgione.

"Such a joy, this picture." Kastein had come up behind him. "You will do it, my boy?"

"Yes. I will do it."

"And how much time do you think it should take?"

"Did Prezniewski tell the prince?" Cassebeer replied, inspired.

"Of course, of course." Kastein was delighted. He deserved the reproof, but he was delighted nonetheless. "And compensation? Certainly, we can wait and see when it's done, since you can't estimate the time it will take." Kastein had regained the initiative, but Cassebeer was indifferent. He was still absorbed by the picture.

"Now, then, Herr Kastein, what will I need? Cotton, the finest cotton. Surgical sticks, no more than a half inch in width, preferably round, not flat depressants. And the cleaner? Alcohol and perhaps linseed oil. That should begin the work. When the cleaning is done, then we can see what we have. I can see that the picture was varnished much later than it was painted, very much later. One hopes it isn't copal (nearly insolvent, you know). I doubt it. More likely Dammar resin or mastic. Did you know, Herr Kastein, that mastic comes from trees grown on the Greek island of Chios?" Cassebeer was pleased with himself. The Giorgione was filling him with a kind of life he had rarely known, a sort of confidence and conviction that all but overwhelmed his tentativeness with an authority he had almost despaired of possessing.

Kastein had been making notes while Cassebeer spoke, expecting no doubt a much longer list of *desiderata*, but Cassebeer in fact still knew only the rudiments of his craft, and what he knew he had already revealed. With a swab of cotton and a mild solvent he could take care of much of the visible problem, but while he was about that slow and painstaking task he would be learning more. He intended later that week to meet with a disciple of Max Pettenkofer, a chemist from the University of Munich who had developed several patented techniques for restoring surfaces of Old Master paintings, and one or two other Berlin cognoscenti who possessed, he hoped, bits and pieces of the alchemical art. He vowed to make himself the equal of the Giorgione when the time came. He worried most about his Virgin's face. He could see, beneath her right eyelid and near the hairline, slight blisterings of paint; it would be necessary, he thought, to see beneath to determine whether that almond cream was overpainting or by the master's hand. That would be the test—the Virgin's face.

"When will it be convenient for me to begin?" Cassebeer asked, returning the shawl to the picture's face and reluctantly turning back to Kastein.

"Tomorrow, I should think."

"And where? At your gallery?"

"No. Too exposed. Here, here would be best," Kastein replied ruminatively. "It's quiet, off the street. I'm nervous about the best, you know. These Cézannes and Kandinskys, my little treasures—not valuable by general standards, but my treasures. I don't like them visited. And the Giorgione, our Giorgione, how much more reason for protecting it from the merchant's gaze. No. No. Right here."

"Excellent," Cassebeer responded drily. It seemed to him quite appropriate.

"Upstairs in Madame Schwann's dressing room. A lovely room and excellent north light. It will be readied for you tomorrow. Shall we say eleven in the morning?"

Cassebeer was momentarily shocked. It did not seem proper. The invasion of odors and dust, he thought. A curious way to regard such an extraordinary woman, entering her rooms, setting up tables and easels, leaving open bottles and jars, filthy cleaning swabs, as if putting the surgery next to the nursery. But, he temporized, the unguents of his trade would be more than offset by the perfumes of Madame Schwann. And perhaps she would, he allowed himself to think . . . perhaps Madame Schwann would one day watch him at his art.


### Five

The following morning, Cassebeer presented himself once more at the home of Lazare Kastein. The butler passed him to the young man, and the young man, his flannels flapping against his ankles, preceded him up the stairs, drifting from one side of the spacious staircase to the other as if, Cassebeer thought, to attract his attention. When they arrived at the second floor, he turned to the right and at the end of the corridor opened the doors of a sitting room beyond which, through cascades of drapery, Cassebeer could see the sun-drenched dressing room.

The little suite contained no bedroom, and Cassebeer surmised, embarrassed by his imagination, that the beautiful woman was obliged to walk down that somber corridor to the master bedroom, which he assumed to be in the other wing of the house. The little sitting room was furnished in shades of green, with walls the deep green of emeralds and furniture the azure of the Mediterranean, while the dressing room was unpredictably severe. Cassebeer had expected light and air, sky blues and rose. The room, however, was dominated by gray, mat gray becoming silver; the chaise lounge alone was covered in another color, a textured mauve silk. The only dazzlement of color was a grotesque portrait of the beautiful woman by one of those Munich artists so much in vogue since the war—her face panels of green, her cheeks outlined in strong black lines, her hat a layering of colors, and the background a floral pattern of crudely painted blue and red anemones. The room undoubtedly belonged to Lily Schwann, for it breathed of her; its aspect was one of majestic formality: the carpet a rich tapestry, the dressing table a cabinet of mirrors before which rested a silver tray holding a half-dozen opalescent vials and a gold-handled brush in which several strands of hair glistened in the morning light.

There, amid the refinements of her dressing room, stood the music stand, and upon it the beshawled Virgin of Giorgione.

The young man motioned Hans into the room. He had not yet spoken. "Herr Cassebeer," he began, returning to refinement, "this house welcomes you. If you should wish me, ring twice." He motioned to the brocaded sash that hung near the dressing table. "My name is Rolf, Rolf Diamant. I should be pleased to assist you." As he said the last, he exaggerated, as though momentarily distracted from his succulence. His eye had caught something. With an irritated groan, he went behind the chaise and withdrew a long white stocking, crumpled it, and put it into his pocket. "Madame Schwann is sometimes scandalous," he smirked. "Good day to you, Herr Cassebeer."

The remainder of that first day and the day that followed, Hans Cassebeer applied himself to a very close examination of the picture. He prepared an exact tracing of the work, dividing its surface into quadrants an inch square; within each square, in a minuscule hand, he detailed, in signs and symbols of his own devising, his observations on the condition of the painting. A magnificatory loupe, which he held to his right eye and passed with snail-like slowness over the picture's surface, gradually revealed to him its texture and touch. With practice, he felt certain, he would be able to mime the master's hand.

Cassebeer's method of self-education, scarcely intelligible to the layman, was hardly conventional even for professional restorers. But then Cassebeer was not a professional restorer. He was not a neat gentleman with gartered sleeves and trimmed mustache conducting his craft like a bank clerk. He was Hans Cassebeer, swollen with the spoils of destiny.

By the third day, the work of inspection and annotation was done, and he arranged to have the painting photographed to document its exact condition before he began his work. He did sectional photographs, which he enlarged and then constructed into a composite photograph that transformed the intimate votive painting to the scale of a mantel portrait. He was angered by this necessity, for it seemed to him a vandalization of the painting, but he had no choice. That was the procedure, the procedure of a new science, and it was called for in all the manuals he had consulted. Of course, the enlarged photographs were grainy and coarse, but they endowed the early sixteenth century with a sepia cast that enabled Hans to discriminate little abrasions virtually invisible to the naked eye. He chafed at science, as witches ought, but he took advantage of it nonetheless.

The second week, having passed Sunday in a solitary walk through the public park near his home, wrapped in the warmth of late spring, he was ready to begin the work of hands. The swabbing began with the lower right patch he had first uncovered in Kastein's presence: beneath the grime of centuries emerged a loamy richness, into which one could almost put one's finger and know for certain that one would find there the good slithering worms of the earth. He had been working in a neatly described rectangle, perhaps two inches in length by an inch and a quarter—so tiny, so very tiny. Utterly concentrated, his eyes narrowed upon the patch of umbrous flooring. Only the tip of the Virgin's toe, shrouded by drapery, extended into the rectangle of his labors.

It was past four in the afternoon. He had worked nearly five hours without an interruption. He stood up from the painting, threw back his arms to stretch—and heard a low laugh from the dressing room. The younger Hans Cassebeer would have jumped, alarmed. In his childhood he had arranged reality in such a way as to prevent surprise; one imagines, for that reason as much as for any, he passed his youth safely but without a significant measure of joy. Joy is so often at the heart of danger (or is it risk?). In any case, Cassebeer had avoided danger by taking no chances, but consequently had left himself unprepared for loud noises, unreasonable cries and shouts, even unanticipated laughter. When these occurred—daily, one would think—his face would whiten, his skin stiffen with fright, his palms itch and perspire, and he would retreat abashed to his room in the Cassebeer household, where familiar things, all inanimate and in place, would receive and restore him. But at this moment, young Cassebeer was unafraid—indeed, the low rumble of laughter delighted him. Here he was, a man in his early twenties, tall, with hair cut like a monk's, falling in bangs over his forehead, with intelligent gray eyes, a remarkably strong nose (more like that of an Italian condottiere than of the son of a middle-class Prussian), and a warm, full mouth ("sensuous," his married sister had called it) that had touched no flesh but his own. He was a virgin like the Virgin, but unlike her he had no reason to remain one, although he had not devised that sector of reality with anything resembling the care with which he had prepared himself against loud noises and cries.

Hans Cassebeer did not turn to face the laughter or its origin. He continued to inspect the work of the day, but his hands had dropped to his sides, and his fingers splayed as he rubbed his pants leg. A feeling of elated prescience suffused him, as though the rose-purple of dawn was at last penetrating night blackness and turning time from resentment to blushing day. The laughter continued, pleasant, mocking, controlled. "Forgive me, Cassebeer," she said at last, laughter licking the syllables of her apology.

"How long have you been watching me?" he asked, not turning.

"Today?" she replied.

"You have been here before?"

"Several times, last week and yesterday."

"That's not at all fair, Madame," Cassebeer chided, not yet turning, although his head had moved in her direction. He felt strangely masterful. She had watched him unrevealed, but he had done splendidly. His workmanship and technique were superb, of that he had no doubt; but then she would not have estimated his workmanship, only the conduct of the worker. And in that, too, he had excelled. He was well turned out, his suit was stylish, his tie bright, his shoes polished. Such externals scarcely interested Cassebeer, but he donned them easily and without fuss. He did not own many clothes, but what he owned he had bought carefully, with the same thoughtful self-possession with which he did everything—neither excessive nor abject. And his conduct during the previous days had been exemplary. He neither pouted nor scowled. He did not chafe or swear. He worked quietly, calmly, efficiently. Of all this he was certain.

"Fair, fair. Fairness has nothing to do with it. Moreover, young man, I am not given to fairness. Fairness has no place in my scheme

of things." She had lighted a cigarette. He heard a series of rapid
taps and then smelled the smoke. He turned and passed through the
door that separated the dressing room from the sitting room. For the
first time, Cassebeer permitted himself to look at Lily Schwann. He
took her extended hand, kissed it, and sat down in the armchair that
fronted a low table separating him from the mauve chaise on which
she reclined.

For several moments, neither Cassebeer nor Madame Schwann
spoke. Cassebeer fidgeted, crossing and uncrossing his legs, locating
a spot on his jacket front and pecking at it with his index finger,
glancing from picture to picture in the room—in effect, avoiding the
obvious fact that he had joined this extraordinary woman, the mistress
of his employer, in her own sitting room, and without so much as an
invitation to do so. "I'm afraid I've been precipitous, Madame," Cassebeer said at last, and stood up.

"Not at all. Do sit down. Since you have sat down already, why
not remain seated? It's all quite harmless."

Cassebeer blushed. "Yes, harmless, isn't it?" He confirmed her
comment and then, brightening, asked, "Do you enjoy pictures, Madame?"

"Yes, in a way I enjoy pictures. Not all pictures. Pictures of me,
first of all. That Kirchner in the dressing room. I adore it. It is very
much my spirit. Imperious, outrageous, ugly, and beautiful. Don't
you find me both ugly and beautiful?"

"You, Madame, ugly? No, Madame, you are exceptionally beautiful."

"But you don't know me at all, Cassebeer. I am superficially beautiful. It all works. You see," and suddenly she wriggled her arm
across her breast and it shivered toward him, her hand coming to rest
at the edge of the table. If she extended her finger, a red nail could
touch his knee. She laughed again, throwing back her head. Her
hair, parted in the middle, flew back and then settled around her
small ears, curling beneath her chin. "Oh, Cassebeer. It all works,

but it works by itself. It wriggles and swivels and turns and moves like a mechanical device. I sing marvelously. I charm. I taunt. I delight. But I should tell you, my friend, that my face is quite green, quite purple, quite gray, as the Kirchner says it is. In fact, I am very beautiful, but I have a quite repulsive soul."

"Madame, I find all this a bit self-indulgent. If this is the way you charm in late afternoons, you will find me uncompromising. I am, after all, only a simple restorer and, I should remind you, the employee of your friend Herr Kastein." The last was unnecessary, but Cassebeer was interested in learning her response.

"Yes, I'm afraid you're right. Am I simply bored? I suppose that's the case. Bored and feckless. The truth is I dislike pictures, Kastein wearies me, and you, young man, are, as you say, only a simple restorer." She snuffed out her cigarette, rose up from the chaise, and left the room, her long dress floating behind her.

It was some moments before the perfume settled in the room. Cassebeer replaced the coverlet over the Virgin and departed for the day.

## Six

The following morning when Cassebeer arrived, he discovered Lazare Kastein seated quietly in the boudoir, sipping coffee. It was the first time Kastein had visited him since he had been engaged. He took it as a matter of course and extended his hand to greet his employer, but it was waved aside and Cassebeer was motioned to a chair facing Kastein.

"Draw your chair closer, young man," Kastein ordered. "Closer still. I want your knees to touch mine. I want to feel your breath as I talk to you."

Cassebeer found the instruction strange, but did as he was asked, drawing his chair so close that he felt Kastein's puffy kneecap against his shinbone. Kastein looked at him for a moment, passing his hazel eyes over Cassebeer's face, arching his bushy black brows in confusion as though seeking out some mark to which he might address himself.

"Now let me be direct and outspoken with you, young man. I am sure you know nothing of this. Yes, indeed, I am sure of it. Your face is too open, too unconcealed for any kind of treachery. Forgive me for using that vulgar word, that contemptible word; but I deal in treachery, you see." He began to wander; his voice was dry and rasping, and drops of spittle collected at his lips. "Yes, treachery, a whole life of treachery, mine. But that's the case. We become used to it. We, yes, we. No, not what you think. We—the universal *we* of my race—are used to treachery. And myself most particularly." His voice was parched and strained. He reached for his coffee, swilled it, and rinsed his mouth, almost gargling the brownish mixture to relieve his tenseness. "Yes. Do you think, my young friend, that being an educated Jew from Riga and studying in the land of Czar Nicholas III was, in fact, a pleasure? Not at all. I knew all the great collectors—Shuikov, for instance. I even helped him procure one or two pictures, but would you believe, notwithstanding all his influence, I was ordered out of the country. Ordered out, mind you, because I refused to return money to the Grand Duke, the Czar's nephew, when he grew tired of a Rembrandt drawing I had purchased for him at great expense. One morning I was awakened and told I had two hours to pack and leave the country. Whatever could fill two valises was all I was allowed to take. I left all my personal belongings, pictures of my parents, memorabilia—and I filled my two valises with drawings and canvases cut from their frames. That little treachery cost me a fortune. Paris next. I was there until the war began and then I fled. The French thought I was a German. What did they know of Kastein? I kept saying Riga, and they kept saying Germany. Off to Switzerland, and the contents of my gallery were sold at public auction like the good Kahnweiler. Another stupid treachery. Yes, my friend, Jews don't travel. They wander, they flee, but they don't travel. So now

I'm in Berlin. I've been here since 1917, and I like this country and I like this city and I love that woman. Yes. Now you see. It comes around to that, doesn't it? My love of Lily Schwann. She visits you now and then, doesn't she? She's fantastic, marvelous, but she is capable of enormous treachery. Yes, treachery." The words gathered force, and the spittle edged through the gaps in his teeth, collecting in little dots about his full lips. "Ah, what's the use? You understand, Cassebeer. You must be merciful. You really must be."

"My God, Herr Kastein," Cassebeer said, stunned by his pitiable revelations. "How can you imagine such a thing, such monstrousness? No, my good sir, not me. You may be certain I shall initiate nothing. And you do Madame Schwann an injustice. She has visited me once that I know of, once, and I am certain, after that visit and this conversation, that she will not visit me again—not without you, most assuredly not without you."

The conversation subsided, and Kastein returned to his gloomy introspection, passing his hand over his forehead and looking about the bright room with such dark eyes that it seemed wherever he turned his head there was a momentary darkness. Not once, however, did his eyes come to rest on the music stand and the shrouded Virgin.

After a quarter-hour of silence Cassebeer stood up and went into the sunlit dressing room and removed the covering from the Giorgione, hoping to attract Kastein's attention. When he turned back, his face molded into a smile, Kastein was gone. Cassebeer rang for Rolf Diamant to remove the coffee implements. When the young man arrived he began immediately to rearrange the furniture, then withdrew from under the chaise on which Kastein had been seated a small oblong lacquer box.

"Did Herr Kastein show you these?"

Cassebeer had not noticed the box. "No. He must have forgotten."

"Perhaps he did not intend to show you. They're quite extraordinary. Contemporary dueling pistols with remarkable pedigrees."

## *Seven*

Cassebeer had been working on the Giorgione for more than a month. The cleaning was virtually completed, although he knew that there was at least another month, perhaps two months, of the most exacting labor: the lifting and replacement of the blistered area and the retouching of the corners constituted the principal and most delicate of operations. He had become accustomed to working slowly, deliberating before contesting a new area, reflecting after it was completed, noting the quality of the dirt removed, examining its possible origin, assessing the response of various pigments to the univocal assault of time. In other words, Cassebeer was not simply restoring his Giorgione but acquiring experience and information that would serve him in the years to come. The hour with Lily Schwann was nearly forgotten, forsworn for the benefit of fantasy, and after more than ten days had passed without her return even fantasy evaporated, replaced by the insistent reality of the Virgin and her Babe. Kastein's panicked plea, however, was more difficult to forget.

It was a murky afternoon in July, more than seven weeks after Cassebeer had begun his work, that Lily Schwann reappeared. He suspected her presence, for when he had arrived in her dressing room that morning he had observed that a rose had been placed in a bud vase on the vanity table. It was not the apparition of the rose—an unspectacular bud not inconsistent with the devotional quality of her boudoir, though Cassebeer had seen no flower there before, no rose, not even a lily, which would have been Kastein's obvious votive offering to his mistress. No. He immediately recognized the invention of Lily Schwann herself. You see, the week before, in the course of cleaning the canvas of Giorgione, Cassebeer had uncovered a remarkable concealment. On the pediment to the left of the Virgin's draperied feet, there upon the cold interior floor, his cleaning had revealed the presence of a single rose blossom, conventional symbol of the Virgin, her sacrificial innocence, animadversion to the destiny of her child. "Madame Schwann," he thought immediately. It was she who had offered the rose to the Virgin. He smelled the rose and began his labors. Later in the afternoon, Rolf paid him a visit and brought him, as had become his habit, a glass of wine. Hans thanked him cordially, although he was disappointed that it was he who had knocked and entered.

"Who," Cassebeer asked, continuing to work, "favors roses?" It was an oblique question, but one he felt confident the intently observant Rolf Diamant would be able to answer.

"No one," he replied, blushing, "no one you would recognize."

"What does that mean? You are sometimes so very obscure."

"Well, not intentionally, Herr Cassebeer, not intentionally. What I mean is that I don't know for certain. Not Herr Kastein, he despises flowers. He says they use up human air. And Madame Schwann, her tastes run to everything. I don't know for certain. I, I honor roses."

"Could it have been you?" Cassebeer turned, smiling.

"It could have been," Rolf replied slowly, "but then it wasn't. Excuse me, I have to go." Rolf stood up, estimating Cassebeer's smiling face and noting the mockery that had accented his question, and departed.

An hour passed. The light of the late summer day, flattened and shimmering in the heat, had tired Cassebeer, and he flung himself down on Lily Schwann's settee. He drank off the glass of purplish claret in a single gulp, flushed, and closed his eyes. He heard no laughter. A hand passed over his head and a finger stroked the down of his hair, passing to the collar of his shirt. He shuddered with pleasure, the sharpened nail scratching at his neck. The perfume enlivened the air, and his face turned upward, her lips passing down to his, touching them gently, touching them again, kissing first his lips, then an eyelid, passing down the river of his eyebrows, returning to his lips. Young Cassebeer lifted his arms and grasped her shoulders, drawing her around to him, drawing her down to him. She came to her knees before him, and he held her head, kissing her hair, and she introduced him to voracious lips. She fell back, her body falling at the foot of the music stand that held the painting, and he, unknowing, found by the instinct of the race the precious passages of her body where, with tongue and hand guided by her knowing shivers, he returned her to satiety.

It was late, almost evening, beyond his hour of departure, when they recovered and Hans kissed Lily a final kiss, stood up from the floor, and made his way down the rear passage of the house, beyond the closed door of the kitchen, out into the early evening. As he passed into the street he saw an old lady crying cut flowers from a cart. He would have wished to buy a rose to take home to his room, but he noted that the heat had curled and withered them, and petals were falling from too many buds. He remembered then that he had not asked, in all that anguish of love, whether it was Lily Schwann who had brought the rose to the Virgin.

## Eight

The Virgin of Giorgione received only desultory attention from Cassebeer during the days that followed the beginning of his romance with Lily Schwann. It was exceedingly difficult to work with sustained attention, for no sooner had he completed his preparations, laying out his swabbings, examining the terrain already traversed, preparing the first moves of the day, than Lily might appear, and if he succeeded in returning to his work before late afternoon, when ordinarily he would be finished for the day, he would have to begin again, to recommence as though it were morning rather than dusk. But on other days, when she did not favor mornings for their trysting, it would be no easier, for whether the hour was early afternoon or three o'clock or teatime, the effect would be the same: work would be broken off, patching and blotchings of the small picture, islands of luminous color surrounded by the murky seas of centuries would have to wait, lacking causeways to peninsulas already cleared. And their lovemaking had progressed from passionate embraces upon lounge and carpet to easy disrobing and mutual assents. They talked little of anything but their pleasure, Cassebeer soliciting her satisfaction and Lily assuring him of his splendid virility—feeling his arms, pinching his breasts, sucking particular nodes of flesh until they rose in little bumps, exploring his body as though it were the *terra incognita* of ancient travelers, except that, unlike those intrepid explorers, she had no sense of danger. She did not even seem to fear Kastein.

Cassebeer would ask if she had locked the door, and she would shake her head that she had not. Once she replied, "It wouldn't matter," which Cassebeer took to mean that she had no concern whether Kastein knew or not. Cassebeer was delighted at her indifference, interpreting it as an affirmation of her satisfaction with him. Yet nonetheless he aspired to a life calling and could not take the risk of being discovered and denounced before he finished his work. At least, he calculated, if Kastein discovered their romance after the Giorgione was completed, he could make off with both his mistress and his achievement. Cassebeer therefore half-locked the door, turning the lock until it caught in the jamb without falling fully into its appointed hole, but nevertheless would have to be banged if someone tried to enter. Lily always watched his efforts to arrange this protective ruse with amusement, waiting behind him with her arms open to embrace him when he finished and turned to meet her.

So it continued for more than ten days, and work progressed betimes. The Giorgione was cleaned. Two months had elapsed since Cassebeer had first come to Kastein's residence. He had learned an enormous amount about the two most important things in the world, love and work. In both he was content and fulfilled. He intended the following day to invite Kastein to inspect the Giorgione and to deliberate with him whether he should press further—add paint to an abraded area, perhaps a half-centimeter overall, which would be hardly noticeable to any but a scrupulously attentive eye, and touch up one scuffed edge nearly lost in the distant landscape that looked in upon the seated Virgin in the upper right-hand corner—or declare the work fully restored and ready for delivery and exhibition. (It should be noted that Count von Preissendorf hoped to unveil his Giorgione in September, at an exhibition of his collection in the provincial museum of Posen, near which his family maintained their ancestral country home.)

### Nine

At eleven o'clock the following morning Hans Cassebeer entered the boudoir where he proposed to invite Kastein to an inspection. He hoped that Lily Schwann would be there, that she had not dressed quickly enough and would be awaiting him, lazily drawing a stocking over an outstretched leg, giving him permission to hug her thighs and fasten the snap. Or perhaps, hearing him approach (and he made a point of whistling a tune as he reached the top of the landing and turned to the right in the direction of his atelier), she would emerge from the bathroom adjacent to the boudoir and advance toward him, peignoir sheer and loose. He entered the boudoir and for the first time turned the lock completely behind him. But Lily Schwann was not there awaiting him, and, though the boudoir shone with sunlight, the Virgin was no longer honored by a rose. Only the painted rose at her feet remained. He frowned—petulantly, you might think, but really not so, for Cassebeer had persuaded himself that he loved Lily Schwann as much as he imagined she loved him and was quite simply annoyed that reality had confounded fantasy. Since it was his first love, authentic in its way, it seemed destined—by indulgence of sixteen hours of imagination since they had last made love—to endure forever and therefore to be considered true and trustworthy love.

All this took only a moment. No sooner had he removed his suit jacket and put on the alpaca coat in which he habitually worked than he heard a shouting in the hall. He could hear Lily's piercing laughter and Kastein's infuriated shrieks and foot-stampings. Suddenly there was a banging at the door of the sitting room, and he saw the handle turned back and forth with rapid, agitated motions. He threw the lock, and Lily entered.

The door remained open behind her, but she ignored it. She walked about the room with an exaggerated arrogance, her back arched, her shoulders pushed forward with outrageous indifference. But her lips quivered and an edge of swollen rosy flesh clung to the tooth that had bitten it. Lily did not turn to acknowledge Cassebeer. He was there, she was certain, but she had no intention of yielding to him and his outstretched arms. She came to rest before her Kirchner portrait and contemplated it. She drew a cigarette from a beaded purse, and Cassebeer hastened to light it. She did not acknowledge the gesture, but continued to face the portrait. Then with sudden, startling contempt, she approached her image and, lungs filled with smoke, kissed the lips of the picture. The smoke rose up, enveloping both her own and the picture's face.

"It's disgusting. I loathe it," she said, turning away from the picture on the wall. "His rage. Disgusting. He's in another rage. Another. Always the same. My God." Lily Schwann addressed her exasperation not to Cassebeer but to the room, to the eaves of the room, to the vault of the ceiling. Her words were there, sullen and hanging in the air.

"Can I do anything, my love, anything at all?" Cassebeer ventured.

" 'Love,' is it? Let me tell you, Hans, several lovings do not make a love. I wish you'd understand that, but then why should you? Kastein understands it no better than you. *Ach*, you men are such contemptible idiots and, worse yet, indulgent romantics."

Cassebeer was appalled. It was clear that she had told Kastein. Why? It was senseless and cruel, cruel to both of them, senseless and cruel. "You told him?" he asked, his voice trembling with anger.

"Yes, what? Yes, of course, I told him. Why not? He always

suspects me, suspects me constantly. I don't sleep around, as the street expression has it. But I have admirers, like you, Cassebeer. One lover, that's quite enough. One protector, friend, counselor, that's also quite enough. And Kastein is both, but he's dreadfully jealous. He thinks himself unworthy. He isn't, you know." Her voice thinned and she looked toward the window glinting with sunlight. "He really isn't, but he thinks he is because he's ugly and an art dealer and a Jew, and all those together aggravate him, and, in the end, I am blamed." She came at that moment toward Cassebeer and rested an arm upon his shoulder on which, for an instant, she laid her head; but then, rethinking the gesture, she raised her head again and sat down heavily on the sitting-room chaise. "I'm exhausted. Sit down with me, Cassebeer?" she asked, her voice weary but imploring.

Hans Cassebeer began to pace in front of her, clasping and un-clasping his hands. He could recognize today that he was foolish, those ancient, time-worn gestures of confusion, the wringings and claspings and scowlings of confused men suddenly confronted with the disarray of their amorous empires. But at that instant, for he was young and only recently become a lover, he wanted only to cover the nakedness of his confusion with the armature of a question, imagining naively that he could conceal his unpreparedness for the answer, even the right answer. "What do you think love is, Lily Schwann? What is it? What do you think of when you seduce someone? Why did you need to have me, to make me love you? Why, tell me?" He advanced toward her and, upon an impulse, slapped her face. She withdrew from the blow, but her face stung and she lifted her hands to protect it, thinking further blows would follow. At last she cried. Cassebeer was grateful for her tears. He fell onto the chaise beside her and took her hand, stroking it.

"Hans, my friend. I deserve your anger, but it's all so foolish. You loving me. Why? All because I made love to you? Making love is just that, making the acts of intimacy. It's not love. Pleasure and perversity, that's all. You're very handsome, dear Hans, but I don't love you. Kastein, whom I love, is most certainly not handsome and for that reason cannot for a moment believe I love him. It's all ridiculous. I've tried to prove it to him in so many ways, but he doesn't seem to understand, ever.

"Several years ago a young count called upon me at the theater and demanded that I accompany him to dinner. I did, since he seemed both determined and, as events proved, a bit unbalanced. But he was nothing compared with Kastein. All he wanted from me was the loan of a shoe, which seemed harmless enough compensation for an expensive dinner. Some months later the shoe was returned, soiled, but with an engraved note of thanks. It appears the count made use of his misbehavior by having his appreciation set in type. But Kastein found the shoebox and made such a scene. He actually threw the shoe out into the garden, where his butler found it a week later. He abused me unmercifully, claiming that this kind of thing happened all the time. Actually the count had been unique. Later it was a French businessman with larger schemes for me and bouquets of flowers seeded with diamond bracelets. I kept the flowers but returned the jewels. And again Kastein was enraged."

"But you made love to them, to the count and the businessman," Cassebeer interjected, his anger renewed.

"Of course not. The count was impotent, obviously, and the businessman was simply enormously rich and had decided the time had come for him to put an end to his misogyny. Who wanted such nonsense? No, I didn't make love to them. But Kastein made so much of those episodes, coming as they did one tumbling upon the other, each a ground for astounding scenes and denunciations, that I decided to show him. And so I began letting admirers become lovers, like you, Hans. There have been more than ten in the past year. Ardent young doctors, writers, millionaires. Each time I leave them I return to Kastein and make deep love to him, deep love, shuddering love. I did that last night, and the moment we were done and lying back in the cool of the evening, he demanded to know with whom I had been proving my love for him. I told him. You can't imagine his rage. He flung me out of bed and beat me with a belt. Not hard, but hard enough to make the point, and then he disappeared. This morning he returned, and you heard the racket. I think something has gone wrong with all of this. It's a sour ritual now, and it has begun to hurt—hurt him, hurt others, hurt me."

It was difficult for Cassebeer to respond to Lily Schwann's speech. Not only was he inexperienced in such matters, never before having had to cope with a mistress, but he realized that he was completely baffled by her apparent sangfroid in the narration of her disagreeable behavior. For a moment he continued to sit beside her, a dumb, half-knowing smile upon his face, his hand continuing to stroke hers, but his intelligence, strained and agitated, was hunting for a recourse he could not find. What to do? What to say? He had no experience to recall, no literature to consult. And so a stream of "wells," "perhapses," "might nots" issued from him without fluency. As nothing followed each opening sally, however, he joined her at last in silence.

Lily Schwann was beyond the reach of Cassebeer's counsel, and his counsel, moreover, was nonexistent. What was left to him and to her was in fact the only communication in which they had achieved any semblance of articulate feeling. They had little alternative other than to make love. Another stupidity, he came to realize later, many years later. Not alone a stupidity, but an arrogance that some men habitually contrive to assume in the presence of more worldly women. Frightened by the authority of sovereign women, they assume that the only tactful and meaningful and appropriate language is that of passion.

Hans Cassebeer began, therefore, to shift his weight, to raise his hand from hers to encircle her back, to draw her to him, to seize her shoulders and turn her, to put kisses upon her tired eyes, to let his small tongue assay the curve of her lips. Lily Schwann acquiesced, but that was all. She allowed his caresses, but did not respond, and the longer she remained passive, the more ardent and single-minded

Cassebeer became. Making love was a restorative, a means of renewal, and a respite from a conversation to which he had nothing to contribute. The sheer emptiness and vacuity of his gestures, lost to him, were not wasted upon Lily Schwann. When he undid her gown, clumsily using one hand to unbutton while the other continued the work of caress, her exhausted indifference turned to tears, and at the end—at the moment when she sat before him, her breasts revealed, her gown bunching at her thighs—her sobs became low growls of laughter, laughter choking with tears, tears repudiating laughter, laughter winning over tears, tears matting upon her cheeks, laughter rising into screams, gasps for air, and laughter returning like a waterfall gusted by wind. Cassebeer understood that Lily had become hysterical and as he raised his hand to slap her again, thinking to jar her back to him, he became aware that another was present in the room, hunched in the chair just to his rear, and at that moment had raised a hand that held a small revolver.

"Stop. Stop. Stop. Stop." The voice was absolutely clear, each order distinct and apart. Cassebeer dropped his arm and Lily Schwann fell forward, her laughter succeeded by low, muffled sobs. Lazare Kastein's voice was very quiet, and he spoke as he stood up and moved toward them. "I have seen enough. The last treachery. The very last." He pointed the revolver at Lily's exhausted body and was about to squeeze the trigger, but instead he stopped, looked for an instant at Cassebeer, and turned the revolver to his own temple and fired. His head fell to one side and his body shuddered and unwound.

## Ten

In the weeks that followed, the scandal made headlines in the afternoon papers, the morning papers being more concerned with the graver details of politics and economic unrest. Hans Cassebeer had fled the house, pushing Rolf Diamant down the massive escalier as he ran up toward the pistol shot. There was an inquest, the episode became public, and, after a period of disgrace, Cassebeer became something of a celebrity. Lily Schwann left Germany almost immediately for the Ticino, where she had friends. And the Giorgione? That had a more decisive aftermath.

The Virgin of Giorgione was exhibited, as planned, by Count von Preissendorf at the provincial museum in Posen that autumn. Cassebeer fortunately did not attend its *revernissage*. Several scholars— a Signor Aldo Pignatelli from the Accademia in Venice, himself the author of a monograph on the Bergamo *Virgin*, and a German scholar from Munich, Dr. Rayner Urteil—were present and scrutinized the work with enormous care. Several days later they gave an interview to the Posen *Wochenblätter*, which was reprinted in all the major art periodicals of the country. They made it clear that the work could not possibly have been by Giorgione himself, that however much it was a work of the time, indeed, the work of a Venetian master, and even the work of a master familiar with the visionary clarity and warmth of the great Giorgione, it was unquestionably a rehash of other works, a veritable Renaissance pastiche. The most singular and striking point in their argument was the fact that Giorgione would never have stooped to such an obvious sentimentality as the emplacement of a rose, however subtly delineated, at the feet of the Virgin. No Virgin of Giorgione, they concluded, would have been honored by such a cliché device.

# The Monumental Sculptor

One suspects that coincidence, made routine by repetition, is the origin of superstition. A light reading, this, of our commonplace insistence upon a stern and impersonal causality, but—however one's philosophy—not at all irrelevant to the life of that remarkable sculptor Estienne Delahaye, who died of fright last month in Mougins, where he had passed the winter in his country house, attended by his beautiful wife and their mutual secretary, a young man whose name he had refused to commit to memory.

## One

It hardly mattered to Estienne Delahaye that war was regarded as imminent by all the knowledgeable habitués of Les Trois Flèches, the cool and cask-lined cellar where he went every afternoon to drink a glass or two after his last class was dismissed. The existence of Les Trois Flèches was, it seemed to everyone, quite inexplicable, even to Monsieur Delagrave, its *patron*, who had become a wine merchant by accident several years before. The story of Monsieur Delagrave's inheritance of the enormous stock of wine—amassed over four generations by the family of the late Comtesse Ambrosie de Valois, the immensely capable widow of Comte Victor de Valois, killed during a cavalry charge of the French army in the Great War—is another story and would interfere with our own. (Moreover, there are sufficient resemblances that they can be, at best, suggested, but not exposed.) Nonetheless, shortly after his inheritance of the more than twelve thousand bottles that constituted the *cave* of the late comtesse—and her accommodating stipulation that he be granted a long-term lease at modest rent and permission to reconstruct the entrance to the *cave* if he chose to become a proper wine merchant and leave off his years of cheese-making ("Cheese, my dear, even your remarkable *chèvre*, is still useless without a fine burgundy—*chèvre* serves the wine, not the other way about. Become a connoisseur of wines. Anyone can supply you with cheese")—Hector Delagrave opened Les Trois Flèches to the modest traffic of Vézelay.

Hector Delagrave had undertaken the remodeling of the *cave*, whose entrance lay a half-dozen feet below the street that leads down from the basilica. The *cave* was situated in a stone house that had been added to the considerable castellar construction of the family of the Comte de Valois—originally built, one would construe from its architecture, in the early sixteenth century, after that family had retreated from the countryside and become the largest grain and wine merchants in the region. In other words, the de Valoises were early bourgeoisie, a not unfamiliar development when aristocracy failed on the land and were astute enough to acquire a foothold in the growing merchant towns of France—and Vézelay was not merely a merchant town, but in earlier days had been a great center of crusading Catholicism, hospitable to that ferociously humble saint, Bernard, of

the neighboring monastery village of Clairvaux. At all events, the
*cave* of the Comte de Valois was situated—as were his stocks of grain
and barley, stores of tubbed butter, vats of oil, dried Spanish olives,
and Moroccan dates, his accountants and overseers, the storerooms
of his leases and currencies—in a stone house, connected by an
underground passageway to the magnificent manor house in which
the greatest of his great-grandfathers had established the fortune of
the family. There, in that cool but essentially plain, unembellished
stone edifice, fronting what had become a quiet residential street of
the resolutely medieval city of Vézelay, Monsieur Hector Delagrave
sold the young wines of the district, the whites of Chablis only thirty
kilometers to the north, the Sancerres from a bit further south, and
the Beaujolais and old Burgundies that constituted his inheritance
from Madame la Comtesse. The casks lined the walls, their spigots
dripping; the smoke of large candles on sturdy wooden tables served
by three-legged stools gave the *cave* its intimate, however lugubrious
and unhealthily dank, atmosphere.

On that early February afternoon, a warm sun having turned the
light snow of the previous day into slush and mud, a group of peasants
were gathered playing dominoes and drinking wine from unlabeled
bottles. Monsieur Delagrave, fattened by his prosperity, leaned over
the long oak counter smoking, the cigarette hanging over his lip,
almost singeing the shaggy ends of his red mustache that in previous
years had given his presentably oval head and its soft covering of
tightly curled red hair an aspect of charm, even of sophistication.

Estienne Delahaye descended slowly into the cellar, holding on to
the metal railing that had been installed to accommodate the elderly
and the poorly sighted. Estienne was of course neither elderly nor
astigmatic, but he was fastidious. It was more important that he
maintain his dignity than run the risk of missing a step (as many did)
and tripping headlong into that peasant gathering. There were other
cafés to which he might have gone of an afternoon after his classes
in art history, life drawing, and sculpture at the "Académie Séra-

phique" (as he called the girls' school presided over by the stern and military Argentières sisters, Floride and Isabelle) on the outskirts of the town, where Estienne and five other masters conducted forty young ladies of good provincial (and several foreign) families from puberty to early marriage; but he preferred Les Trois Flèches. His need at that hour was for silence, not salubrious conviviality. When his classes were completed, usually by four in the afternoon, and the girls had gone with Floride Argentières—a husky spinster with glaucous eyes hooded by darkly shadowed lids—to the soccer field for an hour of skinned elbows and bruised shins, Estienne went to Les Trois Flèches for Monsieur Delagrave's hot wine.

"Your glass, Monsieur?" the *patron* asked solicitously as Estienne put down his cap and stretched his legs beneath the table. Estienne nodded without speaking. Monsieur Delagrave shrugged. He was quite tolerant with artists. His wife painted watercolors on silk and never spoke with him when she was in the midst, as she said, of "creating." A moment later the ceramic jug was at Estienne's elbow; a hot poker was plunged for an instant into the ruby liquid; a sizzle, a bubbled surface, and the wine was heated. Monsieur Delagrave went away. Clearly, Estienne Delahaye chose to be by himself.

It did not seem sensible (or, for that matter, quite intelligible) to Estienne that he should be having difficulty sleeping. For the past three nights, however, he had been unable to sleep. It wasn't the bed; he had thought to blame the unyielding bedsprings and an insubstantial mattress, but they were at most the proximate causes of his discomfort. Indeed, he eliminated the bed from the inventory of his scrutinies, since the night had found him insomniac even without the effort of lying down to sleep. He suspected that it was perhaps his own trial of creation. Shortly before Estienne had left Paris to assume his teaching position at the academy of the Argentières, he had received an important commission from a bank in Lyons. Its directors had admired his submission to the Salon d'Automne the previous year and, having reviewed his credentials with old Aristide

Maillol, to whom Estienne had referred the bank officials, they had commissioned him to develop a bas-relief in bronze to elaborate the entrance to their new offices. In due course, after weeks of sketching, Estienne prepared a series of drawings as well as an installation plan to assist the visually unsophisticated bank directors to apprehend immediately the weight and scale of the relief.

The imagery with which Estienne Delahaye worked seemed both intelligent and appropriate. It avoided the obvious vulgarity and commercialism of the neoclassical style then in vogue for the decoration of stock and bond certificates (recumbent ladies with cornucopias in hand from which tumbled coal or ingots of lead or iron), even though Estienne was well aware that the bearded gentlemen who conducted the affairs of the distinguished Banque de Midi-France wanted their sculpture august but unmistakably traditional. He had conceived instead something joyfully irrepressible, having in mind Matisse's *La Luxe*. Installed in his bas-relief tableau, therefore, were three women and a fluting faun disporting about an underground well that burbled and streamed in their midst. The women's breasts rippled beneath a filmy drapery, their heads were clasped by ivy, their bodies turned in the cubist manner toward the faun, who held his pipes in one hand, lowered to his furry thighs, and bore aloft in the other a cutting of grapes, which he extended toward the women, the graces of Lyons. The work, to be executed in bronze upon a panel four feet high by five feet long, was to be called (alluding to other connections in the history of the modern movement) *The Three Graces—The City of Lyons*. Such a simple conceit, in which subject is less significant than execution, is the case, most generally, with the best of modern art. It was not Estienne's intention to narrate or describe; far from his intention was the impingement of literature upon the plastic arts. Indeed, as he conceived it, the art of his century—the twentieth century at the close of its fourth decade—could no longer narrate. The patient accretion of detail that had characterized the historical style of the nineteenth century had degenerated into conceits and stylizations. However, with Rodin and later his own Maillol, what had been recovered were the majesty of the materials and the perception that what a sculptor removed was every bit as important as what remained. In a word, Estienne Delahaye, who had assisted Maillol for three summers when he was working at Marly-le-Roi near Paris, knew that he himself was a romantic abstractionist, an artist who adored touch and texture, the skin of bathing women glinting in the sun, but who adored as well the peeling away of those realistic details that made women too definitely and historically precise, too peasant or too aristocrat, too young or too old, too delicate or too voluptuous. Indeed, what he sought and had the ambition of achieving (no differently, one supposes, from all those great sculptors of human flesh in his time) was to elaborate the universal embedded in bone and tissue, the flicker of recognition that permits the creator for one moment, and the viewer forever, to acknowledge the translation of figure into idea and the latent shapes of bronze, marble, and wood into form.

When the commission bestowed by the Banque de Midi-France was confirmed, Estienne was celebrated by his Paris acquaintances, each of whom was subtly transformed by the bright dawn of his success from peer into admirer—a situation that pleased Estienne, who never dealt well or comfortably with peers. Estienne did think it prudent, however, to humble himself, if ever so slightly, to his master and sometime colleague, Aristide Maillol, to whom he wrote a brief but respectful letter of thanks for having applauded his credentials to the bank directors. As difficult as Estienne found peers over whom he had little or nothing to lord, how much more difficult did he find accomplished masters, masters like Maillol who could, in Estienne's view, afford to be generous, even to the point, it would appear, of tolerating the theft of a commission by a distinctly junior collaborator such as Estienne Delahaye. But this, too, this so-called theft, will be described in its time and can be judged if indeed it was, in anything but a technically moral sense, a theft. At the moment it didn't even cross Estienne's mind as he contemplated the misunderstandings of the bank directors, their refusal to allow him the license they would have never dared to question if it had been proposed by an eminence such as Maillol. Or, lacking Maillol's reputation, if Estienne Delahaye had had the financial independence to stand his ground.

Unfortunately, at his young age (he was only thirty-four), and despite the inauguration of his maturity as an artist and the acknowledgment of his gifts and achievements by astute critics and discerning collectors, Estienne Delahaye was still so poor that he was obliged to teach in a young ladies' finishing school two hundred and fifty-one kilometers from Paris, cut off from the circle of friends who considered him a sculptor of great promise. He would have been content to eke out an existence on the occasional commissions that had begun to come his way, but his old father, who had been gassed during the First War, was failing in a nursing home and relied upon his only son to supply his needs. From time to time, Estienne resented the obligation he had assumed, but having carried that broken body in his arms so many years, he remained profoundly moved by his father's condition and, however tempted, always refused to forsake him. There was nothing to do but teach from October until May, fleeing on holiday weekends for a respite among his friends in Montparnasse, but returning punctually from Paris on the last bus to resume his instruction of the young ladies of the Académie.

His particular gloom then, that dreary day in February, he ascribed to the arrival of two letters: one from the director of the building committee of the Lyons bank, objecting to the manner in which he had delineated the bodies of the three women of grace, contending that they "seemed most unnatural, hence uncomfortable, and for that reason not at all full of grace," and the other from his close friend, no less poor than himself, but carefree and without constrictive responsibilities—a young painter as fluent as Vlaminck—who informed him that he was to be married after Easter. Neither of the letters should have disturbed him (since he could cope with the incomprehension of the bankers and was objectively quite pleased with the prospect of his friend's marriage), but both put him in a wretched mood. Indeed, whether from lack of sleep or the anxiety aroused by the letters, he had ruined a drawing of one of his students that morning, reworking her character too energetically, leaving little more than a smudge when he finished his expostulations on her clumsy understanding of the connection between neck and torso. He had been unaccountably rude to a new student, the fifth to join his workshop in sculpture. He had snapped at this young woman—she was, he recalled, quite beautiful, although he had given himself little time to assimilate her presence—telling her to sit herself down and watch what the others were doing.

"What's your name?" he thought to ask her after his irritation with her unannounced appearance in the studio had passed.

"Helene," she had answered.

"Helene what, child?" Estienne snapped with irritation, not looking up from the letter of his friend, which was on the table before him.

"Helene Miravilla."

"Not French?"

"No, Monsieur, although my father admires France." Estienne merely grunted, looked up briefly, observed the young lady with long black hair, tied in braids that circled her head, and dismissed the interruption from his mind. He returned to contemplate the marriage of his friend and the letter that he had to compose to the bankers, explaining the reconception of the human body undertaken since the cubist revolution.

At the *cave* Estienne drank off the mug of mulled wine and called out to the *patron* for paper and pencil. Thinking that he intended to sketch, Monsieur Delagrave hurried to bring the tablet and charcoal he reserved for notations of deliveries.

"Not these, Monsieur Delagrave. I don't intend to draw. I wish to write."

"Are you a writer as well?" the other, retaining his illusions, demanded.

"Not at all, but even artists write letters from time to time."

"To be sure, to be sure," the latter replied, not without an edge of sarcasm.

Estienne Delahaye had no interest in opposing his own mood of depression to the blunt weapon of the proprietor's wit. He drank off the dregs, put a coin on the table, brushed back his long brown hair with thin white fingers, and, settling his cap securely upon his head, departed Les Trois Flèches before the proprietor returned.

The following morning, after a more satisfactory night of rest, Estienne Delahaye seated himself in the studio classroom in the garden wing of the vast country house of the Académie Argentières and awaited the four, now five, young women who attended his sculpture class. He drew idly, sketching a marble fountain that occupied the center of a small copse of fir and beech trees just outside the bay windows of the studio. Hearing a low knock upon the door, he called out "Enter," and continued to draw. When he looked up he recalled her immediately, with evident pleasure and surprise. "Mademoiselle Miravilla, yes?"

"Yes, Monsieur. Helene Miravilla."

"Won't you sit down?" He rose and, with untypical politeness, moved around the desk to draw up a chair and gestured to the young woman to be seated. He felt exceptionally well that morning. The coffee had been strong. (Obviously the old woman who cooked for the assembly had responded to his pleas for morning coffee that was not only hot but strong.) More important, Estienne had slept well. His tall and lanky body, usually crimped and discomfited by the struggle for sleep, was free of aches and the crackings of his bones. He felt erect, strong, and, exactly speaking, young.

"And now, Mademoiselle, what can I do for you?"

"The truth is, Monsieur, that I have a particular interest in art—more so, I should imagine, than most of the young women here." She spoke with astonishing self-assurance for one so young, eighteen or nineteen he supposed; but her tone, which suggested no contempt for her fellow students, registered her own gravity and self-possession.

"And why is that?" Estienne asked, smiling, delighted by the amusing innocence and seriousness of the young woman's announcement.

"It's a long story but of no particular importance, I should think. My father wanted to be an artist when he was a young man, but it wasn't possible. He had to come to the assistance of his own father, who was a pharmacist on the Ramblas in Barcelona. All thoughts of pursuing painting as his first love came to an end. The remainder of his life—"

"Is he dead?" Estienne interrupted, wishing to register his acknowledgment of the palpable sadness of her story, although its analogies to his own were not exact and unfortunately his father owned no pharmacy.

"Oh, no," the young woman replied, smiling slightly. "I did make it sound like that, didn't I? No, not dead in fact, but there are many ways of dying, are there not? One sometimes dies long before the heart stops beating." Estienne nodded, surprised by the girl's intensity and understanding. "At all events, although he became quite wealthy from several herbal decoctions that he bottled and distributed throughout Spain, he longed to have a painter in the family. No sons, you see, only daughters—and I the eldest of these. I have four younger sisters. There is no need for me to become a painter, but I should like to know art."

"I understand. You wish to please your father, to give him the satisfaction of knowing that his youthful enthusiasm is shared—passed on, as it were, from his generation to yours."

"You *do* understand, Monsieur. You *do* understand." Helene Miravilla looked up from her long and graceful fingers, upon which her eyes had been modestly fixed, and thanked him with a glance.

Estienne Delahaye observed the loveliness of the young woman seated before him. When occupied with her petition, she had sat, her head lowered, speaking through half-closed eyes, with shyness, he thought; but having come to agreement—although it had not yet been formulated properly—she had relaxed her formal posture, lifted her head, and smiled, her even white teeth radiant in the morning sunlight, as though an offering fire had been set in the grotto of her face, a pale white ever so lightly mixed with burnt umber, giving her complexion the richness of milk flavored with *pastis*. Her head was aureoled with long black hair braided and fastened into a bun. She was wearing a silk dress patterned with red roses against a black field and fringed with a white tulle collar that guarded her modesty, hanging down as it did a good three inches to disguise the suggestion of what Estienne guessed must be her utterly white breasts.

"So it is agreed. You will enter my class in sculpture. Besides that, we shall arrange a tutorial for you and review the history of art together." Estienne half rose from his desk and extended his hand toward the young woman to confirm their contract. She stood up as if to accept his gesture, but unaccountably turned away from him and left the room.


### *Two*

It was approaching Easter in Vézelay. The last snow had melted and only the winds of the valley in which that little hill city was situated continued to blow contentiously, reminding the spring planters that the season had not yet changed. The young ladies of the boarding school of the sisters Argentières were already preparing for their recess—arranging their luggage, which had been returned from the manor house basement to their rooms preparatory to their departure the following Thursday. The term was nearly over. During the previous year, the first that Estienne Delahaye had passed in this position, he had looked forward eagerly to the departure; he had written letters to his Parisian friends alerting them to the day when he would be back among them, arranged several rendezvous at La Coupole, and seen to the packing of the small plasters he was taking to the foundry where his work was cast. Unfortunately he had accomplished little during the term and had to make do with a sketchbook full of half-finished notations and *croquis*. He knew perfectly well that his well-disciplined and rigorous schedule had been disarranged. Before the arrival of Helene Miravilla at the Académie, he had had little provocation to distract himself from his work. Women—much less the attractions of a young woman, a Capricorn just beyond her nineteenth birthday—were not on his agenda. Occasionally he fell into bed with one or another member of his group, for there were always girls who took particular pleasure in offering themselves to what they called, vaguely, "creative people"—not thinking that the gift, like gold dust, would make their skin radiant, but rather, like hierophants, imagining that carnality was more efficiently spiritualized and indeed justified if consummated with some young artist. That was the extent of it. Estienne Delahaye, undeniably handsome, was cooperative from time to time, but in general regarded such hangers-on as dissolute and wasteful. He had no time to fall in love. It was much more urgent, he thought, "to get on with it"—a phrase he used to encompass everything from earning his keep to making his art. His best friend, a strikingly ugly and sexually insatiable young poet from the Dordogne, Alain Malburet, always found such phrases laughable. He chided Estienne for his aloof and (to Alain's lights) cold and businesslike conduct of his life; but Estienne dismissed such criticism, always reminding Alain that the latter could afford the luxury of his libertinism, since his father paid him an annual stipend to stay away from the ancestral village of Brantôme. (Alain's father, a wealthy provincial lawyer, settled on this course after the third young woman of the region had brought suit for alienated affections against his son and on one occasion even produced evidence of her pregnancy—happily miscarried—to confirm her claim.)

"I have the advantage neither of your looks nor of your father's self-righteousness," Estienne would reply cruelly when Alain tried to involve him in one of his weekend escapades. It didn't bother Alain Malburet. His ugliness was splendid (overly full lips, puffy cheeks of a purplish cast, and vast soupy brown eyes) and he knew it, but he also knew that the writing of poems—the kind of poems for which he had already a considerable reputation—was not in the least compromised by the adventurous and amatory exuberance with which he pursued his life amid the underworld of Paris, the Gypsies, the ex-convicts, the pimps, the bars and boîtes where any evening he could be found with his marc and a prostitute.

It was all quite incomprehensible to Estienne Delahaye. "Who does he think he is?" he would mumble to himself when he parted from Alain at La Coupole at midnight and returned to his room to sketch before he went to sleep. But he knew the answer and phrased it to himself as he examined his face in the cracked mirror that hung above his bathroom sink. "He's an ugly poet," Estienne would reply to his own good looks. "He needs everything he can arrange," he would add meanly, but in fact he admired the energy and conviction with which his friend pursued life, disappearing for months on end and returning with fabulous stories of a walking tour he had taken in the Dades mountains of southern Morocco, or of meeting a millionaire diamond merchant from Carpathia whom he had served as bodyguard for three months in Persia. There was energy in Alain Malburet, Estienne conceded—electric energy, automobile energy, fast ships and airplane energy—and his poems proved it. Most recently, Alain had published a book of poems arranged on the pages in the shapes of jewels he had handled for his Carpathian merchant: poems in the form of tiaras, pendants, bracelets, single strands, and even a poem admired by Blaise Cendrars, called "Solitaire." He had written the suite of twenty poems in a month, and one of the best avant-garde publishers, Simon Kra, himself an old circus man like Cendrars, had brought it out. Alain had given Estienne one of the copies on Lafuma, not from the very top of the edition—which had annoyed him, since Estienne regarded Alain as his closest friend. Estienne, however, could not help admiring the volume. The jewels were precious, but not the poems. They were not, as might be thought, little evocations of ice or descants to the color of the gems, but rather fabrications of memories, immensely sensuous and concrete, of his days in the Middle East, its aromas and textures, its architecture and its sunsets, its hieratic styles and titivations, all linked by a consciousness explicitly European, explicitly humane, and explicitly vagabond and independent.

The critical difference, if one may describe it precisely, between Estienne Delahaye and his closest friend, Alain Malburet, lay not in the discrimination of their circumstance, or in that of their looks, or of the habits of their sexuality, but rather in their views of the purpose of their art. Estienne Delahaye wished to be successful, whereas Alain Malburet was as indifferent to success as a tree is to its shadow.


## Three

Estienne Delahaye was unaware that he had fallen in love with Helene Miravilla. One would have thought, given the calculation and care with which he pursued his career, that he would have devoted at least the same degree of reflection to the mounting blood pressure and perspiring palms that attended each appearance of his young Spanish student. Not at all. Indeed, a man with the temperament of Estienne Delahaye would not have been aware that the presence of the young Spanish student encouraged his hunched shoulders to relax, propelled his features into bashful smiles and stolen glances. If observed and brought to his attention, such involuntary gestures he would account as accidental, nothing more than a response to fortune.

The word *fortune*, it seems, occupied an exceptionally prominent position in the glossary of Estienne's interpretation of the world. Despite work, study, endless hours of copying the classical statuary of the Louvre and days spent before Rodin's *Burghers of Calais*, Estienne still regarded his achievement, his modest bursaries, his first commission (the curious circumstance to which we have already alluded but reserved for later exposition), his invitation to teach at the Académie Argentières as the workings of fortune—that mottled notion that enfolds coincidence, destiny and fate, chance and causality. Estienne would, as likely as not misusing the word *coincidence*, describe an unfortunate event—a drowning, an automobile accident, the collapse of a building—as coincidence, when, in fact, the episode exhibited none of coincidence's characteristic marks: the conjunction of two independent orders of causality, their intersection at a specific instant, which, bursting with fullness and meaning, overflows into the unforeseen. For Estienne, coincidence was redolent with the heavy incense of the occult, as if the orders and unfoldings of nature entailed conjunctions and synchronizations planned in the caverns of hell or the secret cabals of magicians and alchemists.

For Estienne as a boy, it was not enough to study hard, to help his mother in the tobacco shop that the family owned in a working-class district on the outskirts of Paris, to help his father up and down the stairs of the ancient building in which they had their rooms; these steady and onerous obligations he supplemented with musings about his destiny and the operation of the stars, with reflections on the tarot (whose reading he learned from the son of a Rumanian emigrant who lived beneath his family), with dabblings in palmistry, which he thought foolish (preoccupied as the reading of the hand is with fixities of line that he thought more fatal than free), and lastly with the uses of numerology, which he found particularly attractive, as the numbers lay at the base of all the other devices of scanning the world—the times and degrees of the horoscope, the ranking and station of the tarot's arcana: indeed all the intellectual disciplines of reading fortune turned upon the intelligence and the significance of numbers. Numbers he played with, determining that one day was preferable to another, afternoons preferable to mornings, certain times more suitable than others for special engagements and rendezvous; and among these the numbers one and five were for some reason of particular attractiveness. All this parsing of his world enabled Estienne to transcribe into mystery what was in fact enacted according to the rigors imposed by inadequate diet, the absence of luxury, the obligations of a working mother and a wounded father. The stars, the arcana, the numbers were permutations of release, as though Estienne—having the right word, employing it appropriately, speaking it correctly— would be able to pull the dropcloth from his world and reveal things of gold and crystal and bright color beneath. As it was, try as he would, the dropcloth remained secure; the world beneath remained covered; and, however diligently he tried to plan the escapades and adventures of his adolescence for Mondays and Fridays, for one o'clocks and fives, for January and May, for every option of the solitary one and every five-fingered grasp of the hand, his world remained pretty much unchanged.

After several years of this attention, Estienne Delahaye appeared to give it up; by the age of seventeen he determined that it hardly mattered, that what would come to pass would come to pass notwithstanding, that only talent and work would save his life, that there would be no elf, no sprite, no magic lantern, no secret word, but that everything would come to pass as it was intended it should. Estienne concluded with a sigh that his name was not mentioned in the councils of heaven, that if indeed unseen powers and invisible orders planned out the venue of each day, separating the living from the dead, affixing the numbers to be called by the black angel and the numbers to be drawn by the national lottery, he was too young and too unimportant to be bothered with. When Estienne determined, therefore, to become a sculptor, to leave his father in a home after his mother's death (in Estienne's twentieth year), to give up his job in a foundry where he had learned the methods and techniques of casting, it appeared he had abandoned his pursuit of the world's mystery, packing away his books and manuals, forgetting the tarot, ignoring his numbers, and deciding that in their place there was, at the most, fortune and co-incidence, for which we can read luck.

His meeting with Aristide Maillol in an empty room of the Louvre, where the old master had come to see a small sculpture of Venus, was therefore luck. The fact that Estienne had the courage to address the master and reveal his knowledge of ancient sculpture some would call arrogance, but Estienne thought it good fortune, since normally he would have been tongue-tied; and that the old man was returning that afternoon to his village outside Paris, Marly-le-Roi, where Es-tienne had a friend whom he had promised to visit, and that Estienne had seized the opportunity to accompany Maillol on the train ride— *that* he would call coincidence. It was more complex, undoubtedly. Like a man blind from birth who imagines that the fingers create the face they feel, Estienne had devised a schema for the world: it dis-cerned what conformed to its touch. When, however, the workings of the world, like the chiaroscuro of the face—a matter of light and dark, unrecognized by the blind man's nimble fingers—exceed the premises of the schema, then the interpretation frays and thins. It is at such times that blind men become frightened and that believers in the tarot, in horoscopes, in numbers, and in coincidence become the prisoners of fearful obsession.

## *Four*

At the beginning of his instruction of Helene Miravilla, Estienne was warm and impassioned, feeling the need to transmit to her in a few months the excitement he had won over the years from the re-searches of the impressionists, the *fauves*, and the cubists. She would sit beside him in the classroom, and while he talked of *La Grande*

*Jatte* or the various estates of Cézanne's *Bathers* or Matisse's *La Danse*, his arm would rest upon the back of her chair, his left hand pointing to the color reproductions that he had set upon an easel. Occasionally, when the need to underscore occurred in his conversation, he would employ—almost unconsciously, one thinks—the arm that lay behind her to press emphases upon her graceful shoulder. These gestures— a small tap, a minuscule poke, an indenting depression of his index finger—were at best aids to teaching; only once, when he wished to suggest the sweeping folds of rose silk that swathed a Bonnard woman dressed for promenade, did he move his fingers slowly over her back, suggesting the rippling smoothness and breathing hug of the fabric upon the body of its subject. He was unaware, it seems, that by the end of March, after the first five weeks of their tutorial had passed, Helene's chair, earlier positioned more than a foot from his own, had moved closer by inches with each session, until only the smallest bit of sunlight, the shape of a lozenge of glazed lemon, could be seen between their bodies.

Helene, for her part, although she could not be described as having come to love her art instructor, found him immensely reassuring. She had been ejected, she felt strongly, from a home in which the presence of five daughters allowed no one of them to enjoy the concentrated attention of her father. Competing among four others with his business, his club, his social ambitions for the time and affection that a single daughter would regard as her first dowry—even from the privileged heights of the firstborn—was inevitably unsatisfactory. Even though their father, big and blustery as he was, dispensed love with the same enthusiasm with which he distributed medicaments and the all-pur- pose remedy of his decoction, from the viewpoint of the sisters what each received was at the most a single bite from an undifferentiated loaf. Their father had no interest in personalizing his love. After the death of his wife in a street accident shortly after the birth of the youngest girl, he had virtually separated himself from the love of women, regarding himself as bounteously supplied with feminine charms and coquetry by the presence of his daughters, whose names he had formed into an anagram so that he might call to them all in a single word when he returned to his comfortable apartment each evening. And, indeed, when he returned from the pharmacy approximately at the hour of eight, word had already passed from the youngest, who was watching the street for his arrival, to the eldest, Helene, who by custom assisted him to remove his overcoat or offer him his dressing robe, while the others awaited him with his newspaper, his mail, his glass of sherry, each receiving for her smiles and ministrations an affectionate kiss, a pinch of the cheek, an inquiry about school or a comment upon the weather. "Papá," as they all called him, would disappear into the study, and only reappear when supper was convoked an hour later and the same ritual, slightly modified, would resume. The passing of dishes, the saving of the finest cuts and unbruised plums for him, their father, the weighing of words and the transmission of bits and pieces of information, often in French, which he had obliged them to learn, each serving to aggrandize the offerer in his eyes, left the children by the time of their arrival into adolescence and beyond, to the age of nineteen—to which point Helene Miravilla had come on the fifth of January, a month prior to her arrival in Vézelay—tense and unsettled. The girls had little preparation to estimate, much less to cope with, the formidable passion that lay coiled within them. Each of them, in her own way, despised other women; each, in her own way, thought that only Papá would love and protect her. Papá, on the contrary, thought ultimately only about Papá, his pharmacy, the distribution of his patent remedies, which, interrupted by the civil war, could now be energetically resumed as peace neared. Although he had remained nonpolitical, nodding warmly to Republicans, Anarchists, Communists in the days when Catalonia was securely Republican, he was prepared to serve the Falangist conquerors with equal solicitude. It was the medicine and its dubious therapy that inspired him—"the luck of the decoction," he called it—and, for the sake of its dominion, he served. He confessed once to the foreman of the small bottling plant he maintained in a building behind the Ramblas that he had once dreamed of the greenish-purple syrup covering the globe.

Papá Miravilla determined in the winter of 1938, when his oldest daughter had turned eighteen, that he would conclude her education in an appropriate finishing school in France; he thought it important that he supplement her provincial education with the expanded horizons of French culture. Indeed, it was his ambition that each daughter in turn be sent abroad to complete her education, to decorate the substance of Catalan and Spanish culture with the graces of the French language, the manners of the wellborn, and the conversational aptitudes of the cultivated. He had, after all, to consider his daughters' fitness for marriage, and a finishing school in France would be like so many swirls and curlicues applied by gifted masons to the plain exterior of solid architecture. He could not have known that his proposal, descending as it did most immediately upon his eldest born, would be received less with gratitude than with ferocity. Helene deeply resented his decision, wanting neither to go abroad nor to receive the advantages of France. She was quite content to contest her preeminence with her sisters from the pinnacle of maturity and beauty, and doubted she could maintain her dominion nearly two thousand kilometers from home. She anticipated displacement and loss, but, unable to mitigate her father's decision, she was obliged to accept it, wrapping herself in the coat of misery that she drew more tightly about herself as her sisters, delighted by the prospect of her absence and the consequent redistribution of position and the pelf of affection, became increasingly cheerful and solicitous of Helene's well-being as the date of her departure approached. It passed smoothly, they thought. Papá Miravilla, attended by his four remaining daughters, arranged for her departure on the night train, which would bear her first to Paris and then, by another route, to Vézelay.

Having entered in midyear and late even for the term, Helene Miravilla was installed in a small and isolated room at the Académie

Argentières—a room smaller than most, since she was not obliged to share it with another girl, and situated at the front of the house, away from the noise of the athletic fields and the gossiping chatter of her schoolmates, whose rooms were located on the two floors below. The only other residents of her floor were employees of the Académie: the housekeeper, a slightly deaf and addled old woman who, when she was not about her duties, was locked in her room telling her rosary; the invalid aunt of the Argentières, who, it was rumored, had guaranteed the loan that had enabled them to acquire the property and establish the school a decade earlier; and a young sculptor, up from Paris, a bachelor without ties in the region, who taught the young ladies drawing, sculpture, and the history of art.

Have you understood the mystery of the human back?

The face-to-face encounter is hardly mysterious, even if unaccompanied by speech. Face to face, the imagination conjures from such a wealth of detail: the setting of eyes, the folding and tension of skin, the elaboration of lips and color—yes, color, ruddy or pale, drawn with the beige lines of thought or hued with the reflected color of hair, abundant or spare, deep cast or lightly blended. There is little mystery in the face, for even if the imagination construes in lies, reality—forcing the ultimate correction of its opinion, to meet and confront, and finally to divest plastic silence with speech—deprives the imagination of its erotic trajectory, its commitment to hope, wholly unsupported by conviction and trust. To come, then, upon a mysterious back; to watch it rise up a stairwell, dimly lit by cut-glass fixtures that shelter light without shedding it; to follow behind, each step more guarded lest a footfall be overheard and, head turned, the mysterious back be instantaneously dissolved by face and expression; to have the sense of following behind, to become implicated in the significance of a back by being its follower, as the number five follows the number four, without being necessarily connected or modified by the simple sequence; and yet gradually, as the ascent from the entrance foyer from which the grand escalier rose commenced, having said good night to Mademoiselle Floride and nodded to the few other strangers who remained, Helene on the evening of her arrival at the Académie put her foot to the lowest step and felt a body pass her in a bound as the front door slammed shut. A figure leaped past, calling out its *"Bonne nuit"* and taking the stairs in a burst of energy, slowing to a simple ascent four steps before her, moving upward past the first floor of rooms, and Helene became accustomed to the substantial back at first and as the slow movement upward continued. Becoming aware of trim waist and firm buttocks (since the back was constrained by a brown leather jacket cinched above the hips), agitated and moving as each leg rose and descended, and the shoulders, not too broad but curved toward the connection of arms, which hung loose, dropping to his sides, the thumb of each hand hooked lightly into side pockets, and at the last, reaching the third floor, bounding the final steps, disappearing down the hall, a door opening, a door shutting, and silence and darkness once more, one could not but be persuaded that the back of a young man might prove to be a mystery.

Helene fell behind on the last ascent, suddenly aware of the region into which her imagination was bearing her, suddenly uncomfortable. She realized as she entered her room and removed her dress that in the next that trim and muscled back was now lying lengthwise on the bed or perhaps poised erect before the window facing away from the copse of trees before the residence, and that some minutes later it would be uncovered and bared. She wanted to be anywhere at that moment but here, in a room adjoining one in which could be found a naked and mysterious back.

Helene Miravilla had decided somewhere between Lyons and Paris that she wanted to study art. She was thumbing through magazines, bored by her traveling companions, when she came across a photograph of beautiful women and handsome men arranged about a marble sculpture of an immense and almost mythically gigantic bird. The photograph, it seemed, was advertising an aperitif, but no matter; for neither the beautiful women nor the handsome men appealed to Helene as deeply as the majestic marble bird. Why not, she thought? Art courses, like sewing and cooking, were always favored by women, and she was quite able to handle a fifth course beyond the requirements. It was not her intention, however, to elaborate the origins of her interest in art when she entered Monsieur Delahaye's classroom; but she first observed him bent over a student's sketching pad, his powerful shoulders drawn together, his tapered fingers holding a stick of charcoal, which he moved rapidly over the drawing. He was wearing a brown leather jacket that clasped his slender waist—alluding to, without demonstrating, the contour of his hips and thighs. When he finally noticed her, he had returned to his desk and seated himself; she, for her part, knocked lightly on the door, which she continued to hold open until he had given her permission to enter. The rest— the frustrated artistic career of her father, his need to support his family and forgo his ambition as a painter—all that came to her mind without embarrassment, a natural consequence of her wish to ingratiate herself, to be warmly received and specially regarded. There was no reason to question the authenticity of her confession; it was of that species of deception so intimately bound to the unconscious propensity for the fantastic and for self-enlarging found in all human beings as to be absolutely convincing. The young instructor seemed moved by her evocation of her father's frustrated passion and touched by the tender and nervously delivered confession. Moreover, her accurate description of her father's successful pharmacy and its notorious decoction returned him to sources of envy that he hardly recognized at the time.

Neither Estienne Delahaye nor Helene Miravilla was aware of what had been set in motion. For Estienne it required a brief visit to Paris the weekend before the Easter recess for his ugly friend to confront him with the truth of his own emotion. Malburet, listening to Estienne's

description of his four students, nodded distractedly as Estienne rehearsed their cloddy sensibilities with contempt, treating his work of
instruction as no more than a custodial preservation and enhancement
of trivial skills, art instruction being no different, in his view, from
teaching the young ladies graceful handwriting or the placement of
the pinky finger in tea-pouring. It was only when Estienne came to
speak of the arrival of his fifth and final student and began not with
her name and background or the wealth or aristocracy of her parents,
that Alain Malburet left off twirling his cigarette holder and listened,
his lips parted in a frozen and perhaps ironic smile. Estienne did not
mention her intelligence or her gifts until he had finished with her
braided black hair and burnished complexion. The girl, still nameless
in his telling, he called at first the "girl of the raven hair," or the
"Spanish beauty," one cliché of admiration following upon the other,
until in his description it became quite irrelevant whether she was a
capable and ambitious student or yet another parvenu putting on
culture like nail polish.

"Clearly, old friend, you are mad for her."

Estienne stopped. "Only *you* would say something like that," he
snapped with irritation.

"But it's clear, Estienne, for heaven's sake. Don't be an ass. Have
that beauty, by all means. Have her before you lose her."

In the past, Estienne Delahaye would have dismissed his friend's
effusions as yet another example of his provincial vulgarity or, worse
still, his libertinage, but now Estienne fell silent. After some minutes,
he stood up from the table (they were at that moment finishing a bottle
of wine in a café on the rue de Rennes), flung down some change,
and left without a word, but his expression (quite unlike the haughty
dismissals to which Alain had become accustomed) was one of
confusion—his face drawn, his green eyes squinting as though to see
a microscopic point that had, until that moment, eluded him. He cut
short his stay in Paris, returning to Vézelay on the Saturday-night
bus, which arrived at five in the morning. He let himself into the

country house and wearily climbed the stairs to his floor. As he passed the room he had come to learn was occupied by Helene Miravilla, he heard a cough, light and insignificant, and several sounds—words he thought she had spoken in her dreams—and decided to enter if it was unlocked, or knock upon the door, high up beside the porcelain tablet of the number five that marked it, hoping to rouse her to admit him, drugged from sleep but still awakened to his desire. He did none of these; he went to his own room, fell clothed upon his bed, and slept deeply until Sunday noon.

Mademoiselle Floride commented upon the unusual presence of Monsieur Delahaye at Sunday lunch, observing with not a little tartness that the girls might consider themselves fortunate that their handsome instructor had seen fit to pass a portion of his weekend in their company at Vézelay. Estienne, not to be humiliated by such witless asperity, immediately proposed that he would lead a group to the Basilica of Sainte Madeleine that afternoon at four and interpret to them the splendor of its achievement. And so, precisely at four, three young women of the three score who attended the Académie were awaiting him in the foyer as he descended the stairwell from his room: Helene Miravilla, a long yellow silk scarf wound about her throat and trailing behind her black loden coat, whose infinity of buttons was fastened up to her neck; Mademoiselle Simone, a smart girl whose acceptably docile features were flawed by a birth mole from which a strand of ugly black hair had been allowed to grow; and another young lady, the youngest of the three, whose acquaintance Professor Delahaye had not made (since, as a first-year student, she was not permitted to enjoy the luxuries of art), and who introduced herself as Jeannette, whispering her first name with breathless confusion.

How was it possible for this last child, so new to the Académie, to have conceived an attraction for Professor Delahaye? The question struck Helene with amazement. She had no doubt, however, as they

walked down the road that wound from the high point of the countryside toward Vézelay, that this young Jeannette—her eyes darting
surreptitiously to appraise the face of Estienne while he spoke in
generalities about the rise of Romanesque architecture and the mon-
astic ideals of the Benedictine monks who had founded the basilica
—was in fact enraptured of this man whom Helene, for her part, had
already begun to call, beneath her breath, *"mon Estienne."* It annoyed
her that this Jeannette could imagine Estienne Delahaye would bother
with someone so young and immature, a first-termer whose teeth were
crooked and whose hair hung snarled and untrimmed like a penance.
Only when they reached the courtyard of the basilica and Estienne
had pointed up to the twin towers and begun to describe the history
of its construction, surmounting the secular community that clustered
about its foundations, did Helene emit a gasp of recognition, at which
she was given a cross look by Estienne, whose commentary she had
interrupted. Helene blushed and apologized, but her dismay was too
intense, and she bolted the little group, fleeing down the road that
they had taken. Not until she had left the city ramparts behind her
and retraced her way along the highway that led back toward the
school did she disappear into the high grass and throw herself dramatically to the ground. Weeping with rage, she acknowledged what
she had been unable to face before: she was jealous of that immature
child and must therefore—in the logic of her native Catalonia—be
in love.

It was the day before Easter recess. The girls were counting the
hours before their departure, arranging their dresses, ironing organ-
dies and taffetas for the Lenten gatherings they anticipated in Lyons,
Geneva, and Paris, from which they principally came. Only Helene
Miravilla was obliged to pass the holidays in Vézelay. A long letter
from Papá, arrived the week before, informed her of reversals in the
family fortunes stemming from restrictions placed upon the distribution of his syrupy decoction: it was contended that the little amber

bottles, containing more than thirty percent alcohol along with sassafras root, nutmeg, several other favored occult essences, and water, were more an aperitif than a medication and hence were required to be sold as an alcoholic potable, with consequently higher tax and diminished profit. Of course, this entire procedure was nothing more than interested officialdom's way of extracting from Papá a fearful *soborno*, which he was quite willing to pay, although he rightly suspected that it would become annual; and with such an expense added to the cost of fabricating his beverage, he instituted immediately the appropriate measures of economy. It was decided that Helene could survive the two weeks of Easter recess at Vézelay; the Argentières sisters offered to keep watch over her; and in fact Helene, quite reconciled to the time of solitude, prepared herself by entering that familiar cavern of the Spanish personality, the dressing up to misery. From her trunk she took out a ball gown of peach silk that descended below her knees, but was cut ragged—daringly cut, one would think, for it had belonged to her mother, dead since the late twenties, a vivacious woman who adored dancing at La Paloma, an old-fashioned hall as large as an arena, in which she and Papá had tangoed throughout the only decade of their marriage.

It was for the candlelight dinner that preceded the spring recess that Helene put on the ball gown of her mother, and drew upon her legs gray stockings flecked with iridescent white threads, and stamped her feet into the small but passionate dancing pumps that she knew her mother had favored for contests at La Paloma. She demanded of herself that evening, beginning her descent into a satisfying gloom, that she remind everyone that she was Spanish and beautiful. She put powder on her face, so that the whiteness almost glared at her in the yellow light; and into her braided hair, to which she had added a chignon, she inserted a black tortoiseshell comb over which she formally draped a splendidly worked mantilla of gray lace.

The dinner was called for eight o'clock; a better grade of wine was to be served, and champagne poured with the lemon sorbet. It was a tradition, so to speak, although the school was only ten years old and traditions were still decreed rather than transmitted. The faculty members, the several women who assisted the Argentières, their husbands if they were married, and Estienne Delahaye were seated at the head table, which for the occasion was set with tablecloths and made festive with boughs of dogwood and lilies. The other tables, lit by candles, lacked only tablecloths, although their floral arrangements offset the grim stolidity of Burgundian oak from which the tables were hewn. Everyone was seated; the clock in the hallway had struck; indeed, the familiar benediction was about to be delivered by the curate invited for the occasion, when the double glass doors, already closed against intruders, were opened, and Helene Miravilla entered. She had not wished to create a commotion; a commotion was not at all her explicit intention. She had designed herself for herself, noting at most one other for whom she dared to dress. It was not from the wish to shock that she had dressed herself for the Lenten dinner but, as we have said, to celebrate her entrance into the lonely world where she would be obliged to amuse herself by herself.

The curate had already risen to his feet and was about to rap his crystal goblet with a teaspoon to silence the chattering assembly when Helene made her entrance. She found her seat and stood behind it as the other girls rose, anticipating the grace, and while the priest struck his glass and beseeched heaven, the Argentières sisters opened their eyes wide in consternation. It appeared that only Estienne Delahaye turned away from the inspection of Helene Miravilla, the erratic flicker of candlelight concealing the pleasure that flushed his cheeks.

Helene Miravilla was unaware of the assembly; she knew without a doubt that she was very beautiful that evening, very beautiful indeed, and it would not have mattered to her if she had dined alone, she was so secure in the knowledge that she had pleased herself in her dress-up for the occasion—pleased the memory of her mother, pleased her father in her loneliness, and pleased the imagination of a lover who remained, up to that moment, hidden around a bend in time. The dinner became curiously subdued, the assembly almost solemn. It was true, as Estienne told her later, that her presence imposed a new solemnity upon the gathering, making all the girls painfully aware that none was as beautiful as Helene Miravilla—the new girl who lived above them, removed and separate in a private room. It goes without saying that on that evening Helene Miravilla, dazzling though she was, acquired many enemies, young women who would have been quite willing, given the opportunity, to tear her apart or at the least to compromise her name and reputation. Already they whispered that her dress was a scandal, her mantilla an affectation and so "typically" Spanish, her stockings and shoes brazen, her pallor anemic, her high look of serene indifference provocative and pretentious. But the fact remained, a simple truth, that she was exceedingly beautiful and that if her appearance was daring, even a bit outrageous, it nonetheless became her. She had passed over the fragile line of unawareness, shattered by deliberation and decision. Helene Miravilla had determined to assert, indeed to celebrate, that what she had endured silently until then—that is, her father's embarrassing exclamations about her beauty—was now a fact, one that she was prepared to detail and exaggerate at will. Throughout the dinner she refused to flinch, her head high, her black eyes, warm and affectionate, moving from face to face, discerning envy and appreciation mixed with wonder. She scarcely spoke; she was hardly addressed. Only once, toward the end of the festive dinner to which shrill voices and gay laughter had returned, did she turn away from her dinner partner—with whom she had been exchanging perfunctory comments, wishing her a pleasant dinner dance and exclaiming politely upon her good fortune to be seeing opera and ballet on successive holiday nights—and caught Estienne Delahaye eyeing her; his words were addressed to Mademoiselle Floride, but his glance passed over her head to the first table, where for the longest time all he could see was the gentle curve

of a peach shoulder, a shoulder graceful and inclined, a thin line of
strap visible beneath the silk, a thin line of strap holding with tenderness another beauty he could only imagine.

The first morning of the Easter recess was incredibly busy. Every
floor, excepting the third, resounded with shouts, for the train from
Vézelay to Paris departed at noon and the young girls, packed since
dawn, dressed in their city clothes, with hats and suede gloves, in
stockings and walking shoes, their suitcases assembled in the down-
stairs hall, were tense with excitement. Breakfast had been leisurely
and casual: the special jams, the croissants warmed and abundant,
the aroma of chicory and tea; cheerful faces, light glaze of rose
lipstick, young girls moving from table to table, shifting places, ignoring their familiar assignments, promising to write, remarking on
grades, noting addresses and telephone numbers, bliss of adolescence, unaware that the earth was already shaking, that the foundations of their secure world were trembling, that it was the last feast
of resurrection that would be celebrated in peace. And the girls did
not notice that neither the master, Estienne Delahaye, nor the beautiful Spanish girl, Helene Miravilla, had made an appearance.

The third floor was still silent. It was as it might have been on any
morning, musty and dim; the windows at the end of the hall remained
unopened, for Estienne had not bathed at the end of the corridor,
throwing open the double window to the courtyard below, touching
briefly the breezes that blew down from the hills before shutting the
door to the bathroom and turning on the hot water, an activity that
had always dominated the ritual of his levée. Estienne had not appeared; nor, for that matter, had Helene. Indeed, consummations of
the mind, they had slept beside each other through the night, fully
clothed, dreamily embracing clothing, pants and stockings entwined,
flannel and silk, gray bestriding peach, black tie descending like a
hand, gently caressing the treasure of a breast that the true hand had
merely described in the sculptor's manner with a cupping of flesh and

a weary sigh that signified willingness to remain outside long after the imagination had entered the very grain and density of the material it sought to model.

It had almost, but not quite or not just yet, not for a little bit, still around the bend in time, come to pass early in the morning of that day of recess, a number of hours after the dinner had concluded and the lights had been dimmed in the drawing room, where the girls had taken their coffee and a special fruit liqueur, after several hours in which Helene Miravilla lay fully dressed upon her bed, her head concentrating a kiss upon the wall that separated her room from that of Estienne Delahaye, and he, also still dressed, one shoe unlaced, lay with his head turned toward the room of Helene, his lips, not unlike hers, pressed to her face through the distance of a dozen feet of empty space and wall. The only difference, perhaps, was that through it all Estienne Delahaye smoked, addressing a languorous kiss, puffing his cigarette, touching his body, kissing the emptiness again, and tamping a cigarette into a tin ashtray that lay beside him on the bed.

It was three in the morning, deadly silent, moon-silver streaking the room, when Estienne got up from his bed and opened the door. It creaked—an almost desperately slow and attenuated sound that struck his ears like a boom, so loud to his fright that he almost slammed the door in alarm; but hearing nothing, no echoing sound, the silence continuing, he pushed it further, edging out his body, folding his slenderness around the door and withdrawing himself from his room into the corridor, carefully holding the doorknob, replacing the door in the jamb, releasing the knob by slowly turning, turning until it clicked into the lock. He breathed deeply and passed a sleeved arm over his damp forehead. At last, although in reality but four feet away, he stood before the door of Helene Miravilla. He put his ear to the door, hoping to hear her wakefulness, but she, on the other side, thinking she heard a sound—a muffled thickness in the air as though suddenly a body massed before her door had stifled the free passage of breeze from the floors below, cramping the air, constricting space into a form—and fearing to provoke what she conjured, bit her palm, holding back the cry that wanted to escape from her lips. She heard him knock. Could it have been a wind, the scurry of a mouse at her door, a bat's wing brushing the panel, a sound he prevented from reaching the corridor by muffling it with his cupped hand, obliging whatever noise his single rap produced to be focused inward; it struck her ear like the breaking of an immense wave, so many hours had she hoped that it would come to pass. For her part, she got up from the bed, moved before the mirror of her armoire, which caught the silvered face, white powder glistening with moonlight, and went on stockinged feet to the door, pressing her lips against the knuckle and whispering the name she had fantasied a thousand times, now to speak aloud and to be heard.

"Estienne. *C'est toi?*" The tall figure stepped into her room, closed the door carelessly, although no sound could be heard, so deep was the silence of the night, and then drew the white face toward his own until face upon face passed into each other and the moon disappeared into a bank of clouds.

## Five

It depends most upon your willingness to construe the world according to its manipulators or its victims (and the admiration or sympathy that you might feel for the one or the other) whether you regard Helene or Estienne as the seducer. There is no clear opinion on the matter. Many who discussed it later (for it became a matter of discussion in the years after the War, when Estienne Delahaye began his precipitous rise to eminence and wealth and his wife Helene made public a succession of handsome and unqualified secretaries) found for one or the other. At the very least, there was no unanimity. It depended. *Ça depend.* The fact remained that by the end of the spring recess—that is, by April 20, when the girls returned from their Easter holidays—Helene was already married; and Estienne, aware of the dangers (for it was neither his inclination nor his style to philander like his friend Alain), had begun to fantasize the comforts and ease that would enter his life if it was cushioned by the doting Spanish bourgeois who enjoyed wealth from medicines and decoctions.

Estienne found his good fortune delicious. It smiled upon him, this fortune of events. The beautiful Spanish girl would remain behind at Eastertime and he, already her lover (although the act of love had not been consummated in more than word and expectation), would cancel his plans in Paris and play her guardian. No one would suspect; the coincidences would be immense, the excuses dangerous, but there seemed no reason to imagine that they would be exposed. He wished for the affair; it seemed a splendor. The black-haired student of room number five, which adjoined his own, would become his mistress; and by year's end, knowing her well, perhaps obliging her with a child, he would compel her to accept his plea for marriage, his wish to do right by her, and reject her willingness to be noble and leave his career unimpeded; they would marry and her rich father would be morally constrained to support them through the early years until his turn of success arrived. Indeed, the new Estienne seemed quite able to model fortune to his needs.

The lovers spent their holiday idyll wandering the countryside near Vézelay, visiting historical sites, eating in local inns, and fixing picnic panniers, which they enjoyed at the side of the road. However, they conspired to produce each evening, for the approval of the Argentières sisters, decently turned charcoal studies of trees and farm horses, each drawing outlined by Helene and corrected by Estienne (crudity of line softened day by day into talented little sketches upon whose gift Estienne would exclaim, which Helene, smiling silently, a trifle smugly, would accept as both truth and ruse).

The sisters did not discover them until the holiday was nearly over. Quite by accident the bead-telling housekeeper had knocked at an irregular hour upon Helene's door to clean her room, and Helene, thinking it was Estienne, had called his name, a curious fact that the housekeeper had noted and remarked upon to Mademoiselle Floride the next morning. While the young lovers were off that day, exploring somewhere or other, passing the afternoon in an inn a dozen miles away, the sisters had entered both rooms and discovered the shoe of one in the room of the other, an errant sock, a mysterious odor that neither could identify but that they considered suspicious, and finally a half-dozen hairpins under the pillow of the young instructor, and they concluded that something disgusting, an indecency, a compromise, had taken place.

When Helene and Estienne returned in the afternoon, they were confronted and accused. Helene bit her lip stoically when she was told her father would be notified (in fact, Mademoiselle Floride attempted to telephone her father's pharmacy, but was informed that it would be at least fourteen hours before the lines to Barcelona would be free), and Estienne was dismissed on the spot and ordered from the Académie within the hour. Despite their efforts to restrain her, Helene resisted; strong-willed as she was, and quite mature enough to deal with even the more muscular of the two sisters, she determined to accompany her lover when he departed the school. Estienne protested Helene's incaution, proposing rather that she wait out her father's anger, pacify it, and then follow Estienne to Paris; however, she insisted. They had little money between them, the sisters having refused to return to Helene the small deposit of spending money that had been given to them by her father; as for paying Estienne's monthly salary, they would hear none of it, telling him instead to sue if he hoped to be paid. The two had a hundred francs between them, perhaps a bit more, enough to take the bus to Paris with sufficient left over for several days of modest living. When they arrived, they made straight for Alain's hotel, where Estienne felt certain he would be received and given a room on credit until they could straighten themselves out, communicate with Señor Miravilla, receive some advance on Helene's dowry, and make arrangements for their living.

None of the spirit of calculation, the combination and permutation of sums and essences that characterized Estienne Delahaye's habitual transactions with the world, seemed to pervade his actions. Viewed dispassionately (but that would not be quite in order, since the seduction of Helene Miravilla was in fact an affair of passion, despite the truth that not all passions are amatory), Estienne Delahaye's behavior, always so careful and circumspect, removed from casual flirtation and transitory involvements, was inexplicable. Alain, who sat with Estienne in his room for several hours in the late afternoon while Helene napped, was quite literally *bouleversé*.

"It doesn't make sense, old friend. My God, the girl's beautiful, but she's still after all just a girl, a child, just nineteen. What's a man of thirty-four, a promising sculptor, doing with a nineteen-year-old? Tell me it's madly erotic, that you can't live without her—my God, tell me something stupid like that, and I would at least understand, even though I would still counsel caution and a night in the Turkish bath to think it over—but, *poof*, my unromantic friend, proper teacher, serious artist, falls into bed with a student, compromises her, gets dismissed, and is talking marriage. And all in the matter of a week. No. No. There has to be something else. Let me see. But of course. She's rich, isn't she?"

Estienne looked crossly at Alain and replied, "What's that got to do with it?"

"But is she, old friend? It doesn't bother me. All the better if she is. You know what they say: 'Better a pearl in the oyster than a grain of sand.' "

"I don't know for certain, but I imagine she is. It costs a bit to go to the Académie. At least six thousand francs without the extras. Oh, I suppose Helene is rich or will be. But you're disgraceful, Alain." Estienne was embarrassed and delighted. He had had no doubt that

Alain would guess his motive, and it pleased him somewhat that it proved so unalarming when it emerged. "But she is ravishing, isn't she?"

"Absolutely. A stunning girl. And Spanish, is she? The first crop they export after their war, and you're there to pick the best. You are a devil, aren't you?"

Estienne glowed. He was pleased again. "Yes, beautiful and rich. Beautiful and rich." He repeated the phrase several times, embracing Alain and hugging him with delight.

Outside the door, Helene stood a moment listening. Her face, impassive and beautiful, betrayed no emotion. Perhaps she heard and perhaps she was surprised, but again at this point it is uncertain. At all events, she did not knock. She turned away after a few minutes and went down the hall to the stairwell, considered returning to her room, but after a brief hesitation descended to the street. At the first café she passed, she sat down and ordered a *pastis*. She had never had a *pastis*, but so many events of recent days were absolutely new that it did not seem unusual to add another, although she confused *pastis* with absinthe and knew that too much of that kind of alcohol could destroy one.

The lovers had determined to write, rather than telegraph, Señor Miravilla. They had composed the letter together, announced their love, described its good fortune, intensity, and miraculous coincidence, signified their willingness to struggle and endure, begged his blessings, and besought his assistance. Having mailed it the first evening, they received a reply in eight days, a simple letter accompanied by a postal order for five hundred francs. Estienne was relieved, as their money was almost gone and the postal order was more than enough to get them quite comfortably through several weeks. Señor Miravilla's tone was, however, not as generous as his gift. He began not by congratulating his daughter or, for that matter, reproving her. His emotion seemed impersonal, directed less to her and her welfare than to himself and his own situation. Intelligent Catalan that he was, he interpreted his eldest daughter's announcement not as a betrayal, but as a cost. The first daughter to leave his home and board meant ultimately a considerable saving—whatever the cash outlay of the dowry, for since the couple was going to elope there would be no wedding and the necessity of display would be obviated. He described his shock at her decision, cautioned the lovers perfunctorily, encouraged them to marry immediately, and invited them to visit him whenever they went south. The check for five hundred francs was, he asserted, a down payment; more would follow when his own financial embarrassment ("about which Helene can tell you more") was relieved. It was the first Estienne had heard of an embarrassment, and Helene observed his concern as he reread the letter. There was little disingenuousness in his inquiry, and when Helene had finished her description of the difficulties of living in post-Republican Spain, the dislocations of the war, and the precarious profits from an herbal decoction, Estienne's expression of concern had turned to a frown. But Helene dismissed her father's nervousness, asserting that, as far as she knew, the business was thriving, the decoction was now advertised throughout the country (and parts of South America); as best as she could judge, his income, given the precarious times, was substantial. Estienne's relief was palpable; he kissed Helene tenderly and left her to rest before lunch. Indeed, they had determined to be married that afternoon, with Alain and his girlfriend—a massive black girl with a vast laugh—as witnesses, at the local registry.

A month later their lives appeared settled and resolved. A letter of congratulation arrived from old Maillol, containing an invitation to the young couple to settle in the deep south at Port Vendres, near the Spanish border, in a cottage not far from his own atelier, with an ample shed in which Estienne could work in peace, and, if she chose, his bride could take up spinning and weaving, a craft in which Maillol excelled as a teacher. Estienne was delighted by Maillol's suggestion.

He had had no idea until the letter arrived that the old master was, indeed, that fond of him. He had assisted him many times during the previous years, and had supervised the construction of a number of public commissions, but he had doubted that Maillol cared for him, particularly after Estienne had succeeded in taking for himself a small design competition for a bas-relief to be installed in a railway station in Bourges. It had not been at all clear to him at the time—two years earlier—that Maillol could not have been less interested in a competition for a work described with such aggravating detail by the town committee of Bourges, and carrying with it a fee that could be described best as niggardly; it was required of the artist as well that the maquette be approved, cast, and installed in four months' time to accommodate the Armistice Day commemorations of that November. Maillol had left the letter lying unanswered on his worktable in Marly-le-Roi, and Estienne, accidentally discovering it, had removed it without permission, replied on his own, and submitted photographs of several works in fact designed by Maillol but rejected by him; and receiving a letter of acknowledgment addressed to him as assistant to Le Maître Aristide Maillol, went for the interview and took the commission for himself. Maillol never missed the letter; he had probably had no intention of answering it, trusting to the passage of time to desiccate its urgency. Estienne was pleased with the ruse; never once did the mayor of Bourges suspect that really and truly it was not Aristide Maillol, but Estienne Delahaye, assistant from time to time to the master sculptor, who would be the artist. A stroke of good luck. Throughout the interview Estienne had so skillfully bound his name to that of Maillol that the committee of town fathers could not but have thought that they were acquiring a work, if not directly from the hand of the master, at least supervised and approved by him— sufficiently so that when the work was installed and unveiled, it carried beneath the signature of Estienne Delahaye the legend "*avec l'accord du Maître Aristide Maillol.*" It satisfied the *mairie* of Bourges to consummate this deception, for they took Estienne's appearance as an answer from the master, but realized quite well that the great Maillol would not work to such distracting specifications and in such a short time for a sum that did not much exceed ten thousand francs. They were pleased, however, to rationalize. Estienne had counted on precisely this confluence of cheapness and provincial cupidity, the wish of the town fathers to have their cake and eat it. Fortunately it worked well because Estienne was an intelligent, indeed a gifted, sculptor. The work was elegantly turned, the somewhat classical soldiers—clothed but still visibly striving in the flesh, frontal in the attitudes of death but transfigured by the various nobilities of youth, courage, clarity of face, and strength of arms—pleased the crowd that gathered for the commemoration.

Estienne Delahaye had passed successfully from struggling artist to maker of monuments, albeit on the strength of a bit of deception, but one which neither party to it—the *mairie* of Bourges or old Maillol—would ever fully discern. From that bit of good fortune Estienne Delahaye had begun to prosper. Several reliefs and table sculptures followed as commissions; he had had the installation in Bourges photographed and sent the photo with an accompanying letter to nearly fifty *mairies* throughout the country, soliciting their interest in case they wished to commission memorial monuments or celebrations of labor, produce, viniculture, or any historical personage of France. Several inquiries resulted, including the project for the Lyons bank on which Estienne had been working at the time he met Helene Miravilla. An accident—reading Maillol's unanswered letter—was converted by guile into luck and thence, by degree of work, invention, and energy, into fortune. Coincidence, the concatenation of wandering eye and unscrupulous hand, had augured well for the beginning of Estienne's career.

The career of Estienne Delahaye had, so to speak, grown on the back of Aristide Maillol, whom he had served well, whom in his way he admired, but whom, quite clearly, he had betrayed. At all events, Maillol's letter replying to Estienne's announcement of his nuptials contained no present of funds or the gift of a work of his art (as Estienne had foolishly hoped), but an invitation to live and work with him, altogether a more appropriate and generous gift. The young couple left Paris for Port Vendres after enjoying a private dinner tendered them by Alain, who promised to visit them once they were installed. Moreover, since Port Vendres was virtually on the Spanish border, Estienne suggested they take the train from Paris to Barcelona, where they could visit Helene's family before moving back across the border to the little village where they would establish their first home.

## Six

Helene Miravilla, now Delahaye, did not whistle during the journey south, as did her husband. She kept her eye on the six pieces of luggage in the rack above their seats, making certain that the parade of travelers who entered their compartment and departed it at each of the principal stops along the route did not steal any of their possessions. She became positively obsessed with their belongings, after each stop counting audibly the two suitcases, the basket that contained a set of fragile glass given them by Alain, a footlocker of shoes and books, a wicker hamper in which Estienne had packed his carving tools along with a number of plasters on which he had been working in Paris, and a large umbrella. Her brow furrowed with anxiety at each stop, and she climbed upon the seat opposite their own to check and count, noting to Estienne that everything was present and in place. He, for his part indifferent to the prospect of robbery, wandered through the corridors of the train, whistling contentedly as he roamed, descending into each station for a look around, a magazine, a box of sweets. The progress of the train was slow and, to their view, interminable: stops of thirty and forty minutes at Lyons, Marseilles, Perpignan, until late afternoon, when they changed trains at the frontier between France and Spain.

The delay at the frontier was exceptionally long. Both the French and Spanish police were protracted and scrupulous in their examinations. With the civil war in Spain concluded, it happened that Spaniards were trying to sneak back into their homeland without proper papers, or with papers validated by a republic that no longer existed. It was no surprise that when they came to the Delahayes they questioned Helene with particular circumspection. They were obviously disturbed that she carried papers in her maiden name, that her Republican passport was clearly that of a Miravilla, whereas Estienne introduced her as his wife. When she explained, producing the marriage license, that she was just married, the police, even more dissatisfied, suspecting such marriages to be political, asked her for the address of her father's pharmacy, indeed even questioned her about the politics of her family. Helene's answers were innocent, insubstantial, and obviously unsatisfactory. She said that she didn't know if her father had a politics, a reply that the officer of the *Guardia* found ridiculous. Throughout these inquiries, Estienne Delahaye stood to one side. It was not really his business, he temporized, even though this woman was his wife. Clearly, however, the police knew that the young and beautiful woman with her limp and crumpled documents was neither a spy nor a Communist trying to reenter her country illegally. It was only that she was beautiful, and they derived some obvious pleasure from her discomfort. When the police left, after nearly a half-hour interrogation, Helene and Estienne, alone in the compartment, fell silent. After some minutes, when the train commenced its slow descent from the Pyrenees, Helene began to cry softly. Estienne, no longer whistling, put out his hand to cover hers, but she hid it behind her.

"What's the matter, *chérie*?" he asked teasingly. "Did the police upset you?"

"Finally, not at all. You did, however. Very much! You said absolutely nothing to protect me."

Estienne looked at her with something like amazement. Her complaint was hard to understand. It wasn't that he didn't understand what she meant. It was more that he had never really thought of other people that way—needing or wanting or, much less, deserving his protection. He thought of his dying father in the nursing home. Nobody protected him. And of himself. No one, absolutely no one, had ever bothered to protect him. Whatever he had made of himself, he had done by application and gift—elaborated, to be sure (although on this occasion this was not recalled) with occasional descents into stealth and guile. Her complaint stood, however, as a reproach, and the reproach dismayed him. It was the first time in many years that a criticism of his personal behavior, made by a virtual stranger, had caught in his flesh like a fishhook. Whenever his friend Alain took him to task, it was always with a lightheartedness, a bantering, an attitude of teasing that enabled him to dismiss it as unserious and irrelevant. But this woman, whom he thought he had married simply as a delicious convenience, had obviously become something much more. In the three months that had passed since she entered his classroom and told him the story of her father and his love of art, he had somehow contrived to dismay even himself, whom he thought he knew so well. He had fallen in love with the astonishing woman, this woman, who was able, tears falling from her eyes, to criticize him for not intervening to protect her from the police. *Tiens*, he said to himself. Obviously he had to take notice.

## Seven

Estienne Delahaye examined the living room of Señor Miravilla's apartment slowly. His wife had joined her sisters in another room, and he heard bits of laughter and the lowing of muffled voices while they awaited the return of their father, who had been notified that his eldest had just returned home. At the very least, the atmosphere of the apartment was lugubrious, it being customary never to turn on lights unless at least a gathering was present; hence the maid had seated him upon a sofa, the curtains having been drawn much earlier against the afternoon sun—curtains sewn, embroidered, and tasseled in gold and blue thread. Estienne scrutinized his surroundings with the aid of a single lamp, held aloft by a scantily clad nymph whose gilt sheathing was pocked with age: a room stuffed with bric-a-brac and ungainly furniture, heavy and monstrous. Cheap oils of village scenes, painted by incompetents, were particularly surprising; lace coverlets were everywhere—on headrests and tables, on little footstands tucked under each chair.

It would have been an unbearable passage of time—alone, already the ignored husband in the assembly of his in-laws—had he not been fascinated by a cluster of photographs, fading sepia and waning tones of gray, that formed a company of intimates upon the lamp-lit table. There he could examine each of the daughters in their unfolding, grouped before a cathedral, dressed in communion white, their hands clutching rosaries and bunches of sweet peas; Helene among the girls, staring off into a space above the photographer's glass eye, already aloof and removed, half a head taller than the next girl, enfolded by the large—immense, it seemed—open arms of their father, who gathered them to himself; and to one side, smiling, her mouth shyly opened to lovely teeth, a woman he took to be her mother, it seemed not many years older than her eldest; frail—petite would be correct—with little bones, small hands, black hair pulled back to a barely visible bun, but immensely beautiful, a reminiscence in prophecy of what would come to be, presently, laughing in the next room, the bride of his seduction. The photographs were principally of the father of the household, the Señor Miravilla he awaited, as a young man in his early maturity, remarkably thin, his suit tightly buttoned, the dark trousers rising above his patent pumps, only bushy eyebrows anticipating the suspicious corpulence that would emerge by the time of the communion photograph, and by degrees, a photograph in his smock behind the marble counter of his apothecary shop, behind which rose the sensuous curves and carvings of his turn-of-the-century establishment on the Ramblas, his widening girth and drooping jowls competing unfavorably with the grace of his art-nouveau environment; and pictures upon each birthday, stuck like calling cards into larger picture frames, snapshots really, memorabilia of the progress of the body, a personage, but impersonal, nothing revealing the time through which the photographs had passed, time in which the streets of his world had been torn up and flung in riots, formed into barricades, blown apart by revolution and war. The timeless indifference of a bourgeois, it seemed, who cared that the photographer note and observe him alone, as if time could observe the aging of a man without reference to his epoch.

"My gallery," Estienne heard a voice remark, and he stood up and turned from his examination to receive the hand and the clumsy irony of the unmistakable Señor Miravilla. No sooner said, the voice in fact booming with pride, than the double doors opened wider, and the graying gentleman (he was in his middle fifties at the moment of this telling) was inundated by his girls, the rituals unfolding as we have described them—business jacket removed, home alpaca opened to his arms, slippers, sherry, his mail upon a tray, footrest—but he ignored these and turned to look at Helene, who stood to one side not resuming her role, perhaps wanting to resume her role but avoiding it, watching her husband, who remained standing, one hand in his pocket and at ease, comfortably smoothing his hair with the other; Helene looking from one to the other and back again, her eyes passing quickly, nervously like a sparrow hunting provender, nervously, darting with agitation, not knowing yet to whom she belonged and who would feed her.

"My beloved eldest," Señor Miravilla said, hugging Helene warmly, "and her husband Señor Delahaye, I take it. My pleasure, I suppose, although you deprived a father of his first pleasure, the wedding celebration of his eldest daughter." Helene flushed with embarrassment; Estienne began to reply but stopped. The other girls, the four younger sisters, had disappeared as quickly as they had appeared, although one imagined them breathing heavily behind the double doors, listening to the first interview.

"And so, sir, you are an artist?" the father began. "Not a very promising career, is it?"

"In what way, Señor? In money perhaps not, but in fame quite considerable. I am mentioned in many articles, if you'd care to see the clippings."

"Not necessary, young man. Not at all. I'm hopeful—no, more to the point, confident—that you are talented, as they say. But talent doesn't put food in my daughter's stomach or clothes upon her back. How do you propose to deal with that, although it's a little late to be having this conversation?"

"I thought, sir, that with your love of art, you might give us some help in that regard," Estienne replied, not brazenly but with professional dignity.

"My what? I don't know where you get that idea, young man. I don't care at all for art. Look at those paintings. Junk, undoubtedly. Pleasant scenes, painted by *gitanos* and bought for a few *pesetas*. The frames cost more than the pictures. No. No. I don't give a damn for art, so put that out of your mind." Helene smiled at this, but Estienne turned white with confusion. "It's much more to the point that you will need some help from me, and I propose to give you some, although my favorite daughter should really be thrashed for allowing you to embarrass her against her will." (Helene opened her mouth to protest, because the truth deserved to be spoken even if it did involve protecting her husband.) "Don't interrupt me, dearest, with some explanation or other! A man can avoid these things if he wants. A woman can't. That's the way it is in this world. So you took advantage of my daughter's youth and frailty, embarrassed her and her family, and I should thrash the two of you and send her to some damn fool convent for a life of penance and incarceration. But that went out long ago, and I made a promise to my dead wife not to punish, and I will keep the promise. It's too stupid to punish people. The long and the short of it is that I'm not a rich man at the moment. I will be rich again soon enough, if we can stabilize this country, but it takes time to make money. It's not something you fall across like a coin in the road. It will take time. I've put aside a sum for each of my daughter's dowries. I can't pay it all at once, but I suppose it will do." Señor Miravilla removed a pad from his jacket pocket and with a pencil wrote a figure on it and handed it to Estienne. Estienne received it and nodded, and the transaction was concluded. No money had been discussed. Like two persons bartering in foreign languages who resort to number notations as the common language of exchange, the sum written was sufficient to seal the understanding. Estienne said "Thank you," and Señor Miravilla observed: "Instruct me what bank you propose to use, and the funds will be sent monthly without fail. I'm like clockwork, you understand. My word can be trusted. But now, time for my nap. We will meet again at dinner. By the way, Helene, are you with child?"

"I don't think so, Papá."

"Ah, then he loves you as well. *Bueno.*"


It was not discussed again. A sum had been arranged, enough to keep the young couple provided against hunger and cold—not munificent, certainly not what Estienne had imagined, or for that matter what Helene had supposed, but sufficient. For the remainder of their days in Barcelona, the loving father provided: restaurants (what there were of them so soon after the war's end), a picnic in Montjuich, an evening at El Molino, a turn in the bay aboard a rented sailboat. Señor Miravilla could hardly say that he admired Helene's choice of husband; Estienne developed a nagging summer cold that left him irritable and snappish; however, it surprised her sisters that Helene was not in the least solicitous of her husband's health or wishes, refusing to forgo a visit with friends on their last night despite Estienne's mild fever. They, for their part, found her husband handsome, his manners terribly exotic, casual and informal, quite Parisian they thought, and they attended to him in a ratio of four to one, treating him to the regality they had habitually reserved for their father. Estienne was, needless to mention, given tumbler portions of the family decoction, which he found more potent than therapeutic. He packed several bottles against his departure.

The following week Helene and Estienne left Barcelona and Spain. They were not to return again together, although the train that bore them beyond the borders of that exhausted land protracted their departure by an abnormal six hours, stretching each kilometer of terrain into an indelible memory, so slowly did the train proceed northward to France. It appeared that the track had been blown up near Gerona by a band of Catalan loyalists who had held out in the mountains near the border. They had been forced into the open and defeated only hours before the train passed through. By the time the train arrived at the frontier, no sign of the violence that had just claimed five lives remained.

It was a serene summer day. August. Yellow dust had settled back upon the olive trees. Even the birds were lethargic. It was silent, as if already night, when they crossed the checkpoint into France.

## Eight

Europe went to war the week that Estienne took up his tools in old Maillol's work shed and Helene went by bicycle to spend the afternoon sunning herself on the beach at Collioure. When she returned to the cottage at about seven on the evening of September 3, having struck up a conversation with a young fisherman who insisted to her smile of incredulity that he had posed for the painter Matisse several summers earlier, she was flushed but pleased. She liked the young fisherman, who was gold and blue and brown, and he had bought her an aperitif and she had agreed to meet him the following

Friday when his trawler sailed into port with the week's catch. She wasn't at all certain whether his name was Jean or Joan, since his accent seemed to her like Catalan, although he spoke a French of the region filled with expressions she did not understand; but it hardly mattered, since she would certainly recognize the wave with which he had said good-bye and the unguarded candor of his face. As she pedaled home, turning into the lane that led to their cottage, Helene realized that although she was married to Estienne, many words had been spoken, many conversations had been overheard, many gestures had been described in the air that made her bond to him, if not fragile, at least less than secure. "Rich and beautiful," the words she thought she had heard his friend Alain speak indistinctly through the closed door, returned to her, and although she knew that they referred to herself and, like the episode of the railway compartment, that her husband had not bothered to protect and guard her from such misrepresentation, she was not quite ready to charge him with guilt. Complicity, or not even complicity but complaisance, a readiness to succumb, was the extent of her reservation with Estienne; young as she was, young and in love (but careful about love's nurture and sustenance, as though love were really an emotion felt privately rather than a feeling exchanged, which either grew and extended in the sharing or, humiliated, withdrew and withered in solitude), Helene refused to judge Estienne harshly, at least so far as she was aware.

When she entered the living room, snug and fitted like a ship's cabin, everything in place, she smelled the dinner Estienne had prepared: a sea bass grilling on the outdoor brazier, salad chopped with dandelions and fresh basil, small tomatoes and red peppers, and a running Camembert alongside two exquisite peaches (perfect "sunsets," Estienne called them when their orange, red, and purple skins glistened) on the sideboard. He came in from the garden, which dropped off toward the sea, and embraced her, but she hardly paid attention. It wasn't until much later that they made love, although Estienne had stopped work hours earlier, smashing a plaster in disgust, and paced the atelier waiting for the time of her usual return.

They had arrived in Port Vendres three weeks before. There hadn't been very much to do. After several days of scrubbing and cleaning, turning out the blankets, airing the cabinets, stocking the shelves with dry goods and the hamper with onions and potatoes, Estienne went to work in the atelier across the road. Helene heard him hammer and bang, curse and whistle, and only once during the week that followed did he return unannounced to show her a little head he had carved. It was rough, unfinished, but she recognized a suggestion of her face, although she disclaimed its fidelity and dismissed it as a poor likeness. Estienne muttered something like "That's not the point," shrugged, kissed her nonetheless, and returned to the studio. Helene read several books, studied the French subjunctive, in which she was maladept, glanced at some magazines, walked to the village several times during the first week to shop, but claimed that it tired her out and persuaded Estienne to let her buy a bicycle. By the end of the third week, despite Estienne's concerned warning that she had better find an interest—indeed, consider Maillol's offer to teach her weaving when he returned to the south—Helene had begun her little tours of the region, covering a dozen kilometers daily, begging rides when the roads were hilly, visiting old villages, examining churches where occasionally she lit a candle; or she sat in the town square under a bell tower and wrote long letters to her sisters, to whom she described her peaceful life, her empty and carefree days, her boredom; "although I do love Estienne very much, he really has so much work to do, there's terribly little time for me."

The outbreak of the war, however, changed the order of their days. It was being fought very far away in the north of the country, but it reached down into their valley of contentment. The second week after war had been declared, Estienne Delahaye was notified that he would have to report for the army, but that exigency was disposed of when the army doctor noted that his heart was unusually large and beating irregularly. Estienne, not having considered seriously the possibility of being called to war, took the news of his exemption as casually as if he had been told that a mysterious benefactor had paid an outstanding bill for him. It wouldn't have mattered. He didn't think in terms of an outside world, except insofar as matters of his art were concerned. He could not help regarding the outbreak of war and the inevitable death of his countrymen as an opportunity to be seized, as inexorably as Maillol, a generation before him, had fallen into the good fortune of producing monuments on commission (except, of course, that Maillol had done comparatively few, and those under very special circumstances). Estienne Delahaye had fewer reservations. The war, foolish though he regarded it as being, was something to keep the idle hands of men engaged, and its conclusion in death or armistice would elicit the wish of survivors and patriots to recall its dubious accomplishments. By early 1940, Estienne had already devised several alternative schemes of commemoration that were easily adaptable, with movable and removable parts, which could be employed to memorialize soldiers, sailors, pilots, civilians, innocents all, children all, transfigured faces, the resurrected flesh that memory wished to conserve. Indeed, it was during April of 1940 that he received a letter from a family in the Gironde whose patriarchal head, shot down over Belgium during the first weeks of the war, had been returned to be buried in the historic crypt of the family; Estienne was requested to devise a relief incorporating an abstract bust portrait of the colonel in uniform with the inevitable MORT POUR LA FRANCE incised beneath his name and dates. The commission encouraged Estienne, and he set to work; Helene, for her part, undertook to work in the *mairie* every morning folding bandages, and in the afternoon to help a neighbor, whose son had left for the war, take care of the chickens.

The war created a regimen of busyness, and days that had been blown dry by the mistral were suddenly filled with enterprise and martial elation. Of course, it didn't last. By the end of the spring of 1940, the war was being lost; the Germans were destroying the French army, and the unconquered part of France was soon to be turned over to the authority of sentimental patriots and political miscreants. Every Frenchman of the south came to understand that survival was no longer a responsibility shared with other Frenchmen, but an enterprise to be pursued alone. Estienne and Helene Delahaye, the industrious sculptor and his young wife, who was carrying her first child, had to devise ways of enduring. Despite the deposits of money that Señor Miravilla continued to make, although the sum decreased and the regularity of its transfer was impaired by the difficulty of even such simple transactions (there were several months when it would have been easier and quicker for Helene to take the bus from Port Bou to Barcelona and return with the money in hand), the support assured by Helene's dowry was modest. On each occasion in the month when the bank informed them by post that the sum had been credited to their account, Estienne would become irritated. "My rich bride," he snorted once in her presence, and she replied with anger that she had never promised him riches. "That was your friend Alain's idea," she added, although Estienne failed to understand the reference. Nonetheless they managed. Their rent was nothing; old Maillol assured them by letter from the north that they could stay on without payment if they wished, and the rest of their requirements— food, clothing, artist's materials—were amply provided by occasional commissions, the sale of an odd wood or stone carving, and gifts of eggs and poultry that Helene received for helping the chicken farmer down the road. They managed.

On May 5 Helene lost her baby. She tripped in the chicken house while carrying a tray of eggs to be packed for market, fell, and, covered with egg yolk and slime, began to hemorrhage. It was necessary that she be hospitalized. Old Dr. Malebranche, superannuated but recalled from retirement to active practice in the absence of all the younger doctors, told her the grim news: "No baby now, my dear;

no baby ever, I'm afraid." Helene Delahaye received the news with tears, bit her lip, and reaching out to find her husband, who had been standing near the bedside only minutes before the doctor came, touched air, her fingers groping to find his absent hand. Estienne, as he explained later, had become so unnerved by the doctor's arrival that he had fled the room. "I couldn't take it," he said. It was, Estienne believed, the beginning of a run of bad luck.

The months that followed were marked by intense industry on Estienne's part. He worked constantly, almost feverishly; he had received another commission to undertake a monument for the defeated army of France, a small pyramid to be placed at the entrance to the new section of the national cemetery at Verdun, and, regarding the assignment as both a challenge and an opportunity not to be missed, he was diligently occupied for many months with the drawings, the maquette, a trip north to present his conception to the colonel in charge of Graves Registration and the Ministry of Monuments and Public Works.

It was during his absence, when he was pursuing the intricacies of this prestigious and profitable commission, that his wife took her first lover. She had never seen the young Jean or Joan again; when she had returned the following week, war had already been declared, and the young sailor had joined up. But Helene had returned to Collioure to meet him, and it was there, late in the fall of 1940, that she met Octave Picone, already a veteran of the war—or should we say a victim of the war, since he had lost an arm to shrapnel during the retreat from the Lowlands. Octave worked in his father's bar, which fronted on the wharf, and Helene—attracted, she admitted, by the fact that he had been wounded in the war—was determined to win him if it was at all possible. During the weeks of Estienne's absence she bicycled to Collioure every day in the late afternoon, and by the time the town closed down at eight and the regulars had gone home to supper and the evening news broadcast from London, she had Octave to herself. The flirtation lasted about a week; the affair, about three months. It was satisfying; it persuaded Helene, as apparently Estienne had not, that to be beautiful was sufficient. Being rich didn't matter at all to Octave. Her body was quite enough reward.

It was not the return of Estienne from Paris and Verdun that ended the romance. Indeed, for several weeks after his return, Helene revised her routine only slightly, persuading Estienne that it was preferable to dine in the Spanish manner (that is, beginning their supper not earlier than ten o'clock each evening) and convincing Octave that, since there was no business after seven and he could close the bar an hour earlier, at least two hours of intimacy could be managed. Octave obliged, knowing full well that Helene's husband had returned, and Estienne, preoccupied with his pyramid and two other small commissions he had received while in the north, was quite willing to wait for his light meal until a later hour, since this allowed him more time to work. He obviously did not suspect; he thought Helene's little trips were amusing recreation appropriate to her youth. It was not a matter of discovery that ended the affair, but rather a fatuous and casual remark of Octave's.

"Will you be my mistress even when I marry?" he asked her one evening. The question concealed not one, but a suite of alarming implications. It suggested that Helene was not uniquely loved (a bearable supposition), but more, that since she felt herself obliged to ensure the ignorance of her husband, Octave or any other married lover would be bound to do likewise; moreover, as they would both be married, she could count upon little more than occasional afternoons or odd evenings of passion, artificially fabricated and rushed to completion against the demands not of one clock, but of two. But, even more important, she realized that were Octave or any other lover to marry and take her as a mistress, she would cease to steal her pleasure, to deceive her husband, to control, as it were, her little universe of recreation, and become instead chosen and controlled. It was a terrible question that Octave had put. When she did not answer, he repeated the question, adding as though it were common information: "You know, I am to marry the postman's Blanchette next spring. It was fixed long ago." Helene got up from the bar stool, pushed away her aperitif, and left. But only when she approached the turnoff on the highway leading toward her village did she realize the full extent of her decision. She had no intention of ever again having an affair with a man even remotely marriageable. And on the two occasions, during the several years that still remained until the war's end, when she became briefly involved with men whom she discovered to be married, she punished them mercilessly for their deception before she terminated the relationship. No, in the seeking and seizure of her lovers, some lasting nearly a whole season, others an escapade of a weekend, she drew at first from a wide range of ages and proclivities, from elderly widowers (including an old baron who insisted upon rouging and wigging himself before he took her to his bed) to the exceptionally young and precocious. While Estienne struggled with art, maintaining an exemplary discipline, securing commissions from the occupied as well as seeking them from the occupier, collaborating—if that is the appropriate term—in the hope of decorating and monumentalizing the victorious German army, Helene, increasingly isolated and alone, became exacting and scrupulous in the refinement of loving, deciding that all her lovers should be not more nor less than five years her junior, raising the age of requirement with each year that she advanced, determining that these flirtations were best pursued with young lads too unskilled to be her masters and too young to desire her bed *en permanence*. By 1943, when her lovers were in their eighteenth year, her pleasure and her romance were at their most exalted, for the sexuality was intense and satisfying, the exuberance unabated, and the quality of thoughtfulness and fidelity minimal. Nothing was paid, no gifts exchanged other than movies or perhaps a meal, no pledges demanded or given, and no seriousness invested in her behavior. Estienne, whatever curiosity he professed in her activities and whatever gossip Helene's association with the young men of the region aroused, drew little more than passing interest. It was a precarious time. The gossiping propensities of the bourgeoisie were otherwise employed; Estienne's relative ease in wartime was more sourly observed than the apparent waywardness of his beautiful Spanish wife.

## Nine

It was during the summer of 1944 that Aristide Maillol, Estienne's master, indubitable friend, and unwitting patron, was seriously injured in an automobile accident while being driven to Paris from his summer home in Marly-le-Roi. The old man, then seventy-seven years of age, suffered immense pain, and—recognizing that his life was coming to a precipitous conclusion—asked to be returned to the house in which he had been born, in the village of his childhood, where he had passed his productive youth and the genius days of his early maturity: Banyuls-sur-Mer, four kilometers from the cottage and atelier that he had lent his former assistant and erstwhile colleague, Estienne Delahaye, and his beautiful wife, Helene.

The old man was installed in his home, and a message was sent by his housekeeper that Estienne should come to call and be so kind as to bring with him his wife, whom the master looked forward to meeting. Estienne received the message spoken in haste by the housekeeper, who frowned while she delivered it. He thanked her for her trouble and she replied: "*Je suis ici pour le maître, pas pour vous, Monsieur. Pas de remerciements.*"

Estienne was aware, increasingly aware, that the townspeople disapproved of the contact he had with the German conqueror; although he had explained to the mayor that he was given little choice in the matter, and was promised even less compensation for his work, whenever he passed through the village of Port Vendres or took a cognac in the café, hardly anyone spoke with him. The resistance had begun in the southwest, and even if there were many who took no part in its activities, working for the Boches was considered equal to collaborating with them. Clearly Estienne had done little more than take advantage of good fortune, of being the only sculptor of his generation who had accommodated himself to do monumental work in the classical style, and at a time when all sides—the French, France's allies, and the enemy—wanted commemorative stones, memorial marbles, bronze reliefs. The German dead had as much right to be remembered as had the French, Estienne temporized, and it was in the spirit of this rationalization that he made the mistake of flying to Berlin in the early fall of 1944 to consult with the adjutant of Albert Speer, who was under orders to plan a heroic monument to the German army that would be built in all the occupied countries of Europe.

When Estienne Delahaye returned from Berlin, ten days after Maillol's housekeeper had delivered her message, the master was dead. Estienne was in time for the funeral, but not to say a living good-bye. It struck him, at that moment, that something was wrong with his life, that he was mistaking the proper order of events, the correct priorities. Helene, who had failed to meet the old sculptor, sat beside Estienne in the village church of Banyuls-sur-Mer. The sun was brilliant, streaming through the tinted windows behind the choir, bathing the unadorned casket in gold. The priest, an elderly monsignor, spoke affectionately of Maillol, citing his achievement as a sculptor, noting the breadth of his internationalism, encompassing the friendship and patronage of noble Germans like Count Harry Kessler as well as the admiration of modern Greeks who thought him the legatee of Praxiteles; but more than all this, he celebrated the utter simplicity of Maillol's vision, its clarity and precision of focus, its celebration of the human form ("ideal and transfigured," the priest said, "as if already in the estate of resurrection"). Not a word was spoken of Maillol's fame—his immense and diffused fame—his success, his glory; none of these notions had apparently struck the worthy monsignor, who tugged at his chin diffidently as he spoke, as though engaged in drawing out his thought by depressing a hidden key beneath his lower lip. Indeed, the monsignor scarcely addressed the congregation, some of whom had come from long distances to be present at the obsequies. It seemed rather that the priest, his soutane shining, his leather boots cracked with age, was performing an introduction of Maillol to his creator, making certain that the Good Lord learned well in advance who was en route to his serene kingdom— a fine man, a passionate man, a loving man, and, above all, a great celebrant of the world, which God had created.

Helene, strained by the funeral—the first she had attended since the death of her mother—sat with her hands folded in her lap, hardly looking up, although once she started and almost rose in fright. Estienne, however, was immobilized by the funeral—not moved or overcome, but immobilized. *Petrifié*, the French say, or "frightened and turned to stone," the double meaning that curious process of carbonization has in most languages. His plane had landed in Marseilles the night before the funeral, and he had been returned in a German staff car to the village very late, after the public vigil had concluded and the mortal remains of Maillol had been given over to the care of a sodality of nuns from a neighboring convent. The meetings in Berlin had gone well, he had been flattered and admired, and his work at Verdun was complimented; but it was clear to Estienne that the commission would go elsewhere, to a German undoubtedly, and that his invitation to Berlin was a courtesy extended to the Vichy government; his picture had been taken and was published, but that was the extent of it. Estienne was nonetheless quite satisfied. He was well regarded, and one day, he assumed, he would be rewarded for his gifts. Judging by the atmosphere in Berlin, he supposed that the war was not going well for the Germans, and he concluded from the idle jokes and drawn faces in the Chancellery that the end was not far off. It was just as well that he had not received the commission to design a German victory monument. And with Maillol's death, which Helene had reported to him as he came through the door of their cottage, he supposed the authority and reputation of the master would fall upon his assistant, his disciple—in fact, the one among all others who had strained to apply the principles of "ecstatic naturalism" (as he was fond of calling it) to all manner of public monuments.

The death of Aristide Maillol, however fortuitous its occasion, was not unforeseen. The man was old, indeed frail. He had been moving slowly for some time now. Even at the time of their meeting in the galleries of the Louvre, Estienne had taken the elbow of the master and gripped it as they descended the slippery marble stairs to the entrance foyer. Maillol was an old man even then; death was not a stranger to him, and Maillol acknowledged once in conversation that he regarded its advent not with horror but with interest. He suspected death of wearing the disguise of youth, of being not, as popular imagination would have it, a skeletal anatomy with grisly visage, bearing scythe and hourglass, reminder and scourge of mortality, warning and threatening by turns, but rather a youth, well boned and muscled, splendid in his carriage, full-haired and fair, through whose luscious cheeks and reddish lips the blood of centuries ran. Death, then, was a glorious youth, and the master delighted in such an image, being unafraid of the attentions of such a memorable creation. Not a fallen angel, not a species of devil, not punishment or rebuke, death came in the guise of a messenger, a Hermes who invited his guests to attend upon a more marvelous banquet, one eternally in process, one forever replenished with new guests.

But at the funeral of the master, the preaching monsignor had not known of Maillol's fancy; he spoke, rather, of death as a ministry of release, as the closing of the door to the antechamber of life, as a finality whose only promise of renewal lay in the great faith of the Church that the tomb of Gethsemane had been empty and that the Jesus of the flesh would pass into the Christ of judgment.

"Judgment," Estienne heard and whispered to Helene, his voice hoarse, and she started, hearing the word and thinking her own thoughts, and half rose from her seat in fright.

## Ten

The death of Maillol allowed the Delahayes to pause. As a complex machine, raised upon blocks, is required to respond to the ignition, turning over, whirling, but abrading no surface, the Delahayes were being tuned.

It was not death in an abstract way or even the particular death of Maillol that was the occasion of taking their lives off the road and submitting them to scrutiny; but rather it was the sheer unnaturalness of time that is the proper atmosphere of death. Somehow the vigil, the funeral itself, the interment, the gathering of friends and family at the house afterward, the closing of the house and the inventory of its contents—in which both Estienne and Helene participated, working long and exhausting hours to complete the task—provided a stasis in which to recollect their existence. In the time of death one becomes used to sitting for endless hours—merely sitting, not even talking particularly, sucking on familiar thoughts, old illusions, pulling without real energy at frayed ends and loose buttons, perhaps unraveling, perhaps not; snagging, devising, temporizing silently with one's own history; rising occasionally to pass somebody a cup of tea or a cake, remarking upon the dead, noting one or another gentility or gesture of the departed, and returning again to one's thoughts. And so an hour or more would pass, and distant neighbors come to call would depart, making way for others; the tight circle would remain—the intimates, the family, the servants, the assistants and colleagues, among whom were Estienne Delahaye and his wife, Helene, who returned after the body had been settled in the cemetery and passed the remainder of the day at the house in Banyuls-sur-Mer. Helene rose after a half hour and passed into the kitchen, with which she was unfamiliar, to help the housekeeper and her daughter, while Estienne began a quiet conversation with the monsignor, who confessed, not without a moist eye, how much he had loved Maillol and before him Maillol's old aunt, who had raised the master and given him a smile or two when he was an orphaned boy. Unnatural time it was, vortical time, a cone of time that enfolds death and inserts it like a shaft in the midst of the ordinariness of ordinary days, causing everyone whom it touches to freeze and for a moment to hold steady.

A month after the funeral, Helene went to Estienne's atelier to help him clean the windows. She hadn't been in the studio for more than a year.

"My God, it's been a long time."

"A *very* long time. I don't understand why," he answered. The worktable, long and narrow, fashioned of planks that lay athwart wooden horses, was covered with plaster dust and wood shavings. The storage space at the back seemed like a frozen regiment: every species of soldiery from dwarfs to giants, grimly white, drained of blood, stood upon pedestals, some artificially supported by rods, others standing free, while others hung from the air as if seized by the nape of their necks; and in another corner, separated from the military, observing them wall-eyed, were women of incomprehensible beauty, not as many women as soldiers, fewer than a dozen, several in black marble, one in dull bronze, several roughly carved in wood, a complexity of planes and surfaces; and about their pediments, recumbent at their feet, a sleeping panther carved in sandstone, a smaller puma whose tail curved down in high relief, an Abyssinian cat, ears pointed, its front paws raised upon a bronze base as though about to jump to the shoulder of the naked woman who smiled above it.

"An immense amount of work!" Helene admired.

"And much of it gone already. That's what we've been living on, you know."

"Yes," Helene replied, not quite comprehending, for at the time she knew nothing of the proceeds from the sale and delivery of sculptures.

Helene set about cleaning the table, using a duster that she whisked about the objects, but leaving a thin layer of dust at their base, as though afraid of coming too close to or touching them. She was intimidated by these strange people. Estienne, handing her the scouring brush, directed her to the pail of soapy water that he had prepared for washing the windows. Helene was pleased to turn her back to the room and begin cleaning the large bay windows that looked out upon a rolling field.

They hardly talked for the next hour. Not until they returned to the cottage for lunch did Helene grip his hand suddenly, while they were drinking their coffee: "It's six years we're married, and *you've* made all the children."

### Eleven

A telegram arrived from Alain Malburet one Monday morning in April. Paris was liberated, and the Allies were driving north into Germany. It was a typical announcement: "Ugliness will descend into the midst of beauty any day now. *Amitiés.* Alain." The following week he arrived on foot from Port Vendres, where the bus from Perpignan had left him in the town square near the gendarmerie.

It was late in the afternoon. Estienne and Helene had gone for a walk through the pine forest that came down almost to the sea. Alain let himself into the cottage, which he recognized instantly; Estienne had described it to him in considerable detail when they had seen each other in Paris the year before. No other cottage on the road was painted white and blue wash, with a carved oak door and windows that looked like the gingerbread openings in the house of Hansel and Gretel, small panes of glass through which distorted images and spectral light could pass, Alain thought. "Cozy, cozy, cozy," he repeated with disgust, but he was delighted and relieved that his friends did not lock their door, even though French circumspection dictated a more fastidious and ungenerous response to strangers. He made himself at home in the living room, fetching a bottle of wine and pouring himself a tumbler, taking out his notebook of the road, and jotting in it a line or two he had fashioned on the bus ride and an observation about an abandoned German tank the bus had passed along the highway, overturned but intact—not a mark upon it, but somehow wrecked.

Alain learned the directions to the cottage by asking at the *mairie*. The notary who was busily writing in his ledgers had looked up when he inquired about the Delahayes, and examined him carefully. "Those!" he exclaimed with disgust, but told him nonetheless, carefully and precisely, adding that he was a neighbor although he never talked with them.

"They don't seem well loved, if I can judge by your attitude, Monsieur."

"Quite right, Monsieur. Not well loved at all. They've done pretty well, you know, while all the rest of us have been fighting the war."

Alain, disgusted, although curious about his friends' poor reputation, remarked to the cracked old scribe, "I don't think you've done all that much fighting, sir," and left.

It was after dark when they returned; they had not really enjoyed their walk together and, although expecting Alain's arrival, found him asleep on the living-room floor, his head resting on a cushion he had removed from the window seat. He seemed to Helene too easily at home, perhaps because she recognized that after nearly six years she had still to make this loaned cottage into something of her own; it still belonged to Maillol, the furniture, the crockery, the bedding—

nothing, with the possible exception of the food she bought, had been introduced by her own taste, not even the little head Estienne had carved of her, which stood upon the mantel of the fireplace, since he had neither given it to her nor, as we have noted, had she accepted it as an authentic transcription of her beauty. They began to tidy up around the sleeping figure of their friend, straightening and cleaning, hoping they could finish and have dinner prepared before he awakened. Estienne was returning the ashtrays to their places and Helene was piling the magazines when they heard a voice behind them: "A beautiful head, but not up to the beauty of the living." Helene heard him, flushed with embarrassment, but turned and bent down to kiss Alain's cheek. He was bearded. Neither of them had noticed, as he had slept buried in the comfort of his arm, half submerged in the pillow. "My God, Alain, what have you grown?" she laughed and, thinking again, kissed him. "How you must tickle your girlfriends!"

"They love it," he laughed. "Estienne, *mon vieux*, how glorious to see you and Helene, as I said, more and more beautiful." He stood up and embraced Estienne and kissed Helene, and hugged Estienne once more. He was a bear, a warm, immense bear, with a face turned to sag, his beard, full and black, covering virtually everything up to his cheeks and growing wild beneath his chin, obscuring the ridged and coarse skin that had earlier announced the ravages of his untrimmed life.

"When did you grow it?" Estienne asked when they had seated themselves and broken out a fresh bottle of wine.

"While I was in the hospital," he answered with a sudden note of grimness.

"Hospital?"

"I was wounded ten months ago during a diversionary attack we made on a German emplacement in the Dordogne while the Allies were making a parachute drop. I got one in the thigh. Don't move as smoothly as I used to. Bit of a limp, but while I was recovering I got a long look at myself and, having become bored with my ugly face, decided to cover it over with the beard. I'm quite splendid now, don't you think?"

Helene smiled and touched Alain's leg with a reassuring palm.

"No. Not that one."

"No. No. I didn't mean," she said, flustered. "You're teasing me again."

"Again? We haven't seen each other since you married. My dear girl, we haven't enough history, certainly not of teasing."

"But I only meant affection."

"I know that, dear Helene. Don't be upset by my bearish ways. I am, you see, a true bear now, not simply one shorn and naked. And I can assure you, after the life I've seen during the past years, my bear teeth are all but worn out. Is it all right if I rest up with you a bit? Not long, a few weeks at the most. It's another inferno in Paris. Good to be here. Good to be here. Especially for both of you. They're shooting collaborators right and left."

"And what's that supposed to mean, Alain?" Estienne demanded, suddenly angry and defensive.

"That's all I wanted to know. I know you when you become outraged. It isn't true. Thank God for that."

"It most certainly isn't true. I know what these villagers think. I never made a sou from the Germans."

"But did you work for them?"

"Not a single piece."

"But they say, over at the *mairie*, that you've prospered. Yes?"

"We've just survived, like all the rest of France."

"I see, old man. Let's forget it. It's obviously jealousy. They never understand the artist, do they?"

"Never. Never. Damned bourgeoisie. If it continues we'll have to clear out."

"Oh, it'll pass, once things settle. But stay here for the while. It's too furious in Paris, everybody explaining to each other. It's like a mass confessional—recriminations, expiations. More like a public urinal, I say, everybody pissing on their neighbors. 'I'm a better Frenchman than you.' It's a pain in the ass. I decided to clear out and come down to see my old friends." His face lit up; a smile, Helene thought, came across his face, but it was hard to be certain; only the crinkles beneath his eyes suggested a smile, but then his face was weathered, and she wasn't sure.

## Twelve

During the days of Maillol's decline and death and the period of mourning that followed, and now with the arrival of Alain Malburet, Helene had little time to think about the young student she had met in the village several months earlier. Paul Verace had just finished the lycée that spring, and although it was uncertain whether he would be able to attend courses in the local college in Perpignan—he wanted to become an engineer—he described to Helene the bridges he would rebuild, the highways, tiered and interlocked, with which he dreamed to replace the miserable road that linked France and Spain, as though these schemes were near at hand, awaiting only opportunity to be realized, omitting from his dreaming the years of study and apprenticeship that would of necessity intervene. They had met, ordinarily enough, in a crowded café in the square of Port Vendres. Exhausted from shopping, Helene had asked to sit at his table where he was reading, buried in a biography of Georges Eiffel from which once or twice he raised his head to look off into space, his soft brown eyes wandering, while he cogitated.

Helene had left the cottage that morning after an agitated night during which she had tried to arouse Estienne to love her. Each time she sought to coax him, he had muttered, "Not now, not now, to-morrow," and turned over, indifferent to her need. It had been that way for some time, Estienne unable or unwilling, she had no idea which, to reply to her importunings. They had not made love for ten days, and although she was not desperate, she had at that moment no alternatives, with the result that she began to feel the eerie hollowness in the pit of her stomach, the slight ringing of confusion in her ears, which she always mistook for sexual need. She had left their bed and gone out into the warm night air, where she smoked one cigarette after another, trying to solicit calm. It was something of a pattern; she was familiar with its history although, not dissimilarly from millions of others who at that hour sat in their own gardens, containing the anxieties of the night, she resorted at last to removing it by the indulgence of an easy and familiar release that bore in its wake a vast physical exhaustion into which she sank, falling asleep huddled in the canvas lawn chair. When she awakened, the sun having already risen from behind the wall of cypress trees a mile away, she was again disgusted with the remedies of the night, and her anxiety returned. She wished to speak to Estienne, to ask the few questions she needed to ask, to solicit the simple clarifications her confusions demanded, but she had never learned to speak directly to a man. Such speech had always been conducted in circumspection, in gestures and rituals, and having failed to speak with her father, who, until the moment of Estienne's descent into her midst, was the only man with whom she had had a prolonged contact, she was without the means of securing reassurance, except of course by making love. Unfortunately, as she had come to learn, making love was as much a language of gesture and ritual, without settled meanings—quite as susceptible to deception and misreading—as her father's tender kiss when she presented him with his alpaca each evening.

Paul Verace, on the other hand, obliged her to speak, to find a language to accompany intercourse—to exclaim upon the emotions generated by making love, to describe perhaps too meticulously (for he was an aspirant to engineering), upon the connections and links that enlarged their lovemaking from caressed thigh and kissed buttock into lines from French poetry that he had learned in school. But the point of importance was that the simple machinery of arousal and release had acquired the elevation of engineering—that is, process with design—and hence a kind of eloquence, although he inevitably resorted to ergs to describe passion and ohms to signify resistance. He used that language; she nonetheless responded happily, for it was metaphor, and making love required more than Estienne's delicious smile of contentment and falling asleep.

She and Paul had made love more than a dozen times during the weeks when Estienne was busy with the monument to German conquest, but by the time Maillol returned to die, Helene had become alarmed by the increasingly desperate intensity of Paul's loving. He held her long after they had been satisfied, and once he cried when she rose from their bed and announced that she had to return home earlier than he had supposed. He despaired of keeping her interested, and at subsequent meetings he had arrived almost prepared with new material to fascinate her; but she had exhausted her curiosity about engineering, and although he had, it must be acknowledged, spoken marvelously of the difference between the Egyptian and the Mayan pyramids and of the flying buttresses in the cathedrals of medieval France, her own intellectual curiosity was flagging. But this was not true, really. It was what her smoking during his little talks, which he conducted upon her naked stomach (building the pyramids upon her groin and demonstrating the flying buttress in a way that might be considered obscene), was construed by him to mean. As he became persuaded that he was losing her, his importunities increased and his desperation became more severe; but actually it was her feeling for him, growing deeper and more frightening, that required the smoking in bed, the application of lipstick, the need to pee just as he became excited—all means of evading not him but herself, her own feeling that this was a young man who loved her not because she was beautiful, not because she was rich, but merely because she appeared to love him in return, to be there when they agreed, to be always on time. It was in fact the case that she began to feel something that might have been love for this dark-haired, moody, serious young boy.

The return of Maillol to die in Banyuls-sur-Mer was an intervention, obliging Helene for the first time to leave a written message at the shop where Paul worked that she would not be able to keep their rendezvous and that for some time to come it would be impossible for them to meet. She had thought to leave the note at that, but recognized that its bleakness constituted an inexplicable termination, which would undoubtedly bring Paul to despair. Of course, had she been certain that she wished to end it then and there, it would have been appropriate to leave the message without hope, but she added a "*Je t'aime*" and followed that with a series of exclamation marks that could not but soften the blow and transform it from rejection into something more mysterious, the declaration that, despite her love, she was prisoner to another obligation. And such it was, an obligation that Helene sensed, not alone to Estienne, who was her first love, her husband, father of her uncompleted child, and artist—let us not forget artist—but even more to her own father, whom she adored and, one assumes, despised, and to whom the haste and thoughtlessness of her marriage and the succession of her lovers (essentially carnal boyfriends) were offered in tribute and rebuke.

During the weeks that had passed since Helene had last seen Paul, the passion of "I love you" had waned to the evocative and sweet "I remember you," as she did at odd moments, sitting with Estienne in the garden at sunset or recalling Paul's face with a shudder in the church when the monsignor had spoken of the Judgment. Even these faded, and only when she made love to Estienne in the desultory and offhand manner to which she had become accustomed did she superimpose upon the occasion the remembrance of Paul's tenderness and enthusiasm. She understood, however, that it was no longer Paul himself whom she recalled but only a ritual memento that enabled her to bear the irresolution of her marriage.

In all this, however, the recurrence of memory and association, the Paul Verace of life, the lanky boy who worked in a stationer's shop and dreamed of becoming an engineer, was all but forgotten. Several times she encountered him unavoidably, but on the last occasion she did not even see him. She had bought a newspaper the day after Alain Malburet's arrival in Port Vendres. She had paid the money to the old woman at the kiosk and was about to thrust the paper into her shopping basket when her eye was caught by a photograph on the front page. A woman, her head shaved, was being marched past lines of citizens who shouted at her, their fists raised in the air; the woman, no older than Helene, shielding her face with her arms, walked through. The photograph, taken in Bordeaux, carried the editorial caption: "A Warning to Collaborators!" Helene gasped in horror and Paul, who had undoubtedly noticed her from the stationer's shop and watched her reaction, rushed out to help her, but she had already turned and begun to run down the street.

When she arrived at the cottage, Estienne and Alain were sitting over a drink, talking about art and poetry. Helene did not give them a chance to speak, but threw down the newspaper on the floor before them. "I don't want that to happen to me," she cried, bursting into tears. "I'm no collaborator. I don't care about politics. I don't know anything about politics." On and on she went, shouting, until her speech became incoherent, virtually hysterical, and Estienne, who had taken her around the waist and held her to himself, quieted her. When she was seated, rubbing her red eyes and sipping a cognac that Alain had poured, Estienne began to speak with remarkable quiet and firmness. "Once and for all, let's be done with this business. The Germans wanted sculptures from me. I made the mistake of meeting with them on several occasions to discuss the work. I was probably misguided, but like you, Helene, I have no politics. I make my work and I sell it; I am asked to make work and I execute it. In this case, it turns out, it is best that no work was commissioned by the Germans and I made none for them. I did make a number of pieces for Vichy, but they were not political pieces—they were commemoratives that honor our dead, French dead, and who can blame me for that? Don't be afraid, Helene. I will protect you." And then, as an afterthought, as though what he had said had not been enough, he added, "I will certainly protect you. I owe you that much."

It was later, perhaps a week, and several days before Alain announced he was returning to Paris, that Helene asked Estienne casually, "And whatever did you mean by that line about owing me something?"

Estienne, who had been drawing at the dining-room table while Alain paced before the fireplace cracking walnuts, stopped and thought. Alain remembered instantly, but Estienne, perhaps genuinely not remembering, asked, "When did I say anything like that?"

"You remember. It was last week, when I was upset."

"Did I really speak of owing you something? I can't imagine what I must have been thinking. Do you recall my saying anything like that, Alain? It doesn't sound like me."

"Indeed, it doesn't, but you said precisely that. I remember the line. You said, 'At least I owe you protection.' "

"How remarkable! Well, of course I owe Helene protection. She's my wife, after all."

"No, Alain, that wasn't it. It meant something else. I can't remember the exact words, but the phrase caught me like a fishbone in my throat: I can neither swallow it nor, it appears, am I able to bring it up again. But the sense was different, as though Estienne were saying that, having failed in other respects, he at least owed me protection."

"Failed? Do you think I've failed you?" He paused and then continued. "We might as well. It's easier with Alain here. He can moderate the dispute," Estienne added with jocular unease.

"I'm not looking for an argument, although it's about time we argued. We haven't stopped for a minute pretending that we're miraculously happy, but I must confess, Estienne, I have not been miraculously happy since our last week in Vézelay, and that was before we were married."

Helene spoke with unfamiliar directness, unqualified by the tentativeness of phrasing that had always marked her almost supplicatory questions to Estienne, as though she were afraid, not of the confrontation itself but of what it would reveal. The same afternoon, while she was sitting in the cottage bedroom, combing her hair, Estienne's curious phrase had come back to her and for the first time in years she had decided to leave her hair loose and long rather than wind it about her head and bun it at the back. She kept repeating to herself, as her resolve to speak grew, that she could take the consequences, that she could leave, that she could go to Paul if she wanted, that she could return to her father if that were necessary, but that she couldn't stand another moment without understanding.

"I didn't know."

"That's true. You didn't know. I have been a very young girl to you for many years, but I stopped being a very young girl to everyone else some time ago."

"What do you mean?"

"Isn't it clear, Estienne? I've had lovers besides you."

Alain Malburet shifted uneasily, suddenly finding the conversation disagreeable, too serious, too full of truth without metaphor.

"Do you really need to go into that, Helene?" he interposed.

"Not you, Alain?" asked Estienne.

"Don't be stupid. Even if I had wanted her, when could I have arranged it?"

Estienne Delahaye sat becalmed. He could hardly speak, although it wasn't the shock of unjust betrayal, but that the simple disclosure of what all along he had hoped for had come to pass. For his part, over those years of war, while he had applied himself to his work, each day rationalizing yet another decision of compromise and complicity—for he had desperately sought commissions from the

Germans, but had been denied them—he had hoped that Helene would betray him, but he had had no wish to learn of it. He had lost passion for her body, if indeed it had ever been authentic passion. Estienne was not a man beset by such emotions; he was too troubled by the struggle to stretch his talent into a major career to allow himself the indulgence of wild passions. Of course, it is true that many minor talents press the faulted energies of their imagination into the living of large and exuberant lives—drinking and drugging their flesh into an excess that remains memorable long after their works have been sold off to interior decorators—but Estienne, born poor and understood as oppressed, was not allowed the license of such a burning-out; for him, the avoidance of renewed poverty, the conversion of talent into wealth, was a project that allowed no interference. Helene was beauty (and adornment) and wealth (and a buffer against poverty) and youth (and passive). Unexamined, this was all true, and the decision to seduce her was consummated precipitously against the background of irritations and competitions. In fact, however unde-niable her beauty and youth, her wealth proved modest, and whatever function it served until Estienne Delahaye's career was securely launched, it was not enough to justify the decision to marry. Helene was, in a word, used; and she, surmising the use, was using in turn. The familiar and desperate human orbit was activated and spinning. The punishment of which Estienne had dreamed when he observed Helene's discontent and unhappiness was to be betrayed. He was well aware that he had served her badly, that he was virtually without interest in the marriage or its consolations, that he would be childless, which the world could use to explain the malaise of their relationship, although he knew more profoundly that children would have been a diversion, not a solution, and that the absence of them was a blessing. He wanted Helene about for her enumerated virtues, but he wanted her free of any obligations. In effect, he wished the appearance of being married—industrious artist and his handsome wife—but was perfectly willing to be punished for having betrayed her first.

"And so what's to be done?" Estienne asked, rousing himself, having run through the argument in his head. Confronted by the question, Helene was suddenly without ideas. All those that she had entertained now appeared foolish. She could not admit to him that she had thought of returning to her father, and Paul Verace had become a memory. She, for her part, was losing the conviction of her resolution to understand. It was a relief to both of them that Alain began to speak.

"It's quite amazing, the two of you. The world is just emerging from the most disastrous war in its history. Armies are still fighting. Most of Europe is destroyed, and the two of you sit at the foot of the sublime Pyrenees, hidden away from history, and discuss your domestic infelicity. Why don't we have dinner?"

## Thirteen

History, of course, was to be the occasion of the considerable financial and social success of Estienne Delahaye. Not history construed by the historian who wishes to describe the complexity of the course of men and nations, but history conserved by popular imagination, a record of large events and oversized persons, its victories and its victorious, its catastrophes and its dead.

During the fifteen years that passed after the end of the war, Estienne Delahaye succeeded to an enviable uniqueness, having become the most celebrated of monumental sculptors. He had expanded his repertoire from *memento mori* to the living, being called upon by the cities of France not alone to commemorate their fallen but to immortalize their rich and powerful. He was sculptor to the government, but he was also sculptor to industry, commissioned to make large historical reliefs for public centers and concert halls, to provide for them improvisations of French history in a style that would be willingly appreciated while remaining significant and modern. He preferred marble for those of his sculptures that stood free in gardens, and for those in the foyers of industrial centers and for wall reliefs, polished brass afforded the shimmer of gold. Whatever original talent for sculpture Delahaye had possessed as he had learned it in the atelier of Maillol had been suppressed in favor of a pleasing style, virtually anonymous in its palatability, but always dated and signed with his monogram. He never exhibited his sculpture in museums; he had no need for galleries and dealers; he had contempt for art critics and connoisseurs. He knew, perhaps, although his behavior belied the recognition, that he had passed over from sculptor into maker of sculptures, as very often architects of promise end as wealthy builders, and as abstract painters, losing nerve, resume the craft of portraiture. He served society to replicate its vanity, enhance its misconstruction of the past, and in the process acquired the styles, manners, and habits of luxury that expressed his gratitude to the society for having favored him.

Estienne Delahaye complained about success no differently than he had remonstrated with the tedium and difficulties of poverty. Both entailed concentration, long hours, unflagging energy, and the connivance of fortune; in the case of poverty there was added the nagging hostility of impatient tradesmen, the condescension of patrons, the wearying contentions with an imagination that dreamed on a generous scale but had to be content with modesty of proportion and meanness of materials; while success, no less exacting, placed an unfamiliar value upon social flexibility, the willingness to be employed as artist to fashionable tables and salons, wit without acerbity, opinion without repetitiveness, and throughout—keeping well dressed and attractive —the continuous production of works that commanded attention (that is, money), and in its train public comment (that is, enough controversy to provoke and secure both jealous enemies and sympathetic friends), and, in consequence of all this, to be talked about and hence to be desirable and sought after. Estienne Delahaye knew that patrons collected art and paid for it; his wife had learned and come to understand, even better, that patrons collected artists and, paying less for them, paid longer.

## *Fourteen*

The country house in Mougins, white and wicker, had been built during an earlier prosperous decade by an English family whose money derived from land in Lancashire. In the aftermath of the war, death duties and the decline of rents obliged the Playfairs to dispose of the property, and, although amused to think that an artist could afford such an establishment, they were willing to allow the local estate agent to effect the purchase at a price somewhat below their original stipulation. Helene, not at all impressed by the distinction of the country Playfairs, bargained astutely, and telegrams passed between them and the agent for more than two weeks, while she and Alexandre, their secretary, a young aspirant to sculpture whom she had met at a *vernissage* six months earlier and invited home to take up his duties, drove about the countryside, eating splendidly and rising late.

Estienne did not begrudge Helene her trip south to negotiate the property. It had been an exhausting fall; two enormous sculptures, one for a garden in Neuilly-sur-Seine and another for an automobile plant in the Midi, had to be installed and the press openings coordinated, and in both of these activities Helene's dexterous management was called upon to the fullest. He did not begrudge this to her, nor, for that matter, did he question her casual announcement that Alexandre, whose impossible Slavic surname he was unable to remember, would accompany her so dictation could continue. He accepted the young and attentive secretary, whose eyes fastened upon everything with a glow of interest and familiarity that belied the fact that he was, like most of his generation, virtually without information or opinion. Alexandre Whatever was nonetheless handsome and he pleased Helene, whose age, though still less than Estienne's, was advancing with the same inexorability.

When Estienne Delahaye joined Helene for her birthday in the south of France on the fifth day of January, he already felt unwell. He had been urged to visit a doctor, but, other than for an attack of bronchitis, he had seen none since an army doctor had declined his services at the beginning of the war. He contended, as do most robust and industrious workers who are unfamiliar with sickness, that all he needed was a rest, but his ashen complexion and unusually slow pace, walking from the train station to the automobile, suggested differently. They arrived at the country house about noon, and the cook had prepared a small birthday feast—a terrine, a fish soup, and a simple *poulet à l'estragon*—which they consumed slowly, taking their brandies to the garden, where they sat in sweaters and admired the view. Estienne suggested a nap, while Helene urged a drive through the countryside. It was agreed that both should have their way and meet again in the late afternoon.

Estienne Delahaye slept, awakened several times by a pain in his right arm. It was probably after four in the afternoon that he awakened fully, his arm smarting as though he had slept upon it and suppressed its circulation, but that explanation, good for the arm, did not explain the constriction in his chest and his difficulty in breathing. Imagining that he was suffering a further implication of his weariness, he put on his robe and walked to the study, where his desk had been straightened to await his arrival, the papers from his briefcase unpacked by the secretary and arranged, and the appointment pad, turned appropriately to the day of his arrival, set out near the telephone. He would not have known the time of the attack had not the white porcelain clock, which Mrs. Playfair had insinuated as appropriately "country" into her husband's subdued study, sounded the hour. The small chime and hum of the mechanism, the striking of five, at the first stroke a pain, but with each successive stroke oxygen arrived more slowly, and with the last, as silence returned to the study and a group of birds to the feeder outside the window, Estienne lost consciousness.

It was during his recovery that his doctor in the hospital in Nice set in motion a course of recollection that—like the disjointed road markers on a map through which the anxious traveler has drawn a line, binding together into a route what had been merely arbitrary notations on paper—obliged Estienne Delahaye to convert simple coincidence into fatality.

The doctor's interview, begun the week after intensive care and the lightheaded confusion of sedation had passed, commenced with his innocent assertion, "And so it all began at five o'clock on the fifth." The doctor continued, eliciting from Estienne's brief replies the patient's observation of his symptoms. Only after his departure did Estienne recollect the phrase and with it fragments of his life, long ago accessioned in the vast and dusty archive of his memory.

"At five o'clock on the fifth," he kept repeating, urged by some prescience to pursue the phrase, to compel fives and fifths to reappear, until the first approached, unbidden: the oldest daughter of five, and fifth among his students, the accidental fifth who entered the classroom to win compassion with her tale of an art-struck father. He annotated these fragments within a numerical order of abstraction, signifying by five and fifths not a stream of recollection but a determination of his fate, fixed long ago in the experiments of his childhood, remembering as though yesterday his grave preoccupation with one and five, his plottings of the tide of days, Mondays and Fridays, January and May, one beyond midday and five in the afternoon, until by the end of the evening, when the nurse came to give him his night pills, he was so alarmed that he dared not fall asleep until the ticking clock was covered with a towel and the lamp in the corner of the room was illuminated.

By the time he returned to Mougins, the list of coincidences had lengthened into a coherent document of obsession, each five diagramed to form a configuration of his life; events of the seduction (even the number five above Helene's room at Vézelay was now installed into the system) crossed with interpretations of sculpture, with hidden significances that none but he would have observed, such as the placement of five panels in his commemoration of the Allied landing at Cherbourg, a commission he had won in competition with fifteen other sculptors; and thereafter, even though he was obliged, as Helene pointed out, to force and misconstrue, he insisted upon the discovery of pentagraphy in each and every one of his major works—until, listening to him discourse upon the subject, one would think that where before there had been an enlarged heart that, strained by work and exhaustion, had weakened and collapsed, a febrile five had now been inserted by a malign divinity.

The obsession became awesome. Days that he should have passed in the sun, warmly wrapped in blankets, drinking nourishing beverages, reading books, visiting with friends who, learning of his illness, passed through to cheer him, turned now into tiresome discourses on the fatality of numbers. Helene, hardly suspecting the implication of his obsession, was at first baffled and disturbed, confusing the fixity of his notions with a derangement of his mind, and repeatedly telephoned to Paris, consulting with a specialist who treated such disorders, but was advised by him to disregard this manifestation and to trust that as strength returned the obsession would pass. The attack, however, had been massive enough to require that Estienne alter his habits: only morning work was permissible, late-day rests were mandatory, and modest diet and modest drink vigorously enforced. The judgment of the learned specialist was for a time confirmed, for it should be noted that the obsession retained its almost heraldic character, never acquiring—as it might have done were Estienne Delahaye to become paranoid—bizarre patterns of magical contrivance. Estienne did not object, for instance, to five people in a room; or, as a madman might, avoid five successive steps, counting and interrupting in order to move but four, and then stopping so that the sequence might be recommenced; or alter clocks to abolish five from the repertoire of time. It was not, therefore, that Estienne feared the assault of five and consequently avoided its presentation, but rather that he imagined his life, having come under the dominion of a number, would unfold according to its regulation. His fear, then, was not of a number but of ineluctability, not of the open course of life but of the certainty of death by which he had already been threatened: this fear prompted his preoccupation. Or so the Parisian specialist explained. "Lightly, then," he cautioned, "treat it lightly. It's not life he fears, but death."

Late in April, three months after his attack, the matter took an unanticipated turn. Helene had driven into the countryside with Alexandre, whose presence Estienne hardly acknowledged other than to motion to him from time to time to bring him the paper or remove an empty cup. Estienne had complained of tiredness, and after their luncheon together, during which he had been unusually irritable, refusing to address a single word to Alexandre and churlishly demanding that Helene pass him something that lay directly in the young man's reach, she had recommended that he rest in bed that afternoon and promised to return not later than six or six-thirty. They drove off, and Estienne, who had not bothered that day to dress properly, contenting himself with a blue silk robe and slippers, returned to his bedroom, where he read, napped, took his medicines, and somehow ignored the time of day.

It was, one would think, sometime before five in the afternoon that he left the room and moved to the sun porch that overhung the garden, a small verandah covered with a retractable awning, which at this hour of day was drawn to conserve the coolness and shade. He sipped a glass of cold water and, stretched out comfortably, admired the valley of pine trees through a glaze of harsh light, no longer hot but nonetheless intense and blinding. His senses charged by the light, the bits of conversation that announced early return of Helene and Alexandre were lost to him; only when they were seated beneath him in the garden, out of his view, turned like himself to the brilliance of the glistening valley, did their voices rise up to him, distinct and clear, their speech apostrophized with terms of affection, each telling by turns the details of their life, an afternoon of autobiography about to be concluded. Alexandre's childhood was soon exhausted, for he had no maturity, but hers she recounted from Barcelona days: the early death of her mother, the other girls, the patriarchal pharmacist who suffered now from kidney stones, the marriage to Estienne, and the loss of their child.

"A child? I didn't know you'd had a child," Alexandre said, unaccountably amused.

"But of course. It's done, you know, at least once."

"And what became of it? Boy, girl? You've hardly made it clear."

"I believe a girl, but I'm not certain. It was long ago."

"And what happened?"

"Eighteen years ago I tripped and lost the little thing. Couldn't ever have a child again. Yes, eighteen years now. For a while I missed it. I've always wanted to make something of my own. It's curious, isn't it—almost confirms Estienne's obsession—that the miscarriage took place (I'll never forget that date), on May fifth."

Estienne had heard it through the sun, which pierced a bank of clouds, burning his eyes; rubbing them, blinded in red, whispering to himself the incantatory fifth, he began to cry. He recognized what he had all his life known he must fear—the conjugation of judgment that is terminated in death. Fives and fifths were little more, he understood, than warnings to prepare and to avoid; make conscious the system that governs life, and a small time—not vast in years, but reckoned in parcels borrowed against collateral accumulated in a lifetime—might still be his. He wept, but not for long; they were tears of resolution, little more. Beyond the point of middle age, but old; the grayness returned; the ashen face, drained of blood; a slight giddiness as though nauseated by the swallowing of a bitter medicine the system requires but cannot easily digest.

The conversation below continued, but he had no wish to interrupt it; softly he moved from the verandah and returned to his bed.

In the days that followed, resolution condensed a strategy, for no longer did any five or fifth disturb him, and he no longer spoke of his obsession. It was a simple maneuver, but one incontestably confirmed by convergence to the fifth and five of days. Several minutes before the hour of five in the afternoon, Helene would join him in the bedroom, a warming cup of chocolate on a tray, and there, hand in hand most strangely, they would sit until the hour struck and passed, and then, putting aside the beverage, he would draw up the covers and sleep through his hour of remission. The consolation of her presence, its assurance that, if the signal sounded and his heart exploded, she would be there to tell him her forgiveness, was enough to inhibit the governing machineries of his fate. The clocks of the house were all checked and certified—a repairer come to call from Nice had spent most of a day examining the mechanisms; the porcelain clock of the study, the night clock with phosphorescent hands that stood beside Helene's dressing table, all wristwatches and pendant watches, and finally an elegant timepiece that stood on the armoire that faced his bed—a splendid mechanism set in semiprecious jewels, fashioned for a general of the czar—were all scrutinized, all synchronized, all monitored by the specialist of clocks and set according to the master clock that somewhere was regarded by connoisseurs of time as absolute.

It could not have been otherwise than that the prisoner of obsession should fall, one day, victim to his own devising. He was so irrational to begin with, so lacking in science, so tied to a melancholy that passed speech and understanding, how could it not be that on the fifth of May, Estienne, full of fear, went up to his room some minutes before five o'clock in the afternoon, having alerted Helene to the awesomeness of the day and the hour. She had heard him warn her of the time, and both at once had looked from the verandah to the porcelain clock upon his study desk, and noting that ten minutes remained before the hour of five, he departed, and she—still irritated by some remark of Alexandre, who sat dark and glowering before her, immaculate in his white flannels—turned back to reply.

How many minutes had passed, who could be certain, for the scream shattered any precision of accounting. They mounted the stairs and reached the bedroom as Estienne died. The hand of the jeweled clock had passed the hour of five—just passed, two minutes now, perhaps three. Helene returned quickly to the study and there, astonishingly, the clock began to sound the hour, to chime and hum, and each stroke of five rang through the quiet room and drifted out to the verandah and the soundless valley.

Helene Delahaye, born into the family of Miravilla, returned to Barcelona several years after the death of her husband, the monumental sculptor. She had managed to conserve his wealth, to distribute authorized editions of his major works, selling several at considerable prices. She invested the money and, during the prosperous decade that preceded the recession still in progress, she accumulated substantial wealth with which, added to the modest inheritance she received upon her father's death, she bought an apartment in the fashionable section of old Barcelona. She kept the shutters closed; she enjoyed her spacious garden; and she managed, her failing beauty enhanced by wealth, to maintain from time to time one or another young man who accompanied her each week across the border into France, not far from Port Vendres, where she gambled in the casino, winning and losing of an evening considerable sums that she could easily afford.

# Malenov's Revenge

## One

It never occurred to me that Joseph Alexander Karnovsky had been murdered by the great painter Yevgeny Mikhailovich Malenov. Moreover, the means by which Yevgeny Mikhailovich eroded the life of Karnovsky, his benefactor and patron, is so odd, so original and unprecedented, that when I came across the documents that revealed his carefully annotated plotting, it took me many months to assimilate my discovery and to determine its accuracy and truth. Finally, in the end, I concluded that Malenov had destroyed Karnovsky as surely as if he had shot him through the heart.

Before proceeding, however, to recount Malenov's history, his entanglement with Karnovsky, and the formation of Malenov's decision of "diabolic revenge" (forgive me for tergiversating, but even as I write the phrase "diabolic revenge," I am obliged to insert it between quotation marks, less to suggest that I am lifting this phrase from a

Malenovian source than to underscore the ambiguity I feel about its employment at all. Did Malenov revenge himself on Karnovsky? and, if so, did second sight constitute his "diabolic means"? or did Malenov only supply the conditions that enabled Karnovsky, with his own aberrations and ambition, to seize the opportunity, so to speak, to *murder himself*—and that not suicide, which is a voluntary act, after all—clearly self-murder, quite unintentional, involuntary, desperate, necessary, fated as if by another hand), I must tell you something about the voice that speaks here so emphatically, for it is I who organize and dispense this narrative.

I—my name is Isaiah Wolff—am not a principal in these events, although I appear a number of times, marginal and in the shadows. Nonetheless I am critical to the narration—a linchpin, moreover, because it is I who discoved that Malenov wished to destroy Karnovsky and in fact succeeded two years after his own death, when Karnovsky was found in his studio surrounded by his finished canvases over-painted in black, dead of what was medically determined (although metaphorically described) to be "cardiac explosion."

All perfectly straightforward, you may think. No, you won't think that at all. You will say: "Curious, bizarre, but no murder." And I, who had known Karnovsky for many years and had sold him all the books, photographs, gallery announcements, exhibition catalogues, personal correspondence, posters, newspaper and magazine cuttings, museum handouts that documented the life and work of Yevgeny Mikhailovich Malenov (items, I might add, that Karnovsky later received in abundance following Malenov's death), would have concurred with your disbelief, until it became my task to appraise the archive of Malenov–Karnovsky papers for purposes of a testamentary bequest Karnovsky had made to the Museum of Modern Art following his own death. Karnovsky's executors, his lawyer and his accountant, chose me because they had been coming across my name for years in Karnovsky's annual account records, each year the sums growing as the prices fetched by every scrap relating to Malenov's life and works commanded increasing prices to purchase and even higher prices to sell. (For example, a simple postcard that Malenov wrote to his friend Naum Gabo when he left the Soviet Union for Berlin in 1926 I bought for a modest sum and sold to Karnovsky several years later for $60—a photograph of a Berlin café, Die Florelle, with the following Russian text: "Not the Stray Dog, but it will have to do and the tea at least has no flies in it. See you soon. Yevgeny." Amusing, intimate, but not an important document. And yet, given the fact that Yevgeny Malenov rarely wrote letters, much less such casual communications as postcards, $60 turned out to be a quite reasonable price.) I thought I knew everything there was to know about Malenov: his mournful celibacy, his second sight, his curious essays about the messianic hope of projectivism (a position he shared with his sometime colleagues and infrequent friends Kazimir Malevich and Piet Mondrian, although Malenov's messianism was of the Russian strain, saturated with references to his beloved Saint Sergius, the baleful eye of the apocalypse, and petty allusions to the shopkeeper mentality of Jews, whom he both loved and feared), his contempt for most painting "merchants" (his term for art dealers), as well as his occasional lapse into paedophilia, a preoccupation he indulged vicariously through the gathering of a substantial collection of photographs of naked children ("beyond eight they are already mature"), which he examined principally during the years when he felt utterly abandoned and alone, and then only at night, when the moon was a sliver of orange, and its nauseous light streaked his bedroom, and he reinvented his childhood in the countryside near the village of Gradiesk in the Ukraine.

I was amazed by Malenov's melancholy, his self-doubt and no less monumental certitude, his mad religiosity, his paedophiliac amusements and passion for dancing the fox trot, but I never thought him capable of murder. He seemed so conventionally a genius—that is, a worker with such absolute pitch and profundity—that I, with the habit of the world, rationalized and excused all the rest of his anomalous conduct as quite fitting, suitable, "to be expected of genius" (an American accommodation to *comme il faut*), and never thought him the worse for being simultaneously a misanthrope, a religious fanatic, and among the warmest and most tender of human beings. But that was my illusion. I had no idea, therefore, that Malenov could harbor such a deep resentment, annotating the details of each provocation and interpreting its gravity and significance by construing every seizing, prizing, mandibular gesture of the insatiable Karnovsky as one more move by his adoring disciple to despoil him. Persuaded by the voluminous Malenovian archive of diaries, scraps of screed, notations of implied insults and indirect humiliations administered, Malenov believed, by his wickedly competitive patron, it was not surprising that the conception of revenge was installed as a blood ruby in the crown of Malenov's program of accomplishment from almost the very beginning, when Malenov first met Karnovsky in Berlin during the late 1920s. Not surprising, but nonetheless wholly unpersuasive, for Malenov's revenge upon his fellow artist and patron requires a reading of Joseph Alexander Karnovsky's character wholly at variance with my own.

I will set down the facts and try my hand at an interpretation or two, but the ultimate decision will have to be made by the reader, who constitutes a jury of one to pass judgment on the issue of the crime. I do not know; I cannot be certain.

## Two

The Russian community of Berlin, a mélange of exiles and itinerant revolutionaries, often gathered during the late 1920s at Die Florelle, a large café in shouting distance of the Kürfurstendam.

It became customary after 1921, when Die Florelle opened (and was discovered by the considerable Russian-speaking population of Berlin to be fortuitously situated near the most frequented public thoroughfare in the city, not far from the popular émigré nightclub

Die Blaue Vogel, around the corner from an efficient travel agent
who specialized in bookings to the Soviet Union, three blocks from
a street of moneychangers and small banks, a kiosk that dispensed
hot borscht and meat pasties, and two restaurants devoted to Crimean
and Georgian cuisine), for the left side of the café to be crowded with
revolutionary sympathizers, comrade members of trade commissions,
visiting Soviet poets, artists, and ideologists, while to the right of the
central service area glared antirevolutionary social democrats, aristocrats and nobles and exiled members of Lenin's bureaucracy, as
well as landscape painters, lyric poets, and angry journalists. The
infrequent German who strayed into Die Florelle, unaware of the
ideological combat of its habitués and their seating arrangements,
was sometimes caught in the crossfire of insult and the occasional
stream of hot tea thrown with screams by one or another enraged
partisan of left or right.

It was generally the case, however, that Die Florelle was calm. It
was regarded by the principal agents of both the revolution and its
opposition as an oasis in the mined terrain of postwar German politics,
and, despite the excitable character of its clientele, partisans of all
extremes thought it wise to keep Die Florelle clear of violence so that
its patrons could be counted, identified, and even surreptitiously
photographed. At the front of the café, looking out toward the broad
avenue where flâneurs ogled and sniffed throughout the day, was a
single row of tables—not more than sixteen, it appears, if the photograph before me that I found among Malenov's mementoes is not
deceptive—separated by a narrow walking space from the packed
and jumbled partisans of left and right. That single row was regarded
by Die Florelle's clientele as confirmation of its management's neutrality. There, at those sixteen tables, sat tea drinkers and chess
players who claimed political unaffiliation (what the Soviets inimitably
called *smenavekovtsy*). From time to time, their neutrality compromised by the discovery of an acquaintance in one or the other camp,
they disappeared into the passionate embrace of left or right, surren-

dering their privileged position near the café's vitrine to yet another visitor, who took up transient residence at the front tables, awaiting in turn persuasion or relapse into ideology.

The manager of Die Florelle, the complaisant Carlo Zuchotti, born in the Ticino, raised in Zurich, and now café owner in Berlin, was superbly indifferent to politics. He stood beside the double doors, a clutch of menus in his hand, waiting to see who would push through the doors into his café. It didn't matter whether it was a weary count dressed in riding clothes, just off from teaching young girls horsemanship, or a consumptive artist from Vitebsk, or a communist journalist such as Ilya Ehrenburg. Carlo Zuchotti was indifferent. He smiled, assessed his guest's relative prosperity, and led him to a table appropriate to the cut of his suit and the quality of his boots. He concerned himself with social notes, not politics. It was for this reason, perhaps, that he made the mistake of conducting Yevgeny Mikhailovich Malenov to a central table in the file of the *smenavekovtsy*, the uncertain and undecided. Yevgeny had insisted on such a table (he wished to keep his eyes peeled for the arrival of a dear friend he had arranged to meet there at 2 P.M. precisely), and Carlo Zuchotti, imagining that Malenov's pointed index finger marked an assertion of political neutrality, seated him at a front table commanding a view of both the boulevard and the sector occupied by counterrevolutionaries. For his part, Yevgeny Mikhailovich, suffering from a tenacious head cold, wished to be seated at a table swimming in warm spring sunlight.

As though in duet, a baritone voice called out from a table of flanneled émigré intellectuals seated near the rear of the café surrounded by other members of the declassed nobility and anti-Bolshevik intelligentsia, "Yevgeny Mikhailovich. My God. You, here, now," at the same instant as a rose-lipped voice, throaty with tobacco, gaily shouted in antiphon, "Beloved Yevgeny, at last." Both speakers stepped into the neutral area where the waiters circulated and disappeared into the moil, and both reached across to seize Yevgeny's weary hand. He smiled, distracted, uncertain to whom to turn. He half rose from his table, embraced Masha Dmitrievna, and, reaching around her somewhat chunky amplitude, shook hands with the tall, lanky young man in his early thirties whose drooping mustache and watery gray eyes suggested breeding and exhaustion. The salutations done, Masha Dmitrievna nodded brusquely to Captain Nikolai Alexandrovich Plakhov, late of His Imperial Majesty's Horse Guard, and both seated themselves at Yevgeny's neutral table. They knew the rules—unspoken and most certainly unenforced, but nonetheless clear by custom. It was understood that politics were to be avoided at the neutral bank of window tables. They could be alluded to, animadverted as screens to insult and humiliation, but they were not to be openly discussed at the tables of the uncertain and undecided.

"But are you uncertain, my dear? Do you still preserve your neutrality?" Masha Dmitrievna inquired, a blue fingernail scratching at a crumb of cake left behind on Yevgeny's table. Captain Plakhov scowled, but she was a beautiful woman, after all, he thought. What she lacked in tact and diffidence she more than compensated for with radiant black eyes and a mouth of almost criminal sensuality.

Yevgeny Mikhailovich was not well that day. He explained later that he sometimes found his mind suddenly overcast, as though a cloud had befogged him or an iron vise, like a medieval instrument of torture, had settled around his forehead, electrifying his eyebrows, which in such episodes he believed to be aflame. He felt a weight, a bitter constraint that prevented him from thinking normal thoughts at all. During such bouts of physical oppression and incandescence, he came to await—after the battles of denial were done—an insight of premonitory vision, so startling, so terrifying that he had no way of dealing with it except to surrender to its instruction and do its bidding, whatever it was. It was a tradition, after all, that ran in his family. Like his great-aunt and a second cousin, Yevgeny Milkhailovich possessed second sight, unpredictable, fortuitous, and for the most part not at all prophetic. That is to say, Yevgeny Mikhailovich saw into a future that was already past or, to be more accurate, he knew of an event's occurrence in advance of all notification, and these gifts of illumination, bridging space and time, allowed him to take measures of self-protection or self-advancement well before he had been given eyewitness reports or detailed information. He saw into the future, but his seeing could not alter events or forewarn their participants. He was always just on time. But then, that was miraculous gift enough. For instance, he had awakened one cold morning in Moscow several years before, absolutely persuaded that his younger brother, then a boy of sixteen (later killed during the civil war), was in great danger. He dressed quickly and hurried to the telegraph office to send a message to his family, living at the time some fifty versts from Novisibirsk. Late that day he received a reply from his father: SASHA PULLED FROM BENEATH THE ICE IN SKATING ACCIDENT STOP HE WILL LIVE PRAISE GOD FATHER. It turned out that at precisely the hour of seven in the morning—the time noted on Yevgeny's telegraphed message—the boy had had his skating accident. A peasant driving sheep to market had seen it happen; quickly he unwound a rope coiled around his waist, threw it to the boy, and pulled him to safety. But such episodes of second sight always left Yevgeny Mikhailovich with a terrible headache and in a mood of such despondency that he was unsociable for a month. He often wrote of the "heavy burden" imposed on him. "So much for so little," he once complained. "At least, if I were prophetic—" But he never completed his blasphemy.

There were other incidents, less dramatic but no less exemplary. He was warned in second sight that such and such a collector would not show up to purchase a painting; that his dog, Petka, had died of old age; that his apartment building was aflame, but that the blaze had been put out before it reached his studio. All these episodes settled upon Yevgeny a mood of constant attention to omens and alarms, hints and allusions that everyday occurrences thrust before him, demanding appraisal and estimation. Fortunately, most were barren of hidden meaning and revelation.

Masha Dmitrievna had entered Yevgeny Mikhailovich's life one evening late in the winter of 1925, after a meeting of the artists of UNOVIS, who were planning an exhibition to celebrate the anniversary of its founding. Yevgeny, seated in a corner of the artists' clubroom, drinking a fruit juice while everyone else was drowning themselves in vodka, was stroking a vagabond cat who had ambled into the gathering and had slowly threaded her way from legs to laps, rubbing against them and rising to each crooked nail that promised scratches of affection. With Yevgeny, the black cat came home to serious and considered adoration; his strokes were rhythmic, his purring confirmed her own, his whispered endearments (barely overheard by Masha Dmitrievna, who had singled out Yevgeny for attention early in the evening's proceedings) to the nameless animal movated to a crescendo: "O yes, Nadezhda, yes, sweet Lazar, ah, Kazimir, ah, ah, Kazimir, yes, Alexander, yes, yes, old puss Popova."

"What are you doing here, Yevgeny Mikhailovich?" Masha Dmitrievna inquired, somewhat belligerently, irritated and confused by his insistent nomination of each of the artists of the day as sobriquets for the purring black cat.

"And why not?" Yevgeny replied, without looking up.

"What do you mean, 'Why not?' You have to be a party member, don't you?"

"Not at all. Never, in fact. An artist is enough. A teaching artist, more than enough. And who cares anyway? Let them hang the pictures upside down, my own included, for all I care."

Masha Dmitrievna snorted contemptuously. "With yours it wouldn't matter." She thought to insult him, but he was indifferent.

Yevgeny smiled. The truth is that in most cases his work could indeed be hung upside down, because the pictures had no sides, no top, no bottom, no right, no wrong. They were cuts of the universe and, to his mind, infinite, able to be hung on the aethers of space and to fit in, blended into clouds and rushing wind, immense black, deep blue, indifferent to bourgeois space and domestic architecture.

"What are you doing here, Yevgeny Mikhailovich?" Masha Dmitrievna now repeated, poking a ringed finger at weary Yevgeny Mikhailovich, whose head had suddenly begun to ache.

"Plakhov, do me the kindness of expelling this Cheka agent. I couldn't stand her in Moscow, why should I tolerate her in Berlin?"

"Cheka? Never! Independent always. A private operative," Masha Dmitrievna replied, her eyes flashing with anger.

"Nobody is independent in the Soviet Union," the captain replied, rubbing his hands on his sweaty jodhpurs as though to clean them before pushing Masha Dmitrievna.

"You would know? How would you know, you czarist lackey?"

"Plakhov, please, lift her up and throw her out. Hurl her into the heavens."

Captain Plakhov stood up and pointed arrogantly to the sector of Die Florelle where the revolutionary cadres had put down their glasses of tea and were wiping their mouths, waiting with excitement. The counterrevolutionaries, pent up and ferocious, were shifting in their seats, positioning themselves for something brilliant and decisive. How they wanted to deal the Soviet Union a great blow. "Go to your comrades, you spy agent, you viper villain, you Cheka whore."

"Oh, Plakhov, not that. She's not a whore, I believe," Yevgeny remonstrated at Plakhov's extremity. "Torturer, traitor, cesspool, viper's den, perhaps, but not a whore. Much too pretty to make it business." Yevgeny was watching Masha's eyes, closed with fury, her purple eyeshadow obliterating her pupils.

At this precise moment of insult and acrimony a young waiter, unaware of the brewing conflagration, was stepping deftly over legs outstretched into the open space that separated the Reds and Whites of Die Florelle. He balanced a tray laden with cakes and coffee.

Masha watched the waiter approach, and her crooked smile expanded into a wicked grin as she lifted the tray from his upturned fingers and overturned it on Plakhov. Her rage gave way to gales of laughter, and the Red contingent of Die Florelle burst into shouts and applause. After a stunned moment, the counterrevolutionary Whites each reached for the nearest to hand; instantly a barrage of bread slices covered with jam, dishes of sticky kissel, tea (with and without pots), demitasse spoons, metal ashtrays flew through the air as attack and counterattack transformed the negotiated decorum of Die Florelle into a street battle. Not a fist was raised, no bodies made contact, but words and implements found their targets or slammed harmlessly against the café's walls, leaving behind blobs of cake and splatters of dribbling compote. Amid the festive battle, Captain Plakhov, straightening his tie, wiping glazed fruit from his jodhpurs, and smoothing down his hair, already matted with drying mousse and whipped cream, turned to Masha Dmitrievna and with an open palm smacked both her cheeks, bowed, and fled the café. Masha Dmitrievna, an instant earlier shrieking with joy, now dissolved into humiliated weeping.

Only the occasion and cue of this pandemonium subsided into silence while the din rose about him. Yevgeny Mikhailovich was gripped by his tormenting adversary; a vise of pain settled about his temples and crept out toward his eyeballs. He groaned inaudibly, swallowing his anguish. His guest was an hour late. He was not coming. He had already forgotten Masha Dmitrievna and Captain Plakhov. Who were they? he briefly thought, as he heard the door slam behind Plakhov and observed Masha Dmitrievna collapse in tears. What is this pain? Yevgeny wondered, forgetting as he always did its source and significance. Brain tumor? Stroke? Arthritis of the temples? He invented ailments and catastrophes. He would die momentarily. The pain rose and swelled his head like a melon; he pincered his temples with his forefingers and groaned again, this time aloud. Suddenly, it all cleared, and before his eyes the fog lifted and a path through his confusion became visible. As in all earlier episodes of his remarkable visionary sight, Malenov saw a complete scene, an augury of an event already in process or almost completed: a room furnished with the artifacts of worldly comfort, plush and stuffed, solid, heavy tables and cabinets, and remarkable pictures, including one, he recognized, by himself—painted when he had been a futurist. At the door, two men framed in a bluish-gold light stood talking. One extended his hand to the other in farewell, a strapped suitcase at his side. The other clasped the extended hand in both of his. On the table lay a mountain of manuscripts, papers, drawings, and painted canvases. Suddenly, Malenov recognized the personages of his vision. His beloved friend whom he was to have met at Die Florelle at 2 P.M. precisely, the painter Kazimir Sevenerovich Malevich, was leaving the apartment of his acquaintance, the sculptor Alexander von Riesen, and rushing for the railroad station to return to Moscow. Yevgeny Mikhailovich knew for certain that he would never see him again, knew that Malevich was returning to dissension and hostility, knew that he would leave behind the masterpieces of his youthful years, a hoard of crucial manuscripts, a bundle of canvases, knew that in seven years Malevich would succumb to illness and die, and knew that for a generation or more his name would be obliterated in his homeland and forgotten in the West.

(All of these visionary anticipations suggest, indeed, that Yevgeny Mikhailovich enjoyed some degree of prophetic sight. But I cannot be certain. He claimed for his second sight only a victory over space, not time. Yet these assertions about the future and fate of his friend Malevich appear to be both genuinely prophetic and accurate. Curiously, Malenov dated this passage in his diary in a hand different from that in which he wrote the entry. Moreover, he wrote in parentheses after the date, "Vision of a vision. Written years later when everything is confirmed." I have no way of knowing whether Yevgeny is congratulating himself on the accuracy of his second sight or fleshing out a simple clear sight with facts he learned much later. Either is possible. Yevgeny hardly invented himself; he was a genius and needed no shamanic myth to improve it!)

The battle of the cakes and teapots subsided. Every table was clear of implements. Signor Zuchotti screamed at his customers in German and Italian, interspersed with such vivid Russian curses as he had learned from his more outspoken clients; the waiters began to swab the walls with damp cloths; the shouting gave way to good-natured laughter and squealing. Amid this subsiding clatter, Yevgeny Mikhailovich, his hands gripping his painful head, lurched to his feet, bellowed like a wounded beast, and rushed toward the glass doors. Wrenching them open, he looked back briefly, a vacant and uncomprehending smile on his face, and fled into the sunlight.

## *Three*

Ever so briefly, even at the risk of confusing the reader or boring the most avid enthusiast of narrative, I must tell you a little, a terrible little about the battles within Soviet art that thrust Kazimir Sevenerovich Malevich and his curious doctrine of Supremus to the forefront, leaving slightly behind (his footsteps almost crossing over and filling up to the narrow instep those of the older and more famous practitioner) Yevgeny Mikhailovich Malenov and his projectivist vision, whose architectonic schemes (which he called utopics) were soon enough to be hailed as the successors to Malevich's ideas. Malenov was to become a world hero of art, transcending the ideological culture he loathed and had left behind.

Think of it this way. First the world was a richly painted drapery hung before an unexplored space, filled with figures, nature in glow, transfigured color. Then, it was thought that what lay behind the drapery had somehow to be insinuated onto the stage: light came from within the painting (as well as from the sun behind the artist), and its rays broke up the surface of the image, fracturing its space, splintering its angles, making simple creatures all legs and arms, all planes and angles, all colors of a dizzy rainbow. But then these curious Russians, annoyed that heavy industry and artillery shells, chemical formulae and electrical generators, textiles and rubber boots should all come from the West, determined that at least a native poetry and a private art should claim a Russian progeny. They began as early as 1910 to look at Western poetry and painting, to drift in and out of Western studios, examining what the West had decided to throw away (Vladimir Tatlin, for instance, scrutinized the contents of Picasso's studio) and returning to Russia to make a new art. Vassily Kandinsky came back from Germany to teach and train. The poets Velimir Khlebnikov and Alexei Kruchenykch collaborated with, among others, Kazimir Malevich to make illustrated books that cost only four kopecks but trained Russian eyes to affix words of poetry to their visual icons. A topsy-turvy time. Artists painted themselves green and blue, wore spoons in their lapels, drew red triangles on their cheeks, dressed in castaway clothing and dined on caviar—all to make an impression, to strike up an acquaintance with the bourgeoisie, loathed and envied as the bourgeoisie always is.

The point is this: in the absence of a long tradition of their own, it was easier for the Russians to become Soviets and make a new art. They had nothing to lose by becoming inventive geniuses and writing unintelligible manifestoes that caused untalented hearts to skip a beat, that gave employment to ten nighttime laborers of the poster-posting guild, and that later provoked quizzical looks, scratched heads, creased foreheads, dubious pouts, and, in their train, miserly mimes without gift who paraphrased the same, repeating it until its slogan, "Anything fills space since space is empty," sounded more and more ridiculous, although at first scrutiny it had seemed saturated with oriental sagacity and aesthetic nihilism.

## *Four*

Yevgeny Mikhailovich flung himself into a taxi turning the corner in front of Die Florelle and, although never informed of the address of Alexander von Riesen's apartment, gave the driver an exact street and number. A half-hour later, panting with exhaustion, he stood before a door marked by the discreet, minute, engraved *carte de visite* of the German artist. He rang urgently, tattooing his anguish with a suite of stabs at the button, whose answering sound he could not hear. After what seemed a decade of silence, the door opened a crack and a shrunken old woman, her gray hair raised into a bower that overwhelmed her tiny face, looked at him crossly. "Malevich?" Yevgeny shouted, thinking her deaf as well. She winced before his assault.

*"Kein Malevich hier. Er ist zuruck nach Moskau gegangen."* She scrutinized him once more and slammed the door.

Yevgeny rang again and, failing to rouse her, began to bang at the door with his fist, even to kick the door. But no reply. Malevich had left Berlin. No message. No farewell. The only Russian artist he secretly adored had vanished. Yevgeny Mikhailovich was alone, abandoned in the West. Like all Russians overcome with emotion, he began to weep. Once again he had seen a future, already past.

## *Five*

An incomprehensible sadness flooded his body. Yevgeny Mikhailovich lay on his uncomfortable bed in the room he had rented near the tram station. Malevich had left without a word of farewell, and the moon flooded Yevgeny's room with a silvered grimness that signaled war and battle. Yevgeny wanted to banish the moonlight. It was not an orange moon, heated by the summers of the Ukraine, but a moon compromised by coke fumes, sparkling a little with silver as though a particular lunar effort had been made to harbinger the full moon. Yevgeny lay naked upon his bed. His tears had stopped, and he had made himself a disgusting glass of tea with hot tap water. His stomach had stopped exploding. Yevgeny withdrew the album from beneath his papers and returned to bed. He stroked its cover, mounted in birch bark he had stripped and fashioned into a binding. (Malevich no longer loved him.) The first pages were innocent, hiding from the inquisitive the ignominy of his private fantasy. An ordinary scrapbook, clippings from the press, documents from the classroom, disused ration books and identity cards. He turned those pages rapidly. At last, the first of his delights. A naked child at the beach in Odessa. He had taken the photograph himself. She stood at the water's edge, a crooked finger pointing out to sea, her tiny alabaster buttocks smiling, although the face that looked over her shoulder toward the camera was pensive and withdrawn. Another: a boy of seven, half-dressed, a naval jerkin, naked loins, a tiny member like a button. And then, clipped from newspapers, little children in various states of amusing undress, holding furry kittens, laughing with nothing funny in view, small flesh like kneaded dough, rosy, smooth, hairless, indistinguishable as to sex for the most part, the precious simplicity of undifferentiated nature, childhood before the rage begins. And at the conclusion of the gallery, fifty pictures, clipped, mounted on black blotting paper, and the very last to which Yevgeny came, the very last to which no further need be added, a photograph of a naked boy, his head shaped like a dunce cap, the straggly hair long about his ears, and bright happy eyes turned upward toward a large bearded head that reached down, obedient to the little hands that held his ears, pulling the head toward puckered lips. It was Yevgeny and his father. One summer day behind his natal wooden house, among the goats and chickens. That flimsy joy of childhood, frozen now into a pastiche of remembering other children, other joys of naked unknowing.

For some years now, amid his dark times, Yevgeny Mikhailovich had rescued himself by finding an image for his album, pasting in one more dream-saturated recollection of an irretrievable moment of contentment. He knew perfectly well that he was called a paedophile; he was often caught out mooning about schoolyards, watching the little children walk home, holding hands, their strapped books over their shoulders, little dresses, little uniforms, and high-buttoned shoes. He sometimes photographed them, his eyes stripping them of their clothing until he could see their lucent flesh and observe the modest ripples of their energy. But it was no ordinary perversion, this love of a lost time. Eros was no winged creature in hot pursuit of some nubile Psyche. He took no pleasure from this recollection, no pleasure, no tension, no release. It was so infinitely sad that he likened his album to a breviary and his recollections of sun-drenched love near Gradiesk to the saying of a litany of loss.

## Six

Yevgeny Mikhailovich Malenov could not afford much wood for the small stove that supplied the only heat in his room in the Prenzlauer Berg quarter of Berlin. He had arrived a year earlier, in May 1926, from Moscow. To be precise, he was in self-imposed exile from the Soviet Union. Betrayed by his uncomprehending colleagues, removed from his position as a teacher of painting theory at UNOVIS, denied access to the preferments and sinecures that came with subscription to the triumphant ideology of art as the instrument of revolutionary process and material fabrication, he decided he'd had enough egalitarianism. One day, therefore, Yevgeny Mikhailovich requested permission to travel abroad to meet with German artists at a congress of revolutionary aesthetics that had been convoked by a splinter group in the Black Forest. Although the ministry regarded his petition as curious, they recognized and approved of some of the names on the invitation Malenov had presented to substantiate his request for travel documents, and after three weeks of deliberation his exit permit and passport were ready. Normally, these would be accompanied by authorization to the central bank to release sufficient gold-backed currency to facilitate a traveler's passage to the West, but Malenov had no bank funds. Instead, he kept his cash—an insignificant amount—hidden in a metal alms box he had stolen several years earlier from an antique store that fronted Leningrad's Neva (he had always wanted a metal bank as a child, but the only one he coveted cost fifty kopecks, which his father had thought extravagant). Yevgeny Mikhailovich intended to buy his ticket and as soon as possible thereafter convert the rest of his funds into gold, no matter what the cost, as he was persuaded that paper currency would soon become worthless, banks would fail, and as usual the poor would suffer.

Against the prospect of starvation, he kept the gold wedding band that his father had given his mother a generation earlier and a pair of silver candlesticks that had been left to him along with two cows, several goats, and the worthless contents of a peasant's wooden house when his parents died of influenza during the terrible winter of 1918. Although his family had maintained a religious home, all that remained of traditional piety was an icon of Saint Sergius, to which Malenov had impiously tacked a photograph of his father and mother, regarding them as holy martyrs, no less saints and intercessors than their beloved starets.

Yevgeny realized that his departure from the Soviet Union had to be efficiently masked as simple travel. He was too famous to risk advertising his departure. His closest friends among Soviet artists— Kazimir Malevich and Vladimir Tatlin (themselves raging enemies of each other)—would each construe his defection as a betrayal, neither regarding it possible that he could be friend to the other, but that of course was Malenov's way of negotiating the perilous rapids of Soviet life, sluicing through narrow channels to the sides of which rose sheer and impassable walls of ideology. Friendships took place deep down in the narrow passageway between ideological escarpments, and there, racing against the current, human beings were frequently dashed to death against the implacable stony sides. Malenov avoided extremity by learning early to keep silent and do his work. Careful attention to the ideological battles among the futurists before the revolution and between the constructivists and the naturalists in its aftermath had shown him that the most reckless and endangered were not the artists but the theorists. It was immensely precarious for the artists to set forth their ideas, to supplement their paintings with their prose. He preferred the view that artists should conduct their public careers without tongues or, if they insisted on talking, restrict their interpretations to the weather, the availability of firewood, or the quality of herring. It was not that Malenov was a coward. Not at all. If one judges by the considerable body of notepaper filled with Malenov's unpublished writings—essays in many drafts, undeclaimed manifestoes (besides his celebrated Projectivist Manifesto), copies of Malevich's most famous work, *The New System of Art*, and the brief excursuses on Suprematism that Malevich hung on his initial admiration for Cézanne, all annotated in Malenov's tiny hand, which, even had they been discovered, would have proved undecipherable—Malenov was anything but a coward. It was not that he had opinion and was too scared to set it down. It was that he had opinion but thought it prudent to avoid misinterpretation. The prisons were already filling with the misunderstood, and he had no intention of contributing himself to penal reformation. Rather, he thought it wise to emigrate, to leave the country with as much as possible and virtually nothing at all. He filled two large suitcases with finished canvases wrapped in oilcloth (more than forty pictures), a sheaf of drawings, his notebooks stripped sheet by sheet from their gluebacked spines and, turned face up, used as wrapping paper for his clothing, stuffing for his shoes, lining for his overcoat—in a word, some hundred sheets of theory concealed as junk and detritus. He left behind most of his belongings, virtually all of his books, a dozen works of art by other painters (consigning all these to his landlady, to whom he promised one day to send instructions for shipment), and late on the evening of May 7,

1926, traveling light, he took the train from Moscow, arriving in Berlin some fifty hours later.

For all his apparent unworldliness and inability to marshall power and influence in the society of the arts he had left behind in Great Russia, Yevgeny Mikhailovich was persuaded without compromise or uncertainty of his immense talent. (His notebooks from the period, which I studied carefully after they came into my hands for appraisal following Karnovsky's death, were abundant in their assertion of his genius. It was not uncommon for Malenovian sentences to begin, "Praise God, but my genius does not allow for so and so," or "Genius tells us with the help of God that thus and so is the case"—"genius" being for Malenov little more than a substitute for the personal pronoun. However, unlike most people's assertion of their sovereign ego, genius meant for Malenov something haughtily impersonal, as though seated upon his brain were another creature, not of his own devising or instruction, who pronounced as Genius through the medium of Malenov. One presumes, although there is no independent authority for this, that Malenov's conviction about his genius resembled the workings of the Holy Spirit in the ancient seers of Israel, whose prophesies he continually underlined and indeed lifted for his own proclamations.) In the throes of making art, Malenov believed that his spirit lived outside his body, that the canvases he wrought, although consciously tacked to the walls of his room, were painted by him under the influence and direction of his own divinely appointed daimon, and that what was made, although exhibited and sold under the name of Malenov, was to be attributed to an exalted spirit (also named Malenov) who took up residence within him whenever he was agitated to make art.

Though he felt constrained to ascribe his genius to another, Malenov had, unfortunately, no one but himself—in all his terrestrial mundanity—to blame for his exceptional poverty. He had never, he confessed years later, really thought about how he would support himself when he arrived in Berlin. He did not expect that his train would be met by hordes of enthusiastic collectors, but neither did he imagine that the collapse of the German economy would leave artists totally without means of support, as they were when he arrived. Moreover, he was not aware that the kind of art to which he was committed was virtually without precedent in Germany, even among those nominally associated with interest in pictorial space and architecture. For the first months, therefore, he did little more than keep himself going, doing odd jobs of proofreading for a Russian-language publisher, washing dishes in restaurants, once securing a commission to design a book jacket. From each payment, having set aside enough money for his frugal habits, he extracted enough to buy wood and tools with which to build stretchers for his small canvases, and pigment powders with which to mix his paints. For months he hardly made a picture; each day was consumed rushing after bare subsistence, with neither time nor energy remaining when the day was done to do more than fling himself on his bed and sleep.

By midwinter of 1927 Malenov had exhausted his resources. His little alms box was empty, and the gold ring and candlesticks had been pawned for a pittance. He was quite literally near starvation, and his rent was overdue. It was time, he persuaded himself, for a miraculous intervention, a sign that grace was renewed and his genius reaffirmed. It had to happen; it had always happened before. Sitting in the corner of the cheap bar where he had gone to drink a beer before returning to his room, Malenov reviewed the events and occasions in his life when, down and out, he had been rescued suddenly, unpredictably—miraculously, as he believed. Such a time had come again. He spoke silently to his parents and Saint Sergius, drained the mug before him, put out his few coins, and left. So preoccupied was he with his prayerful beseechings, Yevgeny Mikhailovich almost tripped over the figure seated before his room on the top step of the second floor of the rooming house. At first he was frightened. He had read of murderers hiding in stairwells (Raskolnikov instantly came to mind), but the voice that spoke quietly to him, calling him by name, reassured him.

"Malenov?" it repeated. "You are Malenov, are you not?"

"Malenov. Yes. I'm Malenov. Who are you? What are you doing here? How did you get in? How did you find me?" The questions spilled out, confused, still frightened. Nobody had ever come to Malenov's lodgings, certainly not such an elegantly dressed, odd gentleman as now rose to his side.

"I have been waiting for you here for more than an hour. Please, may I come in and then I will answer all your questions?"

Malenov unlocked the door, entered the room, and switched on the single light that hung from a cord over the bed. The odd gentlemen followed behind him. There was no chair. Malenov pulled out a stool from under his worktable and invited his guest to be seated on the bed. It was chilly in the room. Late October. Malenov opened the grate to the metal stove that stood against the wall, pretending to stoke the coals, although it was clear that nothing was aflame and there was no coal in the metal pail beside the stove.

"Please, don't trouble yourself. I will keep my coat on. We can talk without a fire. . . . And now to your first question. My name is Magnus Fingermann. I was born of German parents in what is now called Leningrad. (It will be easier for both of us if I speak to you in your own language.) I returned to Berlin shortly after Brest-Litovsk. I had no interest in your revolution. I hope that does not bother you, but I am frank with my opinions. On the other hand, I have great interest in the new art you are making, particularly in *your* new art, my dear Malenov. I am by vocation a connoisseur; I live as an art dealer, a private art dealer who buys and sells the occasional masterpiece that falls my way and no less occasionally takes an interest in a neglected artist, whom I help to bring to the public's attention. I become such an artist's agent, and I retain a commission from everything of his that I sell. It is a simple arrangement. Because I am not married and my needs are modest, I make a living sufficient to preserve myself and my habits even in these increasingly dark days."

Malenov instantly recognized that his prayers had been answered, the intercession accomplished, the miracle wrought. He would have hugged this Fingermann, except that he did not believe it was Fingermann by himself, unaided, who had found him; rather, the larger power in the universe who supported his genius was to be praised. He vowed that as soon as Fingermann left, he would light a candle before the icon of Saint Sergius that hung over his bed.

"And you know my work?" Malenov inquired diffidently.

The odd man, his large head wobbling precariously on his slight and subtly deformed body, examined Malenov carefully before answering. "I know your work very well and for many years now, since the early days in Russia when you were near the Jack of Diamonds group and later when you broke away from Malevich to begin your own experiments. Yes. Yes. I most certainly know your work. And you have been here now for nearly six months and you haven't painted, you haven't sold a picture, and you're starving. Oh yes, my dear fellow, I have been following you closely. May I see that stack of pictures turned to the wall?"

Squinting suspiciously as he always did when asked to show his paintings, Malenov moved toward the pile of pictures and then stopped and asked again, foolishly, but with a peasant's incredulity: "So you want to see my pictures, eh? All right." Silently, Malenov turned each picture, lifted it in his hands, held it before the curious Fingermann, and after a minute lowered it, replaced it against the wall, and lifted another. Exactly an hour later the odd Fingermann had purchased four paintings, paid for them in cash, and arranged to return the following day to discuss details of their relationship.

No sooner had Fingermann left Malenov's shabby quarters than Yevgeny, overwhelmed with good fortune, threw the banknotes into the air with an exuberant shout and saluted Saint Sergius, whom he took to be transformed from grave saint into smiling benefactor. Yevgeny Mikhailovich was saved, starvation averted, genius reaffirmed. In deference to such an immense good fortune, Yevgeny took up his brushes and worked the entire night, struggling to effect a new balance between a floating promontory he had launched into a blue-white aether and a series of proportional geometric forms that tipped from its plane. It was a difficult conception because it involved all his notions of a post-Newtonian space combined with visions he had entertained of the Third Rome of Moscow that would harmonize the universe and lead it to perpetual peace. Everything Malenov made in art had two meanings, it now appears: one accessible to the reading of aesthetic judgment (plainly a public, exoteric significance); the other, metaphors and reminiscences of the great wisdom of Sophia (heralded by Vladimir Soloviev and given theological definition by the ex–army officer A. S. Khomiakov and the churchman Sergei Bulgakov, whose religious retreats Yevgeny had secretly attended), defining an esoteric mishmash.

In the days that followed Malenov met often with Magnus Fingermann, who promised him exhibitions and installations, public celebrations and testimonials, magazine articles and interviews, patrons and connoisseurs. Alas, Yevgeny Mikhailovich believed every word. It seemed only right and fitting that his genius should be honored. The work was brilliant, after all. And it *is* true that certain things did happen that might not have happened without Fingermann's enthusiastic support and enterprise. Herwarth Walden would never have come to see Yevgeny's work and selected two pictures for an exhibition of the new Eastern European art at his Der Sturm Galerie, nor for that matter would László Moholy-Nagy have invited him to travel to Dessau and hang his paintings in the student foyer of the Bauhaus (Yevgeny was nervous about submitting his work to student perusal and declined the invitation, impolitely, with a postcard). But beyond the four pictures that Fingermann had purchased that first night, in the months that followed only a half-dozen drawings of no particular importance were sold, and these to a textile manufacturer who extracted permission to adapt and reproduce them on bedroom wall-paper.

Yevgeny Mikhailovich needed money to buy materials and maintain a minimal existence, and still he was always short. Fingermann, pure good will, undiminished enthusiasm, although himself a miracle, was unable to work miracles. By the end of 1927 Malenov was again near the edge. Again the rent was due, and although he still had enough money to see himself through for about a month, he was on thin ice.

"We need to make an action," Fingermann announced late one night, after Yevgeny had spent an evening watching him perched on his mechanical highchair swiveling his tiny body into majesty by raising himself three feet off the floor. "Yes, an action," Fingermann repeated in reply to Yevgeny's silent incomprehension and wrinkled forehead. "A public event, a crossing of swords with the establishment, a gesture so bizarre and ridiculous that you will be noticed— whether for good or ill does not matter."

"I am no fool," Yevgeny blurted gruffly, "no fool, and nothing I do is allowed to be foolish. Genius, thanks to God, does not permit it." Yevgeny huffed and snorted, blowing the words out his nose rather than through his large and generous mouth.

"You do not understand, my dear fellow. Not at all. I should never wish you embarrassed. Never. Nor humiliated," Fingermann emphasized, as though embarrassment and humiliation were inseparable insults. "What I crave is an event whose panache and brilliance is so palpable, so immediate, that artists and public alike will rush to salute you, will admire you, will invite you to champagne dinners and flock to your dreadful studio just for the honor of having met you." He paused, almost rhapsodic in his enthusiasm, whirling himself up and down on the oiled mechanism of his highchair. "And, of course, I will be there, in the wings, so to speak, talking you over with museum directors and collectors, selling a picture now and then, arranging exhibitions not only in Berlin but throughout Germany, even France and Italy. But what kind of action? That's the question. What kind?"

For more than a half-hour they remained silent, drinking vodka, smoking black tobacco, pacing and swiveling by turn. At last, as though Yevgeny's daimon had bifurcated, separating like a paramecium into two, each with a whole nucleus of genius, Yevgeny shouted aloud and Fingermann struck his forehead. Yevgeny shouted, "Projectivism," and Fingermann cried, "A bombing raid." Indeed, the one had conceived the text and provocation, the other its method of delivery. It was agreed that Yevgeny Mikhailovich would set down his radical conception of a new space that he called projectivism, whose ultimate consequence would be the remaking of cities in free space (which he called utopics), and crystallize its doctrine into neatly articulated points, fleshed with rhetoric and underlined with tantalizing imagery. The resulting manifesto, printed with a reproduction of one or more of Yevgeny's drawings, would be loaded into an airplane; four major cities of the German art world would be bombed with projectivism on the same day; two hours before the event the press would be notified by telegram where the manifesto would be dropped and advised to hold open their afternoon editions to accommodate the news.

### PROJECTIVISM: *The New Utopia*

The Black Square of Suprematism was autobiography. It was shot into the clouds, but fell to earth. Constructivism collected the pieces of the Black Square and tried to make housing out of them. Projectivism will make the New City. Its program is the Painted City.

PROJECTIVISM is no longer communist. It has left the Socialist Empire. It is living in a rooming house in East Berlin.

PROJECTIVISM is not only a new art, it is not only a new architecture, it is not only a new urbanism! PROJECTIVISM is the future of mankind.

The art of the past is about self and selfish. The art of the past is about subject and subjectivist. The art of PROJECTIVISM is beyond self and subject. It is the teaching of the new Utopia, and the practice of its teaching is called Utopics.

The constructivists want art to be made rational: theirs is an art for technocrats.

PROJECTIVISM is beyond the mechanomania of the constructivists. We will build a new city of man upon this earth because we will bring down the heavens to earth. The forces of the aether, the vectors of universal planes, the directional signals of light, the beacons of the stars—these will be the elements of the new art. We will project into the universe and, bending, all light and energy will return to earth. Constructivist art is beyond Newton; PROJECTIVIST art is beyond Einstein.

PROJECTIVIST plans for the revolution of art are already devised. PROJECTIVIST cities are under construction in the mind of genius.

PROJECTIVISM is planning its revolution in a rooming house in East Berlin.

—Yevgeny Mikhailovich Malenov
March 11, 1927

It could not be foreseen that such an outrageous text would produce such an immense impact on the populace of the cities where the hundred thousand leaflets were dumped, but Frankfurt, Hamburg, Munich, and Berlin were not tranquil cities in the spring of 1927. Germany was in disarray, militants of all parties and persuasions could gather riot strength in a matter of hours, speeches rang over airways. Sedition was commonplace and sedition was everywhere, but it was no longer clear what constituted sedition—the legally empowered authorities of Weimar were considered as seditious as its extreme enemies on the right and the left. Who, then, was this revolutionary madman that drifted down on them at midday, carrying an unintelligible doctrine that floated into consciousness the promise of mass housing (an end to unemployment, some concluded), the guarantee of a new utopia, the assurance of a noncommunist revolution—and all out of a rooming house in East Berlin?

Fingermann had planned it well. The newspapers had been informed; the radio stations conducted street interviews, impressions were formed of the metropolitan vision of Yevgeny Mikhailovich Malenov, and by late in the day the block in front of his cheap quarters in the working-class district of Prenzlauer Berg was jammed with the mob, with curious oglers and bourgeois enthusiasts, with police on horseback and agitators in leather coats, all wanting to see Malenov.

Fingermann was enthusiastic. Only Yevgeny Mikhailovich was unaware of the extraordinary excitement that his manifesto had generated. He had delivered the text to Fingermann more than a week before its airborne descent, and although Fingermann had tried several times the day before the action to see Malenov—sending him telegrams and hand-delivered messages—Yevgeny was painting in solitude. As was his habit, he had tacked to his door an announcement informing visitors that he was at work and not to be disturbed; however, with a conspicuous indifference to confusion—his mastery of German did not yet encompass the law of contradiction—the announcement read: MALENOV IS PAINTING. NO ONE IS AT HOME.

Until that portentous afternoon during the second week of March, when the action had taken place, no one had bothered to read the messages Malenov tacked to his door. For more than a week, Malenov had not left his room. Supplied with tea, stale buns, tins of soup, and condensed milk, he had worked furiously either painting or writing, sometimes writing on his paintings, sometimes drawing on his notepaper, frequently trying to collage manuscript to canvas, in order to produce an integrated document of the projectivist universe he was in the process of creating. Whenever a telegram was slid beneath his door, he cursed the intrusion of "art merchants" like Fingermann; whenever he heard the landlord's wheezing cough in the hallway, he cursed the existence of landlords. He wanted nothing so much as to be left alone in total silence, submissive to his daimon, working ferociously, living without substantial food and sleep, as if disembodied, so to speak, an astral genius, Malenov.

At last, taking courage, Fingermann mounted the stairs to Malenov's room, behind him a pair of cynical newspaper reporters assigned to track this latest phenomenon of apocalyptic Weimar enthusiasm. Fingermann knocked on the door. No reply. Malenov later claimed that he was sleeping, that he had just gone to sleep after thirty hours of work. Fingermann banged louder, accompanying his thump with the shouting of Malenov's name. Silence. A shoe dropped to the floor. Fingermann resorted to a melodious threnody of raps and bangs. The door was at last thrown open, and Malenov, dark and enraged, stood before them in his long underwear, screaming at Fingermann in Russian. Fingermann tried to control Malenov's anger, pointing nervously to the two journalists, who grinned broadly at this apparition. "Another madman," one whispered. Fingermann denied it. But Malenov, hearing the insult, began in a rapid mixture of Russian and German to celebrate madness in general and his own in particular.

He began, "*Da.* I am mad. Absolutely mad. And who wouldn't be mad living in a mad country?" The journalists began to pay attention, an exchange developed, a conversation ensued, and the journalists, first amused, ended amazed, as this remarkable man seated on his bed in his underpants began to describe the predicament of German civilization with a telling particularity and observation, showing his paintings as examples of health and cure, supplying quotations from his manifesto and unpublished writings to document the visionary ferocity of projectivism. After nearly forty minutes the journalists had enough copy and decided to leave, after persuading Malenov to throw open his windows and salute the thinning crowd below. Shouts of "Hurray for housing" greeted his waving arms; smiling Malenov withdrew, closed the windows, pushed Fingermann from his room, and went back to bed. He slept for nearly eighteen hours.

By the following Friday, when he awoke, two telegrams shoved beneath his door by the landlord announced the sale of five paintings to a Swiss collector and a German industrialist; a commission from Alexander Dorner of the Kestner Gesellschaft to make two lithographs for his museum; an invitation to a conference, Architecture and Pure Plastic Painting; and a long extract from one of the interviews that had appeared that day in the *Tagblatt* under the headline "Yevgeny Mikhailovich Malenov: Visionary Painter and Utopian Architect." The text was all wrong, but it was respectful and generous. Malenov had definitively emerged from obscurity. Although never a celebrity— that dubious estate would overtake artists some time later—Malenov was never again unknown. There would always be someone in the entourage of the arts who would know of Yevgeny Mikhailovich Malenov, who could identify his doctrine and describe his imagery, who knew where his paintings fit in the scheme of modernism.

All this attention did not secure for Malenov a reliable income. He continued to live, as he once put it, "from foot to mouth," displacement with more than an element of truth, since as often as his hand lifted fork to face, it had first to push out of the way the arrogance of foot, which declaimed, spluttered, enthused over his utopic schemes and dreams. Unworldly, indifferent to the machinery of the world, content with little beyond subsistence, wanting nothing more than the acknowledgment of his vision and its efficacy, eager only to get on with the work of incarnation that would show forth the supreme harmony of his genius, Malenov paid little attention to Fingermann's antic claims on his behalf. The more Malenov withdrew into work, the more Fingermann undertook to agitate the recognition of his genius, dogging journalists, sending out photographs of the artist in his "studio of poverty," as he named it, borrowing pictures and failing to return them as promised, arriving hours late at restaurants to which he had bidden Malenov appear for dinners with enthusiastic collectors (Malenov would arrive only to discover that no reservation had been made and no collectors had appeared), wearing Malenov out with endless complaints about his lack of gratitude and appreciation for his efforts on Malenov's behalf.

Malenov was wearying of Fingermann. One day he appeared at Fingermann's home in a fashionable quarter of Berlin and demanded to see him. A butler tried to prevent his entering until he had been announced, but Malenov pushed him aside and strode through the living room to the study at the rear of the house overlooking a charming flower garden. It was late April, and sun streamed through the house; Malenov envied Fingermann the riches that enabled him to buy a portion of the sun. Malenov pushed open the glass doors that sheltered Fingermann's spacious verandah from the rest of the house and found Fingermann lying on the floor looking about him at his gallery of masterpieces—Cézanne, Renoir, Picasso, a Kirchner street scene, Otto Dix, a large Schiele—but where were the more than twenty Malenovs that he had carried away over the past months?

"Where is Malenov?"

"Ah, Malenov, it is you? Why weren't you announced?" Fingermann asked languidly, undisturbed by the appearance of the bull-headed Malenov.

"I choose to be unannounced. How would someone announce a Malenov to a Fingermann?" he snarled.

"Ah, my dear genius, you seem disturbed. Why are you disturbed?" Fingermann inquired, placing joined hands behind his head and raising himself a few inches from the floor.

"Where are Malenov's paintings, Fingermann? I have come for an accounting and settlement."

"Your paintings, my dear genius, are no more. They are all gone. Sold for a song. I am tired of you, Malenov. You are a genius, but like all geniuses you don't produce enough. You think too much. You talk too much. You paint too slowly. I have gone back to the masters. I am finished with living artists. Too much work for a small fellow like Fingermann."

"Then pay me the song."

"What are you talking about, dear Malenov? What song?"

"You sold them for song. That's what you said. Give it to me."

"An expression, dear fellow. I sold them for practically nothing—even the industrialist from Zurich (actually, he makes ladies' hats) paid me so little it was hardly decent taking the money. But if you insist. There, on the desk, there's a pile of banknotes. Take them. They belong to you. It looks like more than it is. Take the money, dear fellow, and go away. I'm enjoying the sun."

There was an instant during which Malenov imagined lifting little Fingermann and throwing him through the window into the garden beyond. His rage was luminous, but it passed as quickly as it had been ignited. He had no intention of wasting his years paying for the crime of murdering an art merchant. Too foolish, too disgusting. Instead, he determined to annihilate the presence of Fingermann, to gather up the moneys due him and without another word to depart. The red of rage had already diminished. Only the tips of his ear lobes remained bright. Indeed, he had passed beyond rage into an equanimity of such supreme indifference that he was unaware that as he returned from the desk (where he had seized the money and stuffed it into his overcoat), he had stepped on the recumbent Fingermann as he passed out of the verandah. He heard Fingermann scream with pain, but he was unsure from where the cries had come. He had almost fractured Fingermann's shoulder, but he could not remember how it happened when it was reported to him months later.

## Seven

Malenov, depressed, wandered the streets of Berlin after he left Fingermann's apartment. The depression was as large and ill-fitting as the threadbare herringbone overcoat that enveloped him. (Depression, anxiety, alarm, fury rarely seized Malenov with an explicit declaration of their origins and force. He was generally unaware of

his psychic states, rushing speedily beyond intimate pains and dislocations to a metaphysical conclusion that snared him in appraisals
of his own energy and production. Everything he felt—all his longings
and disappointments—rarely turned upon the deceits and corruptions
of others. Finally, it was always *his* fault for not doing enough work.
Saint Sergius glared at him, the Third Rome exposed its rotten beams,
all the young naked delights of his album of regrets suddenly frowned.
It was Malenov's fault if the world worked awry, if the Fingermanns
among dealers turned out to be feckless charlatans.) Malenov wandered the streets in the spring sunlight, returning home at dusk,
trudging up the stairs of the rooming house. Upon his bed the landlord
had placed a letter with a neatly typed address. Malenov assumed it
was from Fingermann already, an explanation, an apology perhaps.
But he had no further interest in Fingermann. He had been cheated,
but it hardly mattered. Genius, he believed, was not restricted to a
few works; it could create again and better. He lay down on the bed
and heard the letter crinkle beneath his buttocks. He removed it and,
as he passed it before his face, bunching it into refuse, he noticed
the Soviet stamp and the return address. He shouted with joy and
tore it open:

> Dear old friend. I am coming to Berlin for a big exhibition
> of our new art that will open at the Lehrter Galerie end of
> March. I will see you there, no? They have a beautiful work
> of yours that I sent from my own collection. With sincere
> warmth, Malevich.

Malenov overflowed with happiness. He did love Malevich, love and
honor Malevich, honor and celebrate Malevich, celebrate and occasionally borrow from Malevich. Projectivism was, he admitted years
later, a spark of the Supremus ignited on the anvil of his own genius.
Malenov leapt from his bed and dashed out of the rooming house,

found a taxicab and headed for the Lehrter train station, where the gallery was located. The small gallery was already closed for the night, but he saw his painting hanging beside others less distinguished; it was a radiant composition of 1923, in which a rectangular lozenge of orange floated off a gray-white scaffolding into an immense sea of powdery black. He had forgotten the painting and he adored seeing it again, even if it was lit by a poorly powered night lamp that stood in the center of the forlorn and empty gallery. Malenov was paralyzed before the vitrine and did not notice that an attractive woman in her mid-thirties was attentively watching him, waiting for the opportunity to speak. After twenty minutes, Malenov heaved a sigh and broke out of his delirium of pleasure.

"Herr Malenov? It is you, isn't it? I am so glad that you finally came to the exhibition. We've been trying to find you for weeks. It was only now, with Malevich's arrival and your press interviews, that we learned your address and have written inviting you to come. And here you are at eight o'clock in the evening, more than an hour after our closing."

The pretty girl, with lips painted like sticks of cinnamon, sweetly hummed her greeting. Malenov turned and in a kind of reverie, still delirious before his painting, nodded to her, as if to query her identity.

"Fraulein Kammerer. Francine Kammerer. The Lehrter is my gallery. Let me tell you. The exhibition is a great success. Your very original publicity stunt quickened interest; attendance has been much greater than we had anticipated." Malenov wasn't quite certain to what she referred, but he smiled radiantly at her attention. She reopened the gallery, walked him through the exhibition, and took him for supper in a café around the corner from the station. At the very end of the evening, Malenov remembered his old friend. "And Malevich, dear young lady. Where can I find Malevich?"

"He is out of the city. He insisted on visiting the Bauhaus in Dessau. I told him that I had called and that the school was closing for Easter holidays, but he went nonetheless. He said Kandinsky was enough reason. All of you Russians are so incredibly stubborn. It doesn't matter. He will be back tomorrow, he promised me."

"And his address?"

"He is living with von Riesen. I don't have the address written down, but here is the telephone number. Riesen has installed a telephone. It is probably easier to send a telegram, but then without the address? No. Try the telephone or come by tomorrow in the late afternoon. Malevich is usually here at that time."

Malenov watched her write the telephone number of von Riesen. A small, sinuous hand, each letter and number embellished like a baroque woodcarving. She did it unself-consciously, without pretension. Clearly, it was the way she had learned to write. Malenov watched her with smiles of appreciation. A lovely woman, he thought. Dare I fall in love with a grown-up? He suddenly blushed; his reverie of love had frightened and embarrassed him. He turned to Fraulein Kammerer and stumbled his apologies. "I am sorry. Rude and vulgar. Rude and vulgar. I must go now." He snatched the bit of paper from beneath her pen and fled into the night.

The following morning Malenov fell into the center of an unfinished painting. He worked steadily throughout the day into the evening. It was almost ten o'clock when he remembered that he had promised to go by the gallery in the late afternoon to visit with Malevich. He tried to call from the corner café, but the gallery was long since closed. The next day was Sunday, and everything was closed. By Monday he had totally forgotten the gallery in the Lehrter train station, the exhibition of new Soviet painting, the charms of Francine Kammerer, and Kazimir Malevich. He had promised himself that he would take a holiday in springtime, before Easter, a walking holiday in southern Germany, and he set off by train for Munich. He planned to be away for more than two weeks, hiking in the woods, sometimes sleeping out of doors, once or twice perhaps finding hospitality in a cheap inn or the haybarn of a peasant. He adored hiking, although Bavaria was completely different from the Ukraine, where flat surfaces, undulant with waving stalks of grain and corn, predominated. In southeast Germany, hills and mountains, valleys and ravines compelled the traveler to watch his step lest he fall off into a charging river or tumble from a rock and break a leg.

Malenov was always excited by the dangers of nature. Nature was for him a metaphor of his painting; it supplied atmosphere and tone; form was in the brain; the painting was reality. One morning he trudged out into the countryside carrying a large sketchbook, his pockets bulging with colored pencils and crayons; he crossed a field, dodging cow droppings, and descended a narrow path that approached a rocky wall that sheered off to a river below. Swollen with the run-off from melting mountain snow, the river careened over jagged rocks and monumental boulders. Jamming his feet into the trunk of an uprooted fir tree that fronted the chasm, Yevgeny began to draw the wall of rock on the other side. Amazed by the geological strata that formed this outcropping of the mountain range in the distance, he devised a pattern of colored surfaces, shading them to suggest their interconnectedness and linkage, gradually erasing the sharp lines that marked the actual divisions of nature, until hours later what had emerged from his concentrated reading of the landscape was a Mal-enovian abstraction. It could have been executed in his Berlin studio, although Malenov insisted that this first drawing of what became a suite of images would have been impossible without the suggestion supplied him by that sheer wall of layered stone, the dashing river below throwing spume into the air, and his increasingly panicked attempt to get it all down before the light changed. The original drawing was rectangles and projectiles as before, although the palette had moved downward from the aether colors that Malenov favored for his heavenly ascents to the earthy tones of ochres and umbers that enriched his transcription of the essence of this animated abstraction he called nature.

When he returned to the small inn where he had been settled for the last days of his holiday trek, the innkeeper greeted him warmly: "Ah, painting our scenery. May I see?" Malenov opened the sketchpad and watched the innkeeper, crestfallen and confused. "But what is this?"

"The canyon and the river outside town."

"I've never seen this before."

"It is there most certainly. It seems, sir, that you look but you don't see." Malenov was content with his day's work. He laughed when he accused the innkeeper. Usually, he growled. The innkeeper was nonplussed; shrugging his shoulders, he went off to make Malenov his afternoon grog of hot wine, lemon, and cinnamon.

The following day, although it was now early May, a spring storm descended on the village, unseasonable winds shattered the calm of the valley, and an enormous tree was dislodged and fell into the roadway, cutting off the village from the dirt road that joined it to the small Bavarian hamlets that clustered the mountain range. Yevgeny Mikhailovich awakened with a chest cold of such magnitude that his coughing shook the quiet of the inn no less than did the battering storm winds. He remained in bed for nearly a week, tended with soups and suspicion, for his execrably accented German, clearly Slavic in origin, unnerved the conservative women of the inn as much as his odd drawings of the surrounding mountains and valleys, which he tacked to the walls of his room, annotating them with titles in Russian while describing in German their complex abstract vocabulary with such banal simplisms as "Mountains and Rivers" or "Prehistoric Bavaria." The mother of the innkeeper, a shuffling woman in her seventies, muttered to herself about Yevgeny's German, persuaded that his drawings were spy codes for a Bolshevik invasion of southern Germany. She mentioned her suspicions to the local constable, who arranged to sneak into the room when Yevgeny was down the hall in the lavatory, but he found nothing suspicious about the drawings, although he declared with certainty that they were "not art."

After six days in bed, Yevgeny decided that he was recovered and appeared one morning for steaming coffee and hot rolls in the common room below, his scarf wrapped about his throat up to his nose, leaving only the smallest of apertures for the insertion of food and liquid. In the days that followed he stayed near the inn, walking down into the village square to introduce himself to the various tradesmen of the village, sketching occasionally, reading the out-of-date newspapers the innkeeper received by mail from Munich, until, in the third week in May, he announced one day at noon that he was prepared to leave, having already arranged to ride in the back of a horse-drawn cart that was about to set forth with cut wood for the trading center of Rosenheim some miles away in a lower valley, from which he could catch a train for Munich. He paid the innkeeper, embraced the mother with eager enthusiasm, hugging her immensity with such ferocity that she cried out in dialect that he was assaulting her, tipped the young girl who cleaned his room, and, having packed his rucksack and strapped his sketchpad to his back, climbed up onto the mountain of cut logs and shouted to the young driver that he was settled and ready for the journey.

Yevgeny Mikhailovich did not return to Berlin until May 26 at dusk. He found many letters and local telegrams, inviting him to salons that were long since over and dinners he would never have enjoyed. There were two messages, however, from Malevich: "What has become of you?" read one, and the other, somewhat more plaintively, "Am I never to see you? Are you angry with your old friend." Yevgeny retrieved the slip of paper on which Francine Kammerer had written the telephone number of the von Riesen apartment where Malevich was staying and rushed across the street to the local *bierstube*, where he phoned the apartment. An old woman answered. "No, Herr von Riesen is not at home. No, the large Russian is not at home. Yes. I will give them a message."

"Tell them to meet Yevgeny tomorrow afternoon at Die Florelle. Two o'clock. Yes. Two in the afternoon. Please promise to give them the message. Please. Please. You have it clearly? Yevgeny. Die Florelle. Two exactly."

But the old lady had hung up the moment he had begun to repeat his instructions. Yevgeny thought for a moment to call back to make certain that he had reached the right number and to give the message again, but he thought the old lady might well sabotage him if he called to repeat himself. Yevgeny contented himself with waiting ten minutes, dialing the number again, and, when the old woman answered, putting down the receiver. Yes, it was the same cracked and weary voice. He had reached the right number, he believed.

And the rest is known. Die Florelle. Precisely at 2 P.M. The battle of cups and cakes, the seizure of premonition and the precipitate dash for the von Riesen apartment only to discover that Malevich had left for Moscow, departing without ever having seen again his younger friend and colleague, the great successor to Supremus, master of projectivism, severe theoretician of utopics, then penniless and abandoned in Berlin.

## *Eight*

Joseph Alexander Karnovsky disembarked at Hamburg early on a glistening January morning in 1928. He had departed three weeks earlier from New York, determined to search out and impress Yevgeny Mikhailovich Malenov. It is true that he did not have Malenov's address, but that seemed hardly an obstacle. He had accumulated a considerable collection of what he correctly called "traces of the Master" and had ordered them in such a way as to provide him with an only slightly blurred profile of his quarry: several photographs (all enlarged and retouched); reproductions of a number of Malenov's paintings; a brief biographical notice appended to the one gallery catalogue that had reproduced Malenov's work; three terse discussions of Malenov's oeuvre in otherwise uninformed comment on the post-revolutionary Soviet avant-garde; and, most significantly, a translation of the text of the Projectivist Manifesto dispensed over the major cities of Germany some months before, which mentioned that the artist lived "in a rooming house in East Berlin." The field was narrowed considerably, and Karnovsky was confident that if a New York art periodical had reproduced Malenov's manifesto, it had presumably been published previously by the German press, which would have elaborated the cryptic allusion to Malenov's dreary quarters with a specific mention of the street and number. He had no fear, then, that Malenov could evade him, much less would wish to evade him. Why, he reassured himself, would the painter want to avoid an ardent, a young acolyte, a potential disciple, particularly a disciple of some means (with more means to come) who only wished to aid and assist the Master, to learn from him, to profit from his presence, to assimilate everything, from the ideas of his art to such minor matters as how genius disposed of rejected drawings.

Karnovsky sat in the lounge car of the Hamburg–Berlin night train smoking thin cheroots and drinking brandy, watching his pleasant face glint and wink in the various mirrors disposed about the sofas and shiny mahogany tables with which the car was furnished. He enjoyed the salubrity of elegance, seated in the warmth of his floor-length beaver coat as the cold crept in and the air began to smoke with chill, smiling to himself almost triumphantly. He had crossed the ocean to find a genius in Berlin to whom to apprentice his own modest but swelling talents.

It had to be. It had to be, he kept repeating to himself, sometimes saying the words, sometimes seeing them before him like the dire warnings written on the plaster wall of Belshazzar's palace, sometimes outlining them with his finger on the befogged windowpanes that blotted the night lights of the countryside past which the train speeded.

It had to be. (What had to be? I wonder now. The victory of

determination over obstinacy is the most that one can construe this phrase—repeated and underlined in Karnovsky's journal of his Berlin hegira—to mean. It had to be, one surmises, because it left out of account everything that was not controlled by Karnovsky's will and what he took to be the omnipotence of the largesse he wanted to bestow. He knew nothing about Yevgeny Mikhailovich Malenov. Indeed, in those early days of the maturity of Joseph Alexander Karnovsky, he hardly knew the details of himself. He had, as all attractive young men, a consoling naïveté that imagined reality curling in fright before beauty and intelligence, the filling cheek, the open smile, the intense and passionate eye, the casually cut hair, long and short, rippled and straight, the generous mouth, all ornamenting an intelligence that organized these discrete items of masculine beauty into a face that was, indeed, passionate and intense, that bespoke intelligence, that was occasionally, in fact, very intelligent and always— in Karnovsky's case—somewhat frightened, somewhat calculating.)

Somewhat frightened, somewhat calculating. (Dare I say this with certainty about the young man of twenty-two who descended at 6:30 on the morning of a snowstorm that stalled Berlin for two days during early January 1928? Can I be certain? I worry about my temptation to pass such judgments on young Joseph Alexander Karnovsky. And yet it seems hardly possible to resist them. Item: he had boarded his ship, the S.S. *Intransigent*, as Joseph Alexander Karnovsky, but minutes later registered for his table assignment and deck chair as J. Alexander Karnovsky. Item: I found years later among his papers of the period a snarly and contemptuous aside about the ancient origin from which his English name was expanded. Our Joseph Alexander thought his biblical antecedent boring and punctilious and preferred to retract him to a mere initial, focusing his favor instead on Alexander, whether thinking of the Great Alexander or considering the liberal czar of all the Russias who had freed the serfs and perhaps facilitated—through many permutations and misjudgments—the flight of Karnovsky's parents and himself from the Old World to the New, I do not know. Moreover, it didn't matter. In those days, he preferred being a bright Alexander to acceding to such a stern monitor as the ancient Joseph.)

A porter rushed forward to seize Karnovsky's valises. Karnovsky was exhausted; he had passed the night in an almost somnambulistic contemplation of his destiny, flitting between various schemes and dreams of his future, reviewing his coming to be in this hour, abroad in the world, fled from the comforts and securities of domestic succor—his father's scrutiny of his enterprise, his mother's bourgeois dismay at her only son's seduction by the world of art. Karnovsky had already left behind several snakeskins of permutation upon the beds and bureaus of his family apartment, passing through moultings that had jettisoned without apology all his father's commonplace expectations for his son.

Markus Israel Karnovsky, a tea importer of renowned connoisseurship, had been a principal purveyor of Russian and oriental teas to the family of the czar and the nobility of the Russian Empire. Wisely, Markus Karnovsky had never sought to capitalize on his mercantile involvement with the aristocracy to petition permission to live in St. Petersburg, with the result that when the revolution occurred, he was far from the scene of early hostilities and near enough to borders of escape that he could prepare wisely and well his departure from the embattled nation. He quietly sold his several shops, happily accepting losses and smiling cheerfully as the new owners fleeced him, each month converting cash into gold and jewels with a calm and deliberation that belied the financial debacle he had accepted as inevitable. A man of forty-eight with a nervous wife and a fourteen-year-old son would do well—he counseled himself—to move slowly, without attracting notice, condensing his holdings to a few treasures that could be sequestered and smuggled across borders. He knew that inevitably he would come to the attention of the Red au-

thorities for being a merchant and tea supplier to the czar's family
and to that of the Whites for being, despite his indifference to matters
of nationality and religion, a Jew of Odessa, an acquaintance of Jewish
nationists, Yiddishists, Hebrew poets, and rabbinic scholars, all of
whom made a practice of requiring Markus Karnovsky's advice in the
mixing of their breakfast teas and special decoctions.

During the summer of 1919, with the war between Reds and Whites
already raging, Markus Karnovsky arranged an unpretentious holiday
for his family at a small Black Sea village near Ovdiopol, on the
Rumanian border about twenty miles from Odessa. He had already
negotiated the sale of his apartment and its furnishings, making certain
that the documents of sale passed between intermediate friends to the
gentile physician who was eager to expand his practice and improve
his social standing with the purchase of the Karnovskys' spacious
apartment. They fled safely from Odessa, carrying little baggage and
what might be taken for a holiday pannier, all jewels hidden in bottles
of jam or pressed behind the anchovies of pitted olives or stuffed into
silver bugle beads that decorated a peasant blouse his wife had made
for the occasion of their flight. They arranged one morning for a young
sailor to take them for an idle day on the Black Sea and then, beyond
the sight of land, to make sail for the nearest settled habitation in
Rumania, the small city of Sulina, where one of the mouths of the
Danube disgorged into the sea. All the way across, Markus Karnovsky
distracted himself (while his wife groaned from seasickness and worry)
by instructing young Joseph Alexander in the mysteries of sums and
subtraction. His wife was irritated with his meticulous instruction,
her anxiety mounting as the gentle sea swelled and rolled the fishing
vessel down the coast toward Rumania and the young sailor, unaware
of her nervous condition or the momentousness of their escape, sang
songs to himself in a language the Karnovskys were certain was not
Russian.

The lights of Sulina were matted by the distant gloom; the fishing vessel turned in toward shore, deposited the Karnovskys on a rocky beach, and abandoned them. They trudged in to the highway, found an inn for the night, presented themselves and their papers at the police station the following morning, and secured the travel documents necessary for them to proceed to Constanta, where they boarded a freighter for Istanbul. There, two weeks and one day after their flight from Odessa, they embarked for New York City. The migration of the Karnovskys was wrought by energetic flight and bribery, a jewel here, a gold coin there, a family moved from the misery of war-torn Russia (where in time what assuredly awaited them was impoverishment and death) to the principal metropolis of the new world, which in their unsophisticated imaginings they had not thought larger or more dense than Odessa, that two-story, wood-and-stone city of southern Russia.

The Karnovskys settled down. They learned English; they refused to forget Russian; they read Russian books; they declined to read Russian newspapers and magazines; they had no interest in politics or historical events; they cared only for what Mrs. Karnovsky called "culture," which included Markus Karnovsky presenting his thick Russian accent accoutered in velour hats and soft alpaca jackets. No rebuke to Markus Israel Karnovsky; he did his best with what he was, with what he knew, with what he construed his future in America promised. He devised and he dreamed, always taking into account the indefiniteness of his wife, who fluttered and sneezed over his arrangements, caring more for the proprieties than for the substance of events, and his growing son, who mooned and affected very long hair and sad eyes.

The Karnovskys did not think of themselves as immigrants, certainly not as exiles. They were "sojourners," and when they came upon the word and mastered its subtleties, they described themselves as such. They had left Russia behind because its atmosphere had lowered and become inhospitable, but their indifference to events was so ingrained that for Markus Israel Karnovsky the mention of his middle name became sufficiently discomforting that he dropped it entirely. They were not Jews in exile or wanderers from a nation of wanderers; they had come to New York because it was no longer possible for them to be tea merchants to the noble houses of Russia. That was all there was to it. (And, let me make clear, Markus Karnovsky was not intent on wealth or power; he thought of dealing in tea the way other merchants thought about fine wine or antiques. His was a calling, indeed a vocation, that required for success an incredibly sensitive nose and an astute and uncorrupted palate, fingers that felt boding staleness in the slightest crackle of a leaf, and a knowledge of the scores of variations that marked out the teas of China and southeast Asia from the black teas of Russia, varieties that alluded to smokiness or the aroma of burning fall leaves, that promised a loosening of catarrhs or a tightening of flabby chins. The tea merchant was a born homeopath, one step from professional medicine, akin to magician and alchemist, but also unsentimental trader and merchant, who mixed and blended, branding his name on certain teas as being his very own.)

Within a year of their arrival, "Karnovsky Selection" was inscribed in elegant serifs on fine boxes and metal containers sent forth to such distant and exotic places as Denver, Portland, and San Francisco, across the nation back to the borders of the Pacific amidst which the many tea-growing lands were situated. In time Markus Karnovsky branched out, acquiring on his staff a pepper expert and a master of herbs, buying contracts that ran into the tens of thousands of dollars, speculating on growths and deliveries, buying up and selling short, taking delivery of rich cargoes and selling their contents to large food shops and new conglomerates that produced tinned soups and seasoned vegetables. In time—that is, near the end of the 1920s—the House of Karnovsky had become one of the best-established importers in the nation, with a staff of thirty tasters and sales personnel clustered around the mahogany tables in the inner rooms, where annually the tasting of the new teas would be conducted with solemn formality in the presence of Markus I. Karnovsky, a figure of portly solidity, now bearded and framed in fur lapels.

Despite his preoccupation with tea, pepper, and herbs, Markus Karnovsky did not neglect the education of his son. On Saturday mornings he walked with Joseph Alexander through the park, from their apartment on West End Avenue toward the reservoir, stopping beside the bridle path to mark out with his walking stick mathematical problems that he wished his son to solve and simple French sentences into which he had installed an error that he required his son to catch and correct. No reward for success nor punishment for failure, he believed. Simple performance, that was all. He was surely unaware that wresting a smile of satisfaction from him became so important to the uncertain young man that when he failed—as happened, if not frequently, at least some of the time—and Markus Karnovsky's eye clouded, a furrow of consternation appeared, a bit lip, a clucking sound of disapproval (all involuntary), the ensemble of grimaces and sounds struck deep into the heart of the young aspirant, who shook his head with horror that he failed and was often inconsolable for several hours beyond the moment, refusing to release himself from the judgment of worthlessness with which he assailed himself. "He wants so little of me," the young boy said to himself, "and even then I fail him." Had it crossed his mind that his father had spent little more than a brief hour's walk on Saturdays in the company of his child, a mathematical mistake or a brutalized French construction would not have weighed so heavily. But that was not the case. In time, what began as the wish to give simple pleasures and rewards to his otherwise preoccupied father became a monumental struggle to impress and overwhelm him (and perhaps, *sotto voce*, to strangle his instructional chords). He loved him so much and yet remained so unsatisfactory a loving son that he found it hard to imagine loving anyone else, loving another, loving a woman, settling finally some years beyond this adolescent interregnum with attending to himself only, loving himself—if such muddled and ungratifying self-love could be called loving.

Of course, there is more provocation and incident behind the introspection, self-enamorment, and nerveless certainty that finally emerged from the welter of beginnings as the grown Joseph Alexander Karnovsky, but too much detail would take me far off course. The misery of the Saturday trial by ordeal, for example, would have returned to the miasma of gestures by which most human beings conduct the work of the affections, had its implication of insensitivity not been confirmed by many other passages of formal rightness with which his father and later his mother conducted their relationship with their only child. Everything from the clothes Joseph Alexander wore and the amount of time he was expected to spend in earnest effort in the bathroom to the fixing of permissible times for reading and obligatory times for roller-skating (which was called a "healthy exercise") were fixed by what his father—remembering czarist times—called "Papa's ukase." Joseph Alexander was never asked to do anything; he was always told in a voice of peremptory loftiness, his father's voice swooping down on him from elevated heights where decisions were presumably made only after consultation atop Olympus. But if such examples fail to persuade us of the depth of injury sustained by the young man, think only on the grotesquerie of the following episode, underlined in red crayon in the recollections of childhood I found among Karnovsky's papers after his death:

> When I was nearing my fifteenth birthday, my father ordered me one day to make myself ready for my first trip to his tailors, where, I assumed, the passage from knee pants and cutaway jackets furled with a velvet collar would give way to a proper suit. Father ordered me to dress with particular formality for the visit to his tailors—"they are imported gentlemen like ourselves"—which I took to mean that he wished me turned out in shirt and tie. I presented myself as his breakfast concluded; the maid—a young girl of particularly striking attractiveness—was clearing the table. Father

took one glance at my get-up and called me to his side. Reaching into his pocket, he withdrew his complicated pocket knife, one of whose gold appendages was a small but deadly scissor. "Your tie is improperly balanced," he declared sourly, and seizing the errant end, which drooped foolishly below the line of the front striped streamer, he summarily scissored it off. The maid giggled. I shook violently and then burst into tears. Many weeks elapsed before a large package was delivered from Father's tailor. The suit intended had been ordered without my seeing it. *Hoc pater fecit.*

Enough then. You know Markus Israel Karnovsky sufficiently; since he plays a minor role in the events that follow and disappears to an early grave before J. Alexander Karnovsky has been four months in Berlin, it is enough to have briefly annotated the characteristics he exhibited as father. He somehow knew that he had failed as father, but always imagined that it was much more to the point of pater familias to serve both wife and son by a single, efficient enterprise: his vocation as expert on the various leafs and buds and fruits that constituted the mysterious world of teas and condiments. He never complained about his son; he took it for granted that he would never become an expert at anything. Indeed, he rationalized the success of the House of Karnovsky by believing that his own eminence would protect his son from the need to become eminent himself. It did not surprise him, therefore, that his son, having mastered languages and mathematics, later science and mathematics, and subsequently science and history, would refuse to become what his father had marked out as the only alternative to a vocation in tea. Joseph Alexander had no wish to become "a technical man," as his father called chemists, engineers, physicists, even astronomers and medical practitioners. The arts were exhausted by teas and herbs, wines and scents; the rest was consigned to the dominion of precision and exactitude, where the laws of the universe groaned. Since those laws were as recondite

and untransmissible as the secrets of nose and palate, it was assumed
that his son would become "a technical man." However, Joseph Alexander would have none of it. He began to visit museums when he
was sixteen and never left off; when other boys rushed from school
to the playground, he began to draw, compelling himself through pens
and pencils to combat his father's decision regarding the life he had
selected for him. By the time he had spent two years at Columbia
University, enrolled in engineering but preferring to ignore its requirements in order to audit lectures in the history of art, it was clear
to the father that to oblige his son to become "a technical man" was
to risk driving him from home or, worse, mangling his spirit. Markus
shouted at Joseph Alexander, berating his stupidity and arrogance,
contending passionately that "the new world is a technical world" and
artists would be crushed, but in the end he accepted the inevitable,
settled on his son an allowance that varied as the yield on speculative
futures in the black peppers of Madagascar determined, and turned
him loose. Joseph Alexander, for his part, grateful for an income that
ranged between $2,600 and $3,400 a year, depending on the fluc-
tuations in his pepper endowment, rented an apartment in Greenwich
Village, arranged his books on a windowsill, acquired a companion-
able alley cat, and spent his days drawing. In time Karnovsky decided
to formalize his study of art and registered for courses at the Art
Student's League. His father, before agreeing to pay the fees, conducted a scrupulous examination of the institution, even going to the
length of pretending to enroll himself for beginner's courses, to test
the manner of instruction, the temptations posed by live models, and
the canons of legibility and imitation observed by its faculty. He
wanted to make certain that his son would become a creditable artist,
if artist he wished to be. At least, he imagined, let his son's studio
be immaculate, his scenes and views bright and attractive, his dress
and manner polite. To be sure of Joseph Alexander's acquiring such
decent habits, he wanted to assure himself that the boy's teachers

would be unexceptionable. After a month of close examination of the league's teachers and students, Markus Karnovsky reluctantly concurred in his son's decision and paid over his fees.

It is important to note that young Joseph Alexander Karnovsky (then approaching his twenty-first birthday) was not without talent. His eye was acute, his hand cunning, his sensibility—fresh and unjaded—receptive to enlargement. It is unclear to what vision he pinned his talent, but it was indubitable to his assigned teachers— a large woman with hair drawn tightly into a bun and an evanescently thin academic draftsman with a pince-nez—that Joseph Alexander Karnovsky, former student of engineering, was more exuberantly committed to making canny marks on paper that signified body and form than to casting sums and devising mechanical theorems. However, what might have satisfied his teachers who regarded their teaching enterprise with indifference (believing themselves to be wasting time with the bourgeoisie when they should have been making revolutions of their own at home) hardly sufficed for Karnovsky. By the end of his first year at the league he knew perfectly well how to draw from life, to shade and hue, to adumbrate and allude in charcoal, pencil, and watercolor. He had even executed in oils—more to prove that he could than from any conviction about the work's importance—a large canvas depicting two nudes seated on gilt chairs, their bodies crumpled with weariness, each with a hand raised to a furrowed brow, one (the male) so foreshortened that he appeared to be suffering from collapsed lungs and advanced consumption, the other (the female) with breasts pendulous and sagging, an old woman, thickened at her hips, stockings falling about her ankles. They were not a cheerful pair, and, although the picture won a prize in the annual exhibition of the league and Joseph Alexander was able to present his father with a check for $25, he derived no pleasure from his ability to make presentable drawings, neatly considered, evocative, but finally second-rate. There had to be something more, a way of reconstructing the universe that would accord with his growing demand for an alternative that could efficiently challenge both "the technical world" vaunted by his father and Madagascar gold, as his particular peppercorns were collectively known.

## Nine

Joseph Alexander's first whiff of the existence of Yevgeny Mikhailovich Malenov occurred fortuitously. He overheard a conversation—more precisely, he eavesdropped—one day while he stood in line at the white-tiled cafeteria on Broadway where students of the league usually gathered between classes for coffee. An elderly gentleman, clearly an émigré, was shouting in Russian to an old woman: "Projectivist Manifesto. *Kvatsh!* Lines in empty space, poking God." The man snorted, his hand trembling so violently that his tea sloshed over the metal tray he was carrying to a table at the rear of the cafeteria. Intrigued, Joseph Alexander followed the pair and seated himself just behind them. "What does it mean, Elena? What? *Kvatsh.* Double *kvatsh*," the old man continued to growl. "I have read it carefully and not one word makes sense. And who signed it, you may ask, Elena? Who? None other. Our old friend, the Muscovite, Yevgeny Mikhailovich Malenov. Naturally! Malenov. Projectivism? *Kvatsh!*"

Alexander Karnovsky had noted the name Yevgeny Mikhailovich Malenov in his little sketchbook, opening to a clean page, where he wrote beside the name in giant Cyrillic majuscules, "WHO IS THIS?" Until that moment Joseph Alexander had had no idea that any artistic ferment accompanied the hue and cry of revolutionary Russia. When the Karnovskys arrived in New York from Odessa in 1919, although they continued to chatter in Russian at home, his father's interest in things Russian waned. They had come, after all, to America, and it was problematic enough to be Russian Jews without being thought communist sympathizers as well. But Joseph Alexander's interest in the artistic enthusiasm of revolutionary Russia was piqued by this chance encounter with Malenov's manifesto. He diligently searched the Russian-language press for mention of Malenov and found two references, both respectful—but inconclusive. It was in an issue of a German illustrated monthly, *Der Querschnitt*, which was gathering dust in the stacks of the New York Public Library, that he discovered a photograph of Malenov, seated on a straight-backed chair, a cane plunged between his open legs, his enormous peasant hands resting like chunks of cubed beef on its gnarled handle. Malenov stared out at the photographer like a guardian lion, a large body surmounted by a vast head framed by straight black hair that dropped down about his ears. Malenov's eyes, hardly visible beneath hooded eyelids, were particularly unsettling, at odds with his sharp, pointed nose and capacious mouth, clamped shut. Behind Malenov (which explains his aspect as guardian lion), rose a wall filled with unframed paintings of various magnitudes. Karnovsky sat in the reading room of the library and whistled aloud. Heads turned, but he continued for some moments to whistle with amazement. An attendant came to silence him. Karnovsky vowed to return the following day to vandalize the copy of the magazine, to slit the picture from the page and bear its leonine subject to his Village lair.

So this was Malenov. So this was Malenov's projectivist image. So these were the Malenovian visions—ellipses poised in space, hovering on the aether, borne on winds, each latticework of ellipses, perpendiculars, floating triangles, painted with what he guessed were serene shades of cobalt blue, cadmium yellow, roses and reds, light grays, desperate blacks, tribunals of space, revealing a new dimension of the universe, where ordinary things, familiar nature, conventional events were excised and a new space, a beleaguered time, an atmosphere void of history and humanity was presented for the contemplation of the metaphysical eye. This was the sublime art for which Karnovsky was searching. His heart surged, the adrenalin flowed like gushing sex, his head pounded. He was ravished by the sight of this score of miniature pictures—each less than postage-stamp size in the photograph—hanging on a wall behind a monstrous beast of an artist.

It was remarkably easy for Karnovsky to give up literal figuration and artistically plausible renditions of what the hoi polloi took to be the real, and to begin to refashion the universe as an abstract underpinning of line and shape overlaid with color. He had read enough philosophy to be aware that everyone uses abstract ideas but generally has no notion that they are speaking in abstractions. All language, he understood, was an agreement upon significance, settling on the heads of little words like *good* and *God* meanings that stripped them of all their richness and complexity in return for the easy possibility that human beings could invoke both without the requirement of even scratching their heads in wonder at what they meant. He began to believe that everything—every style and convention of the species—was marked by stupidity, ignorance, and compromise. It unsettled him to realize this, but did not bother him sufficiently to make such accommodation corrupt or capitulation to such shoddy employment invidious.

All these reflections had the consequence that Karnovsky vowed to become an abstract artist. He concealed this decision from his parents, showing them old drawings of street scenes and rosy nudes when they inquired after his work during their infrequent visits to his apartment. He had no wish (nor need, for that matter) to make his parents any more alarmed than they were already by his artist's life. His reluctance, indeed his fear, of disclosing his resolution to his parents was only slightly less bizarre than the fundamental fact that he had *vowed* to become an abstract artist, as though this, too, were an act of will.

Abstraction, of course, is a work of the mind, and at first it caused him no end of problems. He thought for a while that abstraction would arise before him with the same clarity and power as rain sweeping the streets or sunlight bathing a tenement. It was some time before he came to understand that everything finally was an abstraction of something else, not simply a reduction to elements, as naïve thinkers imagine. Abstraction was not removing and simplifying, but actually a kind of adding, a putting on of different eyes. His first abstract drawings in the Malenovian mode were ridiculous, anatomies of line that treated everything like a skeleton. His hand was nervous; he used a ruler and red and blue pencils. The results were thin and neat, as though he were designing street maps and did not dare to get them wrong lest pedestrians lose their way. He was, you will understand, still trying to hold on to a notion of imitation, as though abstraction were merely a technique of easing confusion. One day, however, as he sat by his window overlooking Ninth Street between Fifth and Sixth avenues, he noticed that the sun streaked through the old wavering handmade glass of his windowpanes, separating the light into bands of color. Thinking that the effect would disappear, that his eyes were playing tricks, he nervously arranged his pencils by his notebook and began to trace the bands of color. The light did not alter. It was midday, and the brilliant sun remained for many hours, the light separating invariantly into bands of pure color, striking a patch of floor and saturating it with beam mixtures that glowed, humming with new arrangements of colored lights. He worked quickly, suddenly freed from the constraint of representation, producing sheet after sheet filled with closely valued streamers of colored light, hastily rubbed, some narrow, others dense and deep. As the light changed, so did his reflection of its intensity. He was unaware of the passage of time, the light dulled and darkened into rich blues and purple blacks. Later, as rain overtook the sunlight, his sketches began to glower and gloom. He had made dozens of drawings, each filled with patterns of streaking light, the color analyzed and weighted, the drawings no longer resembling anything but a cool eye and a contemplative brain joined to fingers that moved the pencils quickly over the cream paper. He had rendered the light as cuts and patches of color; he had made a suite of abstractions. Granted, they were not yet beautiful; the drawings were not held by a formal counterpoint and drama that communicated fluency to the colored lights. But they were indubitably genuine abstractions, conventional notions of reality having given way to transformation, light become color, color become motion, motion become rhythm, rhythm achieving an intensity and contrast that promised a new way of seeing.

It was done; Joseph Alexander had made himself into an abstract artist and he adored the nomenclature, calling himself an "abstractionist" from that afternoon on, announcing that evening in a bar on University Place, where he sometimes went for a drink before supper, that he had done something new that day. To himself, he confided that he was ready to find Malenov and begin his apprenticeship to a master.

## Ten

As we have established, Joseph Alexander Karnovsky arrived in Berlin during a snowstorm early in January 1928. To be precise, he arrived on Wednesday morning during the first week in the new year and went immediately to a small hotel, the Atlas, behind the Kürferstendamm, where he booked a modest suite. He had no idea how long he would remain in Berlin and determined to be comfortable during his stay. The manager of the hotel, her ring of keys jangling at her hip, conducted him through the apartment, prettily arranged with solid peasant furniture; a large eighteenth-century ceramic fireplace dominated the room, and pink, purple, and blue floral wreaths battled on the wallpaper. Karnovsky would have preferred the suite naked and undecorated, furnished with spartan severity, because he had come to believe that his newfound vocation as an abstract artist required a lean and disciplined atmosphere for work, but he announced, after reflecting some minutes, "I guess it will do. I'll have it by the month. In advance?" Frau Liebkind nodded and extended her hand. "Here it is," Karnovsky said compliantly, handing her a packet of small green and brown banknotes. "And now, Madame, could you direct me to the largest newspaper in the city? I need some information."

The manager knitted her black eyebrows, virtually joining them in a bushy assault upon her pallid complexion. "*Ja.* The biggest? It must be the *Berliner Morgenpost.*" Joseph Alexander set off at once, hailing a taxi and giving the driver an address not far from his hotel. By late morning he had found what he wanted: the address of Yevgeny Mikhailovich Malenov, back issues of newspapers that described in detail the bombing action organized by Magnus Fingermann (whose little head appeared in an oval inset that invaded a large photograph of Malenov's room in the Prenzlauer Berg), several interviews with Malenov, and additional commentary that Karnovsky found later in the Kunstbibliothek. By midafternoon he had accumulated enough new material to justify a leisurely coffee in order to study his trove of documents and extract from them odd details of Malenov's history —his fondness for cats, the recent walking tour of Bavaria, his icon of Saint Sergius, the death of his parents from influenza—which, he thought, subtly dropped into conversation, would help to persuade Malenov that he had before him a genuine enthusiast, a disciple without guile or deviousness, an ardent student of his life and work.

It was already too late to call on Malenov. Anyway, Karnovsky had decided that it would be more delicate and less overwhelming to send Malenov a hand-delivered letter, written on the notepaper of his hotel, the following evening.

Karnovsky had determined that only subtlety and patience would convince Malenov to trust him. He had picked up several odd clues during the course of his newspaper inquiries and concluded (erroneously, I believe) that Malenov was suspicious of the young, imagining them to be incapable of loyal affection, constancy, and good sense. Karnovsky decided, therefore, upon a less frontal assault, persuaded that geniuses like Malenov do not succumb to naked flattery.

"He has to be seduced," Karnovsky confided to his notebook. "If he believes that I need him desperately, that I will starve without his nurture, he will be less likely to regard my helping him as patronage. The Malenovs of the world, I am certain, hate patrons—at least such bourgeois and crass patrons as exist today." As Karnovsky regarded himself as neither bourgeois nor crass, his stratagems were carefully devised to avoid Malenov's confusing his good will with the suspicious maneuvers of someone like Fingermann, against whom Karnovsky had conceived an irrational dislike, regarding his looks as sneaky and his attitudes—quoted in interviews—as no different from those of a circus barker.

Above all, despite the absence of any admission of this fact in Karnovsky's considerable writings about Malenov dating from this period, Alexander was clearly afraid of Malenov, persuaded (as he was justified in believing) that Malenov would reject him. It would have gone so much easier, I am convinced, if Karnovsky had simply appeared at Malenov's lodgings and asked to study with him. Granted that Malenov had little or no experience teaching, but then most painters who have students hardly teach them. The master painter exists as example—everything he does reflects a kind of sureness and no less sovereign experimentation, which cannot fail to instruct the attentive student. The young painter watches the older as he prepares his canvas, mixes his paints, struggles for certain effects, and in the process of watching comes to understand painting as a necromancer's art, for what is put down hardly dries the way it first appears, and every painter has his special secrets. Had young Karnovsky gone to work for Malenov, stretching canvas, doing errands, cleaning the studio, serving him as indispensable assistant, he would have learned without being tempted to imitate. The problem was built into the procedure by which Karnovsky insinuated himself into his master's life. He could not accept their inequality and, failing to recognize the absolute and indispensable inequity that exists between master and assistant, was tempted from the beginning to lean too heavily on his teacher, to think himself entitled to receive the magic of the master without the requirement of first becoming a magician in his own right.

## *Eleven*

Karnovsky's first communication with Yevgeny Mikhailovich Malenov was thrown into a corner with considerable annoyance. Malenov was once again at war with the world. His door displayed at least two announcements: the first declaring rather politely, for Malenov, his total unavailability and inhospitableness; followed by a smaller paper, neatly written in crabbed majuscules, that clarified the first: I AM METAPHYSICALLY AVAILABLE (THAT IS, I EXIST), BUT I AM INACCESSIBLE. I PAINT ALWAYS. LEAVE ME ALONE. PLEASE. ALONE. "Alone" was underlined three times in a gradual of black, red, and blue stripes.

Malenov's landlord was indifferent to these front-door exhortations. He read them, laughed hoarsely, and pounded on the locked door with malicious ferocity. The door opened, and Malenov greeted him with a large red tongue projected with animus. "Button your pants," the landlord smirked, laughed again, and spat into his green handkerchief. "You artists," he muttered. "Who needs you?" He threw the letter on the bed, turned quickly, and slammed the door with renewed violence. Malenov almost wept with rage. The landlord's initial assault on his door had so startled his hand that the line he had been drawing quivered slightly. He now had to paint over the inch or so of canvas and begin again.

"Shall I feel sorry for myself? Do I have time? An indulgence," he answered, finally, and relaxed. He knew perfectly well that artists parade before others, conducting small scenes of petulance and temperament. It was required. He practiced on his landlord. The stuck-out tongue was one such. He had caught his profile in the mirror over the sink and winced. "Foolishness. And Malenov is never foolish. *Aargh.*"

Malenov told Karnovsky the following evening that he was exhausted. He hadn't read the letter until early morning of the next day when he awakened. The light had disappeared; he was painting amidst shadows, the naked electric bulb, which he sometimes shaded with a green-visored cap he had found in the market, threw grotesque shadows on the wall, but paintings like Malenov's thrived on internal light, light that glowed from the imagination, transformed by colors whose harmony and warfare bustled through the intellect before they were even mixed.

"Will the world ever be as wonderful as this?" he asked himself, observing the curious projectiles and spatial displacements he had wrapped in a shadowy penumbra of slightly roseate milk-white. "Never. It can never exist, because it only exists in my dreams," he answered himself, poking his brush menacingly at the window beyond which lived a billion or so people unaware that Malenov was reconstructing their universe. He stepped back from the easel and collapsed upon his bed. Hearing the paper crinkle, he withdrew the letter and threw it in the corner. It was only in the early morning, when he had awakened and had made himself a cup of strong tea, that he saw the letter on the floor and retrieved it. He was quite calm. He had slept deeply. "And what is this? Fingermann reborn," he grimaced. He almost tore the letter into bits, but restrained himself. After all, he had not heard much from the world for several weeks. His brief bubble had burst; he no longer existed; he was already forgotten. Who then needed him so urgently that a telegram-letter from the Hotel Atlas was required?

The message began in flawless Russian, the script somewhat cramped as though written by a young and inexperienced adept of his mother tongue.

> Honored Yevgeny Mikhailovich Malenov. I have come a very long way to meet you. In fact, dear sir, I have voyaged across the ocean from New York, to which my parents and I—fled from Odessa nearly ten years ago—have come and, so to speak, settled.
>
> I am a young painter. Painting is my life. That is the way I have chosen. So much so, Yevgeny Mikhailovich, that I can now say with confidence that painting chooses me. But I still risk losing my way. I have rejected the figure. I can no longer paint from nature. What happens with me is that everything I paint is imagined form, a working through ideas that have no counterpart in nature but are nonetheless natural, because they are true.
>
> In other words—and you above all will understand me— I am an abstract painter, a painter of new geometries and alternate spaces. But I am afraid that in my new country there is no one to teach me. Or to be frank, honored Yevgeny Mikhailovich, no one here is a master as you are. I do not need a teacher as much as a model—someone who will show me more than method and technique—someone, indeed, who is a kind of—how shall I put it—moral master of paint. And so I have come to Berlin to find you and to ask whether I might be of use to you, work for you, assist you in your great labor, and by my working for you, alongside you, under your tutelage learn indirectly what I cannot learn by myself.
>
> Will you do me the kindness of meeting me for supper tomorrow evening at 8 P.M. in the lobby of my small hotel, where I will be waiting for you with warmth and anticipation. Of course, if you do not choose to come, it will break my heart, but I will be forced to accept your decision. I will not pursue you, you may be sure. I know how much you have already suffered from foolish sycophants and dishonest impresarios.
>
> Do you need help, honored Yevgeny Mikhailovich? If you do, may I add—and I do so with embarrassment—I expect to be able to pay you well for allowing me to assist you. I

know that my assistance will be unimportant to you, but your assistance to me (the very fact that you exist already assists me tremendously) will be more than enough reason to help you. Perhaps the $100 that I will be able to pay you each month will make life easier for you; perhaps you will wish to move your quarters; perhaps you would like a larger apartment with a well-stocked kitchen so that you can eat more than tea and rusks; perhaps having paint and canvas, colored pencils sharpened and at the ready, and new brushes will make it easier for you to be what you are already, one of the geniuses of modern art.

Please, dear Yevgeny Mikhailovich, come to dinner.

Yevgeny Mikhailovich read and reread the letter of J. Alexander Karnovsky—as the letter was signed—numerous times. He laughed as he read it; once he danced jubilantly until he fell exhausted on his painting stool, his eye entranced by an unfinished corner of one of the pictures he had been working on the night before. He attended to the corner, mixing an almost transparent blue that he applied with an infinitely patient evenness that belied the presence of a hundred strokes and a tremulous hand. Finishing the work, he remembered the letter and read it once more (regarding it first with his eyes as though it were a fresh and original discovery), then he repeated it aloud (evenly, like the application of paint, uninflected, flat, unpunctuated), and then again chanting it like a church choir, and lastly singing it like a lover's ballad. He was aware that there was something in the letter that eluded him, a missed beat, a slightly tinny note that he could not place. But he rushed from the apartment nonetheless and, drafting a reply at the local post office, cabled the Karnovsky youth that he would come to dinner that evening. His reply, so characteristic of Malenov's soul-baring demeanor, read as follows:

To my host, J. Alexander Karnovsky.
I dive to the heart of your invitation. Dinner. Dinner.

Dinner. The prospect of a dinner delights me. Indeed, yes. I starve, you know. Of course, I starve. (But I think to myself. How much time you save starving, Yevgeny Mikhailovich. Less eating, less cooking. Less cooking, less waiting for water to boil. Less watching eggs until their shells crack and announce their hardness. And if no eggs to watch, none to buy in the grocery, where, once or twice even, I was forced to steal eggs in order to have something substantial to eat.) Of course, I agree to dinner (we will see, however, about the $100 a month—that makes me suspicious—not you, sir, but the *fact* of $100 a month, each month, every month—such money makes me suspicious). Yevgeny's stomach moans so loud it sometimes startles him when he works. Yevgeny is sick from starving. Yes? Yes, indeed, Yevgeny Mikhailovich is most certainly sick from starving. He is so happy to take dinner with young Karnovsky.

But then you write, "Do you need help?" I reply differently than I do to an invitation to dinner (in a good restaurant, I hope, where I can have borscht and pirogi, a piece of boiled beef with potatoes and more cabbage, good, yes, and beer, maybe a vodka? O wonderful invitation!). Yevgeny Mikhailovich does not want help. Help is help, sir. It comes or it doesn't. If I have to ask for it (which I am required to do since I am expected to answer the question you put: "Do you need help?" honored et cetera, et cetera), it is no longer what it starts out to be. It becomes instead conversation in the air. If I have to answer the question, the burden falls on me. I am compelled to please and supplicate. Rather than do that, I would tell you to put your offer back into your mouth and grind your teeth. I do not ask for help. (But for God's sake, young Karnovsky, take the trouble to read between these lines.)

It will interest you to know that I have thought a great deal about the time I have saved by not eating during the past six months. If I could make time into space and lay minutes end to end, my savings would not mount to the heavens, but I would have saved at least several miles of time. Counting up my daily savings: not less than eighty minutes saved each day. Multiplying, I gather for my art 560 minutes in a week—enough for a few drawings, enough for a small oil, also enough for a large headache and an irritable stomach, interminable dry belches and sour farts. And yet, with all this saving for art, I grow weak and tired. Perhaps it is not wise making virtue out of such a grave deficiency as food. I am a drought and a famine. How can I make utopics the glory of God if I starve to death? I long to meet you. 8 P.M. this evening at your hotel.

The letter was signed in full, the letters carefully written. It was not an afterthought, since the pen pressure was even and fluent, but Yevgeny Mikhailovich felt constrained to add to his identity the single word "Painter," as though Karnovsky had not known to whom he had written his letter.

## *Twelve*

J. Alexander Karnovsky had installed himself at a small table in the hotel dining room, separated by large potted rubber plants from the small lobby that fronted the street. He wanted to see Yevgeny Mikhailovich before he was seen. He needed to measure and appraise. (*Who is that large mass that has just shouldered his way through the glass doors? It couldn't be Malenov. It is not even twenty minutes to the hour of our appointment.*) Karnovsky needed a preview, a foretaste. (*What's he doing? He's thrown open a large bear coat, shivering with icicles. He's tinkling like a chandelier and melting sound into the carpet. He's left a small puddle at the desk.*) All afternoon, Alexander had paced his hotel room. He drew a little; he composed sketches and drafts of ideas as though already on Malenov's staff; he imagined conducting tours through the Malenov Museum of Abstract Art, of which, naturally, he was director, exhibiting his own work in a small gallery where disciples and epigones hung their second-generation reflections. (*Now he's talking to the desk clerk, wagging his large head from side to side; at last, he has removed his fur hat and, in a single gesture, wriggled out of the bear coat, which he has dropped in a heap on the rug, and thrown his hat on the pile. He's laughing uproariously. What's so funny? Could it be Malenov? The vast body turns; seizing his fur in an enormous fist, he lifts the wet and dripping arctic apparel and flings it on a smooth leather couch, slumping down beside it. Oh. God. It is Malenov. So large!*) Alexander couldn't imagine anyone so large. Not tall, although he was reasonably tall, but packed, congealed, massive, as though his body had been carved from an ancient tree of spectacular girth. He was a lumbering creature, with rounded shoulders and slabby sides like a well-padded animal, his hair—he remembered the image in the first photograph he had razored from *Querschnitt* months before—dropped down his head, matty, stringy, like flaps that obscured sound and interference, provided warmth and cover, and imparted to his head an effect at once formidable and childlike. Alexander lit one of his cheroots and drank off a glass of wine. He was suddenly unnerved; his heart stuttered, caught on the same beat; his lower lip began to quiver. So this was the great artist whom he had traveled from America to meet.

Malenov sat now in the lobby, leaning forward slightly, his head turning from side to side, watching every movement, expecting J. Alexander Karnovsky to enter from the street, to descend by the stairwell, to exit from the elevator, to emerge from the restroom, to materialize from behind a potted plant. Several times Yevgeny's eyes had passed over the face of Alexander Karnovsky, blinking nervously, but his glance continued to peregrinate the lobby, engorging a small dog that dangled from a leash tied to one of the rubber plants while its owner ate on the other side, narrowing to entangle a young man —much too young, Yevgeny muttered, dismissing him with a wave of his hand and refusing to tie him in the snares of inquiry—returning to Alexander Karnovsky, who answered a stare with fascinated curiosity, once half-rising to break the strain, but falling back, as there was still time before the hour. Yevgeny Mikhailovich belched and covered his mouth with the back of his hand; he reached into the side pocket of his threadbare jacket—a thin weave of indistinction and brown—and pulled out Karnovsky's letter, flattening it and laying it beside him on the couch, imagining that if the young American passed through the lobby, undecided as to who (although Malenov and the dog were the only creatures waiting in the lobby) had been the recipient of his dinner invitation, he would see the letter, understand instantly, and approach. And then, suddenly, the bells of the city began to strike the hour. 8 P.M. J. Alexander Karnovsky, dressed in gray flannels with a silk tie of conservative stripes, stood up from his table and calmly—so it appeared—walked from behind a rubber plant, his hand extended. "So you are Malenov, whom I have crossed the ocean to meet."

Yevgeny Mikhailovich remained seated. Too lethargic and disarticulated, he could not instantly come to his feet and seize the white hand ribboned with delicate blue veins that hung in the air before him. He let the hand remain extended, watching it intently, ignoring the face of Alexander Karnovsky. When the fingers began to curl and bunch, dropping with indifference to Karnovsky's side, it was Yevgeny who saluted him, lumbering to his feet, towering over Karnovsky, his mouth open, lips drawn back into a rigid smile of amazement. As little as Karnovsky had anticipated the immense Malenov, Malenov was startled by what he perceived to be Karnovsky's physical insignificance, his precarious slightness, the elegant, somewhat troubled features of face, his light complexion, his thin eyebrows. Karnovsky didn't add up to much. He seemed weightless. However, Yevgeny had seen the nerveless focus of the eyes, black and ungentle, examining him rapidly with the precision of a professional appraiser who was expected to observe quickly and in detail anything of value that might fetch a price at the bankrupt's sale of personal possessions. Karnovsky's small black eyes hardly flickered. They seemed dead and yet they were alive, tugging at one of Yevgeny's ears, hooking into Yevgeny's tattered shirt and frayed cuffs, dropping disdainfully to Yevgeny's scuffed high shoes, whose laces were knotted at several places where they had snapped. Alexander's eyes, hidden in deep sockets where they swiveled in their clandestine orbits, conducted his brain over the outcroppings of Yevgeny's face. Yevgeny knew that he was focused on and observed; Karnovsky was certain that he had caught everything.

An instant of silence; traces of suspicion; the last shudders of fright; and both burst into greetings that rose higher and higher until over-arched by Yevgeny's fluted cry of hunger. "Aaay! I starve. I must eat. Now. If you don't mind, young gentleman. I must eat. To the first business, first." Alexander's face relaxed, the eyes rested, and the fair face shone suddenly with warmth and generosity as he turned toward the dining room and, with a wave of his arm, bowing like a master of ceremonies, conducted Yevgeny Mikhailovich to a table set in a quiet corner of the restaurant. A splendid dinner unfolded: a rich soup bubbling with hospitality, a platter of roasted chicken with specially cooked side dishes of kasha and mushrooms, red cabbage and cranberries, a green salad with cheese, and strawberry tarts. Vodka and wines. Eat and eat. Talk later after stomachs were filled and Yevgeny lay slumped in contentment.

"And so, now, are you satisfied?" Alexander asked quietly when coffee arrived accompanied by a small dish of chocolates.

"Indeed. So much so that I thank you, young gentleman, for your kindness." Alexander nodded. It seemed to be going all right. The bear was sated.

"May we talk now about art?" Alexander inquired, moving his chair back from the table and crossing his legs. "May we talk about art? That is what brings me this distance, Yevgeny Mikhailovich. For nothing else would I be impetuous enough to cross the ocean during winter. The sea was malevolent. Monstrous waves and powerful winds. I stayed below throughout the journey. Sick the whole time. Yes, a dreadful passage. But it's all behind me now that I see you, Yevgeny Mikhailovich."

"Yes," Yevgeny grunted, snatching up a chocolate and dropping it into his upturned mouth. "I see. Of course. And all to see *me*," he twinkled. "So young man, what do you see? And what do you know about me?"

Karnovsky gulped. The examination begins, he winced. "Too little, I'm afraid, but I have done some work on you, rather more than you would imagine. If nothing else, I am ingenious."

Karnovsky described his first hearing of Malenov's name in the Broadway cafeteria. Malenov listened, trying to guess the identity of the old couple who had spoken of him so knowingly. ("Who could they be?" he wondered aloud.) Karnovsky proceeded to review the articles and essays, documents and photographs that he had accumulated. Yevgeny was impressed by Karnovsky's ingenuity. He was clearly useful. Of that Yevgeny was certain. Whether he was talented, a gifted artist, that was another matter and—Yevgeny readily confessed to himself—one considerably more ambiguous and even, perhaps, of less importance. It was unclear to Yevgeny whether he wanted Karnovsky to be gifted. (A secretary, an amanuensis, a body servant need have no comprehension of the master; indeed, for the performance of indispensable but modest tasks, the less critical the eye, the less judging the raised eyebrow, the less scrupulous and appraising the servant's intelligence, the more likely the work will be done promptly and without reservations.) But, already, Yevgeny Mikhailovich knew that he would have to compromise. The young man before him knew too much, was too worldly, too accomplished in the fashionable to be content to receive orders and be expected to obey them. Yevgeny was thinking to himself, half-listening to Karnovsky's artful quotation of passages from the press, already somewhat bored with the accomplished ventriloquism of his young acquaintance.

"And what does all this have to do with me? Yes. Yes. You know all about me, everything that they"—he waved dismissively about him, implicating the others ostensibly filling the near-empty dining room—"know about me: surfaces and exteriors. But I am not there at the surface. I do not hang on the body of the universe like a flesh pink or a wispy violet. You know that. I am more than all this press nonsense. Let's go see. Right now. Let's go see. We will go to my room and we will look at paintings. What do you say to that?"

Alexander Karnovsky was delighted. He signed the check, organized a pile of banknotes for the waitress, retrieved his fur coat from the cloakroom, and hailed a taxi at the entrance to the hotel. Twenty minutes later they were standing before Yevgeny's door, reading the memoranda posted for the importuning public. "These notices are serious?" Alexander asked quietly. "I find them frightening."

"They are meant to frighten. Surely. How else should it be? If we artists behaved exactly the way the world expected, it would destroy us. It is a Malenovian rule: never assimilate! Anything that the world asks you to do, consider whether it would not be preferable—on principle and even if it goes against self-interest—to refuse. There are, for instance, many times that I would love to be interrupted while I work. It goes badly. I am hungry and I stop to make tea. I hear shoe-shuffling before my door. I know it is someone who hopes to catch my attention—a journalist, a dealer, perhaps even a collector. They come all the way to this filthy slum; they climb the stairs; and what do they find on this door but another in a long train of Malenovian rebuffs: Go away. Malenov is not at home. Malenov is painting. Malenov is in a nasty mood and will bite you." Growling and gnashing of teeth. "Actually, the truth is that I am desperate for a human face. I am tired of my floating projectiles and empty space. But if I give in, if I behave like an ordinary bourgeois, I am doomed. Word will get out. Oh, that Malenov, it's all theater. I had a nice chat with him today. Dear fellow, even gave me a cup of tea. Oh, you say he's a genius. Not at all. Pleasant, ordinary sort. That's what they'd say. The myth would dissolve. I would go on making great paintings. It wouldn't affect my work, but it would be harder to get them to believe that what I'm doing here is desperately important not only to my salvation but to theirs. Yes, truly, my stay-away notices are meant to frighten off the packs of wolves that gather at my door, sniffing, scratching."

Karnovsky was impressed. Malenov had spoken to him privately, personally, revealing a hidden side, an unknown reason. He resolved to write it all down when he returned to the hotel. He would make a beginning at keeping notes and records, gathering the information he would need one day for a definitive study of the Master. The door was opened, the bulb tightened in its socket, and the green-visored light diffused a slummy hue. The bed was unmade, a candle burned before Saint Sergius, and paintings were stacked by the score against the wall. Yevgeny pulled out his stool and seated Alexander upon it. Without removing his coat, he began to show his work. Each painting was presented for several minutes, hung on a nail, bathed in the mean light. Raised up, each of the paintings was exposed in a kind of logical sequence as though the order had been planned, the continuity formulated as a strategy of presentation and conversion. The paintings unfolded the elements of the projectivist vocabulary, spatial forms, architectural masses, signs and symbols of the new grammar of affirmation and denial out of which Malenov conceived the universe to be fashioned: elements and devices, painted with a perfect simplicity and flatness, without narrative allusion or indication of similitudes, direct and uncomplicated colors on a white or black ground. Small, iconic pictures. And then as the paintings proceeded, the elements came together, several elements appeared within the same space, spaces embraced and coalesced, combined and passed through, shadow space, real space, objects projecting into infinite worlds where the Malenovian vision of reconstruction was to be consummated.

Three hours later it was done. It was past midnight, and the streets were silent. The taxicab that Karnovsky had ordered to wait, its lights extinguished, was the only vehicle below. Cold frosted the windowpanes. Malenov no longer moved. He waited. Minutes expired while he waited. Karnovsky thought intently. It would have to be right. There would be no second chance from this genius.

"We both come from Great Russia," Alexander at last began. "I come from a different world than your own, but I know something about your world. Our worlds were never the same, although they touched and passed each other in language, in literature, in memories and affections. These paintings. They are like nothing I have ever seen. But they do remind me powerfully of something out of the tradition of Great Russia. Mostly the color. Where have I seen such remarkable silk colors, such amazing diaphanous blues, such rose, such grays as those from which you build your humane abstract spaces? The icon. The great Russian icon. It is as though you have taken all the miracles of the icon—all its eternal power—and retold them as stories of divine space." Alexander stood up suddenly and embraced Malenov, folding his arms around his shoulders. And then, mysteriously, he burst into tears. "I don't understand what you've done. It is a great body of work, so great. I will have to study it and learn. Will that be possible?"

On that unanswered question the evening ended. The two artists agreed to meet the following day for another meal, this time a luncheon, after which they promised to visit museums and galleries together. The education was fated to begin.

A brief extract from Malenov's journal, which I found under the date of their first meeting and had translated.

> Today I met this young and not unappealing Jew from New
> York who travels the ocean to learn more of my work. He
> insinuates it that way. I am become a project of learning.
> Ha! My work is no problem to be examined. If there ever was
> a problem in painting, my paintings have solved it. I have
> no doubts about my work. Why should I have doubts? If my
> achievement were recognized and celebrated, then I would

have doubts. Otherwise, as it is, I am entitled to be sure. I am so alone. Will this Karnovsky make me happy? Or will he mock my loneliness and—when I least suspect it—rob me of my genius. . . . And do I take him seriously when he celebrates our icon? He, child of a race of iconoclasts, how can he understand our flat little depictions of sanctity? He is quite right, of course. My pictures owe a great deal to the icons—not their subject, but their application of paint and their frontality. But how can this young Jew understand all that? It worries me that he speaks of icons. Either he lies about his feelings or, worse yet, he has no feelings about the subject at all. And so his tears are lies and he tries to deceive me. I do not know. But be watchful, Yevgeny Mikhailovich. Be watchful. Enjoy yourself, but be watchful.

The following days were delicious for the Master and his young friend, for Alexander Karnovsky and his new paternity in art. They were inseparable, meeting for a late breakfast, trudging through the snow and observing the curious Germans, visiting museums, taking in the art galleries, seeing a Charlie Chaplin film, going to theater, eating meals and drinking wines, running into Fraulein Kammerer at Die Florelle, taking coffee at the Café des Westens, rummaging in bookstores, visiting nightclubs, dancing fox trot with the girls ("I love the fox trot and I'm also good—you don't believe me—at tango. Watch me, young Sasha"). By the end of a week, Alexander was allowed to call his teacher, now friend, Yevgeny, sometimes even Zhenya, most often Yevgeny Mikhailovich. He found calling him Master uncomfortable and vaguely unsettling, although he had done so repeatedly during their early meetings. But it was particularly discomforting to Alexander when he went to buy tickets or pay a check or hand change to the program seller or the cab driver. Yevgeny had no money, and here Alexander was calling this impoverished, unkempt genius Master while he continuously paid out money on his behalf. He wasn't sure what made him uncomfortable. If anything, the older should be attending to the needs and follies of the younger. Not the other way round. And yet here he was, a young man approaching his twenty-second year, fumbling for bills and scooping change from his coat pocket to amuse and recreate this unworldly, indeed unaware, artist in his early forties. However, it pleased more than it unsettled Karnovsky; he had a sense of his power and enforced it, buying more for Yevgeny than was required, certainly more than was asked for (a warm button-front sweater, a wool scarf, a new teapot and an assortment of Russian teas, a pair of fur-lined winter boots, and a book on Russian icons with a particularly marvelous reproduction of the famous icon of Saint Sergius on which Yevgeny's was modeled). Some of the gifts he bought when he was by himself, wandering, cut adrift, shopping, but more often he bought most cannily when they were together, admiring the displays in the great department stores. Karnovsky would observe Yevgeny's eyes coveting something, and the moment Yevgeny had gone off, attracted by another counter, Karnovsky would return, surreptitiously acquire, say, the black woolen scarf, wrap it, hide it behind his back, and, as the attendant pushed open the doors to shuttle them back into the winter of Berlin, Karnovsky would reveal the package, ceremoniously untie it, produce the scarf (or gloves or beaver cap) and present them to an embarrassed Yevgeny.

"Too much. It embarrasses me."

"What embarrasses you?"

"These gifts." He pointed to a chair at the table in the konditorei where they stopped for late afternoon coffee and counted off four items of vesture and garb, some still in their boxes, some already worn and frosted with snow. "It embarrasses me. No. I feel humiliated, Alexander." He became passionate and rapped the table with his knuckles to emphasize his unhappiness.

"It would be better, wouldn't it, if the arrangement were different? Yes. You know, I would prefer if you gave me gifts. Yes. I would really prefer it. But that will take time. These gifts, dear Zhenya, these are money gifts. They are of no importance. What you will soon give me—all the intangible gift of your genius—well, that will really be a priceless gift, an incomparable gift."

"Yes? So!" Yevgeny Mikhailovich fell silent, thinking about his incomparable gift. It almost made sense, the young man's logic, but he caught himself breathing with difficulty, a sudden constriction tightening his chest, and he touched his heart lightly.

A second week had gone. Yevgeny Mikhailovich hadn't painted since Karnovsky's arrival. Karnovsky, for his part, had stopped sketching and had begun writing voluminous entries in his journal, annotating Malenov's person, history, remarks and observations, his predilections and preferences in art, his ferocities and rages (rather more general and diffuse than his enthusiasms). On a separate page he noted expenses in order to satisfy, he claimed, mere curiosity. Karnovsky wrote every night with his final brandy and every morning with his waking coffee. And another day would begin, very much like the previous one. He worked exceptionally hard with Malenov. One night as he fell exhausted into bed, he realized for the first time that it had all ceased to be pleasure. It was without interlude, relief, interruption. No other person intruded. They were a most unlikely, inseparable couple, seldom out of each other's sight, seldom far from each other's ear. Sometimes Malenov spoke uninterruptedly, imagining aloud, re-creating the history of his youth or describing in detail the early adventures of the Russian avant-garde, recalling his arguments with Livshits, his fights with the Burliuks, his gambols, drunken, with Mayakovsky—all liveliness and wit. But at other times he plunged ahead into the snow, leaving Karnovsky behind, refusing to speak, clenching his jaws shut, while Karnovsky tried to relieve Malenov's sudden melancholy with the offer of a bunch of flowers or a plate of steaming pirogi from a street kiosk. Nothing had been resolved, no arrangements had been discussed, no program of association defined. It had to be faced. Rich though he was, with more than enough money to pay for the diversion of the Master, Karnovsky was fast approaching the point where something formal needed to be settled if he were to avoid having to cable New York for funds. He preferred not to deal with his father at this juncture. There would be time for that.

"The time has come, Zhenya. We have to settle something." They were seated in the dining room of Karnovsky's hotel having a drink before going off to supper. "Don't you think we have to settle something?"

"I don't understand, young friend. What are you talking about?"

Karnovsky was amazed. It was as though nothing had happened, as though more than two weeks of gift-giving and generosity had no significance (indeed, in one description of those weeks, Karnovsky referred in his journal to the absence of a "pay-off"—the precise phrase). "Talking about? Am I mad, Zhenya? Am I going mad or already mad? I wrote you a long letter, my very first letter in fact. I said it all there. *Clearly*! I wanted to work for you, to collaborate with you, to learn from you. More than two weeks have passed since we met. We haven't traveled out of each other's sight for a minute. We are to all the world like odd—the phrase would be—lovers and yet we aren't lovers, surely, but rather acquaintances who have become friends, who having become friends must now become fellow workers in the cause of projectivism and utopics. No? Isn't this a correct description?"

Yevgeny Mikhailovich again felt a sudden tightness in his chest. He could barely breathe. He pulled at a button of his shirt and opened the collar, loosening the new striped tie that throttled his throat. "I can't speak yet, my friend. Give me a moment to breathe. I need to think. But continue, yes, continue. Let me hear all of it."

"The major questions," Karnovsky continued, "remain unresolved. May I assist in supporting you? How much may I give you each month? May I work for you? (Payment enough for my support.) Do you wish to continue to live here and work in Berlin? Do we live together? But even if we don't, you need more space, better space, proper materials, and, most important, Zhenya, most important of all, we need a program. How shall we bring you to the world?"

Yevgeny Mikhailovich flushed red; his temples began to pound. He groaned. He was convinced that he was about to have another visitation. He waited while his temples pounded and his head, streaked with pain, swelled and diminished, expanding his brains and crushing them beneath his weighty carapace. "Aaaaay," he groaned aloud. Several heads turned and frowned. Germans disliked public display. ("A noisy Slav," somebody muttered behind him from a table of stocky businessmen.) But nothing happened. The rush of terror washed through his body and drained away; his feet, once heavy as though the fluid of anxiety had pounded through his thighs, descended his legs, and caused his ankles to swell in size, now drained out into the rug through his fur-lined boots. Karnovsky was frightened. It was all embarrassing, these displays and tantrums. It reminded him of the little fits of his own childhood, childish demonstrations of terror. But here, before him, was a man he believed to be one of the great artists of the age, still unknown and unrecognized, but clearly a genius of modern art, who heaved in front of him and moaned as though an electrical charge had just coursed his body.

"Are you all right?" Karnovsky asked timidly after some minutes of watching Yevgeny's agonies.

"Nothing. Nothing at all. It was only," he paused and thought a second, "it was only that I thought I was beginning to see the future. But it was nothing." He did not explain, and Karnovsky, his own terror renewed, did not dare to ask. The conversation was definitively interrupted, and they went off to dinner. It was only much later, seated beside each other on a banquette in a spacious ballroom, watching elegant couples glide and whirl, that Yevgeny suddenly began to speak, remembering each phrase that Karnovsky had used hours before, addressing himself directly to the matter before them, as though the conversation had never been broken off.

"Indeed, yes, you have a point, Karnovsky. You have come a great distance to meet me. We have been, yes, yes, inseparable for two weeks. You are convincing. I have watched you carefully. You seem to be telling the truth. Not what you say. But what you do. You have been greatly generous with me and you have kept your distance. I don't think you harm me. No. I agree then. Let us find a nice studio, with a few rooms attached, and a small kitchen. Not much, but better than now. You will have a room for yourself. We will see how it goes. Yes? What do you think? By the way, does Karnovsky cook?"

Karnovsky was stunned, but he agreed. (January 21, 1928: "He has caved in—quite unpredictably. I thought it would take much longer.") The following day, they began to look for an appropriate apartment and found one on Sigmaringerstrasse in Wilmersdorf, not far from the Preussen Park, where of an afternoon they could sit, surrounded by trees and shrubs, and drink tea from a thermos. The rooms were spacious and well lighted. The largest, with solid walls and a parquet floor, became Yevgeny's studio; in the rear were two bedrooms, a narrow, sufficient kitchen, and a generous bath where Yevgeny sometimes took himself for an afternoon of hydrophilic indulgence. Nothing to do then but move in. The furniture was adequate, even stylish. Their landlord, an aging doctor who had come up from Swabia during the war to work in a military hospital, was now retired and living on the income from his small country estate. He was descended, he announced, from a convoluted line of Swabian aristocracy who, he insisted, were all inbred and, therefore, slightly mad. His eccentricity consisted in little more than wearing a moth-eaten woman's wig atop his own thinning hairline; he laughed at himself, but persisted. It bothered no one in postwar Berlin. He, for his part, thought the ménage of Yevgeny Mikhailovich Malenov and Alexander Karnovsky equally strange and, hence, never removed his woman's wig when he came to bring them their mail or deliver a package.

The first weeks were tense. Neither Yevgeny Mikhailovich nor Alexander Karnovsky had ever had a roommate. Each was hardly suited to living with another. Their ways were irritatingly dissimilar. Yevgeny Mikhailovich scattered papers and trash, dropped paint on the floor, never shut doors, endlessly chattered to himself, explaining the universe to each of his paintings, and allowed himself the luxury of large and expressive eructations. Alexander Karnovsky thought Malenov a peasant—coarse and vulgar like a peasant, but also strong and resilient. Yevgeny did not mind carrying out the garbage, moving heavy furniture, trudging up the three flights of stairs with baskets of vegetables and bottles of milk. Karnovsky, by contrast, was a cat, silent, gliding on felt paws (he walked about the apartment in his bedroom slippers), sitting in a darkened room accustoming his eyes to shadows and gloom, or else, unpredictably, bursting into song, playing tinny records of Chaliapin, Caruso, or Lucrezia Bori. But somehow they managed not to get on each other's nerves. They acknowledged their difference, spoke about it openly, admired the ingenuity of God for having brought such unlikely creatures together into an association of art and service. Their world composed itself, the Odessan Jew from New York, the Ukrainian from Moscow, seated side by side in a bright apartment in southwest central Berlin at the end of the 1920s.

Bizarre, but also idyllic, you might think. I thought so for a time, until I found an outrageous passage in Malenov's diary that referred to the tremendous argument that broke out between them on the 26th of April, 1928. Karnovsky's journal for that day, on the other hand, said nothing further than "A brief discord."

"The swine," Malenov's diary began.

> Now I begin to understand what is going on. I knew it couldn't be as simple as it seemed. Nothing as simple as that he loves and admires me and will do anything to serve my art. The swine! He saves everything I throw out. Everything. I thought it helpful of him to do the house cleaning, to dust the rooms occasionally, even—although not often—to make my bed, to pick up after me, to put my brushes in turpentine. I thought

all of this an unexpected kindness. He did all this when I went out for a stroll or to visit Die Florelle. He said he would stay behind and keep house. Sometimes, I would return after several hours in the late afternoon and a large tea would be ready and we would sit in the last light and talk about painting. But all that nice nice was simply a trick, a way of putting me off guard while he collected my leavings, gathered up everything I wanted burned and saved it. Why, Alexander Karnovsky? Why do you save up my shit bits? If I don't want them, how dare you save them? It's all business, you think. Everything to do with Malenov can be made into business, you say to yourself. Well, I'll show you, young man, I'll show you.

It had come about this way. It is true—undeniably—that Karnovsky had been emptying the trashcans, salvaging bits of paper on which Malenov had drawn, even saving ends of canvas where Malenov had tried out the colors he had mixed. Karnovsky had gathered and sequestered, marking each drawing with the date of its disposal, noting the painting to which it pertained (because Malenov's paintings were never given titles until they were exhibited, the only way a sketch could be correlated with the finished work was by drawing on its recto a miniature of the finished work with which it was connected). During the three months that they had lived together before Malenov made his discovery of Karnovsky's oversized album, Karnovsky had removed and identified several hundred sketches, drafts, visual notes, and color swatches.

The day Malenov decided to check up on his colleague by going through Karnovsky's belongings, Karnovsky had decided to spend the afternoon wandering by himself in Berlin. That is what he told Malenov. Actually, he had arranged a luncheon with Francine Kammerer to discuss the career of Yevgeny Mikhailovich. Fraulein Kammerer had no idea that Yevgeny might be interested in an exhibition. By the end of lunch, it was arranged. Alexander Karnovsky thought it would make Yevgeny happy. He rushed from Die Florelle to the house on Sigmaringerstrasse. He was eager to tell Yevgeny the news that the Lehrter Galerie would mount a major exhibition of Malenov's Berlin works, to open at precisely the time that tourists flood into Berlin during June. Francine Kammerer was enthusiastic. "It is so important to see his work. Even I hardly know it, but if Malevich swears by Malenov, who am I to say otherwise?" she said smiling. (Alexander Karnovsky watched her smile and shivered; a bit of lipstick clung to her white teeth, as though a drop of blood had fallen from a slow leak in her brain. It excited him oddly.)

Alexander quietly opened the door to the flat. He smelled smoke. Easter was just past, and Yevgeny had spent the better part of the previous week swooning in the Russian church; he always grew a beard at Eastertime, his gesture of mourning for his wounded and murdered God. It had turned warm, however, so what was fire doing in the grate? "Yevgeny," he called out, but received no reply. And yet he knew that Yevgeny was in the studio, sitting before the grate. He felt Yevgeny's lumbering presence like a black cloud hovering over a spring field. "Yevgeny," he called again as he opened the double doors into the studio.

"My God," was all he said. Yevgeny Mikhailovich was sitting in front of the fire, slowly ripping each drawing from Karnovsky's album and throwing it into the flames. "You swine," Yevgeny mumbled. "How dare you save what I throw out? Who are you to decide what is to be saved? Are you the artist? You swine. How dare you?"

Whatever it was that Yevgeny expected to elicit by his spring bonfire, it somehow failed. Alexander Karnovsky was neither humiliated nor abashed, nor was he stricken with guilt and apologies. Rather, he kept repeating a softly spoken American curse until Yevgeny Mikhailovich finally turned and, curious, inquired, "What is this 'asshole'?"

"You, Zhenya. You're the asshole. What do you think you're doing?

Embarrassing me, trapping me in some secret activity, catching me out doing something you didn't authorize? Listen, Yevgeny Mikhailovich, you may be a genius, but you're also an asshole. Now, what that means, in case you don't know the expression, is that you sometimes have your brains up your ass instead of in your head." Alexander Karnovsky said all of this in a quiet voice. He didn't lose his temper; he never lost his temper. In fact, having heard reports of other episodes not unlike this one, I can suppose that Alexander Karnovsky expressed all his outrage in a conversational tone, without his cheeks reddening, without ever stamping a foot or pounding a wall.

Yevgeny Mikhailovich had imagined that, caught out, the young scoundrel would confess to something outrageous, but there was nothing outrageous to confess. Quite the opposite, as Alexander Karnovsky went on to explain. He saved all this random detritus covertly so as not to make Yevgeny self-conscious. He annotated and marked everything in order to provide the basis of a documentary archive, without which Yevgeny's work could not be correctly described in years to come, when all that would remain would be the work itself. Speaking quietly, his calm explanation punctuated by an occasional "asshole" of diminished annoyance, he eventually calmed Yevgeny Mikhailovich sufficiently that he stopped ripping work from the album and burning it. At last he closed the album, lifted it from his lap, and shoved it beneath the sofa. The one-act drama had come to a close: "Yevgeny is truly sorry. Please forgive him." Alexander went over and squeezed his neck affectionately.

(It was never clear to me, however, whether Yevgeny's description of this incident in his diary was made before or after Alexander Karnovsky's return. It seems hardly likely—given Malenov's psychology—that he would, in the midst of fury, take time to write even an outraged entry. Hardly likely. In that case, it must be assumed that despite his apology he remained enraged; that his suspicions once aroused were not so easily allayed; and that hours after the confrontation he wrote out his condemnation of Karnovsky. All this remains, however, my conjecture.)

Alexander decided not to tell Yevgeny Mikhailovich about his visit with Francine Kammerer of the Lehrter Galerie until the following day. Yevgeny was immensely pleased, though he did not dance to the news as was sometimes his habit when overwhelmed by the un-expected. But when Fraulein Kammerer arrived at the studio the following week to discuss the exhibition, make a preliminary selection of the works to be presented, negotiate terms, dates, Yevgeny was almost charming, his bullishness withdrawn, and he listened passively as Alexander Karnovsky raised all the necessary questions, made notes on their discussion, and served coffee.

"You choose well," Yevgeny announced generously as the afternoon waned to a close.

"That pleases me," she responded. "It is an achievement, this work of yours. It is the line between Russia and the West that has been missing. Nothing more is heard from Malevich, and Lissitzky is also back in Moscow (and not well, you know . . . his lungs)." She added ominously, "It's all up to you, Herr Malenov." Yevgeny seemed mo-mentarily troubled; he resisted carrying the burden of modern art. Alexander Karnovsky was, however, delighted; the young woman seemed well able to appreciate his Master. "And the gallery would like to purchase in advance of the exhibition those three paintings," she stated matter-of-factly, pointing to three canvases that described the link between Malevich and the De Stijl paintings of Mondrian and van Doesburg. It was a wise choice. Those paintings, after all, now occupy a position of considerable importance in the collection of the Stedelijk Museum in Amsterdam, whose director bought them some years later to document the connection between the Soviet avant-garde and Western abstract painting. Yevgeny Mikhailovich for an instant seemed deliciously happy; a smile broke through his cloudy, overcast face, and he shook Francine Kammerer's hand with both of his, saluting her on her good judgment. (It seems an oddly sententious gesture, but if you have observed, as often as I have, painters suddenly overcome by delight amid their ongoing social ineptitude, it frequently turns out this way: the artist congratulating the collector on his intelligence, or prudence, or good sense, but really meaning, how good to make a sale, to have money to put aside, to be at last recognized by the coin of the realm.) They discussed the price, briefly, Karnovsky keeping silent but attentive, and when the price was settled and paid over, it was arranged that Yevgeny Mikhailovich would come to the gallery later in the week for a visit with Fraulein Kammerer, at which time the paintings would be delivered. An unbusinesslike transaction—this paying first and delivering later—but trust is always unbusinesslike.

"In the meantime," she concluded pleasantly, "keep those pictures for me. They are my treasures now."


## Thirteen

Yevgeny Mikhailovich fell in love. Hardly credible. Everything we know about Yevgeny Mikhailovich denies it. Vast though he was, in the domain of sex he appeared stunted and diminished, restricted to his nighttime fugues of fantasy and voyeurism, staring at the album of his little delights, delights of both sexes caught in their wavering androgyny. He had never shown interest in grown-up women and yet (surprisingly to Karnovsky) he seemed suddenly overcome by Francine Kammerer. Yevgeny had first thrilled to her solicitude when they had met the year before at the Lehrter Galerie, but he had forgotten about her during his Bavarian holiday. It was only when they encountered one another by chance at Die Florelle and Yevgeny had introduced her to Karnovsky and they had shared a table and drank a musky pot of Lapsang Souchong together—brewed and stirred to perfection by the son of the master of teas—that Yevgeny thought again about

Fraulein Kammerer, installing an image of her kindness and attention in his small cabinet of private images. During that second meeting, while Alexander was brewing and stirring, swishing hot water, and compelling their aging waiter to learn the methods for properly offering fine tea, Yevgeny had engaged Francine Kammerer in conversation, doing more than rumbling and growling, actually undertaking to speak sequentially about the new Russian art, looking if not in her eyes then just slightly above them to her lofty forehead, and in the course of their hour together agitating a perplexing unease that caused his hand to tremble as he helped her into her coat and bade her farewell. She smiled deliciously and thanked him for having struggled to explain himself in German. "I hope we will meet again." Yevgeny Mikhailovich, suddenly agonized by his forwardness, retreated into Russian, saying something unintelligible, and they parted.

Karnovsky, for his part, was disconcerted by Yevgeny's interest in the woman. She seemed unlike the girls he invariably chose when they went out to dance. On those few occasions, Yevgeny selected only tall and undeveloped young women, whose long faces, deadened with layers of powder, made them appear more like mannequins than agile and swift dancers whom he led ponderously through the required steps. Yevgeny danced poorly, despite his conviction that he moved like Valentino, but he conducted himself with a kind of gravity that pleased his partners, and they always presented themselves again whenever he appeared at the spacious dance hall. But Francine Kammerer was unlike Yevgeny's dancing girls, somewhat on the short side, with blond hair that she pushed back from her right eye with a red index finger. Whenever she talked, her blue eyes flashed comprehension and her white teeth, gladdened by conversation, were slightly parted; she was always attentive, ready to join in, to respond, to carry forward the interlocution. Francine Kammerer was highly intelligent and knew it. She understood her business and accepted both the responsibility and the embarrassment of being the owner of an important little art gallery that had enough sense to be ahead of fashion and not enough aggression to become rich.

Yevgeny Mikhailovich was obviously delighted by the explicit con-fusion in Francine Kammerer of enthusiasm and ignorance, familiarity and inexpertness. It relieved him of the tortures of silence and banality that always afflicted him during his dance tourneys, where he never knew what to say after the dance was over. He thought he was obliged to do more than offer his partner a glass of wine and pay her for her time; indeed, once, persuaded that his young partner wanted to engage him in conversation, he announced to her as he poured her a second glass of champagne, "You know I am Russian painter," to which she replied, "How splendid! Will you paint me? I've always wanted a little portrait to send my old mother." "Not portraits of people, but of universe," Yevgeny replied, and the conversation stopped as abruptly as it had begun. But with Francine Kammerer, Yevgeny had gone on and on. Karnovsky knew that Fraulein Kammerer was sympathetic to Malenov's work and he determined to test her interest, but he somehow feared Yevgeny Mikhailovich would waste time with her.

"We must thank Fraulein Kammerer for our food and lodgings. Yes?" Yevgeny announced after she had departed, putting all the money he had received for his paintings in Alexander's charge.

"It comes at a good time. My bank transfer is late again," was all Alexander replied.

Several hours later, Yevgeny burst into Alexander's room, throwing open the door and startling the sleeping young man. "I think I am in love with Fraulein Kammerer," he announced. "You think—maybe —it is possible? I don't know. I have never loved anything alive before." He beamed with pleasure. It seemed such a novelty, an incomparable prospect, a remarkable occurrence, unknown to the world, unfamiliar to others, and hence for Yevgeny Mikhailovich a phenomenon of unspeakable originality. "I must go out," he con-cluded. "I must find her. I must tell her Yevgeny loves her." He disappeared before Karnovsky, shaking with drowsy incomprehension, could reply. And it was more than an hour before Karnovsky absorbed the revelation Malenov had proclaimed (after all, he had been asleep with dreams of his own). In love? Malenov in love? And what would become of Karnovsky if Malenov went off after Francine Kammerer? Alexander became ill, promptly and disgustingly ill, vomiting what he was persuaded was more than his last meal. His stomach ached from alarm, and he felt a certain soreness near his heart. He drank off a vodka to calm himself, but instead he became drunk, his head buzzing with fright, his stomach sour and turning with nausea. In love? How little Karnovsky mattered in such an equation, he complained. Just money. That's all he took himself to be—a source of money to be emptied and replenished. A damn Jewish banker is all he thinks of me. He began to cry with rage. He desperately hoped Malenov would return and find him beside himself with confusion and jealousy.

It is fortunate that Malenov never found out. Jealousy was well beyond the repertoire of emotions that occupied a central position in Malenov's life. Malenov was never jealous, certainly never envious. His estimation of himself was so well formulated and secure that he could regard the fortunate or miserable careers of others without drawing comparisons. If anything, Malenov's sense of the world was defective. Since he did not bother much with his own situation— taking poverty no less than well-being as an accident—he would never have understood why Alexander Karnovsky suffered such anxiety because he, Yevgeny Mikhailovich, had decided—improbably, to be sure—that he was in love.

Malenov was gone for hours. When he returned, he entered Alexander's room and, thinking that he was awake, announced in a sober and careful voice that he had finally found Francine Kammerer at her apartment. "I have told Fraulein Kammerer that I love her. She smiled at me when I told her. She did not punish me for telling her I love her. Good, no? I think she loves me back. Yes? Don't you think so, Sasha? I gave her cheek a pat. Even a small kiss goodbye.

I am so happy to love her. What do you think, Sasha?" He waited for several minutes for Karnovsky to answer, but Karnovsky was deep in a drunken sleep. "Aah, poor boy. He waits up for me and I come home so late. Tomorrow, I will tell him of love."

It went on like that for weeks. Yevgeny was besotted with Francine Kammerer. It never occurred to him that perhaps she was being uncommonly generous and available because he had joined her gallery and she was engaged in all the details of exhibiting his work. Every day, he went by the Lehrter Galerie to speak with her, to take her for luncheon or for tea. She was always polite, always smiled, always answered his questions directly and without guile. To his professions of love and fidelity, she replied unambiguously that he was a great painter. The inappropriateness of the reply never struck Yevgeny. Quite the contrary, he believed that every time he said, "My dear Fraulein Francine, how much I love you," and she answered, "You are a marvelous painter, Yevgeny," that a logical synapsis had occurred, that the appropriate and correct reply to his love was celebration of his genius. It made sense to Yevgeny Mikhailovich. It even, one suspects, made sense to Alexander Karnovsky, which made him all the more anxious and unsettled. Yevgeny no longer worked; he had bought a secondhand balalaika on which he picked out moony Russian ballads; he sometimes drank too much and curled up on the floor of his studio and fell asleep.

Alexander Karnovsky began to wonder why he stayed on. "Cut it, cut it," he shouted aloud in his room, but it was not easy to cut his losses, to cut his ties, to cut off and break for home. And, Alexander had begun to paint when Yevgeny stopped. There were so many hours now when Alexander was left to himself that he knew he had either to get to work or become hysterical. He began a series of black and red pictures, into whose undifferentiated ground he inserted letters of the Cyrillic alphabet, small verbal icons painted in contrasting black or white. (Severe little pictures of a certain handsomeness and indubitable derivation.) Alexander worked long hours on his suite of

pictures. Once Yevgeny entered without knocking while he was working. Alexander tried to cover the picture, but was too late. Embarrassed, he stepped back and watched Yevgeny think about the canvases. At last, "Very good, but too centered. Even the universe is
off its axis." That was all, but enough, quite enough. Alexander was
not thrilled, but he was encouraged. He began to work even harder,
deciding that it was best not to bother anymore about the ridiculous
love affair of Francine Kammerer and the Master.

Karnovsky's work, in fact, began to go well. What made Karnovsky's little series of alphabet paintings intrinsically interesting was
that he worked up the surface of the pictures to ensure a kind of
textured complexity in which brush, trowel, even finger could be
recognized. As well, Karnovsky began to mix up the Cyrillic alphabet
so that the letters ceased to be read as simple words but rather as a
jumble of marvelous shapes, whose literal meanings became the least
arresting aspect of the whole. Clearly, Malenov's praise had been
enough to excite him: the letters no longer sat on an invisible ruled
line but seemed in some cases to be thrown at the canvas, in others
to be falling off an unstated diagonal, and in yet others, like fat little
creatures in a children's book, to be tumbling off a wall. Karnovsky
worked every day, breaking in the afternoon for a stroll, sitting in the
park near the apartment, or drinking cognac in a café. He continued
to attend to Malenov, but his enthusiasm for documenting his every
move had somewhat diminished, particularly now that those moves
included trailing after a younger woman who, the Master had persuaded himself, understood his deepest soul. Karnovsky's reaction to
Malenov's infatuation was profound, but hardly audible.

The week before Malenov's exhibition was to open, Alexander
Karnovsky heard from home. He had written several times, brief notes,
little more than reassurance that he was alive, that he had met his
teacher, that they were working well, that life was promising. His
mother wrote him every week, a detailed letter of meticulous unim-
portance; his father sent him clippings from the newspapers that

mentioned the House of Karnovsky—one contained a photograph of his father tasting tea. It was the last communication he was to receive from his father. Shortly after that letter reached Berlin, a cable arrived announcing his father's illness. The message trembled with anguish: "DEAR FATHER HAS HAD A STROKE STOP I DO NOT KNOW IF HE WILL LIVE STOP BESIDE MYSELF STOP COME HOME MY ONLY CHILD LOVE MOTHER." Alexander had virtually no time in which to conjure the paralyzed and incoherent father who survives a stroke before another telegram solemnly confirmed the hour of his death. His mother was apparently distraught. The family lawyer cabled demanding Alexander's return to settle the estate and take up his responsibilities for the House of Karnovsky.

The telegrams arrived at the beginning and near the close of the day that Yevgeny Mikhailovich had rushed to the gallery early in the morning to supervise the arrival of his paintings from the framer, to plan their hanging with his Fraulein Kammerer, to be interviewed by a journalist, to rehearse a lecture on abstract painting that he was to give for a private audience of specially invited critics and connoisseurs the night before the public *vernissage*. He was not expected to return home much before eight in the evening. Alexander had agreed to prepare a buffet supper for a group of friends of the Lehrter Galerie, who were to come back to the studio for an evening with Malenov. But entertainments and soirées were not uppermost in Alexander's mind. His father was dying; his father was dead. He stared at the first telegram and tried desperately to suffer for his father. Without success. His eyes wearied of the effort to cry. No tears. His body seemed like stone. The second telegram was delivered in the late afternoon. Finality, and the distorting confusion of experiencing death without ever having understood tragedy. His father, relatively speaking a young man of fifty-eight, gone without a final word. Alexander dropped the telegram and, with the only mark of hysterical grief evoked by this sudden, premature, and first death of his experience, felt his body with a gentle hand, covering every surface of his chest, his stomach, his groin. And then, quietly, he wept, not in grief and mourning, but in anger.

Yevgeny Mikhailovich returned to the apartment surrounded by his new friends and admirers. The rooms were dark. He clapped his hands to announce his arrival, but there was no reply. He imagined that Alexander had devised some fête, some surprise, some theatrical invention to greet him and the friends of the Lehrter Galerie, but there was nothing, only a bulky envelope containing an advance against his expenses for the next six months and a brief letter of farewell:

> Excellent Yevgeny Mikhailovich.
>
> My father has died suddenly and I am recalled to New York. I have taken the afternoon train to Hamburg and will catch a ship leaving for New York tomorrow morning.
>
> Forgive my sudden departure. You certainly have no need of a mourning son at this time. My presence could not be more burdensome to you in the midst of your success. The funds I leave you honor my commitment for the coming six months.
>
> Paint well and think of nothing else, dear Zhenya. There is nothing else of any importance. I wish I could be as single-minded and total as you; it would make it easier to say no to my father's legacy, but unfortunately I am much weaker than I thought possible and, even though I do not mourn his death, I am strangled by the power of what he leaves me.
>
> Honoring you,
> Alexander.

Only a few letters between Yevgeny Mikhailovich and Alexander Karnovsky over the succeeding months have been located. (There may have been others, but I doubt it.)

*June 27, 1929   Berlin*
Young Alexander. It has been a triumph. Dear Fraulein Kammerer sells my work with great confidence and intelligence.

The paintings fly from the Lehrter (nine paintings so far and the exhibition is open only two weeks). I am so pleased. And to good collectors, too. The Kestner Gesselschaft has reserved two pictures and many artists have asked me to make exchanges with them. Isn't that good? The press has been unusually attentive. I think they may be catching on.

But, you know, it is still a silly business. Today, I eat. Tomorrow, I get ready to lose weight again. That's the way it is.

I know, Alexander, I should have written you. I apologize. I should have said how sad I am at your father's death. But I did not know your father. How could I be sad? And you, how many times I heard you complain about your father's coldness toward you. I was not certain that sympathy was what was called for. Have I been wrong toward you? Tell me if I hurt you.

Your painting friend,
Zhenya.

*July 19, 1929    New York*
Zhenya. I have your letter. Don't worry about it. I think I understood your silence. It doesn't upset me. I am beside myself with work. My father's estate was not at all tidy. He kept his papers in a terrible mess. But it appears now that he was richer than any of us imagined. By far. Everyone advises me not to sell the business immediately. They say it is much wiser to operate the business for another year or two before trying to sell it. (There are at least three companies that have asked if it is for sale, which makes me suspicious about selling now.) To my amazement, my father left me in charge. He knew that I was ignorant about his business and cared little or less, but he still put me in charge. I consult daily with Mr. Salomo—Father's trusted adviser—who understands everything. Do you think Father did this to trick me into submission? (Painting. What is painting?) It depresses me—all this worry about money and business. What do you think I should do?

Alexander.

*September 24, 1929    Garmisch*

Young Alexander. It is more than two months since you wrote
me last. What am I doing here in the mountains? Recovering,
that's what. Recovering from love. Clearly, Francine Kammerer does not love me. (I am finished with women. I was
right to have been celibate all those years—not that I was
not celibate with Kammerer. We did nothing but occasionally
hug. Pinch was more like it. Pinch and squeeze. I was quite
foolish about her. How little I understand about women. In
this, so terribly an amateur.) She was never untruthful. I
admit that. She thought I was a great painter. That was all
there was to it. I was a great painter. She was a splendid
dealer. I confused her loving my work with loving me. (She
sold fourteen paintings. I earned much money. It will see me
through the coming year.)

One day, she told me at dinner that I was becoming so
possessive and demanding that it could not continue this way.
I was horrified. "Where did you get the idea I loved you? I
never said that to you, Yevgeny Mikhailovich. I said I admired
you, that I admired your work, that I admired your art. But
love, devotion, marriage, household living, I never gave you
to believe that was possible. Now, did I? No. Never." I was
beside myself. We were around the corner from the gallery
having dinner. In a rage, I battered in the locked door of the
gallery and went out the door with the six paintings she had
left and my portfolio of drawings. She screamed for the police.
They arrested me and kept me in custody overnight. I paid
for the damage to the door. *Ein verruckte Kunstler*, was what
they kept calling me. Yes. I am mad. Very mad. Anger and
madness make for me a wild liquor.

                                                    Your Zhenya.


*November 9, 1929    New York*

Zhenya. It had to end that way. I was certain long ago. She
was not for you. No woman can be, I suspect, unless she is
prepared to obliterate herself taking care of you. Not that I
was any improvement over a woman. Our living together would
have come to an end no less decisively, although not as
violently. It was a good fortune in at least this respect that

my father died when he did. We were able to separate without a battle.

You did not answer my question. I asked you what you thought I should do? Do I have any talent? Should I continue to paint? Please address yourself to this when you reply.

Alexander.

*January 1, 1930    Berlin*

Sasha, straight away, yes, paint, paint, paint. Painting is not something you put on and off like your fur coat, a luxurious outer garment. Painting is all transcription, registering mental facts sensuously. There are days that I do not touch my paints, but I think of myself as painting nonetheless. Those days, I think painting (not *about* painting, but painting itself, and my body shakes as though I were actually making the movements that result in the mysterious passage of ideas from the brain to their forms to their colors). Sometimes, I imagine I am a tube of paint and want to squeeze myself all over the street. Those days are quite insane, almost pathological, but they are part of the process: you know, the more I think about painting, the more I realize that the first idea and the final painting are not what counts, but what goes on in between is everything. Painting is all process, thinking sensuously and out loud.

You have the talent, but you do not have the resolve. Maybe it is because you are young. Maybe it is because you are rich. Maybe because you do not understand the poverty of Saint Sergius. But let me tell you one thing, Alexander. Even if I were to tell you that you had no talent, if you believed me, *you would have no talent.* The issue of will and conviction is everything. What other people say is of no importance. So, paint and paint and do not be distracted from paint.

Your friend,<br>Zhenya

There was no further communication between them for many months. They were in touch, to be sure, but there were no further letters.

Yevgeny Mikhailovich sent Alexander every newspaper article, catalogue, casual mention that appeared in the European press regarding his work. Attached to these were little notes: "See, my old friend. They do not forget me," or "Several more for your scrapbook," or simply, penned in the margin of a newspaper article, "From Zhenya." Karnovsky never acknowledged Malenov's little packets of celebration. He couldn't. If he were to begin to write, he would have tempted an explosion of anger. And yet, he knew that Malenov was only partly to blame. It was simply that having found his Master, he had lost him again. His father had ultimately triumphed, imprisoning him not in the world of technology and science whose authority he had trumpeted, but snaring him in the coils of commerce. Every day, Karnovsky awakened to a three-piece suit and white shirt, to somber neckties and conservative overcoats. Every day, Karnovsky ordered from the hotel kitchen his juice and coffee and consumed them in the rented suite he had decorated with paintings by Malenov and Karnovsky. At the hour when he would have begun to work in Berlin, he descended in the elevator, entered a taxicab that awaited his appearance, and sped downtown to the House of Karnovsky. It was always the same: meetings with Mr. Salomo, the senior member of his father's staff, reviewing expenses and sales, conferring with advertising and marketing strategists, pretending constantly that he was fascinated and delighted by the aromas of tea and the redolence of spice. He loathed the enterprise, but succumbed to its aura of power and inheritance. An oil painting of his father stared down at him. Sometimes, it glowered in the rain or sparkled in the sunlight, but it was always the magnificent founder, whose ingenious gifts of smell and taste had built a little empire of exotic commodities.

Karnovsky had no release. Mr. Salomo, occasionally sensitive to his fidgeting and inattention, would advise him to take the afternoon off and perhaps treat himself to a Broadway matinee; once, to Karnovsky's horror, he suggested that it was such a lovely day, perhaps he should set up his easel in the park and make a landscape. Karnovsky replied sourly: "I don't like nature as it is."

This dispirited young man was barely noticed in the conduct of the House of Karnovsky. He was allowed to come and go, to be present or absent at meetings, to approve or disapprove a decision of his subordinates; but whatever he observed, having evoked polite nods of approval or condescension, hardly mattered to the inexorable course of commerce. Mr. Salomo complimented Karnovsky if he said something appropriate or to the point. For the most part, he ignored him. Karnovsky never objected. For nearly two years after his father's death, Karnovsky accepted the regimen imposed by his inheritance. One day at luncheon with Mr. Salomo following a meeting with the firm's auditors, who had presented them with the figures for the year just concluded, Karnovsky suddenly interrupted Mr. Salomo's pleased recitation of their healthy balance sheet and confided that he had every intention of selling the company at the first opportunity. Mr. Salomo was horrified. The House of Karnovsky was his life, and his life, at sixty-eight, was hardly over. He protested, but Karnovsky was adamant. "I loathe this business, Mr. Salomo. Loathe it. Clear enough and unmistakable. I want to paint. Do you understand? I want to paint. That's all I want to do. Paint, paint, paint." Apoplectically overcome, his voice choked with emotion, he stood up from the restaurant table and fled.

The subsequent months made it easier for Karnovsky to abandon his father's company. Karnovsky's mother, increasingly estranged from living after her husband's death, passed through a massive heart attack and died three months later in a sanatorium. This signaled freedom for Karnovsky. There was no one to whom he had to explain his life.

Karnovsky never returned to the House of Karnovsky. It was arranged that he would receive papers from time to time for review and signature, but he never again set foot in the offices. And, as he said, he organized himself to paint, going about it with a meticulous assurance that surprised him. He had a lesson from which to begin, a reflection he had uttered in frustration nearly a year before: "I don't like nature as it is." Read this formula as an utterance of annoyance or pique with divine uncompleteness, and only a portion of its profundity would reveal itself. Karnovsky was closing in on his own visionary breakthrough, a premise of reconstruction that would be as authentic and original to him as Malenov's projectivist architecture in space.

Karnovsky had not wasted time during his tea and spice days. It was hardly possible for him to paint seated at the vast desk beneath the portrait of the founder. Not possible at all, although once or twice he had sketched and drawn a notion or two; but it did not prevent him from shutting off his telephone, announcing to his secretary that he was taking a nap and didn't wish to be disturbed, and then removing from his desk his various treasured books: Paul Klee's *Pädagogisches Skizzenbuch*, Piet Mondrian's *Neue Gestaltung*, Malevich's various Russian and German treatises on the new theory of painting, but even more exciting because seemingly light-years from the world of art, books of meditation and philosophy from Plato's late dialogues, Pascal's *Pensées*, Burton's *The Anatomy of Melancholy*, Spinoza's *Ethics*, Nietzsche's *Beyond Good and Evil*, a gallimaufry of the wisdom literature of the West. He trained himself to read slowly, penciling in the margins delicately formed comments that alluded to his growing conviction that as an artist he stood outside the mainstream of world culture: he had stopped believing that the speeding racket of automobiles, the collapse of world economies, the starvation of the unemployed, the rise to power of idiot demagogues could possibly be influenced by daubing canvas with bits of paint. He had won out over commerce and technology to an appreciation of his friend Malenov's single-minded and, above all, private dream of a reconstructed universe. What could he do now but become a prophetic artist—like those whose works he coveted and whose essays of self-interpretation he considered the visionary literature of his century. He even, remarkably, allowed himself once again to be called Joseph Alexander

Karnovsky, restoring to eminence in his private canon the ancient dream interpreter of the Nile, the old prophet Joseph, whose paternity in Israel continued to discomfort him with an unease and nervousness that he took to be absolutely appropriate to his time and century. What can one say of this Joseph Alexander Karnovsky: he had finally grown up to inhabit himself, his emotions and intelligence at last swelling to fill out the weightless grace of his face and figure. A line appeared on his cheek, crow's-feet crinkled at his eyes. They pleased him immensely. He remained a man alone, still without connections to human beings aside from the distant Malenov. But loneliness is bearable when despair gives way to energetic production.

## *Fourteen*

I have tried with considerable diligence to reconstruct the six years that elapsed between Alexander Karnovsky's flight from Berlin and Yevgeny Mikhailovich's passage out of Europe to New York. The difficulties of such reconstruction are immense. They are, in a definite sense, unfathomable, because documentation is nonexistent. The bits and scraps that Karnovsky culled from art journals and critical press during those years set forth at most the contours of Malenov's considerable international reputation. Of Karnovsky's trials far less is known; virtually nothing that constituted the life of Alexander Karnovsky was preserved. Karnovsky was not writing in his journal about himself. Whatever he wrote—those few entries I was able to find for these intermediate and dark years—dealt with Malenov, only with Malenov. The single entry, for example, of October 21, 1932—a mere notation of fact accompanied by a clipping from a financial page that described the transaction—stated: "The House of Karnovsky no longer exists. I sold it today for 1.4 million dollars cash. It would have been more had we not been in the midst of a depression. They tried to persuade me to take stock, much more stock, but I am not interested in having to spend my years in consultation with idiot brokers and financial consorts, buying and selling bits of paper whose ultimate value is dubious. Better the cash. And now, God, let me paint." The little article that appeared in *The New York Times* stated the terms of the purchase by Consolidated Emporia, a food chain that added the House of Karnovsky to its portfolio of specialized food services. In the first annual report of Consolidated Emporia following the acquisition, the House of Karnovsky was listed in its schedule of divisions under Beverages and Condiments. So much for the vocation of Markus Israel Karnovsky.

It was during this period that I first made Alexander Karnovsky's acquaintance. He had telephoned my office and inquired whether by chance I had any materials relating to Yevgeny Mikhailovich Malenov. As it happened, I had nothing; indeed, I confessed politely that I scarcely knew the name. Karnovsky was only too willing to inform me. Several weeks later, I was fortunate to be able to buy a small library belonging to some Russian émigrés, one of whom was an unmatriculated student of architecture. His contribution to the family collection—mostly issues of fin de siècle Petersburg art journals and books illustrated by Bakst and Benois—was a handful of theoretical treatises on the new Russian art that included a little pamphlet hectographed in purple ink by Malenov, containing very early drawings of the basic Malenovian shapes and their permutations. My command of Russian was minimal, restricted to the alphabet, which enabled me to vocalize titles but hardly to read. I called Karnovsky and slowly pronounced the title of Malenov's first treatise (it was his *Elements of a New Utopics*). Karnovsky was enthusiastic, announcing the rarity of the work I was offering him at, as he put it, to my pleasure, "such a reasonable price." He visited me the following day to collect his purchase, and what began as a simple transaction was enlarged by conversation and lunch into an afternoon of confidences and intimacies. What do I confess about Alexander Karnovsky? I found him awkward and vulnerable, but immensely intelligent, serious, and appealing. His was a look of bewilderment that I have always found attractive—the kind of unsureness that is one minute covered with arrogance and another hidden behind a hand through which the low voice speaks, uncontrollably shy and melancholic.

As we approached the conclusion of our first luncheon, I realized that I had learned virtually nothing about Alexander Karnovsky. He knew who I was. That was transparent, and I had elaborated the history of my coming to deal in the rare materials of European art history—letters, manuscripts, prints and drawings, documents and photographs, illustrated books and obscure periodicals—but I had learned nothing of Karnovsky. Of Malenov I knew abundantly, almost too much, as I was now girded and tied by the cords of Karnovsky's judgment without being able to confirm it by personal encounter. There were no works by Malenov at that time in American museums. I was promised a tour through Karnovsky's collection, which consisted, he said, of some dozen paintings and drawings and a large album of preliminary sketches and drawings that he had accumulated in Berlin and taken with him on his departure. But my knowing whether Malenov deserved Karnovsky's unqualified enthusiasm (or whether Karnovsky deserved my sympathy, if it emerged that he had been duped by a minor artist) had little or no bearing on the phenomenon that, to my mind, seemed most remarkable. Not only the talent of Alexander Karnovsky but—in some mysterious and as yet indefinite sense—his life depended on the existence of Yevgeny Malenov. Malenov, whether he knew it or not, dominated and determined the life of his disciple and enthusiast, even though they were separated by thousands of miles. Speaking of Malenov, celebrating his genius, describing his personal eccentricities and boorish manners, his charming self-confidence, his oddities and peccadilloes was his young admirer's favored occupation. I grant you that it all began to weary me by the third of our meetings, since the only way to relieve Karnovsky's depression was to ask him whether he had had word of Malenov, at which point he would begin to dream aloud, his spirits lifting slowly, until after some minutes—orbiting—I was regaled with the aesthetic navigations of the genius, but it left me with little choice: depression or Malenov, hardly a rich and variegated social selection. He concealed from me completely that he, himself, was an artist, aspiring to greatness.

Boredom, I had come to realize, was one of the unavoidable by-products of being a dealer. Most collectors, I am persuaded, are obsessive acquirers whose passion is rarely accompanied by any fund of knowledge. Unfortunately, I had little to learn from my clients, which left me for the most part bored by them.

Karnovsky was something of an exception to my rule. He was undoubtedly obsessive, but his monotonous absorption focused on a single painter and was not involved in the least with either prestige or power, the twin monsters that inspire most collectors to pursue the prowl and hunt. Karnovsky never celebrated the prices at which he had purchased his treasures or compared his holdings with the purchases of others. Indeed, in the case of Malenov, nobody in the world of money and power really cared. Starvation was commonplace for artists during this period, and virtually every European artist of any importance did something else to make ends meet—designing furniture, printing books and leaflets, teaching, touring as performers, and with all, living scrappy and impecunious lives. (I have just learned, for instance, that the splendid collagist Kurt Schwitters began in Hanover by selling his little works for two and three marks and achieved great success in England twenty years later selling them for five pounds.) Malenov's situation was somewhat worse than most because he was an immigrant to the West, without proper command of any language except Russian, a visionary and utopian whose doctrine was transmissible but indisputably vague and romantic, who was without following, camaraderie, or support, cut loose from the great Soviet artists, who had by the end of the 1930s all returned to their homeland for the rewards of ignominy, humiliation, and death. At the same time, Malenov was immensely fortunate. He had Alexander Karnovsky—introverted Alexander, rich, handsome, dedicated, whose life and vigor were drawn like an infusion from Malenov's vitals.

During supper after the opera one night in October 1935 I remarked to Alexander—somewhat flippantly, I admit, since I suppose I had become enamored of the young man—that he should stop all this mooning and moaning about Malenov and simply bring him to New York.

It had been a wearying performance of an Italian melodrama, the soprano trailing twenty feet of white organza train like a royal gown when she was at most a celebrated courtesan, the tenor indifferently belting his tunes. I had nonetheless looked forward to the evening. I had not seen Alexander Karnovsky for nearly a year. He had been traveling—not to Europe, as I had thought likely, but to the Caribbean, where he had rented a house in Jamaica and tried to begin serious painting again; but he complained that the sun was too brilliant, the flowers too abundant, the undergrowth too lush.

Instead of painting, Karnovsky felt oppressed by the opulence of his life and had retreated into his books. Preparation, he called it. This was the first time he had spoken to me of his own work as an artist. I knew that he was rich (I had noticed the item on the financial pages), but I was unaware until that casual aside that he was also possessed of the same vocation as his friend Malenov. I confess I was stunned by the revelation, so casually inserted into his conversation. Perhaps he imagined—a not uncommon habit of the rich—that I had made inquiries about him and had found out everything that needed to be known. (The truth is that I had tried. I knew many people about town and am not uninterested in gossip. But unfortunately, practically no one had ever heard of Joseph Alexander Karnovsky, and those who had had never met him. He traveled in circles that did not overlap my own, a fact I found upsetting, but no matter. It was only when I brought up his name to a rather sleek and clever art dealer whom I met at a cocktail party at the Morgan Library that I discovered something about his background. Apparently, this art dealer had sold him a Malenov several years earlier—one that Karnovsky had recognized as stemming from the group of paintings exhibited at the Lehrter Galerie in 1929—and in the course of their transaction had learned among other things that Karnovsky was interested in philosophy and painting. The art dealer mistakenly regarded Karnovsky as a mere dabbler, neither a serious collector nor sufficiently rich to be cultivated. So much for making inquiries.) Seated before me at Longchamps, not far from the opera house, Alexander seemed hardly a painter, although admittedly I had readily consumed the cliché of long-hair artists, and Alexander's soft brown hair barely broke the collar of his tuxedo. In the midst of my effort to comprehend his casual disclosure, I was struck by the evident pain elicited by my proposal that he carry Malenov out of Europe to New York. Instead of the long-faced, somber, even solemn Karnovsky to whom I was accustomed, he suddenly collapsed, as though my suggestion had plunged a knife into his *amour-propre*. Karnovsky first groaned, "No. Not that. Not now," and then, recovering from his first deflation, confessed to me that nothing could be more inopportune.

"I've been away from that vast ego for five years now and I enjoy the separation. No, Isaiah, I depend on it. I couldn't bear to have him in the neighborhood. Living with him was difficult, even impossible. I tried to work, but how does one work with a genius next door? Everything I made was covered with a Malenovian pall, as though he had invaded and occupied me. Such a succubus was possible in Berlin, because I didn't have the vaguest idea of what I was doing, but the last two years—Jamaica excepted (and that was as much a recuperation as anything else)—I've been hard at work, and since I came back to New York in May, I've made some objects I think first-rate. And several dealers think so, too."

"And you'll exhibit them?"

"In January, my first show. Isn't that wonderful? But if Malenov were here it would all start again. I haven't left off sending him money. I send. He receives. We don't discuss it. But I couldn't cope with him in the flesh."

"But, my friend, your obsession with him continues. You speak of nothing else. I didn't even know you made paintings of your own until now."

"Not paintings, sculpture. I make constructions out of wood. Sometimes I paint them. Sometimes I use different qualities and grains of wood that emit natural color. No need for paint."

"You should be very happy with yourself."

"I am. Perhaps for the first time, I am."


## *Fifteen*

The first exhibition of Joseph Alexander Karnovsky's work opened in a serious Manhattan gallery toward the end of January 1936. It was a smart opening, well attended, voices modulated, the hum audible, the excitement controlled and well mannered. The major newspapers of the city reviewed the show, and all the critics praised it. Dorothy Miller of the Museum of Modern Art promptly came by the gallery and reserved a piece; several prominent collectors stopped in, and four works were sold during the first week. When the exhibition closed in early March, the reputation of Karnovsky, sculptor, was established. Karnovsky's dealer spoke of him now simply as Karnovsky; collectors referred to "my Karnovsky"; museum curators made diligent inquiries about the possibility of acquiring "a recent Karnovsky." Virtually every sculpture was sold, as were most of the pastel drawings that reflected process thinking about the issue of each construction.

By any standard it was an immensely successful debut. Many people knew Karnovsky as the son and heir to the so-called Karnovsky fortune in tea, and undoubtedly several of his father's friends who had observed young Karnovsky rise up to overshadow his father had acquired his works, but Alexander was indifferent to the implication of such commercial nepotism, precisely because nothing negotiable was to be gained by owning a Karnovsky. Indeed, in those days of the mid-1930s, art was simply the corona of society, and rich people acquired painting and sculpture in the same way that horse people acquire racing prints—art went with a certain level of ease and social self-assurance. The buying of art wasn't to be inspected closely, nor its motives questioned too intently; owning art was much like owning good luggage or well-made shoes: one didn't buy too much of it, lest its abundance send the wrong signals. Having a Karnovsky was daring enough—owning work by a Jewish artist descended from an Odessan tea merchant implied that amid a house full of odd French names and English watercolors, there was an American ethnic who did a sculptural turn. (At the opening, one lady was heard to remark: "How terribly contemporary!" Indeed!) The social chic of an art collection was still monitored far from the modest corridors of the Museum of Modern Art. A Karnovsky remained closer to Picasso than Picasso was to Velásquez. (Today, of course, it's all caught up. Karnovsky is still Karnovsky, but Picasso is an old master spoken of with the hushed respect accorded a bit of bedaubed canvas that commands a million dollars.)

Karnovsky's works were indubitably handsome. (That is the most that my unsophisticated eye can determine.) They were wooden structures built up of irregular boxlike rectangles mounting upward, with occasional interruptions as flanges projected out into space and way-stations imagined by Fritz Lang turned at angles to the primary grid. They were not brilliantly fabricated. No matter. Already collectors understood that the difference between Karnovsky's art and carpentry lay in the formal power of the image and the appearance of fragility: the small nails could be seen, putty was artlessly applied to fill unwanted holes, the wood was rough and poorly planed, but the forms themselves—"architectonic but hardly architectural," as one critic put it—thrust dramatically up from their small, unpretentious black bases.

Is it any wonder that Karnovsky was unenthusiastic about the prospect of Malenov coming to New York? He was having his own success, a success perhaps grounded on imagery suggested and worked out in two dimensions by Malenov, but sufficiently obscure and unknown to the American public as to allow the passing of his own work into modest celebrity unmarred by the cavil of imitation. One critic, to be sure, writing for the French periodical *Art Aujourd'hui*, remarked of Karnovsky's work that he stood in a highly respected modernist tradition that stemmed "from Malevich and Malenov," but that observation suggested neither Karnovsky's borrowing from Malenov nor his transcription in sculpture of what Malenov had asserted in painting to be his projectivist vision. As far as Karnovsky was concerned, his work was original, fresh, and spontaneous. That was all that needed to be said, although surely his lack of enthusiasm about transferring his beloved Malenov from Berlin to New York brooded possibilities that were still unformulated, perhaps even unconscious. What if, I speculated, Karnovsky had in fact made use of sketches devised by Malenov for a suite of unrealized sculptures? What if Karnovsky had seen Malenov drawings and simply filled out their implied volumes in wood? What if, in short, Karnovsky was simply a transcriber who avoided the charge of outright thievery and plagiarism by concealing as sculpture what had been created as painting? But how was I to answer these questions? I was unskilled as either connoisseur of modern art or historian of its complexities.

During the late summer of 1937 Karnovsky received a pitiful letter from Malenov. It was the first letter Alexander had had from him in many months. Earlier in the year, at about the time of the opening of Karnovsky's exhibition, Malenov had written describing a commission he had received to execute a large mural in Stuttgart. He was not clear whether the commission was an official assignment or was financed by private sources. This is a relevant question principally because the American art press had already noted that the new regime in Germany was in the process of stripping from its museums and public collections every painting, sculpture, drawing, and lithograph that reflected, in the judgment of the authorities, the degenerate influence of the Jews and other inferior peoples, including notably Slavs by race and communists by politics. Listed among the Russian-born artists whose work was to be withdrawn from public view was Yevgeny Mikhailovich Malenov. When I brought this information to Alexander's attention, he was instantly upset. I observed his eyelids flutter, a sure sign in Karnovsky that something troubled him; when he undertook to comment on the report, he stuttered slightly, unable to find the right words to suggest both his indignation and his unwillingness to rise at that moment to the implication of the news. He knew that it was all over in Europe for Malenov, that his time of success and recognition was about to be eclipsed, but he was unable to bring himself to the obvious conclusion that what I had earlier proposed as challenge—that he bring Malenov to New York—was now necessity.

Malenov was again in need; Karnovsky was once more to become his succor and savior. Of course, succor and salvation had little to do with uninterrupted financial aid. Karnovsky had promised Yevgeny Mikhailovich a hundred dollars a month and, throughout the years that had passed since they met in 1929, Karnovsky had delivered. Every month Karnovsky's bank had transferred by cable to a bank in Berlin the mandated sum, and every month, notified of its arrival, Malenov had appeared at the teller's window, presented his identification, and received a hundred dollars' worth of German currency. It was efficient and unemotional, a detached transfer, an impassive reception. It would have been much better, I think now, if the ma-

chinery of subvention had been more personal, if each month Karnovsky had been obliged to compose a brief letter and mail a check,
if each month Malenov had been obliged either to ignore his dependence on the benefaction or compose a note of thanks and appreciation. The enmeshment would have been more complex, but no
less would the parties have been compelled to actually give and
receive, to acknowledge and appreciate. When the fortunes of Malenov were rising, he could have suspended the gift, and when his
fortunes sank, he would have been obliged to request that the money
be renewed. The utter indifference of mechanical instructions—face-
less bankers, impersonal tellers—routinized a personal gift and transformed a moral commitment and charity into the anonymity of an
arrangement whose private dimension was elided. Karnovsky was
allowed to forget what he was doing, and Malenov could ignore what
he was receiving. Of course, the deep truth is that neither forgot.
They occasionally chafed under the arrangement, but were too lazy
and casual to call attention to the bondage of their relationship. The
transfer of funds was an enslavement for both, and although they
fulfilled the right regimen of charitable bequests, removing from generosity and receipt the risks of embarrassment that arise when gifts
are made face to face—the proffered gift, the scraping receipt, the
procedures of condescension and humiliation—the impersonality of
their transaction proved, in my view, to be exceedingly harmful. The
large ego of genius accepted the small sum of support, and burgeoning
talent was constantly reminded by his monthly generosity of an in-
debtedness to his master that bruited dependencies and reliances
more dramatic than mere money.

Unavoidable then that in the fall of 1937 the interests of Malenov
and Karnovsky should collide. Malenov's need was reasserted at a
time when Karnovsky's success required that the existence of Malenov
be obscured. An inescapable moral dilemma, which Karnovsky was
compelled to resolve. He did the right thing. Despite his reluctance,

the historical evidence of misfortune could hardly be obscured. Malenov was in trouble; indeed, virtually all of the finest artists of Germany were in trouble, but Karnovsky had little interest in the generality of political misfortune. He could not help all the artists stranded by the barbarism of the regime, but Malenov he could help, and he could not close his eyes to that fact. Reluctantly, he opened his eyes and focused—even if narrowly—on the predicament of his teacher and master in art, Yevgeny Mikhailovich Malenov. With a weary shrug of capitulation, Alexander composed a telegram to Malenov: "HAVE LEARNED YOUR PICTURES WITHDRAWN FROM GERMAN MUSEUMS STOP IT'S ALL OVER IN GERMANY STOP COME TO NEW YORK STOP EVERYTHING ARRANGED STOP ALEXANDER."

There was no immediate reply. However, a month later, a letter arrived that explained Yevgeny's silence.

> My dear friend. Your telegram came the day before my studio was broken into and paint poured over the floor. Many works were slandered. Cut into little pieces. Would you believe it, Sasha? I still do not. It is madness here. Many painters are quitting, going back to small villages and hiding out. Some take up house painting and bricklaying. This is no country any longer. It is a jungle. Yes. Yes. I will come. I don't know where I will live, but we can find something, isn't that so? I will pack up everything. (Francine Kammerer's gallery is closed. Her grandfather is a Jew. I didn't know that. Poor Francine.) Please, dear Alexander, send me funds so that I can leave. I have money to live on from day to day, but no money put aside for big moves like this. I am not sure that I can survive in your country, but I have to go on. The work is wonderful these days, the canvases larger, and I did a splendid mural for an architectural project in Stuttgart, which was to have been inaugurated last month. (It is canceled now. In its place someone has painted a tasteless tableau of thick-chested workers building houses and large-breasted pink women with hair as blond as cornsilk carrying cement. It is called: *The New Germany Builds*.) But I have my own hopes

to keep alive. I could surrender and die, but I cannot give in now. That would be too foolish.

Zhenya.

## *Sixteen*

"It is exactly as I saw it."

Yevgeny Mikhailovich whistled with delight when Alexander Karnovsky threw open the door of the third-floor walk-up apartment on Sixth Avenue and 54th Street several hours after the *Berengenia* docked in New York on November 2, 1937. A large room, light and airy, freshly painted white, furnished with a large couch, dining table and chairs, a spacious worktable, bookshelves, a comfortable bedroom and bath at the rear, and a small, fully equipped kitchen. Yevgeny was presented with salt, bread, and wine to dedicate his new home, and the two friends, the painter in his mid-fifties and the sculptor entering his thirties, settled down to review the history of their separation. "Exactly as Zhenya saw it. First clear sight in many years and good one. On the deck of the ship in late afternoon, I saw this room. Exactly, this room! It must have been the day you signed the lease for it. Exactly. Same day exactly. I saw this room, filled with sunlight, radiant, walls white and pure. Oh, I will make such paintings here. I will make such paintings. I will thank you, dear Alexander. I will reward your trust."

It is hardly likely that Karnovsky would have fallen back into his predictably self-effacing demeanor before Malenov had he been able, early on, to bring Malenov to his studio, to show him his recent work, to elicit reaction to his newfound activity as a sculptor. Surely Malenov had learned that Karnovsky had had his first exhibition and that it had been immensely successful. Such news travels, and Malenov, despite his indifference to other people's success, would have been curious enough to have confronted Karnovsky's work, acknowledged its source in his own, and perhaps been delighted by the progress of his young disciple. He might have stinted his praise or brought out this or that drawing of his own to document an option that Karnovsky had refused, but he would have willingly assimilated Karnovsky's dependence on his own achievement as his point of departure.

Karnovsky's failure to admit to his own work was a serious—I think, decisive—mistake. It set in motion the furious progress of anger and betrayal that was to follow. And yet, it is understandable. Karnovsky had not grown up with the kind of strength and assertiveness that Malenov dispensed so easily. Malenov's ego was so large and expansive that he could distribute in a day assertions and announcements of his genius that would take Karnovsky months to formulate. Karnovsky had achieved something important, but the knowledge that he was reworking in sculpture occasions and possibilities implicit in Malenov's paintings robbed him of the joy and pleasure his success should have brought him. The money his exhibition had earned was nothing beside his inheritance; the few Karnovskys now presented by museums among their new acquisitions were more than offset by the number that stood in entrance halls to summer homes in Southampton and Oyster Bay, mere condiments for the rich. Karnovsky was invited to parties and intimate soirées where the odd writer or painter turned up to amuse for his supper, but Karnovsky soon tired of this. He kept feeling that he was traveling with false credentials, that whatever he had demonstrated of his talent was siphoned from the profligate generosity of his master's genius, that he was still, despite his accomplishment, a beginner who had yet to find a voice of his own. His depression continued, his melancholy was revived, the presence of Malenov, now close to hand, loomed as a challenge to which he should have risen, a threat to his independence that he should have undertaken to combat. The day Karnovsky had sent his telegram of invitation, he was about to assemble two sculptures in his studio. They were as good as sold, his dealer told him and urged him to finish and deliver. Karnovsky looked at the pieces that night, but could barely see them through his gloom. They remained unfinished. By the time of Malenov's arrival ten weeks later, Karnovsky had convinced himself that he was untalented, worthless, and incapable, and had suspended work.

Moreover, the months that followed Malenov's arrival revealed something of which Karnovsky had not been aware. The discovery only served to consolidate his melancholy. He had believed for many years that no one in New York knew of Malenov's existence. Alexander occupied such a diminished world that he was generally out of touch with what transpired beyond its borders. He imagined that the absence of clippings, the failure of American magazines to contribute to his growing collection of articles and essays documenting Malenov, confirmed that Malenov was unknown and unregarded. It suited his fantasy to think that America was still rude and unsophisticated. Although the Museum of Modern Art had opened its doors in 1929, and its sweep and influence were already regarded as innovative, the very notion of American connoisseurs passed him by. Europe was culture; America was commerce. This was the legacy of indoctrination in which his father had raised him, and he had accepted its stricture without examination. Such attitudes, unfortunately, comported with the manner in which Karnovsky did things: he was arrogantly rich, never counting his change or adding up a bill to check a waiter's calculation or examining the contents of a package to see that everything charged had been delivered; he never bothered to make certain that he had money in his wallet; he wrote checks, stepping into banks and shops where, even if he was unknown, his letter of credit—always in his wallet—was sufficient to insure that any Karnovsky check would be honored. He was always out of touch, moving through the city unawares, bumping into people he never saw, passing through reality like a magician who pretends to walk through walls, except that Alexander's misreading of solidity and substance was never willed or calculated to elicit huzzahs of amazement from onlookers. Alexander Karnovsky simply didn't read the world accurately. What he took to be the world's indifference to Malenov was more accurately a reflection of his own separation from the coteries that formed the art world and were generally quite familiar with European developments, following Mondrian in Paris, van Doesburg in Holland, and Malenov in Berlin.

It was to Karnovsky's considerable surprise, then, to discover several weeks after Malenov's installation in his new studio that several American artists had already come to call, that one of the curators of the Museum of Modern Art had left his card and invited Malenov to a museum reception, and that Malenov—the absurdly unworldly painter he had abandoned in Berlin eight years earlier—had puffed out and expanded. Malenov quite easily stepped out into the city, walking briskly down 57th Street, cutting through the park, lying down on park benches to survey the skyscrapers surrounding him, charging into crowds with an unfailingly correct apology for his bustle and rudeness, pushing aside obstacles and obstructions that prevented his movement on subway platforms and buses. Malenov had mastered the indifference of reality to precisely the extent that Karnovsky had succumbed to it—the one persuaded that talent and achievement could bend the real to serve him, while the other, despite being efficiently outfitted with wealth and first success, still cowered before the world, once again uncertain of any role other than the enhancement and celebration of the importance of his older and more accomplished friend.

The means by which Karnovsky undertook his program of enhancement was not, however, determined by a desire to see his friend independent and free, abroad in the land. It unsettled Karnovsky to learn that Malenov kept company with painters who were indifferent to his eccentricity, who regarded the subtlety and power of his paintings as more important than his execrably accented potpourri of languages—part English, part German, trailing off when words failed into a low rumble of Russian—who were amused by his oversized overcoat bulging with notebooks, a small box of pastels, and leaking pens that occasionally stained through his jacket lining and left surreal shapes on his breast pocket.

Yevgeny Mikhailovich quickly became for his fellow artists the "bear" of the art world (the small art world that existed in those days), "bear" having come to signify not only the Great Russia from which he came but the aspect of massiveness, almost monstrosity, with which he wheeled through the city, his head lowered as if preparing to charge the unsuspecting and devour them.

Alexander Karnovsky was unable to revel in his friend's modest reputation. It was, I suspect, an authentic reputation, marked by the admiration of those who know what it is they celebrate—painting, the act of painting, the quality of paint, and not cleverness and novelty or the ability of painting to comment on this or that recognizable nomenclature of social vulgarity. Oh, these New York friends of Yevgeny Mikhailovich knew he was the real thing, the genuine article, a proper genius, who fashioned a mysterious universe of space and populated it with shapes that neither told a story nor narrated social muck. Yevgeny was a great painter, and younger painters knew the difference and admired him. They sought him out, invited him to their studios for comment, took him to tea and slipped him vodka in his water glass, loved him sober, preferred him drunk, but with everything respected the fact that he had survived, that he had fled Russia (but rarely spoke politics, which made it possible for even avant-garde radicals to tolerate him) and had already fallen in love with New York (which delighted everyone else).

Everyone, that is, except Alexander Karnovsky, who confessed to me one day that he was losing Zhenya.

"What do you mean by such an insane remark?"

"Just that. Just that. I'm losing him. He's on his own. He's off on his own. He doesn't need me anymore. Except, yes, sometimes to pay the bills."

But it was hard to interpret this last. It wasn't said with anything like the sneering bitterness such words imply. It was offered as fair comment, an extenuation of an otherwise frankly descriptive assessment: He's doing all right, but sometimes he needs help. To myself I had observed: And what did he need from you before other than money, and listen, young Alexander, who found whom? Who traveled to Berlin in search of a master and turned up Yevgeny Mikhailovich Malenov? The reversal had transpired, the upside-down version of the universe that is at the heart of all envy and all malevolence. All that any reversal requires is one act of superlative forgetting, dropping one critical, holding stitch from the fabric of the universe, and, pressured, the frayed thread can unravel the most carefully contrived and persuasive tapestry. What had he wanted from Yevgeny Mikhailovich? A lover? Bizarre, but possible, an authentic genius of no particular physical charm who could overwhelm and subdue him, turn him out of his virtually sexless and smooth neutrality toward a delicious perversity of sublimation, which might have enabled him to show his contempt for his paternity while submitting to its gender. But more. Denied by his history that indispensable species of trust and confidence that enables parents to die and allows children to survive and prosper, Alexander Karnovsky had devised an alternative route, a means of egress in art, which took him out of the kingdom of fathers and installed him under the authority of masters. A neat parallelism, but it hardly describes the reversal. How came it to be, then, that Alexander Karnovsky, one minute obligated to bring his master to New York, now chafed that the Master had come and was able to survive, no, thrive on his own?

A revealing example of Alexander's nervousness and unease before Malenov's fluent and unself-conscious mobility. Once, not more than three weeks after his arrival, Malenov visited the Metropolitan Museum of Art. He planted himself before a Renaissance painting dominated by a blue and pink sky lowering upon an Adoration of the Magi, and there he stayed for nearly three hours, quietly, transfixedly examining the painting. It was approaching the closing hour, and the guards, having observed him earlier, were by then persuaded that this monstrous enlargement of a man was going to do some violence to the little painting. As the hours passed and Yevgeny's nose approached closer and closer to the canvas, the number of guards observing him rose from one to four, and a small assembly of spectators filled a half-circle at the perimeter of the room, expecting something terrible, something vile, to transpire. At precisely the moment that one of the guards decided to approach and inform him of the museum's imminent closing, Yevgeny Mikhailovich whirled about and, tears streaming down his face, cried out: "How does a God settle among us?" No one understood his Russian interrogation, but no one undertook to pursue and question him. (He fled the museum and did not return for a month, when he appeared with a false beard, convinced that the entire staff of the museum was awaiting the next visit of the hysterical Russian, armed to the teeth and prepared to do battle.)

When Yevgeny Mikhailovich told the story to Alexander and myself that evening, we laughed until the tears came. We laughed; Yevgeny was finally persuaded to laugh, although he warned us that his next visit would be in disguise, but Alexander Karnovsky, although he had laughed, added: "Oh, dear Zhenya, you shouldn't go on such expeditions without telling me. I would have come with you."

Clearly, Karnovsky needed to regard Yevgeny Mikhailovich as somehow unable to conduct himself in the world—not as madman or dangerous, rather more as a genius incompetent, like those amazing defectives whose brain is stuck on an infinitesimally minute synapse and who, despite idiocy, are capable of adding in their heads immense columns of figures or recollecting dates going back to the beginning of history. And why this need? And even more so, why in New York, with an exaggerated insistence not at all evident during their Berlin months together?

One explanation, of course, is that during those early days, despite ample funds to organize and conduct his life with Yevgeny Mikhailovich, there was not much experience left over. Alexander could still dream paintings with an energetic will to make them; he could still regard Yevgeny as his discovery, his secret authority, his unknown master. He could pretend that everything he saw in Yevgeny's work and reconstructed in his own was an original creation. There was no one to gainsay his borrowings. Yevgeny would never comment, amused, perhaps flattered by Alexander's diligence and attentiveness, perhaps regarding his often academic translations of Malenovs as a legitimate device of pedagogy, even encouraging Karnovsky to find a vocabulary that would help transmit the Malenovian doctrine to others. Moreover, during their Berlin idyll, when neither could communicate efficiently with others, they were capable of bolstering each other's confidence and optimism without the need of checking their own judgment against a judgment being offered in a language foreign to both. But in New York, all the hermetic enravelment and self-infatuation that had characterized their life in Berlin before the advent of Francine Kammerer was dissipated by the commonplace directness of American speech and manners. There was no way that Karnovsky could prevent Malenov's entrance into the world. It was possible then, long ago, when Malenov was starving and Karnovsky was a rich aspirant, but by 1937 all the conditions had changed. Malenov was internationally regarded as a master; still poor, still uncelebrated by the coteries of fashion, he was nonetheless highly prized by the only world that mattered to him, fellow artists and utopians like himself.

Karnovsky, for his part, despite his reluctance to own up to the fact that he had stretched his talent to the limit and had accomplished the making of a body of work, establishing the foundations of a respectable career, still felt himself trammeled by his unspoken recognition that he was borrowing heavily on aesthetic capital he had not earned. In everything else immensely rich—itself a sufficient difficulty for a young artist—he had built his idiom on the transformation of ideas derived from his long and serious consideration of Malenov's painting. Where Malenov was quite willing to imply his utopian vision, Karnovsky was determined to formulate sculptural skyscrapers that signified heretofore nonexistent architectures. He was undeniably original, but he was not a genius, not a talent of first rank. He worked out the implications of premises he was unable to formulate. That was his achievement. It was also his curse and his predicament.

Several days after Malenov arrived, he asked Karnovsky whether he had been working well during the years of their separation. He admitted openly, indeed with considerable warmth and interest, that he was curious to see Karnovsky's work, to learn of its unfolding and development. They were sitting in the sun-drenched front room of Malenov's apartment drinking coffee Alexander had brewed. Dozens of half-opened cartons and broken-down suitcases lay about the room, and pictures were stacked against the walls, but Malenov was more interested in Karnovsky than he was in settling in. "All this can wait. Let's see what you do in art," Malenov asserted, waving dismissively to his belongings.

Karnovsky answered simply: "I've done nothing worth seeing."

"Oh," was all the comment Malenov made, and he jumped up from the table to show Karnovsky a box of Russian books that had arrived in Berlin with all the belongings he had left behind in Moscow eight years before. Karnovsky took this to mean that Malenov was perfunctory in his curiosity, that it didn't matter to him what his young friend had accomplished. Not true at all, as I discovered later from Malenov. The truth is that he was upset and alarmed by Karnovsky's self-effacement. It was so unlike the Karnovsky he had known, assertive, energetic, once prepared to work in a bedroom adjacent to Malenov's studio (certainly not the best of working conditions), but now, although completely freed from the wheel of necessity, apparently unable to make art. ("Something is wrong with Sasha," he admitted ruefully. "The whoosh has left him." Although I could not identify the rush of air that signified Malenov's *whoosh*, I took it to be an audible metaphor for inspiration.)

But it hadn't ended with Malenov's simple "Oh" of disappointment. Karnovsky put down his cup and tried to explain; almost stuttering, he admitted that he had left off painting and begun to make wooden constructions. He even drew for Malenov several little figures that suggested the complex structures he was undertaking to build, but all this description and allusion was after the fact. It was as though Karnovsky were trying to introduce Malenov slowly to the idea that his young disciple was not simply attempting sculpture but had in fact exhibited some twenty of them, that the exhibition had occurred months before, that most of them had sold, that Karnovsky was already an independent, working artist. But he could not bring himself to admit this. It would be like a mere mortal admitting to a divinity that he had wrought something on his own, unauthorized and without permission, and now, confronted by divine curiosity, was guiltily trying to hide his creation. Such evasions and deceits are as deadly to human transaction (where it is hoped candor and trust would obtain) as they are corrupting of all relations between divinity and creature.

Malenov was perplexed by his young friend—even more deeply perplexed when Alexander concluded their breakfast conversation by laying his monthly stipend upon the table, this time in banknotes, resuming, it appears, the habit of giving that had characterized their earliest transactions. Malenov resisted picking up the money for several days. He put coffee cups, dirty plates, filthy paintbrushes down on the bills, hoping to soil and transform the banknotes into something else, but they did not disappear, although they were now covered with rings of brown and splotches of yellow and red. He began to hate taking the money from Karnovsky. He sensed that taking and receiving from his benefactor was beginning to work an insidious influence on both of them, compelling the one to silence and evasion, the other to an almost childlike dependence. Picking up a ten-dollar note, soggy with spilled soup, Malenov suddenly cried out: "I will give back all money. *All.*"

The following month, when he needed to fix a leak in the bathroom, he asked Karnovsky to call the owner of the building. And then regretted the request. "Why should he call that man? I will go to the landlord's office and introduce Malenov." But that was not as easy as it appeared. The lease for the apartment was in Karnovsky's name. The landlord would not have known who Malenov was. "You mean this is not my apartment," he asked Karnovsky. "Of course it is, Zhenya, but you weren't here to sign the document. I signed the papers. I paid the deposit and the security and the rent." (And so I ask, why didn't Malenov ask that the lease be transferred to him, even if Karnovsky were required to guarantee it? And why didn't Karnovsky propose the transfer and be done with it? But nothing as simple as this was possible.) It continued as before: Karnovsky paid and Karnovsky paid and Malenov vowed to pay back and nothing was resolved. It cost Karnovsky several hundred dollars a month, what with the stipend and the rent and extraordinary expenses such as a new winter coat, a reconditioned icebox when the old one burned out its coils, the replacing of a door that Malenov admitted kicking in during a fit of temper early one morning after a sleepless night.

Malenov had been constantly assailed with inquiries about his obscure enthusiast and benefactor, whom his American friends had seen at his apartment either preparing drinks and coffee or else sitting diffidently among them, hardly speaking. Malenov was unable to escape rumors of Karnovsky's work and exhibition. It was discussed by the painters he met at a gathering of the Association of American Abstract Artists, to which he was invited during the fall of 1938. A painter from Oregon, for instance, who wore a red-and-black-checked lumberjack's shirt that Malenov instantly coveted, had been pointed and direct: "You know, that friend of yours, Alex Karnovsky—the guy I met at your studio last week—he's making some good stuff. Not bad at all. But it all comes out lookin' like blown-up Malenov. And he's got some good moves of his own to make. Malenov, listen here, why don't you stop him taking a bead on your work and make him fire away at his own target for a change." Malenov didn't quite understand the painter's language, but he caught its sense. Karnovsky was admired, but everyone suspected him of trading on Malenov's ideas. In itself, that didn't bother Malenov. What bothered him was Karnovsky's unwillingness to bring him face to face with the work, to confront the situation, to be open and direct about his supposed dependency. If Karnovsky had had the courage to deal with his derivativeness, Malenov might have shown him the way out or, at the very least, given him his blessing to go on adapting. But Karnovsky's refusal to invite Malenov to his studio came to signify for Malenov that something was being concealed from him. Others knew Karnovsky's work—everyone else, in point of fact, except Malenov—and, for his part, Malenov regarded himself as the only person who was absolutely entitled to know what his young disciple was making.

The advice given by the painter from Oregon was excellent and to the point, but unfortunately it came too late. If all along there had been a stream of work flowing from Karnovsky, if the work had never stopped, and if the sculptures had continued to accumulate, refined, strengthened, governed by a critical eye that could mark the difference between the working through of new ideas—however clumsily realized—and mere rehearsals and rung changes on notions cooked and served by Malenov, it would have been possible for Yevgeny to check Alexander's fall into recapitulation of the ideas and images already proposed by his master. But Malenov could not tell Alexander what was going wrong and, more to the point, he had no interest in doing so. The Malenov journals make this clear. As well, they reveal something else: the guilt and embarrassment at being in Karnovsky's debt and the consequent reservations Malenov maintained about his disciple, his suspicion that by accepting so much over the years, he himself was being hobbled. Not that Karnovsky interfered with Malenov's art. Never. Malenov's art was always beyond manipulation and control. Indeed, as long as Malenov worked, Karnovsky raised no objection, never chafed, never complained that he was blocked and unproductive.

It was only when Malenov went out into the city without leaving a note of detailed itinerary tacked to his door that Karnovsky became anxious. "Where can he be at this hour?" he complained, seating himself before his door, awaiting his return. But Karnovsky was back in less than fifteen minutes, carrying a bottle of cream and six cakes filled with cheese in a little box. Karnovsky followed Yevgeny into the apartment. Malenov disappeared into the kitchen, and Karnovsky smelled coffee brewing in a saucepan (Malenov boiled it with egg shells and then strained the thickened mixture into a porcelain coffee pot). Shortly, Malenov returned to the atelier, carrying a tray filled with cups and saucers, the cakes displayed on a blue plate, the coffee pot redolent with his concoction.

"People are coming to visit."

"Wonderful. Do I know them?"

"No. Not friends of yours, I think."

"Shall I stay?"

"Not a good idea. Very nervous people. They may buy something, you know. Best I do it myself."

"Oh. I didn't think I'd interfere."

"That's not the point, Sasha. You come here at all times, day, night. I never know when you come. No telephone. I am usually home working. Don't you think you should see me not as often? I feel you sometimes around my neck like a rope."

"You want a telephone? Tomorrow. I'll get you one."

"I hate telephones. I never want a telephone. Don't you dare telephone me in this room."

"What is it you want then, Zhenya?"

"Alone. I must be alone. You follow me like a sad animal. Yes. Yes. Like a small, sad animal. But you are a good artist and you have work to do. Go home and do your work. Let me alone."

Karnovsky left immediately. He got up from the sofa, pulled open the door, and left. He managed to reach the street, dizzy with confusion. He wanted to disappear; for an instant he even wanted to die. A taxi stopped in front of the building and four people got out, three women and myself. We had an appointment with Yevgeny Mikhailovich Malenov. As we approached the door, Alexander saw me and screamed, I thought melodramatically, "Traitor, traitor," and rushed down the street. My friends, an Italian marchesa and her sister and a friend of theirs, who were in New York after spending six months in Palm Beach, wanted to meet the remarkable artist. They had seen paintings of his at the Biennale a year before and, learning that he was now settled in New York, asked whether I would introduce them. I had arranged the meeting and had inquired whether Yevgeny would invite Alexander—a courtesy on my part, as I had no idea of the mounting tension between them.

I was annoyed with Alexander's little outbreak of pet. I thought it rude. He never even allowed me to introduce him to the charming marchesa and simply ran off down the street, shouting "Traitor." My friends were alarmed by the scene and, when they reached Yevgeny's flat, insisted on telling him of the meeting. I wasn't certain Yevgeny had understood their heavily accented English, but he did catch the marchesa's repetition of *traditore* and understood instantly that Alexander was infuriated by my presence at the gathering. The ladies were amused by Yevgeny, too amused in fact to take him seriously. He tried to interest them in his work, but after discoursing about his understanding of the universe for several minutes, during which their faces froze into polite incomprehension, he stopped, and I conducted the gathering through chatter and gossip for another half-hour, at which point we all left.

"Even you usurp me," Alexander shouted at me the moment he opened the door to my insistent ringing.

"You're mad and you know it. What kind of nonsense is this? Usurp you. Traitor-talk. What stupidity. If anyone is at fault, it's your friend Yevgeny Mikhailovich. I didn't keep you from being present. In fact,

I asked him whether he would invite you, and he said he would think it over. It's between you and him. Leave me out of your little melodrama."

"Yes, yes. I know. He's getting tired of me. I don't blame him at all. He said I'm a noose around his neck. And he's right. Completely right. I'm terrified of him—terrified that he should see my work and recognize his own in every corner of what I made; terrified that if I own up to what I've accomplished, he'll tell everyone I'm a thief. What do I do instead? I stop working and follow him around like a concierge waiting for a tip. I disgust myself. I'm weak, goddamned weak, and I can't do anything about it."

"But you can. Show him the work. Invite him here and show him what you're doing. You told me the same story about your time in Berlin together. You were making your alphabet paintings in the next room, hiding them from him, and one day he came in unannounced and praised you, and from that day on you worked like a demon. Why shouldn't it work again?"

Alexander took my advice. More than a month passed, during which he hardly saw Yevgeny Mikhailovich. He never visited Malenov's apartment. Sometimes he circled the building, standing in the street, his eyes straining to see into the studio, to catch a glimpse of Yevgeny, but he never went up the stairs. Of course, he had written Yevgeny and apologized, but had received no acknowledgment. Yevgeny sulked every bit as strenuously as Alexander became pensive and melancholy. Their moods of rejection and unhappiness were immensely compatible. At last, however, after nearly forty days of this ridiculous separation, I persuaded Alexander to write and invite Yevgeny to his studio. When the letter was written, I took it from him and delivered it myself, handing it to Yevgeny, who opened it, read it, and said that he would come.

Both Yevgeny Mikhailovich and Alexander were happy that I was present at their reunion. It would have been impossible without me. They would have been unable to speak. When I arrived with Yevgeny

Mikhailovich, Alexander had already had a drink of cognac, and Yevgeny dived for a bottle of gin, which he poured into a water glass.

"Well, I guess you want to see my secret work." Alexander laughed nervously and opened the double doors to the studio. He had arranged to borrow back from collectors several of his most severe and imposing sculptures, to which he added three new pieces that he had assembled and finished at four o'clock that morning.

Yevgeny Mikhailovich shambled into the studio, his large body stalking the room like a predator. But suddenly a look of calm came over him, his face relaxed, and he stood up erect before one of the largest of the constructions, a smile of delight kneading his features, filling them with his familiar warmth. "Amazing," he said at first and then lapsed into silence, moving slowly from piece to piece. Alexander stood behind him, trembling slightly, biting his lip. I remained at the entrance to the room where I could see them both and observe their remarkable confrontation. At last, "Amazing," again and then a flood of words: "Yes, yes, yes. I think you do something amazing, Sasha. Ha, ha, ha. I worry from other people you make sculpture out of me. No. No. What you do all your own. Malenov take no credit out of this. None at all. I think your work original, you know, something you make up out of Karnovsky. Very good. Fine. We show together, no? Good idea. We show together and put stop to all this nonsense about Malenov giving away genius to Karnovsky."

Karnovsky was overwhelmed. He took it all as it was offered. A superlative gesture of generosity from the older artist to the younger. Of course, I had listened closely to Malenov's testimonial and never once heard the words of praise that Karnovsky insisted he had heard. I heard words of amazement; I heard exclamations of originality, expressions of pleasure that Karnovsky couldn't be accused of being an impersonation of Malenov, but never an assertion that Karnovsky had made beautiful works of art. Karnovsky, however, was completely persuaded by Malenov's apparent enthusiasm and grasped him around the neck, hugging him with delight.

"May I give you one of these pieces, Zhenya?"

"You want to give Malenov one of these?"

"It would make me very happy. Yes. May I?"

"You need to make much more work before you give away. Save them for our exhibition. Later, well, later, you can give one to Malenov."

Malenov had interrupted the festival of their reunion with a reproach of realism. Not enough work to give it away. Keep working. Make lots of work. Then we decide if you're an artist, a working artist, or an uncommitted epigone who makes art from time to time whenever everything else becomes boring. Malenov still held the hammer in his fist and saw no reason not to bring it down, when it suited him, on the head of Karnovsky.

During the weeks that followed the entrance of the United States into the war, neither Malenov nor Karnovsky worked particularly hard making art. Both were agitated by the proximity the war assumed to their lives. After the fall of Kiev, Malenov was galvanized into fierce patriotism, inventing wildly imaginary wars in which his familiar spaces were filled with screaming projectiles embedded in circles of red. These paintings—the half-dozen he made in a burst of energy during the summer of 1941—were contributed to charity bazaars to raise funds for the Red Cross and to supply winter relief to the embattled Soviet armies. Once, overcome by reports of the devastating losses that afflicted the Red Army during the spring of 1943 at Stalingrad, Malenov even attempted to enlist, but was rejected with hilarity. Following his rejection, Malenov kept at Karnovsky to enlist, but Karnovsky—terrified by war and violence—avoided Malenov's challenge, knowing full well that in due course the draft would catch up with him and that there was no way of avoiding it once the notice arrived. Karnovsky was called up, reported for a lengthy physical examination, and was finally rejected after the doctor vaguely inculpated his heart in some irregularity. Karnovsky was so relieved at being refused that he paid no attention to the medical reason.

When the tide of war turned during early 1944, when the Soviets began their devastating drive against the invader and the allies landed in North Africa and invaded Sicily, Malenov and Karnovsky felt they had been given permission to resume their work as artists and begin planning the joint exhibition Malenov had proposed almost five years earlier. They were encouraged in this decision by Karnovsky's dealer, who had agreed with enthusiasm to mount the exhibition, even proposing for it the publication of a catalogue that would document the work of each artist and annotate the collaboration and development of their complementary visions. It was agreed, without sufficient reflection on Karnovsky's part, that Karnovsky would write the essay about Malenov and Malenov would introduce Karnovsky.

The exhibition, scheduled to inaugurate the gallery's program during the spring of 1945, was prepared with exceptional care. Special walls were constructed at Malenov's suggestion in order that the gallery space acquire a labyrinthine aspect in which the viewer would be led through small rooms hung with paintings to interior spaces where Karnovsky's sculptures were installed. The placement of the temporary walls enabled a visual counterpoint, paintings offsetting sculptures, sculptures leading into rooms of paintings. There were, of course, many more Malenovs than Karnovskys. As hard as Karnovsky worked, he did not complete more than eight new constructions for the exhibition. Although Malenov visited Karnovsky's studio often during the working months that preceded the *vernissage*, Karnovsky never thought to inquire of him which works he was going to exhibit.

About a month before the catalogue was to be sent to the printer, Karnovsky asked to come by Malenov's studio to see the work he planned to show. He wanted, he said, to be able to write about the specific works intended for the show. Malenov temporized with Karnovsky's insistence. "Not necessary. You know Malenov's work better than Malenov. Write about the whole Malenov. Americans do not know Malenov. A general introduction is a better idea." Karnovsky readily agreed; it seemed the correct approach. Since the works shown at the exhibition were going to be listed on a separate sheet inserted in the catalogue, it wasn't really necessary for Karnovsky to see them. In fact, he never did see them until the day before the opening, when it was all too late. Every time Karnovsky visited Malenov in his studio in the months before the show, the walls were bare, work stacked in closets or covered with a tarpaulin in the corner. Karnovsky was without suspicion. He was still overwhelmed by Malenov's generosity.

The day the catalogue went to the printer, Malenov had not yet delivered his essay introducing Karnovsky. He promised to leave it at the gallery, but it never arrived. Finally, ten days before the opening of the exhibition, Malenov went to the printer and delivered his carefully written text, which, despite an occasional lapse of syntax that he urged the printer to correct, was in presentably decent English. No one saw the catalogue until it was delivered to the gallery the afternoon of the opening.

Even without the catalogue, however, Malenov had arranged surprise enough. He had allowed Karnovsky to install the exhibition, permitting him to arrange the forty pictures that Malenov insisted on showing in the small rooms that swept through the artificial rotundas greeted by the temporary walls where Karnovsky's wooden constructions were standing. Karnovsky was unnerved by some of the recent paintings Malenov had completed for the exhibition. They not only seemed to reflect visual ideas out of which his sculptures had come, but several alluded directly to the turning grid on which his architectonic structures were built, as though Malenov had devised a series of paintings after the fact to antedate and criticize Karnovsky's work. Although Karnovsky had situated those several paintings distant from his sculptures so that at least the untrained eye would pass over the analogy, it was hardly possible for him to ignore the similarity of painting and sculpture when he arrived late in the afternoon for the opening of the exhibition. To his horror, he learned that Malenov had spent three hours that afternoon virtually rehanging the exhibition in order to make unmistakable the dependence of the young sculptor on the master's work. Moreover, that horror was only the beginning. When the catalogue arrived, Karnovsky immediately turned to read the text of Malenov's introduction. It read with almost demonic subtlety and insinuation as follows:

The relationship of Yevgeny Mikhailovich Malenov and Joseph Alexander Karnovsky has been intimate and profound since their meeting in Berlin in 1928. When they met, Malenov was already an artist of considerable reputation, well known in his native Russia, where he was an active collaborator with the great artists of the avant-garde, Kazimir Malevich and Vladimir Tatlin. Malenov left the Soviet Union for the West after losing his position as teacher of painting theory at UNOVIS. His work had been exhibited in all the major salons of the new Russian art both before and after the Revolution of 1917.

What was Joseph Alexander Karnovsky before his meeting with Yevgeny Mikhailovich Malenov? He was a child of wealthy family derived from the mercantile bourgeoisie of Odessa. Like Malenov, Karnovsky was of Russian background. But the difference in their age at the time of their meeting was almost twenty years. And the difference in their education and experience was even more vast than is suggested by the difference in their age. Malenov was bursting with ideas; Karnovsky had only one idea: to meet Malenov.

Malenov will be indebted to the end of his life to the generous support that Karnovsky gave him. Without Karnovsky, Malenov would today be dead; without Karnovsky, Malenov's work would be unknown and Malenov would have surely starved to death.

But it is equally true that without Malenov, Karnovsky would not have been able to realize his ingenious constructions. In order to demonstrate this fact, Malenov has made especially for this exhibition a number of paintings that exhibit within the Malenovian idiom the three-dimensional undertaking that

Karnovsky has so cleverly contrived. Malenov would not have
made them as has Karnovsky, but then Malenov is a painter,
and Karnovsky has learned his art out of the astute study of
possibilities lodged in Malenov.

Karnovsky's work is more than an achievement. It is amazing.

It is a wonder that Karnovsky did not commit suicide that night.
It is a wonder. I still marvel at it, but now, in retrospect, I have come
to understand that Malenov's brutal assault on Karnovsky was simply
preparatory to the bequest he had foreseen and had set in motion to
bestow. He punished Karnovsky with the large fist. Indeed, the punishment worked. The little essay of introduction was sufficiently subtle
and artful that all the critics and gallery visitors received the instruction. Those who observed the relation of painting and sculpture did
not need to read the catalogue; those who read the catalogue hardly
bothered with the work. The result was inevitable. Malenov overwhelmed Karnovsky, buried him under the double assault of his attack
and the sheer number of works he offered. The critics—even those
who had praised Karnovsky's first exhibition—now treated Karnovsky's work as a pendant to Malenov's. Many of the lengthy discussions
of Malenov's oeuvre—excellently introduced and documented by Karnovsky's thorough and affectionate catalogue essay—concluded their
discussions with variations of the following: "The exhibition also exposed eight new sculptures by Malenov's disciple, Joseph Alexander
Karnovsky," or "The catalogue essay on Malenov was excellently
prepared by the young sculptor, Joseph Alexander Karnovsky, who
showed some of his new constructions." No one was heartless enough
to set forth the complex stratagem of subversion by which Malenov
had undermined Karnovsky. They apparently felt it was sufficient to
ignore Karnovsky, to relegate him to the role of mere disciple and
praise his scholarship rather than his art. And for whatever purpose

Malenov had devised his savagery, it was effective. Malenov sold many works and acquired a new and enthusiastic American dealer; Karnovsky sold one construction and lost an American dealer.

It might seem inevitable in the course of most human relations that an episode of such malevolence would destroy the friendship of Yevgeny Mikhailovich and Alexander Karnovsky. Think again. Friendships are destroyed by cruelty and deceit only when friendships have been grounded in equity, when some equivalence has been settled, territorialities defined, boundaries and borders scrupulously adhered to until the hour of the fatal breach. But such equities had never existed in the friendship of Malenov and Karnovsky. As deeply as Malenov had felt Karnovsky's artistic dependence, his punishment was contrived to temporize and relieve the guilt of his own dependence on Karnovsky. To that time, Malenov had no identity that was not supported and vouched for by Karnovsky. He had no documents of emigration, no ration card, no lease, no official papers of any kind that did not carry the guarantee and authentication of Karnovsky. Karnovsky supplied Malenov with his principle of identity; Malenov supplied Karnovsky with his aesthetic. An equity in appearance, but not a genuine equivalence, because art had no public face or credibility, and everything that a human being could claim to be was defined by his face before the law. In that respect Malenov was nothing, Karnovsky everything. And Malenov determined that he would have revenge for his servile capitulation to Karnovsky.

## Seventeen

It is not believable to me that Malenov had foreseen the hour of his death. Indubitably, nonetheless, near the end of his journal, Malenov confirms it, and Malenov is dead, dead of congestive heart failure following a siege of neglected pleurisy:

It is time to be done with all this huffing and puffing that is called life. I accept my end, beloved Sergius. I have nothing more to do. The work is done and I am bone dry and weary. How successful I was, throughout all my years, in fending off the scrutiny of others who might have seen beneath my bluster a soft and vulnerable heart that wept bitterly at its loneliness. I kept off friends and intimates to preserve my solitude. I understood clearly how disagreeable it was for Sergius to go off into the wilderness to found his chapel and then (even saints become famous) attracted by his piety, his fasts and austerities, his conversations with the Holy Spirit, to be suddenly inundated with disciples who wanted to share his understanding, to be conversant with his spiritual genius, to support and settle him despite his wish to be alone. It is all so strange, how God works with his saints. And so filled with confusion! Sergius wished to serve God alone, and God made his pieties so great and magnified his achievement so immensely that suddenly he was surrounded by disciples and was obliged to leave off his pieties to feed them and to tend the beggars who flocked into his wilderness to populate it with their own misery.

Have I done differently? Little Joseph Alexander, my unpious Jew from Odessa, came nearly full circle of the world to find me in Berlin, to make my wilderness habitable, to settle me in triumph, and in return to be nourished and fed by my gift. Is it any different? Am I not a new saint of the modern world, the only kind of saint bearable in the modern world—the end of bohemia and the beginning of celebrity— who wills his work to be his own, and the more he struggles to make it difficult and intractable, the more the world wishes to master it, to translate it into its own idiom, to suck out its indigestible marrow and consume it.

I would have been content to have had a small career of neglect, like Van Gogh or Gauguin, to have had few admirers and fewer buyers, if it could have been done without the waste that both those geniuses expended in disease and madness. Their modernity began when they realized they had sold little or nothing in their lifetime. If we artists could have continued to be guildsmen as in the Renaissance, doing our work for the most part anonymously, giving employment to useful historians who could then have tracked the signs of our identity beyond our death, I would have been content. Let only one of my pictures carry a signature and all the rest be known as Pseudo-Malenov or the Master of the Utopic altarpiece, how nice that would have been! After one's death, all fame is useless, and before one's death, all fame directs the way to dying. It is so with me. I know that my time approaches fast, since I am come into the palace of fame and fame dwells like a vulture over my doorway.

I see my dying as clearly as I saw the apartment from which Malevich fled or the rooms in which Karnovsky settled me. I see into rooms, it appears. My deadly second sight is house-bound, confined to quarters and domiciles. In those rooms I see the lines of my catastrophe. And it is in this very room where I sit now at peace writing out the details of my death that I observe the outline of my dying. Over there, I fall down on the floor near the window. I am too exhausted to reply to the knock upon my door, the persistent knocking that is Karnovsky come to call, his daily come to call, his persistent, relentless dogging of my steps for which he pays me monthly, that earns him the right, he supposes, to make my days unbearable, to keep me from my solitary pieties, from Saint Sergius, from my album of little treasures, from all the ministries of solitude that I have organized and put to work over a lifetime.

And, you, too, Karnovsky (though you did not intend to wear me down by your persistence), you will pay for having destroyed my solitude. I have also made preparation for your death. If all this comes to pass, I will have set in motion an inexorable plan. It is not, Sasha, that I am angry with you. Not at all as simple as that. It is that if I die (as I see myself dying), the balances in the universe will have been jarred. There can be no reconstruction of the universe according to my plans and programs, if the foundations of the world shudder and groan from the tilt of your devising. If I die because of you, you must die because of me. The work is more important than either of our lives, and I would have you dead that the work of reconstruction can go on.

Enough of this. I have seen enough of this. And now it is to the sinew of the real, where bone, muscle, tendon stretch

and turn upon a universal rack, that we must pay attention.
It happens; it does not happen. But all will be ready if it
does.


The day after Malenov wrote this entry in his journal, with dusk
accumulating in Yevgeny Mikhailovich's apartment, Alexander Karnovsky brought me along for his daily visit. I had not seen Yevgeny
for several months. I was pleased to be invited for their time of teacups
and cakes; my own life had been sordid and boring. But it was unclear
why Alexander had insisted on my joining him. It was less an invitation
than a command. "You must drop everything and come with me to
Zhenya's." The tone was so uncompromising that I succumbed instantly. Only later did I become curious about Alexander's invitation.
Why now? Why me? Why the necessity of this moment? Nothing was
anticipated, although everything transpired, indeed everything that I
later discovered in Yevgeny's journal was set in motion that afternoon.
Had Alexander expected it? Had he been forewarned? Was he also
gifted with sight? No. Not at all. Karnovsky came close to philosophy
and metaphysics, but he was not a spiritual man; sensuality at bay,
that is the closest he came to the spirit. But all human beings, I
conclude, have the capacity for being unpredictably unnerved. Something can rise up out of the prospects before us that baits our attention,
sets us at the ready, makes us aware—even if insubstantially and
fleetingly—that there is something that might happen, that is around
the bend of light, hidden in the infinite rooms of time.

As we climbed the stairs to Malenov's apartment, Alexander confessed that he was apprehensive. "Thank you for coming, Isaiah. I
needed someone else today. I feel it." I couldn't ask what he felt, as
the door was thrown open and Malenov invaded the space to hug
Alexander and swallow my hand in both of his. Before we could halt
the progress of events, consume our tea, nibble at the toast, talk
about the unseasonable cold snap or even comment on a vast new
painting that covered ten feet of his wall, Malenov had begun to talk.

The talk seemed rehearsed, as though it had been practiced over and over, learned and memorized.

"Before we talk of other things, I have something to say to you, dear Sasha," Malenov began speaking his curious brand of chopped English, "about which I have thought now for nearly eighteen years. You have been more than helpful in my life. You have sustained me through all these years, good years and bad years. I think the time approaches—fast approaches, I am afraid—when my life comes to conclusion. No. No. Do not argue with Zhenya. You know perfectly well such things are not secret from me. I know they will come to pass. When remains uncertain. But now rather than later is undeniable. I propose to repay you everything that I owe you—the nearly forty thousand dollars that are due to you—by leaving you everything that is in this studio, all the paintings and drawings, all my books and records, all my journals and notebooks, in short, everything. You have wished to be my child and so you shall become my child when I am dead."

Alexander Karnovsky, to my amazement, was not surprised. He kept silent for several minutes, not fidgeting, implacably staring at Malenov. I found the silence like the eye of a tornado, of such immensity and power that it grinds out the living in a whirlwind. "Your figures are correct, however just beyond forty thousand," Karnovsky murmured in a low voice, removing a slip of paper from his pocket on which the precise sum had been noted. "Thank you, Zhenya. Nothing could move me more than to become your child of inheritance. But shall we make it legal?"

Malenov did not object; it had all been anticipated and accepted, even the cautious disbelief of Karnovsky's request. Malenov brought paper from his desk and, leaning on a small drawing board, began to write as Karnovsky dictated a simple testamentary document, naming himself as sole heir and executor. And then it became clear why I had been brought to this incredible afternoon tea. "Will you witness Malenov's signature, Isaiah? I will fetch that cleaning man we passed in the hallway. He will be the second witness." Moments later an elderly Italian, holding a crumpled banknote in his left hand, entered the apartment and put his signature beneath my own, printing his name and address below his nervous scrawl. It was done and witnessed.

"Legal, yes? I am finished, so to speak," Malenov added wryly, as he poured a fresh cup of tea and seized a cherry tart in his begrimed fingers. "You see the painting behind me. Very big, much bigger than the Stuttgart mural the barbarians cut up in Berlin. It may be my last great painting. Quite possible, you know. I've seen it all. My death, that is."

"Oh, stop, Yevgeny Mikhailovich," I exclaimed. "We are all going to die some day, but not just yet." (I never could bear conversations about dying. The only tradition I extracted from my family was their ingenious refusal to speak of death. Death was never final among my folk—it was always spoken of in the euphemism of travel, one minute here, the other out of sight in some other realm where we would all meet up again. My grandfather would leave the table enraged if even the word *death* were mentioned, and my father, until his own death not long ago, spoke of it as though it were an avoidable happenstance, occurring only because of some mistake or error of judgment. He was in the habit of speaking about the time beyond his death in the language of uncertainty: "If I die, Isaiah, you will have to take care of your mother." He did, and I am still caring for my mother. But at the time of these events, several decades ago, when I was a manuscript dealer in my early forties, I found it exceptionally difficult to listen to this bizarre Russian genius, discoursing genially about the time and occasion of his death. Particularly, of course, because I accepted that what he was saying was inexorable and bound to come to pass precisely as he had imagined it and, as I later found, set it down in his journal.)

"My death not important. Everything I wanted to make is done. This last picture is, you understand, kind of summation. See how red planes pass through black solids into blue aether. It's what I've always dreamed to build—vast planar platforms to launch projectiles into space. Malenov's space-travel architecture."

Karnovsky listened closely as Malenov continued his interpretation of the unfinished canvas behind him, once getting up from the sofa to examine a dense area of the composition where the black paint shone like polished ebony. He made no further reference to the testament, which he had simply folded and inserted in his wallet. It was all terribly strange. Alexander had never alluded to the vast sum that Malenov owed him. Indeed, I had never thought of Alexander's monthly generosity as a debt incurred, carrying the obligation of repayment. It was presented as a charity, I took it to be a charity, and yet, clearly, without relatives or heirs, the aging Malenov had conceived of the bequest as the single means he possessed of repaying his benefactor. I was not aware at the time, however, that the bequest carried with it a more insidious intent. Malenov knew that his reputation was continuing to rise, that his works—once valueless—now commanded international attention. With the war concluded and museums throughout Europe beginning the work of reconstruction, demand for master paintings of the century would mount, and the desire to bring together and aggregate holdings diffused by the European destruction would intensify. Of course, I did not learn of Malenov's malevolent construction of his bequest until several years later, but it seemed less surprising when I discovered it, given the cold, indeed calculating, manner in which Karnovsky had received it. He knew to the penny how much he had given Malenov; he was cognizant of all the requirements for preparing a legally incontestable document of bequest. It was as though simultaneously with Malenov's presentiment of his own death—his famous "second sight"—Karnovsky had been suddenly illuminated. Karnovsky denied it when I inquired, but he did acknowledge that during the days prior to Malenov's announcement he had been unable to sleep, had felt incredibly tense and apprehensive, and had—for reasons that he was unable to fathom—counted up not only the money he had given to Malenov but the number of paintings and drawings that he owned from Malenov's hand, as well as the quantity of documents dealing with Malenov that he had accumulated over the years.

## *Eighteen*

Alexander Karnovsky broke down the door to Malenov's apartment during the early morning of February 11, 1948, and found him collapsed on the floor by an open window, gasping for breath. He was near death. After his removal to a hospital, where an elderly doctor tried to make him comfortable, he expired. It is not clear whether he had opened the window and allowed freezing winds from the Hudson River to chill the apartment or whether he was ill before opening the window and then, weakened by pleurisy, had collapsed while trying to close it again. Whatever the sequence of events, because of his debilitated condition, his admitted weariness, the abscesses on his lungs and his overburdened heart, by the time he was found—apparently more than a day after his collapse—there was nothing that could be done to save him. Of course, had Karnovsky gained entrance to Malenov's studio the first time he had come by and listened at the door, hearing him pacing inside, hearing the indistinct cough (hearing the slow and somewhat dragging footfall uncommon for a man who always moved briskly and with resolution), he might have gotten to him in time. But Malenov, it must be assumed, had anticipated this and had resumed his habit of posting notices upon his door to discourage visitors: MALENOV NOT RECEIVING TODAY, MALENOV WORKS, LEAVE MALENOV ALONE. The piling of ordinance and warning had frightened away the postman, who had a registered letter for Malenov. A Swiss visitor who had wanted to speak with Malenov about a commission for a projectivist installation in a local museum had slipped his card under the door, but, obediently, had never knocked. Karnovsky, going by the apartment morning and evening, hoping to be admitted but each time finding the notice of admonition in place, hearing Malenov inside, persuaded himself that everything was all right, that Malenov was working on some large enterprise and did not wish—genuinely—to be disturbed. It hurt him, of course, that no exception had been made for him. (Once, he told me, several years earlier, when they were organizing and planning their famous joint exhibition, Malenov had written a notice for his door that read: NO VISITORS FOR MALENOV EXCEPT KARNOVSKY.) Karnovsky was an exception to all Malenov's rules, and if so then— once, even—why not now, when Karnovsky anxiously paced the hallway before his apartment trying to make up his mind whether to announce himself, to call out, or simply to repeat the low rapping that he had used in the past when he wanted to enter Malenov's atelier at the front of their Berlin apartment. But for some reason he had not knocked.

Or rather, I can guess the reason: ever since Malenov had nominated Karnovsky as his heir, their relationship had changed. For the first time, Malenov had ceased to be oblique with Karnovsky. Indeed, on one occasion he had dismissed a new construction Karnovsky had ventured to describe to him. "Sounds like a packing crate, not sculpture." Karnovsky laughed and persisted in his description. "Aach, Sasha, I do get tired of your making me into solids. One Malenov is enough. We don't need a half-Malenov called Karnovsky." It was cruel; it was intended to be cruel. Karnovsky didn't reply. Malenov had punched him in the stomach; he was winded. There was no reply. It was almost true. But why, suddenly, did Malenov begin speaking this way to Karnovsky? Of course. Now that Malenov had decided he was his heir, he had no further need to guard his tongue. He was quits with Karnovsky. The slate was clean, the scales balanced. Whatever bitterness Malenov had felt over the years when Karnovsky was accumulating the stuff and substance that was Malenov, a junior Malenov, a minor Malenov, there could be no confrontation except by indirection. Malenov repaid Karnovsky all those years with slyness and slights, small reproofs and critiques, driving him away, but also recalling him as unpredictably. All those years he continued to receive money from Karnovsky—no, to take money from Karnovsky—and Karnovsky gave the money as forcefully as it was received. Karnovsky controlled the finances of Malenov and, consequently, controlled his movements. Every time Malenov wanted to take a holiday, to drive with some acquaintance up to Cape Cod for a week or take a train to Chicago to visit the Art Institute, he had to ask Karnovsky for something extra. Money was always around and abundant—banknotes were found after Malenov's death inserted as bookmarks in volumes he was reading (Malenov once explained he couldn't pay his gas bill because he hadn't finished a certain book where he was using a twenty-dollar bill to mark his progress), rolled with a rubber band among his underwear, hidden in the jacket pocket of his suits, flattened in his favorite pair of walking shoes—and yet never organized in one place where Malenov could find it. He treated money indifferently, casually, and yet he had need of it and knew when it was instantly required to fund an excursion. It was then, requiring fifty dollars, that he would touch Karnovsky for an advance against the following month, to which Karnovsky always replied, "No, no. I'm not a bank. No need for an overdraft. Here, take it. I have more than enough." And yet Karnovsky *was* a bank, a benevolent bank who was always beseeched the same way and always responded generously. An uncommon bank, but at last fulfilling one requirement of a bank's reality: there was a never-ending supply of money in the till, and Karnovsky was always willing to bestow it on Malenov.

Malenov obviously despised the fact that he could not support himself; even after a score of exhibitions, after the sale of several hundred paintings, after the praise and admiration of museums and cognoscenti, he was still broke, always poor, always a supplicant to the young man who was unfailingly generous toward him, but who wanted more than anything to become the new Malenov, replacing the visionary paintings with original sculpture, taking from the master as recompense for his generosity a little bit here, a little bit there of the original genius that made projectivism one of the most controversial and argued doctrines of modern art. It was bound to end badly, and this despite the fact that both men admired each other, depended on each other; in the fatality of such hopeless arrangements of trust and mistrust, they were also committed to destroying each other.

Karnovsky sadly arranged the funeral for his dead friend. Testimonials and reminiscences were offered by representative figures of the European art world who had come in the course of war to settle in the United States, artists who had known Malenov in Moscow and Berlin, museum curators who had begun to collect him in Europe and America; and finally, reluctantly, unhappily, Alexander himself concluded the solemnities with a brief recitation of remarkable events in the life of Yevgeny Mikhailovich, episodes and anecdotes, most culled from his vast archive of Malenoviana, some, indeed those of greatest warmth and intensity, drawn from their own intimate but troubled friendship. The service—wholly without religious allusion—concluded with a pianist rendering Scriabin's sonata "Towards the Flame," Karnovsky's single concession to Russian spirituality.

After the service, Alexander invited everyone back to Yevgeny's atelier for a sort of festive wake. When the guests arrived, a long table was ranged with vodka, champagne, beer, and whiskies of all kinds, vast platters of salmon, whitefish, and caviar, trays of cold cuts, loaves of bread, salads, and pirogi stuffed with meat, potatoes, and vegetables. The party went on interminably, but by late evening all of the guests—the forty or so who remained to drink themselves into oblivion—were aware that Alexander Karnovsky was the new son and heir of Yevgeny Mikhailovich Malenov. It was a secret Alexander would have been well advised to keep.

A month after the death and cremation of Malenov, Malenov's dealer persuaded Karnovsky that a second and final joint exhibition of the work of Malenov and Karnovsky should be held the following season.

Karnovsky agreed, although already he thought it unlikely that there would be enough time for him to make new work. He had ready several drawings that he wanted to translate into wood, and he had recently begun to use sheets of colored bakelite to contrast with the graininess of ash and oak, but making art was not something you could start at eleven in the morning and then break for lunch to deal with matters arising out of the Malenov estate. He kept repeating to himself *ars longa, vita brevis*, but he had already reconstructed the meaning for him of this familiar Latin apothegm: art took a long time to make and his life was so short, the working day was so abridged, spans of uncommitted time were so infrequent that he was lucky if he had ten hours a week in his studio to work at sculpture. And ten hours was hardly enough time to consider oneself an artist, much less to make art.

Karnovsky tried; he tried profoundly to return to his work. He thought it a responsibility that he had to Malenov to continue making Karnovskys, to press the future of projectivism by insisting on its visionary architecture and demonstrating its possibility. He even organized a small collective of young architects to work on housing projects for postwar America and Europe that would incorporate projectivist principles in the design of urban spaces, treating highways and mass transit as systems of utopic grids, funding research that might yield a new and untried building material that could sheathe his new constructions. But everything that Karnovsky pressed forward in support of Malenov's principles diminished his own time and prevented him from attending to his own work.

It was under control for a while; Karnovsky did manage a number of hours alone. But as the time approached for the exhibition to open, it became clear that he would have at most one new sculpture ready for presentation. The rest would be Malenov, and, consequently, it fell to Karnovsky to choose which Malenovs would be exposed, to annotate the catalogue and provide an introduction. It took months of work, as everything connected with Malenov went slowly. Because

Malenov had successfully built into his oeuvre a dimension of obscurity and confusion, there settled upon his heir problems of scholarship and documentation that were uncommon in the work of other artists. Malenov rarely signed his work, never titled it until it was exhibited, and dated it in the most bizarre of fashions: "Begun one night in the winter and finished several years later. YMM." Is that a date? What winter? Where? Later than what? The "YMM" passed as signature and authentication, but the anecdotal dating compelled Karnovsky to settle for approximate chronology based on internal evidence of the work—changes in Malenov's palette, shifts in the positioning of certain forms, introduction of the enlarged format, use of collage elements, all these variations in the scheme of Malenov's work were well documented by Karnovsky (he had, you see, put his ledgers of Malenov's working drawings and sketches to good use) and allowed him after weeks of careful examination to decide that a certain painting had been made in Berlin during the early 1930s or in New York prior to 1942 or in the period after their disastrous joint exhibition or in the season before his death. Many of the paintings Karnovsky knew firsthand, having been present when they were made and having reproduced and dated them in his notebooks. The real problems were the little pictures that Malenov had made but never shown to Karnovsky and, more serious still, the work done in Berlin from 1929 until his removal to New York. Many problems, many problems indeed. And all of them—precisely as Malenov had envisioned—fell on Karnovsky, robbing his own time of any concentration that might be considered private and saved for Karnovsky.

The exhibition of Malenov and Karnovsky opened in due course and was hailed by the critics as an opportunity to see the genius of the late Yevgeny Mikhailovich Malenov. The fact that Karnovsky had presented a new sculpture and included four previously unknown constructions that he had sold privately during the previous two years was completely ignored. Of course, Karnovsky's inheritance was discussed, and his enlarged responsibilities as the concierge of Malenov's reputation were duly noted, but Karnovsky the artist was never mentioned. Indeed, that was never discussed again. Karnovsky's dealer became Malenov's dealer and an even closer intimate and adviser of Karnovsky, but he never again asked about Karnovsky's work. Karnovsky the artist simply disappeared or, more accurately, was so confused with the fame of Malenov that one almost spoke of them as a hyphenated enterprise, the work of the one, the authority and scholarship of the other. The Malenov–Karnovsky oeuvre: the dead artist Malenov had made the work, the scholar Karnovsky annotated and exhibited it. For a time Karnovsky was able to bear the intrusion, delighting, in fact, that he was in a sense closer to Malenov in death than he had been to him in life, interpreting the work, defining its intent, formulating its ideology, supplying the world with the language of its exegesis. Karnovsky took upon himself the requirement of making Malenov legible and in the process not only supplied each painting with a history and documentation, but fitted it into a scheme of vision, invented by himself, and supported by documentation that no one could question. But all the while it ate at Karnovsky that he had been obliterated by the new eminence, that Malenov had installed himself in his brain and now weighed upon his heart with a pressure that had become unbearable. Indeed, the first time that Karnovsky complained of a savage pain in his chest—a pain of such intensity that it seemed to be ripping him open—he regarded it as such a fitting metaphor of Malenov's incision in his life that he waited until it passed and never pursued the matter. Not that anything could have been done to relieve the presence of Malenov in the lining of his coronary arteries. Malenov had obliterated Karnovsky, quite simply. By 1950, there was nothing left of Karnovsky that had not been recast by Malenov—all his imagination, all his energy, all his time was devoted to Malenov. And though the bright lights of wealth and money had not yet come to shine directly on the artist and his works, its angular and embarrassed radiance was sufficient that Malenov's unsold paintings and drawings had come to be valued at nearly a million dollars—a modest sum by today's standards, but vastly more than Malenov had earned during his lifetime, and an inheritance that in time would rival and ultimately surpass the considerable wealth enjoyed by Karnovsky.

## *Nineteen*

Finally, the revenge was accomplished. Alexander Karnovsky, approaching middle age, was dead of an exploded heart. The medical description is precise and not unusual. It occurs some two thousand times a year in this country, but despite its relative mundanity, it is a heart disease of such complexity and suggestiveness that I am obliged to regard its occurrence in Alexander Karnovsky as a malign fulfillment of another's will, an intended murder, conceived by another, foreseen in the clear vision whose documentation I discovered and had translated, projected with an almost demonic persuasion into the life and person of another, and brought to pass two years after the seer's own death.

I have described how the last years of Alexander Karnovsky were beset with Yevgeny Mikhailovich—more than beset, encumbered and obliterated. Every day was given over to Malenov, every free minute was spent thinking out the consequence of a loan, a bequest, a sale, an exhibition, a catalogue, an essay, a critical volume, an offering at auction, an interview, an archive, a documentary center and library. What time would there be again for Karnovsky? No time. Never again a moment of time in which the name Malenov would not insert itself through the cracks in the structure of a thought, in the interlineation of a letter, in the syntax of speech, or—as is the case with an aortic dissection—in the transmission of blood to the heart.

Karnovsky's body was found on the floor of his studio at the rear of his hotel apartment. His feet were drawn up as though trying desperately to relieve the pain that tore him in two. Most remarkable is that a half-dozen of Karnovsky's paintings, made when he had lived with Malenov in Berlin, were obliterated by broadly painted black brushstrokes, as though during the frenzy that preceded the explosion an almost hysterical anxiety had seized Karnovsky and compelled him to assert during his last hours of life that he was no painter, that he had no further wish to compete with his master, that he surrendered to him in his final agonies and elected to destroy his past as artist. Indeed, this is further confirmed by the fact that one small maquette of an unfinished sculpture had been smashed with a single blow, and pieces of wood were strewn over the floor. Karnovsky had capitulated in the hours before his death, and Malenov victorious, seated in majesty before a wall of his works in a grainy enlargement of the photograph Karnovsky had cut from the German magazine nearly twenty-five years earlier, gazed down on the destruction that he had envisaged and accomplished.

A handkerchief clutched in Karnovsky's hand suggests that he had perspired profusely before the onset of the fatal attack; moreover, the muscles of his jaw were clenched in that tightly constricted vise by which some fight against excruciating pain. All the elements foreboding such a wild and uncontrollable cataclysm as aortic dissection were present: premonitory anxiety, drenching perspiration, excruciating pain; even a drop of bile vomited during the advent of the attack stained his chin. One can only hope that Karnovsky lapsed into unconsciousness as the tumorous blood-filled swelling ripped the aortic lining, tearing it open before a geyser of blood poured through its wall, drowning him in hemorrhage.

### Twenty

The Karnovsky bequest was enormous, involving gifts and benefactions of many millions of dollars, accumulated slowly over the more than twenty years since the death of his father. Karnovsky had been totally unaware of his investments. All these had been handled by his father's former adviser, Mr. Salomo, a man well advanced in years, who turned over to Karnovsky's accountant an impeccably honest set of books. Karnovsky's only genuine life-interest had been Malenov, whose own records and documents were neatly ordered in eight filing cabinets located in a study abutting Karnovsky's studio. There, in that small alcove, Karnovsky must have sat at his worktable and pursued the study of the Malenov Codex, developing a complex system of archival filing that cross-referenced photographs of every painting with the large folios containing preliminary sketches and drawings, and with files of letters, documents, clippings referring to the work in question. That part of Karnovsky's research was complete at his death.

Incomplete, and therefore of striking importance to this narration, was Karnovsky's biography of his friend and destroyer. The manuscript had first undertaken to describe the complex Malenovian visual vocabulary, to document the sources of his metaphor (pursuing his language through Ouspensky, Bragdon, Steiner, Mondrian, Malevich; various non-Euclidean geometricians on the one hand and mystic theoreticians of the Third Dimension on the other; the vocabulary of the new urbanist architects and Soviet aesthetic theoreticians) and to relate them to Malenov's delirium in the presence of various Russian Orthodox theologians and verbal romantics. Karnovsky had carefully tracked the working of these ideas through the six hundred paintings completed by Malenov and the more than two thousand sketches, drawings, lithographs that Malenov had employed to trace the undergarment of his universe.

Of proper biography there was little or nothing. Karnovsky had explained to me that Malenov's life hardly mattered. The life of an artist was in the work, he argued. Everything else was simply the excrescent bubbling of genius, hardly of importance except as a frame in which to insert the works, to establish their temporal sequence, the birth and transformation of ideas, the dismissal and recovery of visual notions. Malenov's life would come at the end, when the work of deciphering and explicating the painting was completed.

Evidently, Karnovsky was reading through the Malenov journals on the night of his self-destruction. The three thick volumes of letters and writings that constituted the personal memorabilia of Yevgeny Mikhailovich Malenov were piled on Karnovsky's worktable in the archival alcove. He had accustomed himself to using paper clips to draw his attention to a particular page to which he intended to return. The first two volumes were bulging with paper clips, sometimes flagging little pieces of paper on which Karnovsky had noted a remark or internal reference. In the third volume, however, paper clips were evident only throughout three-quarters of the sheaf of papers that made up the album of Malenov's final years. Moreover, at a certain point, the point in question, Karnovsky had affixed a paper clip, although the sheet on which Malenov's handwritten Russian entry appeared had adhered to the next page and two pages beyond. Only by steaming the sheets was I able to cause Karnovsky's profuse perspiration to be condensed; the pages were then freed and swabbed dry with cotton-tipped sticks. Clearly, as I reconstruct it, Karnovsky must have come, at approximately ten o'clock of the evening in question, upon Malenov's remarkable journal entry and affixed the paper clip, as would be automatic in the case of a Russian entry that required careful scrutiny and translation. His eyes dropped down the page, he turned it, and then, as he suddenly perspired, droplets of sweat fell on the pages, dried, and sealed them together. These were surely the last pages written by Yevgeny Mikhailovich Malenov about Joseph Alexander Karnovsky. They were, moreover, the last pages read by Alexander Karnovsky before the beginning of the attack that murdered him within two hours, thundering pain obliterating consciousness while the lining of his heart was breached by a tidal eruption of blood.

Alexander Karnovsky.

In all my life of second sight, I have never seen into the future. Everything that has come to pass in my visions occurred at the same moment as my seeing. I saw but I changed nothing, made nothing come to pass by having seen it. My sights were innocent. But I know from all that has happened during the recent years that this time it is different. As you have demanded of me that I pay up to you, returning in kind for the money you advanced, I determined to leave you everything after my death.

My death is coming inexorably, sooner rather than later, I have no doubt. My obstinacy will make it certain when the right time comes to pass, but your death is no certainty, your punishment no inevitability. Until this moment! Now, I see it clearly. To destroy you, I give you what you desire— everything I have made, everything on which I have put my signature. It is what you want, but it will kill you. You will never make again a work of your own. All your own ambition will be silenced, and you will work only for me when I am gone. You think the Malenov inheritance will make you rich, famous, celebrated. It will do that most assuredly, but it will also destroy you as I know and have decided.

## *Twenty-one*

It is not my way to succumb to tales of demonic prediction and vengeance beyond the grave. We are modern men, without superstition, after all. But this tale is so remarkable, its slow accumulation of understanding and anger so unparalleled, that one gives up rational renditions of the real (which supply us at best with what reason governs) and entertains, even with dismay, alternatives that can encompass more, enabling such mysterious aptitudes as "second sight" and predictive visions to be accredited, if only because what they envisage was accomplished. But, having said this, there is a larger reading that I cannot fail to note. I have survived some three decades beyond these events. I undertook to edit and publish the manuscripts of Karnovsky about Malenov. Malenov's undistributed work was passed by Karnovsky to me. I was named the ultimate heir and owner of the Malenov oeuvre. Karnovsky bestowed on me—along with a generous financial settlement—the labor that he did not complete. It nearly destroyed me, as well. But I resisted; moreover, I had never been a source of anger to either Malenov or Karnovsky and so, when I completed the editing and publication of Karnovsky's study, I established a foundation and consigned all of Malenov's unsold work to its impartial determination. I freed myself of Malenov and Karnovsky, and I have continued to live my solitary and not unpleasant life to its own gathering confusion.

I have told a sad story, a story of incommunication and loneliness, in which two artists—the older master and the younger aspirant—instead of learning how to speak the volumes they formed in paint and wood, broke away from each other, shut themselves off in misunderstanding, frustration, jealousy, and anger, and, instead of learning how they might love each other more wisely, devoted their misunderstanding to projects of revenge and punishment. The truth is that both artists were nearly pure, but they lived at the beginning of that vulgar time when art is no longer understood apart from celebrity and money. Their own proximity to that time of desperate confusion contributed more than anything else to the destructiveness that was unleashed.

*Artists & Enemies*

was set by Crane Typesetting, Barnstable, Massachusetts, in Bodoni Book, a face named after Giambattista Bodoni (1740–1813), the son of a Piedmontese printer. After gaining renown and experience as superintendent of the Press of Propaganda in Rome, Bodoni became head of the ducal printing house of Parma in 1768. A great innovator in type design, his faces are known for their openness and delicacy.

The book was printed and bound by Haddon Craftsmen, Scranton, Pennsylvania. Book design by Virginia Evans.